THE LOGOS PROPHECY

Book One in the Fall of Ancients series

FIRST EDITION
The Logos Prophecy – Book One in the Fall of Ancients series © 2023
by Martin Treanor
Cover art © 2023 by Jasmine Poole
Interior design © 2023 by Brett Savory

a DRPZ Publishing imprint
FireHornetCodex.Com

THE LOGOS PROPHECY

Book One in the Fall of Ancients series

MARTIN TREANOR

Fire Donnet Codex

For Sal

DAENY

A grove of palms stood at the lower end of the village. No one paid much attention to the place. It had always been there, set against the sun. On windy days, the trees swayed like Aspara dancers. On a radiant dawn, they split the sunrise into orange shards. Grass and coarse dirt covered the ground between the tall trunks, and the grove itself was so densely packed it was difficult to see all the way through when the hazy light of dusk came down. There were rocks there too. Big, grey ones. And a dilapidated old hut, with thatched palm leaf walls and roof, the traces of its garden lost to the encroaching grass and trees. Beyond the grove, far in the distance, Ta Prohm temple popped-up like a page from a storybook. It was old. Very old. And, being just eleven, Daeny wasn't alive to remember the time when the foreigners came to gawk at the ancient stones. Not that she would get to meet them anyway. Her whole life revolved around Srah Srang and her rambling village of stilt houses. Anywhere farther than the commune rice fields seemed an alien place, including the officials and Khmer Rouge soldiers showing up on occasion to push people around and confiscate the crop.

The man living in the hut was a foreigner, with black skin and khaki green clothes. The villagers said he was an American soldier who deserted the war in the Vietnam. That war was over now. The Americans fled back home the same year the war in Daeny's own country changed, when the carpet bombing and big guns stopped and other types of killing began. The foreigner arrived four months earlier with two large backpacks, an M16 rifle, three pistols, and several bars of chocolate. Sometimes, he sat in the palm shade cleaning his pistols and rifle, smiling and – at the beginning at least – doling out cubes of chocolate to the local children. He had plenty when he arrived. It was gone now. So, for a while, he sat alone, still cleaning his pistols and rifle. Then he stopped coming out of the hut altogether. At other times, he disappeared for weeks on end. When he returned, he remained inside, also for weeks on end, drinking rice wine out of grubby plastic bottles and staring at the walls.

The Khmer Rouge came looking for him.

They came often.

He wasn't there. He never was when they came around, asking questions and beating people until their bodies were broken and bloody. The most recent time, they shot two teenagers dead and wounded an old man so badly he would never walk again. They, however, left Daeny alone.

They didn't know she probably knew more about the foreigner than anyone else alive. Sitting on the rocks closest to the door, she liked to watch him as he papered the thatched walls with pages from books, maps, paragraphs he'd written on scraps of paper with felt-tip pens, the drawings he made of the buildings and carvings at Ta Prohm temple and Angkor Wat, along with strange symbols she'd never seen before. For the weeks he spent inside, he would sit on his camping bed staring at the papers he had pinned to the walls. He ate food from a can, drank his rice wine, shouted and threw things around, then returned to staring. He was a curious person, this dark-skinned foreign soldier and, before he left for one of his excursions, would remove everything - including the maps, pages, and drawings - pack up and go, leaving the place with no signs of anyone having lived there.

The Khmer Rouge came again.

They hurt and killed people.

He returned when they'd left, went about his rigmarole of wall-pinning, drinking, staring, writing, drawing, throwing tantrums, and staring some more. Occasionally, he might glance out through the open doorway and see Daeny sitting on her rock tracing random patterns in the dirt with the heel of her foot. Sometimes he smiled. Other times he slammed the door shut or at least as much as a it could slam being no more than rickety palm leaf thatch. A night, his candles burned and, when the opportunity arose for Daeny to sneak away to spy some more on the curious foreign soldier, she saw him crouched in the darkness, leaning against a palm tree, cradling his rifle in his arms as if expecting an attack. Then, he was off again. A few weeks later he returned, and so it continued for the best part of six months; him heading off, coming back, pinning things to the walls, drinking, staring, writing, drawing, throwing tantrums, staring some more, all the while remaining just those few steps ahead of the Khmer Rouge who got increasingly agitated and evermore vicious with every wasted journey they made.

More villagers died.

Even more still were infirmed, to be then finished off on their next visit.

It was as if people were reeds, mowed down when they became an inconvenience or had no value in the eyes and minds of the people holding the scythes. Rumour had it that, across the country, many were mowed down, particularly those living in the cities, where the educated were taken out to the fields, tortured, and hacked to death. Daeny had never met an educated person, so she had no idea why they were tortured and killed. Maybe they talked back. Everyone knew it was foolish and dangerous to talk back when the Khmer Rouge came asking questions.

For this reason, if nothing else, the villagers stayed well clear of the foreign soldier.

Daeny kept her observations secret from her family, stealing away when they were busy in the rice fields and hurrying through her own work so she could spend an hour or two, scattered throughout the day, attempting to work out what the curious person was up to. So far, mostly because he was either always there or he removed all traces before he left, she'd come up blank. Then the government officials came back and designated the village a co-operative. The Work Units began. Her days changed. The village houses were commandeered, other ramshackle huts were built, the villagers were forced to wear the same baggy black pyjamas, families were separated, and Daeny now spent twelve hours of any given day digging irrigation ditches and lugging soil for the grown-ups building a dam in the river that ran alongside the rice fields. Her exhausted body had little time or energy to keep an eye on the curious foreigner. Except for this day. It was an obligatory holiday, Pol Pot's birthday, and she awoke to a radiant sunrise painting the sky orange, crimson, and a deep, deep purple, casting shadows across the ground as if the stilts upon which the houses stood were the legs of huge and numerous giants. She rose and prepared the single bowl of salted rice for her mother, father, two brothers and sister to share between them. It was her only morning chore and a full day free of labour permitted her an opportunity to find out what happened to the foreigner in the weeks since the officials arrived and turned her life upside down.

For this one, single day, the murders stopped too, and most of the villagers slept.

The American soldier was still there, inside his hut, awake, with the door open, sitting on his bed and drawing with one of his felt-tip pens in a spiral bound notebook. He looked across at her. This time, he smiled, stood, ripped the page from the notebook and set the sketch on the bed. He came out, went across to the palm tree where he used to dole out chocolate to the children. His weapons remained inside the hut; the pistols on the floor, bullets and magazines on the bed alongside the sketch, and his M16 rifle propped against the back wall pointing up to what seemed to be an increased number of book pages, written notes, and drawings. How he had avoided the scrutiny and violence of the Khmer Rouge bemused her. And yet, here he was, sitting at his tree, his expression every bit as downbeat as those of the villagers forced to work long hours for little food.

A helicopter straked the tops of the palm trees, flew out across the dam-works, turned, came back and landed in a glade where the thicker trees of the grove met the soldier's hut. The helicopter was shiny black and carried no markings. With its rotors sweeping massive arcs, whipping the long grass like the heavy winds of the monsoon, its engine idled and two people emerged, jumped down to the ground and walked with a casual pace towards the American soldier sitting pensively by his tree. They wore dark blue, military-like clothing, their lower faces hidden behind balaclavas. When they reached the soldier, they said nothing, one stood beside him, the other crossed to the hut, stripped the maps, pages, writings, and drawings from the walls and shoved them into a backpack on their shoulder, removed a small pebble-like object from their pocket, set it on the floor and left to join their colleague. Seconds later, the hut burst alight, the gusts of the helicopter rotors fanning the flames whereby cinders, ash, and pieces of burning bamboo whisked upon the air as if churned by a tornado. The blaze flared white. The heat searing Daeny's face, forcing her to take refuge behind the biggest rock. There was a loud bang and the soldier's ammunition went off in all directions, squealing, whirling, invisible dangers punching holes and stripping clumps of bark from the palm trees. For the first time since the strangers appeared, she hunkered down. The new arrivals seemed unbothered by her presence or indeed the bullets that strangely splintered everything but them. The soldier seemed unbothered too, he merely stared at the ground, singing a tune Daeny had heard before, back when villagers were permitted to have radios and recognised as one of the American songs the defeated Republic often played on one of their stations. He seemed sad, or resigned, she couldn't tell which.

The bullets ceased.

The blue-clad person took another pebble-like object from their pocket, dropped it into the soldier's lap, then they both turned, went back to the helicopter, took off and, within minutes, were a dot and a drone fading into the distance.

The soldier looked up and across to Daeny. He continued mumbling his song, repeating the first verse over and over... but didn't touch or pick up the pebble in his lap.

Then, like the hut, he burst alight.

The palm tree at his back went with him, then the grove.

People ran out from the village and, by digging a wide ditch and passing buckets of water, one to another from the river to the grove, they managed to stem the flames from fanning out and overtaking their houses. Daeny helped. And, when the blaze was beaten, she returned to the epicentre of the dowsed fire and found the hut, its wooden posts now just a collection of black stubs poking up from within a patch of glassy earth. Over by the smouldering palms, the soldier's ash-white skeletal remains merged with the scorched dirt, the once towering tree behind him cropped and standing like a charred grave marker for the human remains at its base.

From now on, there would be no distractions, only hunger and back-breaking labour.

The maps, pages, and scraps of paper were gone and, with a thought that panged in her heart, so too was her curious foreign soldier. She headed back to the village. A little way down the dirt track, the fading evening sunlight singled out something white amidst the greener grass that had avoided the devastation of the fire. She picked it up. It was a piece of paper, the uniform fringing along its upper edge indicating where it had been torn from a spiral bound notebook. In a singed arc going from the right-hand to left-hand side, the bottom third of the page had been burned away. The top was intact. As was the upper part of a drawing, which Daeny assumed was the last sketch she'd watched her curious soldier make, blown clear of the blaze by the gusts from the helicopter rotor blades. The drawing was only two thirds there and reminded her of a mandala, something perhaps from the great monuments of Angkor Wat.

She shoved the scrap of paper into the waistband of her trousers and returned home.

Over the next two years, she would lose both her parents, her sister, and one of her brothers to famine. The Khmer Rouge snatched her remaining brother away soon after. One day he was there and then, like the rest of her family, he was gone. Two days after her fourteenth birthday, her Work Unit was sent to Siem Pang to labour on yet another major agricultural project. She was skin and bone when the Vietnamese invaded. A kindly woman soldier took pity on her, fed her rice, and talked about bringing her back to Vietnam, to a place called Cao Bang, but yet another war kicked off, only now between Vietnam and China and, just like her brother Sopheak, the woman soldier was gone. Daeny headed south to Kampot, where she found work in the market selling peppercorns. It was there, after a long time being distrustful of most people, she met and married Ai Long, a demobilised Chinese soldier with a chest wound and family ties to Cambodia. In 1991, three miscarriages later and another baby on the way, she told Ai she wanted to birth the child in Kampot. Ai didn't agree because, should the child survive, he wished a better start for their firstborn and they ended up halfway around the world in a grotty basement flat in cold, damp London, Ai reliving his war stories and Daeny longing to return home and find Sopheak.

A few weeks before their daughter's fourteenth birthday, Ai died. The doctors at Paddington Hospital said it was due to undiagnosed problems associated with the bullet wound in his left lung.

Daeny never made the journey back to Cambodia.

Unlike Ai, she never spoke about the wars either, or about her curious American soldier, how he spent his days staring at maps and scraps of paper, his strange drawing, or the day the people in dark blue came to set him and his ramshackle hut alight.

ARY LONG

Peter was a dick. He'd sent her half the way across London on a miserable grey Saturday afternoon for what she assumed to be a legitimate cosplay gig, but which he later revealed – after she had already boarded the Tube – to be a character portrayal for some fifty-three-year-old bloke, having a party for one and wanted, quote-unquote, *any angel from the original movies* to blow out the candles on his birthday cake. The closest person Peter had on his books to fill the remit was Ary because, setting the blatant misogyny aside, in the right tight-fitting clothes, she bore a more than passing resemblance to one of the said angels.

How many times did she need to tell him about this shit?

She was a serious actor-stroke-model-stroke-face-double. The whole lookalike thing was supposed to be reserved for comic-cons and media events but, then again, her house-share in Kilburn didn't pay for itself and the two hundred quid, less Peter's one-third commission, would go a long way towards the eight hundred she needed to make sure her pokey, dismal, mould-mottled room remained somewhere to lay her head for at least another month. A few years back, before the pandemic, there had been not numerous but sufficient opportunities for an actor-type person of Cambodian and Chinese descent to find work. Mostly professional cosplay, the occasional energy drink or food promotion for online news-sites, and she even landed a TV advert once, where she played the busy sister of a busier mother of three, delighted to arrive home to a bowl of steaming noodles and cup of Golden Guangxi tea.

The advertising industry didn't really get the *don't do stereotypes thing*.

If something worked, they did it to death. Even if it was offensive, or a lie. Especially if it was a lie. Lying on purpose to sell shit no one needed was their raison d'être after all. But the virus had put the bullet in that reasoning too. The post-pandemic planet was in a strange place. The advertising world seemed desperate. Things weren't going to plan. And the rot had spread to politics. Something the king of gas-lighters, puffy-red-face Vladdy Putrid had found out when he tried to start World War III. People resisted. Fought back. Well, some people fought back. Others sulked. And it wasn't the first time, nor will it be the last, that the reality humans had come to covet and trust had all but gone, smothered beneath a heady cocktail of a virus, economic uncertainty, wars, and lack of political will to do anything quantitative that might address the imbalance.

The warmonger blamed a supposed enemy.

The religious pointed to an angered god.

The pragmatist said our circumstances came about through neglect, hubris, and denial of our place in the scheme of things.

The sceptic, however, saw a more malign influence than mere neglect or the petulant tantrums of a higher being. *The world is not an abstract construct*, they might say. *Things are the way they are because of careful planning, pitching human against human, human against nature, and therein against whatever god they chose to devote their thoughts and lives to.* People had become suspicious.

Well, some people had become suspicious. Others sold their souls for the latest phone, a TV, football, sad soaps and reality shows swarming with loud-mouthed wannabes or posh-arsed trendies. They genuflected at the feet of their perceived betters, blundering through life and wilfully absorbing any and all arse-gravy dished out by Etonians, Bullingtons, Bonesmen, those born to the right families, born to rule, powerful people who knew how to both brew it and spew it. Scooby Snacks for the gullible.

Keep'em stupid. Keep'em angry. Give'em someone to blame.

It was a playbook as old as humans had been ravaging the Earth. Accumulate wealth and power, ferret it away and, if unwanted eyes become too inquisitive, find a scapegoat, usually a misunderstood and maligned minority – or perhaps even a few – then lay the blame all of society's ills on their overburdened laps. Throw in a foreign enemy for good measure, either real or fabricated, marry them together with said misunderstood and maligned minority – which the easily led have now come to hate – and, like turkeys gobbling towards Christmas slaughter, the great exploitable public would do anything to preserve the unbalanced and repressive status quo. The privileged had it all sown up. And still they desired more, lusted for it all. Wealthy malcontents bullying those in need to greater deprivation, devoid of empathy, sympathy, or the common goodness of doing the right thing. They were a plague. A swarm of aspiration sucking parasites, stripping all before them and leaving the ragged stalks of anger in their wake.

The usurpers.

The liar clique.

The wasting death of decency.

And yet, much to Ary's surprise, even the easily led were asking questions. In most cases the wrong ones. But questioning existence was a right she viewed as the most important trait a person could possess, and a positive development.

Deep within one of her frequent *brain-rants* – her unwritten streams of consciousness, if you will – she recalled how it had started. Fifteen years earlier. With a book. And, here she was, as the tube-train trundled to a stop at Bethnal Green station, still scrolling through the same pages. Not the printed format, though. When not at home, she read it on her phone, even though the ebook version lessened the impact of the images. Ary didn't do bags either; not hand, side, shoulder, or even a backpack. A few years before, a mugger had slashed the strap on an old, fifties-era munitions bag she'd found in a junk shop and made off with her phone, tablet, make-up, hairbrush, and all of her notes about the lost city of Atlantis being at the centre of an ancient civilization. Luckily, it was the main tenet of her *hypotheses*, as she liked to call them. Her research was well backed up. Since then, however, when outside she took nothing but her phone. And anyway – on top of the post-Brexit accusatory glares she received for having the audacity to sport a Southeast Asian ethnicity – when she read the physical version of her favourite book, the judgemental glances irked her. One time, she actually had one professorial-looking type scoff loudly, his eyes rolling ceiling-ward as he flicked through the pages of his paper copy of the *Daily Telegraph*.

Yeah, as if that was truth.

Ary read other books too. She loved Greek classics - particularly the story of Theseus and the Minotaur. The idea of having to navigate a labyrinth to find the root of a problem epitomised her every thought. These days, however, most of her books were like this one: a comprehensive validation of aliens walking among us. And, although she had grown to dispute some of the author's approach, it had been her first step into questioning, studying, cross-referencing, and seeing the universe without blinkers.

A handful of passengers got off and some boarded the train.

They looked like cattle.

They were cattle.

Ary smiled, not out of humour, but from pity. If they only knew. It was why she started her blog, called it *Hard Truth*. A hard hitting, full disclosure resource for anyone wishing to swallow the red pill and speak truth to malign power.

The train moved off.

Only two stops more and she would arrive at Stratford, home to the 2012 Olympics and the weirdy-weird fifty-three-year-old man who devoted way too much of his time to a movie while all around him the world was heading down a rabbit hole of deepest delusions.

She put her phone in her pocket.

'Does this train stop at Mile End,' a foreign-sounding person asked her from across the carriage, his voice muffled by a blue surgical facemask.

Ary wore a facemask too. Looped over both ears, beneath waves of black hair. She always did on the bus or Tube. A black one to compliment the black skin-tight outfit and plastic thigh-length, uncomfortably high-heeled boots evoking the persona of movie action hero. The mask kind of shattered the illusion but, unlike the misguided denialists, she respected the disease that had ravaged the planet for near on two years. For her, when her mother spent three weeks in ICU and still wheezed when she breathed, it had been all too real. Maybe manufactured, or at least propagated by some kind of environmental mismanagement, but real. She had no intention of either dying or contracting long-term lung damage because some feckless numbnut, thinking such things an insult to their rights, wanted to be a prick and not wear a facemask, or get the vax.

They were also getting distracted by the wrong conspiracy.

She made a mental note to write another blog about the subject and said, 'yes' to the foreign-sounding person, adding, 'We'll be there in about a minute,' to at least show that, unlike the *anti-mask-anti-vax* knob-knuckles, she did give a shit about other people.

The foreign-sounding person left at the next station.

Ary did likewise when she reached Stratford and walked through the centre-complex of shops and restaurants to where the fifty-three-year-old movie enthusiast lived on the tenth floor of one of the newer tower blocks. She went up in the lift, found the flat and rang the doorbell. The man answered, thankfully wearing jeans and, as expected, a T-shirt emblazoned with the requisite movie logo. He was slim, good-looking in a David Tennant kind of way, and not at all creepy as she'd expected.

He ushered her inside to a large open-plan living room and kitchen.

She followed, surprised, although she didn't know why, to see his flat looked much as you expect for a professional type living in this part of London: grey walls, hardwood floors, plush furniture, and a massive television hanging on the wall above an oak sideboard. Maybe she expected to see more movie stuff: posters, figurines, tacky pink cushions with the three actors' faces on them.

He offered her a drink.

She declined.

He asked did she like the movies.

She lied, and said, 'I love them. That's why I play the part.' He smiled, broadly, and Ary got the impression her simple answer had totally made his day.

He said, 'give me moment,' disappeared through a beaded curtain to what looked like a pantry, returning seconds later with a red and orange coloured birthday cake also emblazoned with the logo. A single unlit candle sat in the centre.

He set the cake down onto a frosted-glass coffee-table.

'I kind of expected your flat to be covered with memorabilia,' Ary said.

'I'm a nutcase,' the bloke replied, 'but not that big of a nutcase.' He sniggered. 'I do have my *Angel Room*, though.'

Ary smiled and thought, *there it is. I knew there had to be something.*

'I can show it to you, if you'd like,' he added.

'Maybe after I do the cake thing.'

'Good thinking. Always good to get the main show out of the way.' He seemed nervous. Probably social anxiety. It would explain a lot.

'Now, how do you want to do this?' she asked, taking off her short, black corduroy jacket (the only part of her clothing not in character) and tossing it over the arm of the sofa. 'I say, you light the candle. I'll cut a suitable pose. You take a bunch of selfies, photos, video, whatever it is you'd like to do to preserve the moment. I'll blow out the candle. Wish you a happy birthday in Lucy Liu's voice – and, yes, I can do that – then, that's it. You have an *almost real-life action star* scored into your memory for eternity.'

The guy gestured with an unemotional nod.

The excitement in his gaze, however, spoke of his delight inside.

Ary did her thing, complete with throwing a few character-esque moves, a couple of high-kicks, voiced an authentic '*Good morning,*' and a glare directed at the cake that said, *fuck with me and I'll smash you to crumbs.*

The bloke took photos on his phone.

No selfies, though.

Ary noted how, since she'd arrived, he had kept a respectful distance.

She threw some more moves and blew out the candle, with words, '*And that's kicking your ass!*'

The bloke was beaming. Said, 'Thank you.'

'My pleasure,' Ary replied, still in character, and turned to leave.

'Are you sure you don't want to see my *Angel Room*?' the guy asked again.

'Nah! That's okay. I have another gig to get to.' She didn't, but also didn't have the heart to let him down.

With an outstretched palm, he ushered her to the door and said, 'The money should already be in the account.'

'Not my department,' Ary replied as she went out to the concourse, 'but thanks for letting me know. Anyway, have a great birthday.'

The bloke nodded.

Ary smiled and before the door closed, she asked, 'By the way. Your name isn't Charlie is it?'

The guy tilted his head and nodded.

'I suppose it figures.' She smiled and walked towards the lift.

On the way back to the Tube, she thought about the bloke called Charlie who maybe felt so alone that, to glean some semblance of self-worth, he needed an *almost real-life* fictional character to blow out the single candle on his birthday cake. She berated herself for having misjudged the guy, for having deemed him a weirdy-weirdo before she met him. He was just lonely and found comfort in fantasy characters created by others.

And wasn't that what she was trying to expose in the first place?

The illusion of existence. The fictional reality created by shady persons and organisations designed to smother the truth. It was the misdirection of stage magicians. While the susceptible public were focused one way, the powers that be were manipulating, fleecing, securing power for themselves. It was what Ary was out to reveal.

The *Great Lie.*

She had to do it.

For herself... and for people like Charlie.

HARPER T JACKSON

On the way home, Ary ate a three-bean burrito for dinner and arrived back at her room around seven. Being a Saturday evening, her three house-share-mates were out, probably half-pissed and slaughtering pop classics at the karaoke pub down the road. Not that they were *mates* in the true sense of the word. Her need for a room when she returned from her last trip away had merely solved a financial hole for them and interactions were few and far between.

To them, she had wackadoodle ideas about... well, everything.

And they weren't alone.

Except for Mateus and other likeminded enthusiasts online, most people viewed her as a conspiracy crazy crackpot. *Norms* didn't like being told their whole world view was a manufactured illusion. They thought themselves to be realists. Ary thought them gullible. She knew the truth or was, at least, open to questioning the way of things. They went with the flow: a solicitor and two accountants, three full-on, card carrying, bone fide rats in the race.

She changed into her cosy bunnies pyjamas, opened a bag of plain salted crisps, fired up her games console and spent the next few hours assassinating ancient Greeks. At half past ten, she put down the controller, opened her laptop and wrote a post about the current state of politics for her *Hard Truth* blogsite. Completed, she then opened another tab to a website which was commonly regarded within conspiracy theory circles to be the deepest, darkest and therefore most credible resource. Eleven o'clock, every Saturday night was when *News Drop* dropped. No one knew who the mind or minds behind it were, but it was collectively assumed by the participants of numerous chatrooms that it was someone with access to the most secret of secrets. A kind of gnostic. Dripping truth to the world.

Most of their broadcasts reiterated what she already knew.

On occasion, however, they revealed a real nugget about a new order, the Illuminati, or a shady group they called the Caucus. It was all good stuff. Today's *News Drop* focused on the power behind the oil economies, political influencers, the rich, politicians, and finished up, a half-hour later, with a video of a blurred figure admitting to another blurred figure that they had proof, soon to be released, of the Bilderberg Group's planning for the next global recession.

No surprise there. It was what they did.

The screen went blank. The usual way *News Drop* signed off.

Ary reached across to the mini-fridge beside her bed, popped the cap on a beer, and began her standard Saturday night activity of scouring the internet for material for her next *Hard Truth* blog. She had to be careful, though. Someone was always watching, listening, documenting clicks, and no doubt building a dossier. It was why she learned how to protect her information, had *vanish quality* VPN, and blogged under the moniker, *Harper T. Jackson* instead of her real name. In a world controlled by shadowy organisations, no precaution was too much.

She browsed her usual series of websites, uncovering evidence of ancient aliens, time-travellers, and immortals like *Comte de Saint-Germain* and – hard to fathom but, as far as Ary was concerned, it was true – that shit-stirring war-hawk, Vlad fucking Putin. Must be easy to start wars, when you have no skin in the game. The guy made her skin crawl. He was a real loser. And a dangerous fucker at that. Which was why she tended to avoid politically inclined domains. One or two references to the shite going on in this world was enough. And they tended to be spaces for the ill-informed, serving only angry arseholes, somewhere to vent their frustrations and hate. Not a good resource for information. She drank some more beers and, around one in the morning, with little in the way of anything new to contribute to her next blog post, decided to call it a night. She closed all the tabs in her browser. One refused. Which, when she thought about it, she couldn't remember opening in the first place.

The site had no title.

Or a URL.

Consisting of single page, and a single image.

Her skin felt tingly. Tiny hairs stood on the back of her neck and arms.

The description beneath the image stated: *Machu Picchu*. Nothing else. And, to Ary, the carved stone did indeed appear Incan but with different characteristics to others she had researched. Although carved in the customary blocky style, the detailing looked weird for the setting, more like something found at Angkor Wat or the temple at Ta Prohm. Which, to Ary, also didn't come as a surprise. As far as she was concerned there were undeniable similarities between the ancient Khmer and American peoples. The folkloric sameness of the Orion traditions across the planet were indisputable. The temple at Koh Ker was proof perfect. Save a few defining Khmer characteristics, it was an almost double for any Incan site. And yet, it was the spiral relief in the centre of the carving that intrigued her most. It looked Neolithic, maybe even Mesolithic, definitely North European and not something she expected to see from a Peruvian source.

She downloaded and saved the image, made a note in her *Hard Truth* research journal and bookmarked the webpage. She also didn't sleep much, spending the hours until dawn and into mid-morning resting, waking, hearing the others bang, crash, and shush each other as they arrived home, but mostly scouring the internet for another reference to the strange symbol. At 10.45 she texted Mateus. Like her house-share mates, he was a Saturday night kinda guy and on Sundays didn't respond to anything much before lunchtime.

The text said:

> *Found something really cool*
> *You gotta see it*

Mateus didn't reply. She expected as much.

She got dressed in old black jeans and her grey, washed-out but comfy *Truth is Out There* T-shirt. Apart from her cosplay and performance garb, Ary considered herself distinctly zero-fashion – *couldn't-be-arsed chic* she called it. She added to the ensemble with a grey hoody older even than the jeans and T-shirt, threw on her short black jacket, ran a brush through her hair and tied it into two K-pop style ponytail buns atop her head with a yellow ribbon in one and red in the other. They were the only colour she allowed to her *look*, if a person could call it as much.

She thought them *quirky*.

As in the person on the bus the *norms* always avoided quirky.

Job done, she attempted to transfer a copy of the image of the unusual symbol from her laptop to her phone. The file wasn't there. She looked through her folders, many times, searched in temporary files, recent files, downloaded files. She looked everywhere. The image was gone. She checked her browser favourites. The bookmark was gone too. No image. No website. The oddness of which both intrigued and scared her.

Someone did this.

Someone who might be watching her right now. And monitoring her phone.

Regardless, she texted Mateus again:

> *I'm coming round*
> *There's some real weird shit going on*

As expected, he didn't reply.

She left.

The day was warm for mid-April but grey, cloudy, clammy hot, and exuding the disconsolate dullness that seem to always accompany any given Sunday. In the street outside, a fat tabby sat with one leg bolt upright licking its bum on the bonnet of a grey 4x4. A pigeon pecked at a soggy, half-eaten sandwich in the gutter. Two kids, heading in the direction of the park on the other side of the crossroads, kicked a ball to each other. A well-dressed man got into a car and drove away. Everything looked normal and unthreatening. If she was being watched, whoever it was, was very good at it. Then why wouldn't they be? That's what shadowy agencies did: watched people and were very good at it. And she should know. Because of her *Hard Truth* blog, she fully expected to be bugged, tapped, and tracked. Not to mention, she was one of them too. Her *rat in the race job* – well, her one day at the weekend and maybe another if Nigel was in a generous mood job – was surveillance with Transport for London. The actor-stroke-model-stroke-face-double gigs helped pay the rent. Camera-surveillance with TfL financed her exploratory foreign trips which was the main reason why, at thirty-one she'd never set down roots. It was the second biggest of her mother's many disappointments. The first being Ary's insistence to study History at London Met instead of opting for a nice, normal, secure, career-generating degree like Business and Finance.

There was, however, too much to investigate. Many conspiracies to bust.

Being a *norm* would only get in the way.

That said, she had a six-hour shift today, starting at 3pm. The irony of which wasn't lost on her either. Ary Long, under the pseudonym *Harper T. Jackson* might campaign for the truth but, when push came to shove and cash was short, she full on toed the line for *the Man*, as the hippies in the sixties used to say.

How's that for a hypocrisy?

The great conspiracy warrior, one-hundred percent part of the herd.

BIG FUCKING THING

Pulling her hoody over her head, Ary hurried up the street to the crossroads, went out onto Carlton Vale and onwards to Kilburn Park station. In the concourse, she took her black facemask from her jacket pocket, put it on, took the escalator down to the platform and found a dark corner to wait for the next train. The speaker crackled. A voice uttering an unintelligible message, coinciding with a familiar rush of air that let her know the train was arriving at the platform. She boarded, moved down inside the carriage, and stood by the adjoining door to the next, staring at the floor. A woman, wearing a beige trench-coat glanced up with the haughty expression of an overbearing mother from a made-for-TV Christmas movie. She was working through the *Mail on Sunday* crossword with a gold pen while opposite her, as if in direct antithesis, a young guy with bright green hair, neck tattoos, eyebrow-rings, also wearing a facemask, played a game on his phone. Both were engrossed. Both rendered invisible by the act of doing nothing of any consequence.

All along the carriage people sat or stood, hunkered and brittle behind newspapers, books, phones, and tablets; their chosen form of concealment. Ary reckoned not one of these people, including the cool-looking young guy, would give a flying fart if she proved her hypothesis that extra-dimensional entities controlled every aspect of their lives all the way down to the *Mail on Sunday* crossword and an RPG mobile-phone game.

To her mind, they seemed blissful with the importance of being unimportant.

At Paddington she changed to the Circle Line and took advantage of the onboard WiFi to search for the strange symbol. She found nothing. Reaching White City, she got off and walked to Loftus Road. Mateus had a flat there; three double bedrooms, two receptions, on the top floor of a period mansion block called Prince Albert Court. It was nice. Rich person nice. Mateus kept it well considering, apart from a fervent interest in conspiracy theories or *conspiracy truths*, as Ary called them, he couldn't give a toss about most things other people found important. He had a good job, though: a music producer, ran his own label, Stinky Hole Records, and was one of the business's few successes. It sheltered him from the realities of life. He wanted for nothing.

Mateus answered his door in blue paisley boxers. His eyes were red, his shoulder-length grey hair a bird's nest. He didn't look happy.

'What the fuck, Ary. It's the middle of the bloody night.'

'It's nearly noon.'

'That's what I said. On Sundays, anything before mid-afternoon is the middle of the night.'

He grunted and went back inside without inviting her in.

Ary followed. The flat was a mess. Beer cans littered the floor. Pizza boxes and Chinese food cartons filled the spaces between the room's two sofas. Residual white powder betrayed where someone had been cutting lines on the glass coffee-table.

'What happened here. Not like you to kick the shit out of your own flat.'

'I had people over,' Mateus replied, returning from his bedroom tying his dressing-gown.

'People or howler monkeys.'

'A new band.'

'Any good?'

'They've got potential.'

For someone whose business depended on communication skills, Mateus often said little when asked a direct question. If it came from within his own head, however, it was a struggle to get him to shut up.

'It stinks like a smoke ridden jockstrap in here,' Ary said, gripping her nose.

'How would you know what a jockstrap smells like?'

'I've played with the odd rugby ball... or two.'

'Ah, I forgot, you like 'em sporty.'

'I like 'em any way. And what I wants I gets.'

'Sure. Not me, though.'

'You're in the friend zone. I don't shag mates.'

'I know. I'm just being awkward.' He peered around the room, went across to the nearest sofa and plunged one hand down the back of the cushions, gave up with a grunt, did likewise with the second sofa, before turning to Ary, 'For fuck sake, ring my bloody phone would ya.'

She did.

It was right there on the coffee-table, buzzing away beneath an old copy of a prominent music magazine with the front-cover title: *Mateus Prata – Life After Radon Death*. For two glorious years in the late-nineties, his band, Radon Death was the muso-zines' latest big thing; five *Billboard Rock & Metal* hits, one Grammy, two Brits, a full roster of gigs, television appearances, a butt-load of cash, before the whole thing collapsed; the usual way, through drink, drugs, and lack of commitment. Mateus did alright out of it, though. As the front-guy, he went on to do a solo album which, being moderately successful, gained him the industry creds and moolah to launch an indie label. *To give back*, he'd say. Oh, and to earn even bigger butt-loads of cash.

'So, I see you hauled out the magazine to impress the youngsters again?'

'It's what I do.' He swiped his phone and read his texts. 'So, what's all this *weird shit* that's *going on*? It better be bloody good.'

'It's freaky.'

'Like what?'

Ary swept some empty cans from a sofa and sat down. A dribble of beer dripped onto the hardwood floor. Mateus glared but said nothing.

'What? As if that little piddle makes a difference in this pigsty.'

'The cleaner is booked for two. It's driving me nuts just looking at the place. It's why I sleep through on days like these... but then you turned up. Coffee?'

'Please.'

Mateus went through to the kitchen and, a few moments later, returned with two cups, handing one to Ary.

'Pod machines are the bollocks. Don't know what I'd do without one. He cleared the cans from the other side of the sofa and sat down. 'So, let me have it then. What has you so worked up?'

'An image.'

'An image? You woke me up at fuck-off o'clock on a Sunday for a bloody image?'

'Yes.'

'And what? You couldn't email or message it to me?'

'You never check your emails.'

Mateus smirked, sipped his coffee.

'Or your messages. So, I came over. Anyway, I couldn't send it. But I'll get to that later. Do you want to hear or not?'

'Go on. But it better be good.' He rubbed his eyes, took another sip of coffee and sighed.

Ary took a sip too. 'Anyway, I was doing the usual last night. Tuned into the eleven o'clock *News Drop*.'

'Yeah, I missed that one. Wish I hadn't, though. My head would be thanking me for it.'

'Yeah, right. Well, anyway, after the sign off, I got down to some internet snoopings and loaded a site I don't even remember opening. But it was right there, so I must have. Strange thing was, it had no URL. Just an image and a blank address bar.'

'This is what you got me out of bed for? With a head like this.'

'Yes, I know, you're going to say it's probably just a tech glitch.'

'Pretty much. Yeah.'

'Me too... normally. But the whole site was just the image. A symbol. Said *Machu Picchu*. Nothing else.'

'So? They all say that. *It's Machu Picchu*. People love making connections with Machu Picchu. It's everyone's favourite go to. Or Egypt. Everyone loves an ancient Egyptian conspiracy.'

'I know. Me too. If it's credible. But this one was a carved stone.'

Mateus feigned shock. 'Oh no, not a carved stone. I'm glad you came to me first. I'll pack a bag. We'll need to go underground. GCHQ are probably looking for us right now. Who would ever have suspected there would be a conspiracy about a carved stone?' He sniggered.

Ary scoffed. 'Funny. You're a fucking riot. This one was different, though. Definitely Incan but the peripheral detailing looked like something you'd see at Angkor Wat. And it had spiralling in the centre, more North European Neolithic than South American.'

'So what? You know as well as I do, there are commonalities across the ancient world.'

'Yes. But not all together in the same glyph or symbol.'

'And you think this stone will confirm your theory about an ancient global culture?'

'Not *an* ancient global culture. *The* ancient global culture. A sophisticated civilization built by the dimension-hopping elders. You know this. You helped me research it.'

'I did. And I believe it.' He sipped his coffee. Ary did likewise. 'But you'll need more than one carved stone to prove it.'

'I know. It will be part of my next inquiry.'

'Well, show me then.'

'That's the really weird bit... and why, apart from you being a knob on Sundays and not checking your messages, I didn't email it to you. I was going to. I downloaded it. Saved it on my laptop. But, when I looked for it again, it wasn't there. I searched through all my folders. It was gone. I should've made a drawing in my journal.'

'Are you sure you downloaded it right? Did you check in the temporary folder?'

'Duh-huh! Of course I checked the temporary folder. But why don't you go ahead and dick-splain it to me anyway. I keep forgetting that having a vag and tits makes me thick as shit.'

'I'm not. I just wondered...'

'*Yes*, I checked the temporary folder. And recent files. And downloaded files. I know my way around a laptop, Mateus.'

'Sorry, I didn't mean...'

'I know. Actually, you're one of the good ones. I'm just a bit spooked is all.'

'Because you lost an image?'

'Yes, because I lost an image. One that looked strange in the first place. And also – which is the mega-freaky thing – apart from having no URL, the bookmark I placed in my favourites was gone too. And I couldn't find the website again either.'

'What was it called?' Mateus asked, opening the screen on his phone.

'Didn't have a title. Just the image. On the way here, I searched using: *Machu Picchu Symbols*, *Ancient American Symbols*, *Inca*, and a whole raft of other similar criteria. Nyet. Not a jot.'

He tapped and scrolled several times.

Ary looked on. 'Well?'

'Nope. You are right. Nada. Zilch. But a longer search might pull up something. Are you sure it said *Machu Picchu*?'

'Fuck sake, here you go again. Yes! It said *Machu Picchu*. Remembering strange stuff is what I do, remember.'

'Well, I can't find anything.'

'Me neither.'

'So, what are you going to do?'

'Dunno. Keep looking. You know me, I'm like a dog with a bone. This is something else, though. I've never seen a website disappear two minutes after I found it. And, as for the file just deleting itself from my laptop, that's just total intergalactic space-aliens monitoring you through your fillings kinda shit. Mind you, not that that's not happening too. I just think intergalactic space-aliens might be a tad more sophisticated than employing something any old dentist can go poking around in. And anyway, I don't have fillings. I've never had fillings. I brush. And floss. Squeaky clean. See.' She bared her teeth.

'You're rambling. What's wrong? Is your mother-board malfunctioning?'

'Funny. No, as I said before, I'm totes freaked.'

'*Totes* freaked?'

'Yes, *totes*.'

'What are you, fourteen?'

'What can I say. My inner prom-queen comes out when weird shit happens.'

'But weird shit always happens to you.'

'I know. But this shit is totes cray-cray.'

They both laughed. Mateus reached out and held her hand. 'It might be nothing. You know yourself, Ary, when you get this far down the rabbit hole, most things don't make sense.'

'True. But who has the capability to delete files and bookmarks?'

'If your blogs are to be believed, all of them.'

Ary thought about it. 'You're right. So then, why me? There are oodles of conspiracy theory bloggers out there doing the same thing.'

'Maybe you plucked a nerve. Isn't that what you wanted all along? You always say your life's goal is to uncover the *big fucking thing*. If this even is the big fucking thing. It might be nothing. Archaeologists make weird finds all the time. Most of which turn out to be no more than some ancient priest or other, getting their jollies by soaking their favourite pyramid in human blood.'

'I believe they're all linked.'

'I know. You're cooky.' He laughed.

'Hey. That's not nice.'

'What did the carving look like anyway?'

'Like an Incan Cross but with atypical features... and the centre circle contained spirals.'

Mateus bounced up, dashed into the second bedroom he used as a home office, and returned flicking through the pages of a large, tattered, hardback book:

'Anything like this?' He sat down and set the open book on Ary's lap.

A picture on the page, surrounded by text and other images, depicted an Incan Chakana Cross, carved in stone with a single spiral in the centre.

'Kind of,' Ary replied, 'but set inside a circle. The detailing at the cardinal points looked Khmer, and there were three centre spirals – forming a triskele.' She lifted the edge to view the front cover. It was grey, fraying at the corners and nondescript, with just the wording, *Hidden Peru* written in black. 'Where did you get this?'

'From that second-hand book shop in Muswell Hill. You know, the one that carries all those cool documents and academic papers. Funny enough, I was drawn to the images. And there are a few symbols and Incan texts in there I'd never seen before. Not even in the Dresden Codex. I just had to buy it.'

Ary returned to the image. 'Well, this is similar but not exactly the same. As I said, the triskele in the centre looked as if it came from northern Europe. But, then again, *power of three* symbolism was rife in the ancient world. It's in the Giza pyramids, as well as just about every religion... the symbol itself could just as easily be Indian, Chinese, African... from anywhere really. All I can say for sure is, it was defo unique. And I'd love to know more, but the whole wiping the file thing has me feeling a bit jittery.'

'You'll be okay. It's not the first time you stumbled onto something you shouldn't.'

'Yeah, but those were government sites. I'm way too *cooky*, as you so kindly put it, to be of any major interest to them. It still amazes me that I even got the camera surveillance job.'

'Maybe they've got you where they want you.'

'Or me them.'

'That too... perhaps. So, who do you think posted the image in the first place?'

'I don't know.' Ary replied. 'But I'm going to find out.'

After a few more coffees, Ary left Mateus to suffer his hangover in peace. At five past three, she arrived for her camera shift at the TfL offices and spent the rest of the day snooping on red light breakers, illegal parkers, and London's general populace as they traipsed in and out of overflowing Tube stations. When she'd arrived, Nigel – in that passive aggressive tone he had honed to perfection – ripped her a new one for being late. For some bonkers reason, Ary felt somewhat in awe of her boss; the articulate way he wrapped an obvious bollocking into a string of saccharine sentiments, intended to humiliate while always making sure to skirt a few steps shy of being outright abusive. It was a true art and Ary considered herself well and truly admonished. If she gave a shit, that was. Five hours and fifty minutes later, with today's tour of duty about to end, like the sequel to a bad zombie movie, Nigel turned up again, to remind Ary of the five minutes she had to add to the shift, along with the fifteen extra it took to get chewed out for being late in the first place.

Then, with a swish of bright yellow viscose and cheap aftershave, Nigel disappeared back into his office.

Ary checked through her reports from the day and prepared to leave... in twenty minutes, of course, as instructed. The gig was a handy one. No point winding up the *Dick of the Dead* and getting sacked.

The footage on one of her screens wavered. The image from the previous night popping up where a wide-angle view of the entrance to Charing Cross Station had been a couple of seconds earlier.

Ary looked across to her nearest colleague. 'Talat... can you see this?'

'See what?' he replied, with little interest, deep into the process of registering a silver BMW 2 Series parked on double red lines at London Bridge.

'This.' She looked back at the screen. The image was gone, returned to the view of Charing Cross Station.

Talat peered across. 'What am I looking for?'

'Nothing. Doesn't matter.'

Talat went back to his paperwork and, regardless of Nigel's instructions to make up additional minutes, Ary left. With haste. On the way home, she avoided the Tube, walked to Hyde Park Corner and took the bus to Kilburn Park, snuggling down into the rearmost seat on the top deck, with her jacket buttoned up, her hoody pulled over her head, arriving home no less freaked out for having made it there. Scoffing down the mushroom pie she had bought from a chip shop on the way home, she fired up her laptop, tossed it onto the bed as if the mere touch might prompt a bunch of armed mercenaries to burst through her window, dart her with sedative, and haul her off to their secret basement torture chamber. She laughed at the thought, and then noticed the tremble in her hands.

Arranging the laptop so she could view the screen from a spot by the door, she sat cross-legged on the floor and waited for something to happen. Sometime later, she reached across, disabled the sleep setting, drifted off, and felt both elated and disappointed to wake with sunshine streaming through the window blinds, the weave of the carpet embossed on her cheek, but no reappearance of the image. She sketched a drawing from memory, posted it on her *Hard Truth* blog and asked for help in identifying the symbol. In her persona of *Harper T Jackson*, she felt somewhat shielded from unwanted attention. It was why she chose to create the character in the first place, and used a uber-secure VPN. Truth seeking in the conspiracy network attracted all sorts of whackos. As well as prying government eyes. She would never give up, though. The truths she investigated were too important.

Apart from a trip to the corner shop for crisps and a fizzy drink, she stayed in her spot by the door until night fell. No one answered her call. The image didn't return. And, although returning to the comfort of her bed, she continued like this for next five days, checking websites, checking the blog, watching, checking, taking some selfies for Peter to advertise his *Birthday with a Movie Star* service, watching, checking the blog, filling an emergency sickness-cover shift for Nigel at TfL – apparently even shite employees can be called upon when the regulars don't turn up for work – checking websites, checking the blog, doing a dress-up gig as an Anime fan-fiction art group, watching, checking, watching and, by the following

Saturday, her nervousness had faded to the point she switched off the laptop and even joined her three housemates for a few pints down at the karaoke pub.

She had a good time.

They turned out to be not as stick-up-their-own-arses as she'd expected.

She sank a stack of tequila shots, sang two Amy Winehouse numbers, snogged a super hot woman she met in the toilets, and woke to curtain-dimmed daylight; on her bed, fully dressed, with a crick in her neck and the remnants of a falafel pita strewn over the duvet. Her head thumped. Her mouth tasted like the falafel had decomposed there. The mere sounds of the day were insects gnawing into her brain: a siren shrieking up at the high street, a crow cawing outside, that fucking bluebottle whacking, whacking, whacking, whacking against the bloody windowpane. Her thirst was unbearable. She got up and went to the bathroom out in the corridor, drank from the washbasin tap, did a piss, and doused her face in an attempt to come round. It didn't work. She returned to her room and checked the time on her phone... six forty-three, which explained why, apart from the snoring coming from Madeleine's room, the house was deader than a parish cake-bake. She changed into her fluffy bunny onesie – stumbling a fair few times before she mastered the task – got into bed, pulled her falafel strewn duvet over her head and fell back to sleep. An indeterminable time later, her phone buzzed on the bedside table. The screen brightened. With blurry gaze roaming the room, she reached across and pulled the phone close to her face. No one was calling. There was no text either. Just the image from a week earlier.

Then, it disappeared.

HOME IS WHERE THE START IS... WAS

Throwing her phone onto the bed, Ary bounced up. The sudden effort stung like a bitch, in both brain and body. She grabbed her laptop from where she'd slid it underneath the bed and checked her blog. The post with the sketch was gone. Not that it mattered. Nobody had answered her request to identify the symbol anyway. Or, if they had, their comments had been removed along with the post. By whom or what, she didn't know. She felt vulnerable. Fearful. Wary of her own devices.

Setting the laptop on the bed, she reached out and opened the screen on her phone without picking it up, as if, like greeting an expectant vampire standing in the doorway, to do so might invite some level of malevolence into her life. Everything looked normal. She texted Mateus, telling him about the reappearance of the image and that her blog had been tampered with.

He didn't reply.

As usual, she hadn't expected him to. He would later. He was like that, always indulging her theories. A couple of times, he had accompanied her on her trips; the first to Crete, searching for signs of a possible interdimensional portal, and because she just loved the old Greek classic about Theseus. The second took them to the Yucatán Peninsula, where Ary felt certain she would find evidence for her ancient global culture. Mateus was a good travel companion. Had the energy of a curios five-year-old. And was loaded. Not that she needed such base things as money. He was, however, nice to have around. Especially when they failed to find proof of either theory. It didn't stop her trying, or travelling, though. Or Mateus begging to accompany her.

She went to the window and peeked around the edge of the curtain.

Apart from pigeons and the occasional person walking by, the street outside was as lifeless as any other Sunday. She didn't, however, trust her eyes. If someone could infiltrate her phone and laptop, they could also remain hidden. There but invisible. She got dressed. Thankfully, Nigel hadn't logged her for a shift today. He hadn't logged her for any shifts this week. Or indeed the week after. And Ary got the impression that her boss's passive aggressive bollockings had given way to a full-on aggressive sacking. The midweek emergency cover she'd provided might well have been her last. Nigel just hadn't made her aware of it yet. Might never. He was like that... such a fucking tosser.

That said, Ary was thankful for the lack of obligation.

The day was hers.

She dressed, hastily slipped her phone into her jacket pocket and left. Like everyone else, her phone was a *must have with*, even if it provided an entry point for a shady someone or some-ones to observe her movements.

Taking a vigilant, hoody up, tube-journey north to Stonebridge Park, she walked a kilometre to the comfortable two-bedroom flat her parents had been transferred to when redevelopment razed the concrete shitholes that had once blighted the area with crime and crappy lives. She didn't ring ahead, let herself in, before removing her boots and setting them by the front door.

Her mother came into the hall and seemed surprised to see her.

They exchanged Som Pas.

'Back again?' her mteay asked in English with an obvious sarcastic tone.

Much to her mother's disappointment, Ary never bothered to learn Khmer or even her father's Mandarin. She knew general etiquette, and perhaps the odd phrase or two, in both languages, but rarely used them.

'Don't come with the guilt trip,' Ary replied, 'I was here last week.'

'Only because you wanted food. And take the hood off your head. It's not nice when inside someone's home.'

Ary did as she was told, following her mother into the living room and glancing across to the armchair by the window where Baba used to sit and read his Chinese newspaper. In her mind's eye, she saw him look up, smile, and return to his paper. The memory stung.

'I'll make you something,' Mteay said moving into the adjoining kitchen, 'you look ill.'

'I'm not hungry. And I was out last night.'

Her mother shook her head and cast Ary one of her *thought-as-much* stares. 'You should eat, then. It will help.' She coughed. It sounded raspy.

Ary followed her into the kitchen and sat down on one of the two chairs of a small, square breakfast table. 'I see your cough is as bad as ever.'

'Doctor says I'm getting a bit better.'

'He would. It's part of a secret policy. To cut down the number of people clogging up the NHS. One old Cambodian woman's death is nothing to them. I don't trust him.'

'You trust no one. And sound like a crazy person. I have leftover amok in the fridge, do you want that?'

'Oh, okay then,' Ary conceded. 'What did the consultant say?'

'She says the scarring is permanent.'

'And there's nothing they can do?'

'It's like with Baba. If a person has bad lungs, they are on *borrowed time*, as the English say.'

'Don't.'

'It's true. But I will be around a long time yet.' She took a resealable plastic dish from the fridge, popped the lid, set the dish the microwave, turned the dial, and the oven fan began whirling. As the food cooked, she said, 'You looked stressed. Are you sleeping? You have to sleep. Sleep is as important as food and water. And why are you here?'

'I just wanted to pop round. Maybe spend the night.' Her mother didn't say anything, so Ary added, 'I don't have a shift today and wanted to visit my mother. What's wrong with that? Do you want me to go?'

'Stop. I only asked.'

'Sorry. Actually, I felt a bit lonely in my room.'

'But you're always alone. It's the way you chose to be.'

'Don't start with that again.'

'With what?'

'The whole I should be married by now thing.'

'You should. It's not normal not being married and without children.'

'You didn't lead a normal life.'

'There was no choice. There were wars. It wasn't safe. No one got to be normal.'

The microwave pinged. Mteay opened the door and the kitchen filled with the aroma of coconut and spices. Using a dishcloth to insulate her fingers, she lifted out the plastic dish and poured the contents into a bowl which she set on the table in front of Ary, along with chopsticks, a ceramic spoon, and glass of water.

'Eat,' she said, brushing Ary's fringe with her fingers. 'It will help with the headache.'

She sat in the chair opposite, pushing two newspapers – the Khmer and English editions of Khmer Times – to one side, along with the pen she used to circle certain passages. Even after three decades living in Britain, Daeny Long struggled with some aspects of the language. Comparing text helped her understand the more taxing phrases. Ary thought it was an ingenious solution, and a laudable trait. Much better than her own zero effort regarding her parents' languages.

'This is yummy as always,' Ary said, picking out, sniffing then eating a cube of sweet potato. 'You really do make the best vegetable amok.' Her mother smiled. Ary continued, 'So, do you mind if I stay the night?'

'You are not doing camera watch today? Is there something wrong?'

'No. And not really.'

'But there is something.'

Ary sighed and admitted, 'Yes. But it's no big deal. I'm just trying to work through some things is all. And don't think it's anything to do with me not being married either,' she quickly added. 'I don't need anyone.'

'Doesn't look like it to me.'

'Well, I don't. It's just been one of those days.'

'What about your friend, Matthew?'

'*Mateus*. And no. He's just a friend.'

Mteay didn't push it.

Ary finished her meal, drank the water, got up, set the dishes in the sink, refilled and downed two more glasses of water, before sitting back down in the chair.

'Do you want something else?' Mteay asked.

'No. Thanks. That was enough. And you were right, it is helping with my headache.'

Her mother smiled and, for a few seconds, they sat in silence until, for want of something to do, Ary lifted the English language edition of the newspaper and asked, 'So, what's happening in the old country then?'

'In the what?'

'The old country. It's an expression, meaning the place where someone's parents or grandparents came from. So, in your case, Cambodia. What's happening in Cambodia?'

'Your baba was from China.'

'I know. And it would apply to him too if this was a Chinese newspap… never mind.' She looked at the front page. There was a post-Covid-19 related article, something about a politician, and news of a major archaeological find at Siem Reap. 'That's interesting,' she said and peered up at her mother. 'Have you been to Angkor Wat?'

'No. No one had time.'

'Actually, I don't know why I've never asked you this before, but did you ever visit any of the famous sites?'

'No. No one had time. Just work.'

Ary noticed that her questioning was causing distress, so she dropped it and turned the page to read the rest of the archaeology article. In the past, she hadn't considered that her mother's newspapers might have information she could use for her blog but, in this feature piece, she had found a real nugget; somewhere south of Angkor Archaeological Park, a statue of a *makara* had been found: a crocodile-like sea dragon purported to guard gateways and thresholds and which, to Ary's mind at least, might be a depiction of an ancient traveller from an alternate dimension.

'This is good stuff,' she said. 'I'll have to read your papers more often.'

Mteay just smiled.

Ary continued reading and honed-in on an image of a carved stone, uncovered along with the statue. It depicted an Incan Cross with a plain disc in the centre. A chill ran down her spine. She lifted Mteay's pen and drew a triskele pattern of three spirals in the centre of the symbol.

'Where did you seen this?' her mother snapped, snatching the newspaper and turning it towards her.

'What?'

'This drawing you've made. Where did you see this?'

'It's a symbol. Someone has been sending me... someone showed it to me once. Why? Do you know what this is?'

For many seconds, her mother didn't say a word. She looked shocked, distraught, as if reliving a distressful memory.

'You've seen this before, haven't you? What is it? Do you know what this is?'

Mteay remained quiet.

'Tell me,' Ary insisted. 'If you know what this is, you have to tell me.'

Her mother tossed the newspaper aside, got up, brushed down the creases on the black pyjama trousers she still wore all these years after moving from Cambodia, and went into her bedroom. Ary pulled the newspaper towards her. The article was nonspecific. Angkor Archaeological Park was huge. There was, however, a note at the bottom of page stating that the article had been compiled in collaboration with a university near Stuttgart, Germany. Her previous wariness had waned, making way for full-blown inquisitiveness. They were emotions she was familiar with. The excitement of the chase. An upsurge of blood to the brain. Tingling in her fingers. Neurons firing by the billions. Her feet itching to stand, walk, run, get to where she might find out more, learn more, expose the true workings of the world.

She reread the article and took her phone from her pocket.

Her wariness returned, but she pressed the on-button without hesitation.

When the display brightened, she opened the screen with her thumbprint, making sure to cover the front-facing camera with her other thumb. The thought of someone watching her was frightening and, then again, in some ways it wasn't. There was always someone watching. The modern world– and she should know – was awash with cameras and covert surveillance. It was the reason for *Harper T Jackson*.

She texted Mateus, saying:

He often received this kind of cryptic message.

Being her partner in all things conspiracy theory, he was also her brain dump.

Her texts were less communication and more a method of notetaking, for future reference or, if his investigative urges got the better of him, a base point should he wish to indulge.

Mteay was still in her bedroom.

Ary surmised the mention of a place close to her childhood home had troubled her.

Leaving the kitchen, she found Mteay sitting on her bed. She looked distressed, preoccupied, and had a shoebox containing photographs open on her lap.

'Are you okay?' Ary asked.

Mteay didn't reply.

Ary went inside and sat down beside her mother.

'Was it something in the paper? Did something bother you?'

Mteay didn't utter a word.

Ary placed a hand on her shoulder. Mteay didn't pull away. She never had been one for displays of affection and Ary took this to mean whatever was troubling her mother was pretty major. 'What is it?'

'I never went back.'

'To Cambodia?'

'Yes. Sopheak could still be there.'

'Your brother?'

'Yes.'

'The one who survived?'

'Maybe he did. Or not. I'll never know.'

Ary looked down at the photos. Most were of her as a baby, or as a toddler, and one with Baba carrying her on his shoulders. It made her smile. Her heart panged at the unfairness of having lost her father so young. She recalled, although still travelling in the taxi on the way to the hospital, the gut feeling of knowing he had died. The dread. The heartbreak. The resolution.

She missed him.

'Are there any pictures of your brother in there? Do you know where he is?'

Mteay didn't look up. She said, 'They came for him in the night. The rest of my family were dead. There was just me and Sopheak. Then the soldiers took him away. He was there. Then, he was gone. I was sent to Siem Pang to dig irrigation ditches. I was good at digging ditches. I was young. But they didn't feed us enough. I got weak and nearly died. The Vietnamese came. A woman told me she would take me to Vietnam. But another war started and she left too. Probably died. With the Khmer Republic gone, I went to Kampot, met Ai, married, and we came here. Then he died. They all die. It's better not to have family and friends. Sopheak is probably dead too.'

Aru rubbed her mother's shoulder. 'It must've been so hard.'

'It was what it was.'

'Is that why you never went back?'

'I don't know. Maybe it's better thinking he's still alive.'

'You've got me.'

'Not always. You go away too. On your trips.'

'But I come back.' That made Mteay smile. 'Do you want me to look for him?'

'Who? Sopheak?'

'Yes.'

'No. I wouldn't want to disturb him after all these years.'

'I could, though.'

Mteay reached into the shoebox, rummaged around, and took out a scrap of yellowed paper. 'You could look for this,' she said, handing the scrap to Ary. 'Find out what it means.'

It was a piece of old notebook, singed at the bottom, depicting the top two-thirds of a sketch: a cross, interlaced with geometric markings, with a disc in the centre and what looked like the upper end of a triskele.

Ary's skin tingled. The similarity of the drawing to her mysterious disappearing symbol was undeniable.

'How do you...? Where did you get this?'

'When I was a girl, there was a palm grove close to our village in Srah Srang.'

'Srah Srang?'

'It's a commune near Ta Prohm temple. It's where I come from.' Tears welled in her mother's eyes but Ary let her continue. 'We had a good life there. We were sometimes happy. Even with the wars. But, when the Work Units started, it all went bad. My parents died first. They starved. Mony went next, followed a few days later by Phirun, who got his name because it had rained the day he was born. Both were younger than twelve. Then, the soldiers took Sopheak away. And me too. I was taken to Siem Pang. The Vietnamese invaded. The woman, who said she'd bring me to Vietnam, didn't. So, I went to Kampot, and promised I wouldn't let anyone get close after that, but your father was kind… and sensible. It was his idea to come to London. And he was right. You had a better start here.'

'But what about this?' Ary asked, holding up the scrap of paper. 'Was this something from your village?'

'Not really. And yes.'

'I'm confused.'

'An American soldier came to that palm grove I mentioned. He had his guns with him, and chocolate. He made that drawing.' She gestured with a nod towards the scrap of paper. 'He made many drawings, but that was the only one to survive.'

'Survive? Survive what?'

'The big fire. People came. They burned down his hut and him too…'

'They burned him? Was he inside the hut?'

'No. They had pebbles. The pebbles set everything alight.'

Ary let that go. She wanted to find out more about the drawing. 'And, what is this? Is it a symbol from Srah Sra…?'

'…Srah Srang. And I don't know. I never saw it before that day.'

'The day the people came and burned the hut and the soldier?'

'Yes. He used to disappear – for weeks. When he came back, he'd cover the walls of his hut with writings, pages from books, maps, and drawings he made of the buildings

at Ta Prohm temple and Angkor Wat. He never settled. And he drank too much. He seemed angry. Always angry. He drew that symbol on his last day. I saw him do it with my own eyes.'

'And you think it might be something from Ta Prohm temple or Angkor Wat?'

'I don't know. I was only a girl. I'd never been there, to either place. It wasn't safe to leave the commune. We only had what the grown-ups told us.'

Ary's thoughts raced: *what was this symbol, what was its genesis, its meaning, and who or what saw fit to share it with her in such a clandestine way?*

Mteay didn't ask her any more about the symbol. She only said, 'You keep the drawing. And be safe. I know, if I tell you not to do anything, you will anyway. I can't stop you. So, I thought you should have it. It might help you find out what it means, and why those people killed that soldier.'

'I'll try.'

'But, be careful. They are dangerous.'

'I'm getting that impression,' Ary said, 'What with the big fire and all. I will. I've been doing this a long time. And, if I find out anything about

Sopheak, I'll ring you right away.'

Mteay smiled, but it looked sad, as if she doubted Ary would find anything.

'And, no,' she said.

'No, what?'

'No, I don't have any photos of Sopheak, or anyone else in my family either. I can't even remember their faces.' She closed the shoebox, stood, slipped it underneath her bed and left the room.

Ary let her go.

She needed to talk with Mateus but, if the previous Sunday was anything to go by, he was probably still in his bed.

She texted him anyway:

There's been a development – it will blow your fucking mind
(worried face emoji)

And she rang him. He didn't answer, so she sent another text:

I'm coming round.

Twenty minutes later, when Mteay assured Ary she was fine and had settled down to watch *Antique Hunt* on the TV, Ary left with a promise to return and spend the night. On the back of hearing about her mother's younger life, particularly her exposure to the strange symbol, Ary felt even more wary of going back to her room. And her mother needed her. The simple act of scribbling some spirals onto a newspaper had put her on edge. Something Ary hadn't witnessed before. Mteay was usually stoic about life. She had seen a lot, lived a lot, and suffered as much as anyone who had lost their childhood to war, famine, and persecution.

Even when Baba was alive, she wasn't one to show emotion.

For a short while, during her teenage years, Ary even thought her mother didn't like her.

But, now, she knew better.

Mteay's aloofness had been her crutch, her way to cope, and the story she'd just told was the first time she had opened up about her life before coming to the UK.

And, as they say, the apple never falls far from the tree.

Ary herself could be aloof... but she also cared.

She would find out everything she could about the image.

For herself.

For Mateus and his inquisitive mind.
For the people out there needing to know.
And for her mteay, who had suffered and lost so much.

PAST LIFE IS BUT A DREAM

Mateus was already up by the time Ary reached his place. This week, he was wearing clothes; camouflage print shorts, a blue paisley shirt matching last week's boxer shorts, and plastic sandals – the expensive variety. His flat was tidy. The floor clean. His sofa and coffee table uncluttered. Lavender scenting the air from a diffuser bubbling away atop his lowest bookcase.

He seemed more upbeat than her previous visit, but said, 'You do know that just texting *I'm coming round* doesn't mean I'm ready to, or in a fit state to receive.'

'To *receive*? Who the fuck are you... Elinor Dashwood? I told you to lay off those Jane Austen novels. They're filling you with a false sense of grandeur.'

'Enter,' he just replied, ushering Ary inside and closing the door behind her. 'Maybe next time you should call on my bat-phone.'

'You don't have a bat-phone.'

'I could have a bat-phone.'

'But you don't. So, I text and turn up on your doorstep.' She grinned.

In the living room, Mateus muted the television and sat down on the nearest sofa. Ary sat beside him, noticing he had been watching a series about ancient aliens. She'd seen the episode before. More than a few times. The one focussing on how, sometime in antiquity, Earth people had connected with a race of beings who lived on Mars. She didn't totally dismiss the hypothesis. Some of their ideas sounded credible but, as her investigations went on, she found herself leaning more and more towards inter-dimensional entities rather than tiny grey humanoids scooting around the galaxy in shiny silver space-saucers. Something about it didn't ring true for her. Too many contradictions and grainy photos for her liking.

'I see you cleaned up,' she said. 'The last time I was here, the whole floor had a bad case of the dumpsters.'

'So, how you been?' Mateus replied. 'As gobby as usual I see.'

'Ah, you know me: opinionated, curious, over-indulgent, sometimes twitchy. Always brilliant,' she smiled, 'and – since the talk I had with my mother today – also freaked the living fuck out.'

'You're always freaked out. Living fuck or otherwise.'

'Yup, that's true. But, this time, I have much to tell. And it will blow your bloody noggin.'

Watching Mateus's jaw droop ever closer to his chest, Ary retold Mteay's story about her family, the GI from the Vietnam War, the people who killed him, and the scrap of paper depicting the top half of a symbol similar to the one popping up on her devices. She told him about that part too; how the symbol had appeared a number of times since her last visit.

'So, the big questions are,' Mateus said, 'what is it? Who's sending it? And why you?'

'I think the *why me* is patently obvious. I'm the cooky one, remember. You said it yourself. And I don't just believe this stuff. I live and breathe it.'

'Maybe it's a message.'

'Duh, genius. Of course it's a bloody message. But why now? I've been at this for years. And the whole connected to my mother thing... well, that's just super-extra freaky.' Her head went light. Vision faded. The room darkened. Disappeared. As her sight cleared, she saw Khmer Rouge soldiers, labour camps, fire, death, and destitution. The images were stark and yet blurry, immersed in an ocean of sparkling pinpoints, drifting in and out, hard to grasp but there in all their emotional severity. Amid a glistening, hazy mist, she saw the two uncles she'd never met, still only boys, an aunt as a child and her mother's parents, all of whom had died or went missing long before Ary's birth. She felt their loss. The barren hollowness. Almost unbearable grief. And the tenacity to go on. The vision wavered and then solidified. As clear as day, she saw the American GI, standing outside his hut in the palm grove. A snapshot image, bright, sun-drenched, the place where he stood as real to her as if she had travelled back in time to inhabited her mother's thoughts and eyes.

A burst of light. Bright like a camera flash.

Mateus peering into her face.

'Where did you go?' he asked. 'You spacked there out for a good twenty seconds.'

'I don't know. Have you been on the blow today?' She gazed around the non-smoky room, sniffing the air.

'No. Not today. Why?'

'I had some sort of vision there. It was totally real.'

'Maybe a flashback. Acid? Molly? Mushies?'

'Pr'aps, but it's been ages. And, I was actually inside my mother's head. Totally nuts. I was right there. Where she lived. I saw her life.'

'Are you sure you haven't dropped something?'

'No. I haven't.' She looked down at her hands. They were shaking.

Mateus took the right one. 'It's okay. Just a daydream.'

'A fucking lucid one.'

'Yeah. Us crackpots get 'em from time to time.'

Ary smiled. 'S'pose. But, I'll tell you this, it did confirm one thing...

about what I need to do next.'

'And what's that?'

The answer was obvious. 'Go to Cambodia.'

JORDAN BURKE

Jordan Burke checked the time at the bottom of his computer screen. It was twenty past eleven and, what he had hoped to be a productive morning had, as expected, turned into another trail of wasted leads and unrequited emails. He shifted in his chair and uttered a groan, his back twinging from sitting too long in the same position. His shoulders ached. Stinging eyes. He needed food. The search he'd begun in the wee hours of the previous night, still had no reviewer for his latest magazine feature.

Who in their right mind would start a lunatic venture like this? he berated himself. *A complete idiot, that's who. An idiot without cash. Or connections.*

He stretched and flexed his shoulders. Rolled his head from side to side. His neck crunching like a pellet-filled hacky sack. None of which relieved his aches. He interlaced his fingers and cracked his knuckles. That was pointless too. As it seemed was his search for an academic – any academic – willing to read his piece on *the Copenhagen Interpretation* without obliterating two thirds or going off at a tangent about *deviations of opinion* or *revised consensus on the original conclusions.*

He had sent dozens of emails and dozens more enquiries.

No luck.

Academics were a twitchy bunch. They tended to talk blue sky, but were reticent to countenance any hypothesis diverging from the *approved.* They also moved at a frustratingly languid pace. Delayed acceptance of the KT-boundary-stroke-dinosaur-extinction theory was proof perfect of this approach. Ancient Norse migration to North America was another. As had been String Theory, and the Copenhagen Interpretation of quantum physics, until it wasn't, then was, then wasn't again, and so on and so on ad infinitum. All Jordan wanted was an academic, any academic, who would endorse his essay and, if the science gods were feeling generous, write an addendum for his magazine detailing why the premise had been accepted in the first place.

They had, it seemed, closed ranks.

Too busy.

Not exactly their field.

Away on sabbatical.

Or just down right rude. Ignoring him, which turned out to be the majority response.

Dammit, there must be someone, he told himself, hoping that that *someone* would jump out of his screen at any moment and save him the inevitable meltdown of missing his own, self-imposed and over-rigid deadline. Through his open submissions programme, he had good contributors – never mind more than enough conspiracy kooks to totally kerboom the internet – but, what he really needed was a fulltime feature writer. Someone who wasn't him. Someone with cred. Hell, he needed a cigarette but wouldn't give in. The hankering was there. Like an annoying bongo player on the Subway, it rose up when he needed to concentrate. So far, given the five hours he spent researching and writing the damned thing, combined with this morning's academic search, the whole venture had demolished nine hours of the time he should have spent on the four PhD and two Masters theses needing proofread by the end of next week. Normally, he was rigid about day job tasks; the ones that paid for food, board, to keep the lights on and other such luxuries. But his heart wasn't in it today. Or even for the wasted search.

He gave up, stood, snatched his dark blue puffer jacket from the back of his computer seat, and crossed to the room's only door. There were no windows either. The New York – and sole – office of *The Kitchen Sink Magazine* was a small, dank basement storeroom beneath Cute-icles Nail Bar in Fordham Heights. And *home* was a top floor, studio walk-up on the next block. Opening the door, he squinted as the garish lights from the nail bar upstairs saturated the stairwell in dayglo pink. The stench of chemical treatments came with it. Holding his breath, he locked the door behind him and climbed the stairs wondering if the invisible miasma clinging to the walls also penetrated his skin and, within a few years, his final days would be spent coughing up a lung or two, courtesy of people whose very existence required fingernails embellished with sparkly unicorns. He chased the thought away. Better not to speculate on such things. He also reprimanded himself for being spiteful. It was a free country. People should be able to paint any old toxic crap on their fingernails, if they so wanted.

At the top of the stairs, in the tiny lobby leading from the front door to the nail bar, he avoided eye contact through the window with Lori Cassano, its forty-something-year-old proprietor and his somewhat admirer. It wasn't that he didn't like her. She was nice, called him *Professor Nerd*, even though he'd dropped out of academia immediately upon completing his PhD. She was also the definition of a true upstanding citizen, bringing much needed jobs to a deprived neighbourhood and, although fifteen or so years his senior, might even be the type he would go for if the circumstances were different. He was, however, on a mission. *The Kitchen Sink Magazine* was the start. If successful, it would become the go-to resource for everything that was science but strange. Jordan Burke intended to discover it all – reveal it all. If that meant travelling the world to interesting places, then all the better.

The only weak point in his plan, however, was the small matter of cash.

He had less than squat.

Which was why he'd started *TKSM*. Proofreading paid the rent, but the magazine was to be both the promulgator and financier of his more cherished exploits, even if it meant standing in as his own fake feature writer... with or without endorsement.

He left, walked up to Grand Concourse, crossed at the crosswalk, entered the First Stop Caribbean Deli and Grocery at Park and East 182nd and bought three Jumbo Patties. They weren't as good as Moma's, but he liked the veggie ones, they were healthier–*ish*. He also bought a full sugar (eight spoons) cola. So much for the health kick. Before he reached the crosswalk again, he had already devoured one of the patties, and another as he walked the final few yards to the *TKSM* office. The air had a nasty nip to it for mid-April. With his free hand, he zipped his jacket tight to his neck. Jordan liked it hot. Unbearable for most New Yorkers hot. Ninety degrees and upwards, which he put down to Moma's grandfather having come from Jamaica. Dad was Irish, from Donegal and endured life best when it was wet and windy. *Good gardening weather*, he called it. But, coming from someone whose *garden* consisted of two indoor cacti and a remarkably neglect-resistant spider-plant, his credentials to make such a statement seemed somewhat suspect.

Back in his basement office, Jordan turned the wall mounted fan-heater to max, ate his last patty, downed his cola in one without a hint of remorse, and resumed his search through university staff profiles.

His mind wandered.

Concentrate, he willed himself. *And whatever you do, don't get side-tracked by conspiracy blogs.*

Too late.

He was already there, on a site called *Hard Truth*, reading some nutjob's claim that shape-changing lizards controlled the world. Through which, via some... err...side-*research*, he made the startling discovery that Justin Bieber was one of the said lizard people. The former Queen of England was another. Her whole brood were. Crazier still, so were both Barack Obama *and* Donald Trump. And the list went on: A-listers, B-listers, minor celebrities, influential people and politicians – all reptilian humanoids. Firmly gripped, he circled back to *Hard Truth* and more bullshit about our lizard rulers, a global secret society, something called the *Astronomical*

Reckoning, and other specious nonsense defying both science and logic. The freakshows writing this bunk were clear-cut loons but, on a rare occasion, their lunacy did touch the fringes of credible. That, however, wasn't the case for this particular blogger, *Harper T Jackson*. She-he-they were the real deal. A total crackpot. And yet, Jordan was also cognisant that, in some ways, they both paddled in the same pool. They shared natural curiosity. A need to uncover mysteries. And he wasn't turned off by the notion of some form of ancient civilization either. Like Harper T Jackson, he was open to new ideas. Which was why he had focused on ancient physics and engineering for his PhD at Colombia.

Thinking about it, he had more in common with this blogger than not.

He just wasn't ridiculous enough to invent a pile of spurious crap.

For the next five hours – yes, five whole hours he could have spent in more fruitful pursuits, not least proofreading one of the theses – he wasted his afternoon bouncing back and forth from credible researchers to bone fide fruitcakes, noticing the narrowing gap between both. The line was thin. Something the average conspiracy nut seemed to know and exploit to the max. It was the art of the bullshitter, taking two or maybe three nonsensical scenarios and, with clever manipulation, moulding them into a hypothesis that sounded almost believable.

An example: a self-confirmed *researcher* claims the gods of mythology were actually aliens from the constellation Orion, while simultaneously asserting that a rock, picked up by some guy in the Nevada desert, with unusual but fully accountable magnetic properties, was left there by ancient people wanting to document the visitation of their intergalactic overlords. Two propositions; one ludicrous and independently unprovable, the other verifiable through experimentation, wound together by way of interviews with other *researchers* of arguable credibility, to arrive at a final statement of:

'What if the gods of Egypt were space-voyagers from Orion's Belt?
And what if the strange characteristics of the Nevada Stone proves ancient people
made a magnetic record of visitations?
Does this not prove that our ancestors conversed with aliens?
And are those same aliens still living among us?'

The whole scenario was a masterpiece of affirmative wordplay.

Verbal misdirection worthy of any stage magician and as seamless as it was brilliant.

What worried him most, however, was how otherwise sensible people fell for this bullshit. Fake News and Alternative Facts had become the new normal. So-called *proof* of the Illuminati, shapeshifters, alien bases on the moon, Deep State, QAnon, secret politics, the list was vast and growing in both popularity and adherents. Jordan despaired for the planet. It was why he felt duty bound to shine the light of reasoning into the dark pit of speculation.

All the mad dog's shite, as his Irish dad might say.

And, *you can't fix stupid...* that was another of his father's frequent pearls of wisdom.

Jordan shut down his computer.

His mind wasn't in it anymore.

As the screen went blank, an image popped up.

It was of a carved stone, carrying a symbol that looked Incan in origin, maybe Khmer, maybe North European, or all three, and perhaps a sprinkling of others. That National Geographic subscription came in useful at times. After a few seconds, the image disappeared. The computer switched off. He gave it no more thought, assuming it to be something residual from the madcap sites he'd been nosing around. Putting on his jacket, he went out, locked the door, climbed the stairs, and stopped in the lobby to chat with Lori Cassano about nothing more illuminating than the weather taking a dip in temperature, how her cat-eye glasses steamed up in the cold, and his sister's glasses did the same.

They shared an awkward laugh.

The type that instinctively arises when conversation is bland and forced.

Leaving Lori to lock up, he went home, cracked open a party bag of low sodium/less fat potato chips, a can of full sugar vanilla cola, and turned on his games console. For the next few hours, he drove like an asshole, stole some stuff, butchered some gang members and, at ten, muting his cellphone to vibrate only and setting it atop the wireless charger on his nightstand, he folded out the sleeper-sofa, got under the sheets and opened his laptop. Sitting propped up against the two cushions doubling as pillows, he adjusted his position to lessen the nagging ache that had remained in the small of his back and shoulders since morning. Months of bad posture both at the office and at home had worsened the problem. He had developed a paunch. An issue no doubt exasperated by a diet of sugar-coated breakfast cereals, cola, and his lunchtime addiction to the Jamaican Patties he classed as dinner. His health drive of only eating low-everything chips wasn't working either.

He vowed to work-out.

Perhaps, he might even get around to unboxing the exercise bike.

Tomorrow, though.

Tonight, he needed to find his elusive academic.

The laptop screen lit up and, as always, he was tempted to trawl for a juicy conspiracy theory, whereby he could huff and blow with righteous indignation. The compulsion was getting ridiculous now. It had become an obsession. That and comment threads. Jordan was hooked on them both as badly as his appetite for unhealthy food, soda – and cigarettes.

At least he had put that one behind him. Seven months free and counting.

Resisting the urge for both cigarette and conspiracy, he resumed his search through university staff. A task so goddamned boring he fell asleep with his fingers resting on the keyboard. An indeterminable time later, his cellphone buzzed. The screen brightened. Setting his laptop aside, he reached across and lifted his phone off the nightstand.

No one was calling.

No text either.

Just an image of the same stone carving from earlier.

Then, it disappeared.

CAUGHT BETWEEN THE LOONS AND NEW YORK CITY

'You look like you had a real shitty night,' Lori said too loudly for morning – she said most things loudly – while rolling back the security gates to Cute-icles Nail Bar and the stairwell to Jordan's basement office. She was wearing a fleecy pink jacket, a bright yellow blouse and skirt, over high-heeled boots that looked impossible to walk in, yet she carried off with impressive agility. To Jordan's reckoning, she looked the bomb. Making his ensemble of blue-jeans, black turtleneck, and dark blue puffer jacket look distinctly dull and pedestrian. Fashion sense, however, was for those with the time to bother... and Lori Cassano, who didn't have the time but always seemed to bother.

'I was up late,' he replied.

'That's not wise, you know? Lack of sleep will ruin those good looks of yours.' She smiled. There was intention there. Holding her keys in one hand, she fumbled inside her also bright yellow handbag and took out a pack of cigarettes.

She offered the first pick to Jordan.

He shook his head.

'Shitsticks. Sorry. I forgot you'd given up.' She plunged the pack back into the bag. 'I can be a total klutz sometimes. And I should quit them too. But it's so hard. I've tried a bazillion times and never got past the first week.'

'I suppose it's willpower.'

'Yeah! I don't have none of that.' She laughed.

Jordan edged towards the stairwell and took a step down.

'So, what has you coming in early on a Saturday?' she asked quickly. 'More rocket science stuff? There's a rumour going round the salon that you're building a nuke down there. Or maybe a spaceship. That'd be cool. You could take me for a ride in it.' She smiled again. There was definite intention there.

'No. No bombs, no spaceships. Just science.'

'Don't you get bored?'

'Nah. It's my thing,' he nodded down the stairs, 'and I need to be getting on.'

'Sorry. Of course. I'm keeping you back.' She turned the key in the glass panelled door, dashed into the nail-bar and disabled the beeping alarm.

When she returned, she said, 'Maybe catch you later?' She smiled, it appeared downhearted, perhaps hopeful.

Jordan replied, 'Maybe,' and carried on down the stairs, wondering what the Lori beneath the brashness, make-up, and chintzy clothes might be like. But, then again, who was he to question anyone's image or choices. Maybe he could learn a thing or two. As his squirly sister, Jada (Moma apparently had a thing for names beginning with J) liked to remind him: *all that boring is gonna someday turn you grayer than those lame-assed clothes you wear.*

Inside his office, he switched on the lights, the fan-heater, and the PC base unit underneath the desk he had deliberately located centre of the room to survey the wipe-boards taking up the other three walls. It was why he couldn't work from home. He made many notes and needed space to do it. The wipe-boards also hid the black mould. Even in April, it took hours of intensive fan-heating to dissipate the chill and musty stench. The office was a freezer box in winter and a stale pit in summer. It was also a place of isolation, somewhere *to get to it then*, as he had lied to Lori before he came downstairs.

While he waited for the computer to load, he phoned Jada.

'What?' she answered abruptly. There was hubbub in the background.

'Hey. Get over to the office. Something weird has happened.'

'It's Saturday. I'm at work remember.' Her voice changed, sounding like she had moved the phone away from her face. 'It only comes in black,' she shouted out to someone in the distance, 'but you get the full package: sim, data, and complimentary speakers worth a buck fifty. I have to go,' she then said to Jordan. 'I'll call in five.' She hung up.

For the rest of the day, Jordan scoured the internet for the image that had appeared and disappeared from his phone. He had given up searching for a reviewer. And proofreading theses. There was more interesting rabbit to chase. Contrary to her promise, Jada didn't ring back. She was probably – definitely – too busy. He knew that. He always got in trouble for calling her when something cool popped up. But he also knew, like him, she was drawn to a mystery, and his statement of something weird having happened would have her neurons sparking like fireflies.

At ten-past-five, she barged through the door wearing her best *what-the-fuck* face. Something he suspected the customers at the phone store had been exposed to all day; becoming not so much convinced into their purchases as bulldozed into them.

'It stinks like farts in here,' she said, her nose creased, acidity in her tone. 'And why so damned dark?'

'That would be the no windows.'

'You've heard of electricity, though? Light bulbs?'

'All the lights are on.'

Jada pushed the bridge of her glasses up her nose and gazed up at the ceiling. 'I'll take your word for it. So, what's all the noise about?'

'Pull up a stool.'

Jada moved inside, grabbed the wastebasket, dumped the empty chip packets onto the floor, flipped it over and sat down. 'Shoot.'

'I need your expertise.'

'Well, that's obvious. You interrupted me at work, remember.'

'Yeah. Sorry. I got weirded out.'

'About what?'

'That's it. I don't really know. But I have a question. An IT, phone and PC hacking type of question.'

'You were hacked?'

'Yes. Maybe. Maybe not. There was an image. It came out of nowhere on my desktop yesterday. I had been scoping out some sites...'

'Conspiracy nutter sites?'

'Yeah, conspiracy nutter sites. You know me. I'm addicted. Anyway, as I was closing down, the image came up and then disappeared. But that's not the biggest thing. It came back again, last night, and just for a few seconds but, this time, it was on my phone. Like someone was sending it.'

'Did you check the wallpapers folder?'

'Checked that. But I only use the *TKSM* logo as a wallpaper.'

'What about default images for other apps?'

'Not the one in question. I've never seen it before.'

Jada appeared in thought, rubbing her chin to emphasise the process. Then she grinned:

'That pause was for dramatic effect. Did ya like it? It's something I'm trying out for when people – mostly brothers – think I'm here to answer all their problems. Long story short, you're overthinking it. As usual. It's probably just something you downloaded by accident and it synced across your devices.'

'Then how would it pop up from nowhere?'

'Nothing pops up from nowhere. It's probably in your folders.'

'I looked and nope, nothing there.'

'You left a window open then.'

'On two different devices? When I didn't download or open anything?'

'Like I said, they synced.'

'Maybe you're right,' Jordan conceded.

'I'm always right.'

'Sorry.'

'Sure thing. Next time, though, make sure it's something worth rushing over for. Just because I'm doing a Masters Degree in Computer Science doesn't mean I'm here to solve all your cellphone glitches. I'm not your personal IT department, Jordan. It doesn't work like that. I don't work like that.' She stood up. 'You coming round Moma's tomorrow?'

Jordan was already deep in another browser search. 'Maybe.'

'She'll expect you to be there. And to have done Mass beforehand.'

He peered up at his sister. 'Yeah, well, one of those two things have a chance of happening. So, I'll see you at Moma's then.'

Jada laughed. 'Me too. Not big into the whole zombie-saviour thing. But, don't tell her that. She'll burst a blood vessel.'

'Definitely not. And the same goes for me.'

'Cool. And, to do us both a favour, I'll swing by the Church of the Blessed Suffering Whatever beforehand and check out which one of the priests said eleven o'clock Mass. I'll text you the details so you're prepped. Same as we did when we were kids.'

'Thanks. You're awesome. I take you way too much for granted.'

'Better believe it. You're a complete asshat.'

Jordan teethy grinned, gave his sister a double thumbs up.

Jada flipped him the bird. They laughed. Jada left. Jordan returned to his search to see the image from the night before right there, centre-place on his computer screen. He was about to call his sister back when it disappeared and his phone buzzed with a text from a number he didn't recognize:

$5000 has been deposited to your bank account.

FREAKS PAY OUT AT NIGHT

Within minutes, Jada was back again. Jordan had chased after her. Lost her. Rang her, and she returned, taking her previous position atop the upturned wastebasket.

He showed her the text.

'You know it's just someone fucking with you?' she said. 'Probably one of your homies.'

'I don't have homies.'

'From college.'

'I didn't have any there either.'

'Holy crap, you're fun sponge. It's all doom, gloom, and kaboom.'

'I'm dedicated. I have plans.'

'What? The science magazine? You do know you'll need some serious bills to make that into an actual thing.'

'Well, apparently, that's not a problem now. I'm swimming in the stuff. Someone I don't know just gave me five grand.'

'Yeah – hashtag Nigerian Prince scam.'

'I don't think so. And how did they get my digits? I have two-step authentication on all my accounts. I use a network mask. Have a VPN. And a number block on all my calls.'

'You go bro. Look at you getting all techie.' She sniggered. 'Sheesh, you stoopid, man. Everyone knows you can't stop a dedicated hacker. If they want in, they'll get in. Simple as that.'

'But what if there's nothing worth *getting in* for in the first place?'

'Identity theft. Data gathering. Building a scam. It's all worth something. Even if the information applies to someone as lame as you.' She laughed.

'You're not funny.'

'Yeah, and you got no chill.'

'So, what about the image then? Why does it keep popping up on my desktop... and my phone?'

She pushed her glasses up her nose. 'Give it here.'

Jordan passed Jada his cellphone. 'But it appears on the PC too.'

'I know. I'll get to that. And shut up. I'm working.' She held it out to him. 'I can't do anything if it's not open.' Jordan touched his thumb on the sensor, the phone lit up, and Jada started flicking and tapping on the screen. After a good minute of searching, and shushing Jordan as he attempted to voice questions, she said, 'I can't see anything obvious. It's like a graveyard in there. Where's all your apps. Your music? Photos? Do you even use the camera?'

'I don't do any of that. It's a phone. I use it to ring people and send them texts.'

'Ah, that explains it then. You're not thirty-two at all. You're actually a seventy-five-year-old retired truckdriver, terrified of *all these goddamned noo-fangled machines they keep throwing at us.*' She laughed.

'Like I said, you're not funny.'

'Oh, but I am.'

'No.'

'Hells-yes.'

'Not.'

'Yeah-dat.'

'Stop it.'

'Yerps I am.' They both laughed. Jada handed back the phone. 'There's nothing there. *Literally* nothing there. I don't know how you exist in the 21st Century.'

'What about the desktop?'

'Probably a glitch. Same goes for your phone. Look, keep an eye on them both and, if anything properly weird happens – and I mean, *properly weird* – contact me. But I'm not coming back if it's a waste of time. Have you even bothered to check your bank account... to see if the five grand is even in there?'

'No. I was going to call into the branch tomorrow.'

'Jesus wept, grandpa... nobody goes to their bank anymore. We use apps. Aaaps! On our cellphones. It's called *tech-no-logy.*' She snatched the phone back. 'Open it again.' Jordan touched his thumb on the sensor. 'What's your bank?'

'Westchester Trust.'

'Never heard of it.'

'They're small.'

Jada scoffed and rolled her eyes. She tapped around a bit. 'Well, at least they have internet banking. But you probably don't use that.'

'I like the personal interaction.'

'Yeah right. From the guy with no crew. Anyway, it appears they also have an app. I was worried they'd be using chalkboards or something.' She smirked, tapped some more, downloaded the app, and gave the phone to Jordan to enter the relevant details and security confirmations. 'Welcome to the twenty-first century. It's where all the cool kids hang out. So, go ahead then. Check the account. Five bucks says there's nothing in there but your sadsack overdraft.'

Jordan tapped. His jaw dropped. He showed the screen to his sister. There it was – in *Recent Transactions*:

→ *Anonymous Depositor* *+$5000*

THE STYLE COUNSEL

A sleek, black helicopter burst through the rain, pitched right over Yeouido Hangang Park and set down onto the helipad atop the Shun Corp Building in the heart of Seoul's financial district. Crouching beneath the downwind gusts of the rotors, three men in suits rushed out from a rooftop doorway, hastily opened umbrellas and ushered their also besuited, middle-aged guest from the helicopter into the building.

Taking the elevator down a hundred and thirty floors to the sub-basement, the guest was greeted by Yuze Shun's personal assistant. Without discourse, the three other men peeled away. The assistant straightened his tie and led the guest along a mahogany panelled corridor, down a half flight of stairs, through a door into a spacious museum crammed with glass cabinets displaying artifacts from all corners of the world. Sumerian sculptures. Incan art. The emperor Nero's laurel crown. Carvings from Bharat civilisation. Bone flutes from China. Annunaki gold. Dogon paintings. Engravings from Maputo. Along with armour, dating back the full thirteen thousand years since these basement rooms were established. Crossing to a bronze statue of the Haechi lion, the personal assistant pressed its left eye, in turn opening a false-wall door into another room, its windowless margins stacked floor to ceiling with bookcases containing all manner of literature, from ancient scrolls to first edition copies of *Atlas Shrugged* and *Mein Kampf*. An ornate chandelier illuminated the space and, dominating the centre of the room, thirteen high-backed, blue velvet armchairs – arranged around a circular mahogany table – bore brass plaques on their upper crest-rails, each engraved with a one of the family names of the Caucus:

Rothbauer, Roquefeuil-Borgius, Saxe-Gothe, Romanovich, Pachacuti, Shun, Hanno, Mansa, Abram, Soma, Patidar, Jomon, and *Gildermere.*

Twelve of the armchairs were occupied, containing men of varying ages, from mid-thirties to late fifties. They didn't speak. Or look towards the new arrival, Vilmos Gildermere, who waited for the personal assistant to leave, before taking the vacant armchair bearing his surname.

'We have a problem,' Thomas Rothbauer began without ceremony. 'The first astronomical alignment has happened. And with some success. The event we worked for the last six decades to suppress has finally come to pass.'

'But we built a bulwark,' Yuze Shun said. 'Consumerism. Commodities. The neo-liberal global economy. Thousands of years of planning consolidated into sixty years of promulgation. It was supposed to contain them. Keep them greedy and possessions-hungry.'

'Yes. And it worked. Until now. We thought, if we kept the *plebians* otherwise distracted by cash and baubles, with no one to follow them, the other faction would be rendered powerless. But we underestimated their resolve. In some ways, it's stronger than ours. Something we should have dealt with at the time, but didn't. Anonymity was our greatest success. But underestimating *them* was our most prevailing failure.' He spat the word *them* as if ejecting something foul.

'So, now what?' Gildermere asked. 'We need leadership. Not regrets for past failings.'

Rothbauer glowered.

The others shrank into their armchairs.

Gildermere sat upright, defiance written on his face.

'Plans are in place,' Rothbauer snapped. 'You'd do well to leave such matters to me.'

'And where, after more than sixty years of heightened endeavour, has that got us? A disgruntled, fearful world, verging on rebellion and anarchy. It's uncontrolled. The complete opposite of the sunny upland scenario your family sold us. The Rothbauer blueprint of rampant consumerism backed up by boom-and-bust economies hasn't delivered.'

'It still works.'

'How? Where is the supplicant population you promised? Where's the stability?'

'*It works!*' Rothbauer growled.

'And, the UN,' Gildermere continued with disregard. 'That was a Rothbauer idea too, but has only served to stymie our objectives.'

'Not when we can influence some of the delegates.'

'Your puppets?'

'Exactly. *Our* puppets. You have influence too. All the *families* do.'

'This is getting us nowhere,' Ferdinand Saxe-Gothe interrupted. 'Whatever the state of the world, the Rothbauers have ascendency. They are *Head Family*. Thomas is *Patriarch*, so his plan is sacrosanct. At least until the next election.'

Rothbauer said, 'Thank you,' appearing calmer, and adding, 'Yes, Rothbauer do indeed have ascendency... in all matters relating to the Caucus and our collective aims.' He turned to Gildermere, 'I know it looks bad at the moment. But, you only have to watch a plebian news show to see our climate manipulations are paying off. When the time comes, we will instigate the great solution. Now, back to the problem I mentioned earlier. Through our network of operatives, the other faction's plans have come to light. They mean to co-opt and focus two *plebians*.'

'Focus on what?'

'*Reactivation.*'

'They can't do that,' Shun said. 'They don't have the capability.'

'But the two *plebian* proxies might,' Rothbauer replied. 'And we can't allow that. So, I've initiated a protocol. And, don't worry,' he said with a sly smirk towards Gildermere, 'it will be discreet.'

Agitated mumbling rippled around the room.

Gildermere didn't join in. 'How discreet?' he asked.

'Not your concern. Just know that the problem will be solved with the *plebians* none the wiser. They will continue to lust for needless trinkets. They will bitch, moan, blame foreigners, gods, extra-terrestrials, each other – anyone but themselves for their miserable choices, while wasting their lives pursuing simple solutions to the complex problems we lay before them. Additionally, there is a window of astronomical opportunity in late May that could work in our favour.'

'Mercury Max,' Dario Pachacuti confirmed.

'Yes. With the protocol timed to coincide, the issue of the proxies will be quickly resolved. The other faction's aspirations thwarted. Then, we can forge ahead. Unhindered. Undo all the frustrating obstacles they laid in our paths these last thirteen thousand years.'

'And what about the *plebians*?' Gildermere asked.

His endless questioning seemed to annoy Rothbauer, but he smiled. 'Like I said, they will do as they are told. And, for our part, we will give them peace... between the wars and catastrophes that is.'

The Caucus members laughed.

Everyone except Vilmos Gildermere.

WE'RE ALL OFF TO DUBLIN

A few days had passed since Ary's freaky vision-experience-thing at Mateus's flat, after which the conversation had kind of gone like this:

Mateus: 'I'm coming with you.'

Ary: 'No.'

Mateus: 'Yes.'

Ary: 'No!'

'Yes!'

'No. Nada. Nyet. Nopes. Not happenin'.'

'Why not?'

'Because.'

'Because what?'

'Holy fuck. Because I don't want you to.'

'Why?'

'Because I do these things alone.'

'Not always. I've come with you before.'

'Yes, but that was only to... okay, fuck it... if it'll shut you up, you can come as far as Dublin.'

'Why Dublin?'

'Fuck, here you go again. Because that's where I'm going first.'

'And where are you going after that?'

'Farther. To Asia. Which I defo want to do alone. Gonna swing by China, where I'm hoping to track down my baba's family. Might as well while I'm in the general direction... and then to Cambodia. Which is the next part of the search, but also another family thing.'

'So, Dublin it is then. Go Team Ary!' He'd raised his hand for a high five.

It wasn't reciprocated. 'Don't do that.'

'What, the high five or Team Ary?'

'Both. But definitely the second. It's not a thing... ever!'

'What about Team Dubliner?'

'You're just making it weird now.'

'It's what I do.'

'I know.'

'Look, I know you're feeling a tad wigged out at the moment, but the thing is we can't be sure if any of this is legit or just some knobend yanking your chain. It could be one of your flat-mates. That pushy boss of yours at TfL. Might be no more than a simple tech blip. Or maybe it really is something. Or another fake. Who knows? Most things are fake. All of them maybe. The whole caboodle. The world has always been a dung-heap of secrets built upon a bigger dung-heap of lies. Where, if a truth does happen to lift its head above the noise, an equal and opposite untruth pops up straight away to counter it. An anti-truth. Getting bigger, fatter, untenable to those who can see, but hard-wired into those who never came to anything through reason in the first place. And the numbnuts gleefully lap it up. Gagging to genuflect at the feet of their masters. Just give 'em a heavy dose of shitty talent shows, toilet-paper tabloids, and enough cheap booze to knock them senseless and they'll merrily kiss anyone's backside until cirrhosis shrivels their liver to a walnut. It's how empires are built. The same old same old.'

'It might be *the same old same old*, but I don't have to like it. That's why I do what I do. To reveal the truth.'

'Abso-fuckin-lutely – and you're doing the right thing. You just need to stop getting pissed at everyone all the time. All the doomscrolling has made you over-cynical, and snarky.'

'Only because everyone's a dick.'

'Even me?'

'Even you.'

'Bite me.'

They'd both laughed.

'Anyway,' Mateus had continued, 'the long and short of it is that the powers above know exactly what they want and how to get it. That's why what you do is so important. But it can also be freaky, unsettling, scary, and terrifying. For people like you... like *us*, viewing the world is like watching a dog with worms. It's kinda funny to see it use its front legs to drag its arse across the carpet, but also gross to know that your deep shag is now covered in dog-turds and parasites.'

'Eww.'

He'd sniggered. 'Simply put, Ary, you're one of the enlightened few who can see both the event *and* any downside that comes with it. Especially the stuff you research. Your problem is, however, that you want to appear objective but get caught up in minutiae. The serious shit. And it brings you down. Makes you snarky.' He paused. 'Anyway, I'm speaking to the converted here. You know this already. The connection with your mother has made it personal. More intense. You need to get it sorted.'

'Yeah. S'pose.'

'Definitely. But you will do what you always do... reveal the mystery. So, why Dublin?'

'I have a mate there who owns a pub. He gives me shifts when I need to build up funds.'

'I can give you moolah. I'm bloody loaded, remember.'

'I know. You're Mateus McDuck, the bigwig music producer. That's not the way I roll, though. You know this. And, anyway, if I take your money, you'll be hanging out of me all the way to Siem Reap. This is something I must do alone. But you can come as far as Dublin. I have a job for you at the Trinity College Library, while I head out to Newgrange.'

'Newgrange?'

'It's a Neolithic passage tomb in County Meath. There's something specific there I need to see for myself.'

Dublin was, as always, an absolute delight. Next to Lisbon, Portugal, one of Ary's favourite cities. San José, Costa Rica was another. Gaborone, Botswana was in the mix too. Although bustling capitals, something about these four made her feel welcome. Safe.

They'd arrived at six in the morning. Ary taking in the sunrise. Mateus bleary eyed and crotchety because, in spite of his protestations and repeated demands to throw wads of cash at the issue, Ary had insisted on travelling by bus and Holyhead ferry – not the first-class plane seats as he'd appealed for. Her travelling funds might be few but not scarce enough to leech off a friend. That said, dropping the TfL job, and so dramatically, was probably ill-advised.

'It's very likely Nigel had already sacked me,' she'd told Mateus, during their slow journey to Ireland. 'But the look on his face when I told him to stick his job up his backcrack was fucking priceless. I was sure he was about to burst a brain-vein right there in front of the monitors.'

Mateus had managed a laugh. Despite his dour mood.

She'd reminded him he was only along for the ride, and at her pleasure.

The admonishment helped, but he still maintained a grump all the way to noon of their first day when he discovered the joys of the music pubs in Temple Bar.

That was a month ago now. As promised, her friend, Damo Duff had been good to his word by giving her shifts in his bar – The Square Peg on Trinity Row. So far, however, she had worked only eleven out of the possible thirty-seven slots. *The Covid*, to quote Damo himself, had *kicked* his daytime business *in the teeth*. Thankfully, though, he also had an upstairs room where she could stay free of charge and, on the days she did work, hadn't far to travel when a shift finished and all she wanted to do was crash into bed. Needless to say, her funds were in the pits.

From day one, Mateus had booked himself into the Gresham Hotel and – when he finally gave up browbeating her to join him – spent his time perusing the landmarks, mixing with the locals, drinking way too much and, on occasion, doing what he came here for in the first place: examining books at the Trinity College Library for any references of triskeles in South and Central American cultural history.

This was why she preferred not to take him with her on her travels.

He was too easily distracted. Now proclaiming his intention to relocate Stinky Hole Records, lock and stock and acoustic panels from Kentish Town in London to whatever part of Dublin the local musos called home. Temple Bar by all accounts. To say he was smitten would be an understatement. *The Fair City*, as with so many before, had him enchanted. He seemed happy here. Unpretentious. Contented. Busy with plans. Which was good for him, but not for Ary, who needed him clearheaded and focused on the research.

The clock on the wall of the backroom kitchen of Damo's bar said seven twenty-seven.

Sunshine, spilling through the cracked window blinds, slashed the grey Formica surfaces with the split-toned yellows, oranges and reds that often accompanied a Dublin morning. There was a chill, but it carried the promise of spring warmth. Finishing the dregs of her coffee, she placed the cup in the dishwasher. Damo was in the main bar, a shard of bright sunlight glinting off the bald-spot growing yearly broader atop his head. What hair remained, he wore long; a tangle of ginger curls, tied back in a ponytail. He had a cup of tea in his hand. He always had a cup of tea in his hand, or it at least seemed that way. He took a swig, set the cup on the bar counter, and walked into the back kitchen

'So, what's your plans for today?'

'Newgrange.'

'Again? You've really got a thing for that old tomb. What's it now, three times since you got here.'

'I'm casing the place. Biding my time.'

'Yeah, well, watch your back. The Gardai are not too enamoured with English people poking around our national monuments. I take it's for that conspiracy blog of yours?'

'Yeps.'

Damo smirked.

'I know you don't believe in what I do. But, if I'm right about the world, one day you will... and will thank me for it too.'

'I'll take your word for it. But I'm from the *Rebel County* remember...

and a Corkman is a hard one to convince... about anything.'

'Maybe. And, in fact, because you are always a solid egg about everything, I will tell you first.'

'I'll bate my breath. Sure, you know what, I mightn't even breathe a gasp until you get back and tell me everything.' He laughed.

Ary did too. 'You're a funny bugger. No, I mean it, you've always had my back. You're like Mateus in that way.'

'I'm just pissed I can't give you more shifts. But it's been a slow climb this last year.'

'You've given me enough.'

'I could do more. I was on my last penny when you got me that gig at your girlfriend's café. What was her name again?'

'Gisela. Gisela Joubert. She was great, but probably also the reason why I only date men now. Fuck, she was bossy. S'pose that's because she was Parisienne. And a business owner.'

'I'm a business owner. And I'm sweeter than unicorns and rainbows.' He grinned.

'True.' Ary smirked. 'You're a real prince.'

'Anyway so, fair's fair. One good turn deserves another. The Euros I earned in Paris got me up and running again. In some ways, even set me on the road to owning this oul money pit.' He stared out into the main bar. A change in expression displaying his worries.

'You'll be okay. It'll pick up soon.'

'I kinda know that. And the daytime punters *are* coming back. Slowly. But I could do without the stress. There's not a publican around that hasn't felt the pinch since the pandemic hit. But, sure, it's probably all down to space aliens or zombies or the like.' He sniggered.

'Tosser,' Ary said, smiling. 'Anyway, shouldn't you be getting back to it. Your tea's getting cold.'

Damo smirked, nodded, and said, 'Have good'n anyway, at... whatever it is you're up to,' went back into the bar, shouting back, 'and, remember, don't get caught. I don't want to have to bail you out of no prison cell.'

Ary put on her jacket and texted Mateus – who was probably sleeping off another night on the tiles – with a reminder to get back to Trinity College Library and the assignment she'd allotted him. Leaving the premises by a side door, she then walked up an alley, turned out onto St Andrew's Street, went past the Molly Malone Statue (known locally – along with other deprecating monikers – as *The Dolly with the Trolley*), went onto Suffolk Street, past College Park, and around to her now regular car-hire, Green World Cars, behind Pearse Station. The city bustled. Buses, cars, work-goers, early-out tourists, scurrying here and there, heads down, heads up, running, ambling, getting on and getting in the way. Charity collectors in yellow bibs shook plastic buckets outside the supermarket on Westland Row. Something about a sponsored bed push to Belfast. People on bikes flashed across the intersections, as a black cat sat at the threshold of a corner shop, licking one paw while nonchalantly watching the madness go by. All the while, the crisp morning sun shone down. It brought lustre to the day and, for Ary, a sense of hope that, after a month of surveillance, she would finally get close enough to the Newgrange's inner sanctum to find evidence of the trans-world origins of the symbol that had dominated a couple of weeks in April, but strangely hadn't appeared since.

Its disappearance didn't, however, deter her.

Her interest, and angst, had been piqued enough to continue her search.

Two or so hours later, with a fair portion of the time spent driving through rush-hour traffic, she arrived at the ancient site; one of a collection of passage tombs, known in Gaelic as *Brú na Bóinne*. Parking at the visitor centre, she took the designated coach out to the monument and settled in among a group of tourists; some interested, some not, but all of them here to see another famous *Irish thing* before they embarked on the next leg of their grand European vacation.

And the ancient circular monument never ceased to impress.

Rising over the landscape, it broad sides glistened white in the sunshine; contrasting the rain-fed grass growing green on the high mound encasing the tomb. Three large cigar-shaped stones, confined behind a wooden barrier, marked the entrance to the tomb. The middle one carved with spirals. To either side, two sets of wooden steps led up to and away from the entrance to a long internal passageway.

When her group arrived, they queued up behind another being ushered by a uniformed guide over the left-side set of steps and around to the passageway entrance. For several minutes, this first group were permitted to peer inside. Some seemed awed. Most took photos. Lots of chatter. The guide led out them out again. Then came Ary's group's turn. She didn't go with them, but remained at the wooden barrier, to study the triskeles carved into the central entrance stone. She'd seen them before, from her last two visits as well as internet research, through which she also learned of another located farther inside the passage itself. That was the one she wanted to see. The images available to the collective commons, however, tended to be few, indistinct, never fully revealing the complete stone within its setting. She needed to get inside the mound itself. There was only one snag, only approved archaeologists, researchers, and *important* folk – with influence or money – had access to the tomb. Never common or garden tourists. And definitely not truth-seekers like her, who were no doubt deemed questionable, and maybe downright *cooky*. In their brochure, the heritage authority stated the policies protected the integrity of the site. Ary, as usual, suspected more dubious reasons for closing out those with enquiring minds.

After they were given their prerequisite peek down the passageway, Ary's group moved on, following the first tranche of tourists along the path to the coach park. She didn't go with them. For the present at least, apart from the guide standing by the passageway entrance, she was alone.

'You'll miss your bus,' he called across to her.

'It's okay. I'll get the next one. I want to look at this central stone some more.'

'Fair enough. Knock yourself out.'

For a few minutes, Ary feigned interest before, pointing towards the tourists walking down the path, she shouted, 'Oh dear. Something's happened. I think somebody might've fallen over. They look hurt.'

The guide dashed out and sprinted after the two groups now mingling as one down at the coach park. Ary took her chance. Rushing up and over the wooden steps, she nipped into the passageway, searching for the larger stone mentioned in her research. She found it a few metres in. Along with the single triskele carved into its surface. She had, however, expected to find more. Something cross-like, similar to an Incan symbol, or mandala-like, to fit with her theory of there being links between the European Neolithic, pre-Incan, and ancient Khmer civilizations.

There was only the triskele.

Feeling despondent, she sighed, looked down at the floor and then upwards, noticing how the ceiling rising up to the capstone was shaped like a square or, dare she think, a cross. She took a couple of photos with her phone. And another few of the large stone and carving. By which time, the guide had returned.

Forty minutes later, with a firm bollocking from the *Gardaí* – the Irish police – she was allowed to return to her car. Before driving off, she checked the photos she'd taken of the tomb ceiling and, on closer inspection, determined the area below the capstone didn't appear cross-like at all. There were elements there, but not enough to support her theory. She flicked to the images of the inner stone and its triskele, expecting to be likewise disappointed.

Her skin tingled. Hairs stood on the back of her neck and arms.

Due to the narrowness of the passageway, to get a decent shot, she'd been forced to tilt her phone, the flash therefore picking out certain surface elements of the large stone. Hollows. Chinks. And a pattern, glowing like a halo around the triskele. If she'd been standing off by a degree or two, the effect wouldn't have shown. And yet, there it was, a cross, enclosing the triskele, set inside the shape of a mandala. An exact copy of the symbol that had both spooked and intrigued her since April. And the one Mteay had discovered while a child in war-torn Cambodia.

She rang Mateus.

No answer.

She texted him:

> *Look for info about a halo effect in the Newgrange passageway*
> *And for any references to crosses or mandalas*
> *Am on my way back to Dublin*
> *See you in the Square Peg*
> *Your brain will pop a nugget when I show you the picture I took*
> *(exploding head emoji)*

It was mid-afternoon when Ary got back to The Square Peg. Mateus, dressed in black jeans and a green paisley shirt (paisley being his thing), was sitting alone at a window table, cradling a pint of stout.

His rosy glow indicated he'd already had a few.

There were four other customers. A regular, called Mick Ryan, sitting on a stool at the counter, drinking lager and watching Gaelic Football on the TV, and three office-y types, two women and a man, sat at the table by the poker machine, holding glasses of red wine and picking at a bowl of mixed nuts. The air throughout the bar was a heady concoction of brewer's yeast mixed with brass polish. The source of latter being Damo, behind the counter, buffing beer-taps. He looked spent, camouflaged beneath a concentrated dedication to the perfect sheen and his trademark cheeky grin. The Covid-19 downturn, however, had taken its toll, even postponing his marriage to Mashaka, planned for this summer but put off due to bad finances. In truth, he looked like someone ready to quit. And Ary felt for him but, then again, that was the pub business. If her time with Gisela had taught her anything, it was that, even outside of a pandemic, the average punter was as fickle as any given trend, even when it came to their favourite watering-hole.

Mateus waved.

Behind him, viewed through a frosted glass of the window, people swept by on Trinity Row. Flashes of grey, blurring against a yellow sunshine backdrop. Passing shadows. Serious things to do. Important places to be. To Ary's mind, human cattle. Hunkered beneath mundanity. Unknowing and unwilling to countenance the existence of those who controlled and owned them.

'How's the goin'?' Damo asked from behind the bar. 'Did you get what you wanted?'

'Yes,' Ary replied. 'And a police caution.'

He laughed.

Mick Ryan laughed too, but with a look that said, *I'm laughing but I haven't got a damned clue why I'm doing it.*

Damo winked, said, 'Thought ya might, you mad eejit,' and returned to his beer-taps.

Ary smirked, went over to join Mateus at his table by the window and sat opposite, the photo on her phone already onscreen before her bum hit the seat.

'Would'ya look at this beauty,' she said, puffing with pride at both her success and the audaciousness of how she got it.

'What am I looking at?'

'The triskele.'

'I see that but what else?'

'Fuck sake, Mateus. Look harder.'

'What? I'm not seeing it.'

'The halo. There's a fucking halo.'

Mateus squinted. And smiled. 'Aaaah! I see it now. Well, close the feckin' front door, there it is.'

'I know. Isn't it, though?'

'That's absolutely your mysterious symbol. I only had your word for it before. But, damn, if that's not an Incan Cross and Asian mandala surrounding a triskele, then I'm a space alien's gonad. What do you think's causing it?'

'Dunno. The texture of the stone. It's geological constitution. Shadows in the tomb. Whatever it is, it's totally there.' She grinned, then asked, 'And, *feckin*? Really? Didn't take you long to go native.'

'This city is *fierce*. I love it here. The vibe. The theatres. Literature. Trinity College Library. That place is like a wizarding school. When I was sitting in there, I kind of expected someone to swing by and plonk a massive book of spells on the table. Which also takes me nicely to what I've been doing while you've been criminally trespassing. Something that might confirm what you've just shown me.'

'What's that?'

'I found a book.'

'Not unusual in a library.'

'Nopes. Not unusual at all, you cheeky bugger. But this one was written by one of those English traveller types. In the 1790s. He wrote a few. One on Cumbria. Another on the Scottish Highlands. And one on Ireland, specifically the counties Louth, Meath, Cavan, Monaghan, Armagh, and Tyrone. Did you know that Ireland was mostly forest back then, but by the early 20th Century they were almost decimated?'

'No, I didn't. But get on with it.'

Mateus took a long drink of his stout, looked to be savouring the suspense, so Ary shot him a glare of admonishment.

He grinned. 'Anyway, this bloke – *Percival Greave Thrussington III* – now that's a name and a half... he was involved with some diggings around Newgrange and even went inside the tomb itself. It was allowed back then, apparently. Probably because he had a name like Percival Greave Thrussington III.'

'And what does he say about it?'

'Same as you. When he held a lantern up to one of the inner stones, he saw a triskele surrounded by the faint image of a cross. Of course, being the eighteenth century, he immediately went all god-squad on it and proclaimed the pattern to be *the majesty of Our Lord Jesus Christ, heralding the Christianisation of these pagan islands, thousands of years before the Massiah's magnificent birth at Bethlehem.*'

'Well, that's bullshit.'

'Yes. But also strangely prescient, don't you think?'

'Or just an inter-dimensional secret society influencing the lives of ancient humans.'

'Yes, there is that. But, on the back of what you found, it's good proof for the sources of your symbol. And I have more.' He took another slow drink of his stout, this time spilling drips of the dark brown liquid down his expensive paisley shirt. It didn't seem to bother him. He finished the dregs, wiped his mouth with the back of his hand, and continued, 'You'll give me a parade when you hear this next bit. Tell you what, get yourself a pint. And another for me while you're at it. I have a tab running. We can celebrate me being so goddamned awesome.'

'I think I will,' Ary said, rising from the chair. 'And, if I do, does that mean you'll get on with it?'

'Scout's honour.' he grinned, saluting at his forehead.

Ary went to the bar and placed her order.

Filling a glass two-thirds with stout, Damo set the glass atop the counter to *settle*, and glanced across to Mateus. 'He looks like he's in for the duration.'

'Yeah. He loves it here. It would be unkindly to interrupt him when he's so happy. Anyway, I'll be gone soon and mightn't see him for a while.'

'Where are you off to next?'

'Cambodia. Via China.'

'Cambodia? In Southeast Asia?'

'That's the one – not to be confused with the other Cambodia in South Croydon.'

'I see. I'm glad you cleared that up. I'm always getting those two confused.'

They shared a laugh. Damo poured a pint of lager, topped off the stout, and Ary carried both glasses across to Mateus's table, this time sitting alongside him. 'So, let's have it then.'

Downing a good quarter of his drink, Mateus wiped his lips and announced with a cocky tone of accomplishment, 'I found another source. That image we saw in the Muswell Hill book got me thinking. So, I followed a hunch, and found the personal account of Father José García Velázquez. A little-known priest who accompanied Pizarro on one of his trips into Peru and who, while undertaking his mission to bring the word of the living Christ to the jungle heathens, also liked to document things. Turns out, Father José was a gifted artist too. Sketching folk he came across here and there before his boss, well... before his boss basically hacked them all to bits. He made drawings of farmers. Weavers. The elite. As well as all the magnificent buildings and pyramids he came across on his journeys. Focussing one area in particular – a mountain place he called *Citadel of Damned Souls*.' Mateus left it there. Fell silent.

After many seconds, Ary asked, 'And so...?'

'*Citadel.*' Mateus replied.

'Yes...?'

'*Citadel,*' he said again, this time with more emphasis.

'I heard you. *Citadel. Citadel, citadel, citadel...* what about it?'

'K'in 'ell, Ary. Call yourself a researcher. How many other places in Peru do you know that are called a *Citadel*?'

The penny dropped. 'Oh, *Citadel*? In *Peru*? You think he found *Machu Picchu*?'

'Yes, genius, I do. History claims the Spanish never found it. Even though we now know the city was populated right up to their arrival. But I think our intrepid bible-basher stumbled across the place during one of his excursions into mountain country. A dangerous quest to undertake. But I – and you will be too – am glad he did, because he saw this...' Mateus reached into his jeans pocket, pulled out and unfolded a sheet of A4 paper, and laid it flat on the table. 'They wouldn't let me borrow the book, so I traced the image... and it's bang on for your description of the symbol... as well as that halo thing you just showed me.' He grinned, like a toddler having done his first poop in the toilet. 'So, whatcha think? Did I do good?'

Ary's skin tingled. Hairs stood on the back of her neck and arms.

These sensations had become an occurrence when exposed to the symbol only, this time, her mind drifted with blurry detachment. Became lost in a hazy, glistening sea of light and mist. She lost touch with her surroundings, instead finding herself standing outside a squat thatched dwelling with walls of grey stone. People clad in brightly coloured clothes came and went, others tended fields on the terraces below and, behind her, a monumental pyramid rose up to pierce the clouds. In the distance, a gigantic nub of forest-swathed rock burst upwards through diaphanous mists that roiled through the trees and flowed like water into the narrow lanes of the mountain city. Beneath her feet, the ground was of the compacted clay. A path led to five stone steps, and up to a slight but important-looking circular structure. The doorway was open. A small fire blazed inside. It appeared ceremonial. Somehow, she *knew* it was ceremonial. And, behind it, carved into a granite tablet, was the mysterious symbol: a mandala, outside a circle, surrounding a cross, with a spiral triskele in the centre.

'This seems to be a thing now,' Mateus said from a distance.

'What's a thing?' she asked, as the table, Damo's bar, Mateus, and the world in general emerged from the glowing mist and the mountain city disappeared.

'You spacked out there. Again.'

'Did I?'

'For reals.'

'Well, I s'pose so then. Apparently, I can travel to ancient Peru now. In my mind at least.'

Mateus looked confused, took a drink. Ary did too, a large one.

Her phone buzzed.

The symbol was back. And, this time, it stayed.

FINDING CUSCO

The next step was obvious and, for the trip to Lima, Ary and Mateus had struck a deal.

Actually, they'd quibbled:

'Two grand if I can come,' he'd said. 'After all, it was me who found the link to Machu Picchu.'

'Yeah-but-nah. Not happ'nin.'

'Three grand?'

'Nope. I want to go alone.'

'What about four?'

'Fuck sake, you're a persistent bugger, but no.'

'You'd get my cheery company. And this smile.' He grinned, like a child begging for sweets.

It made Ary snigger. 'No. You're too annoying.'

'Only because I like you.'

'I know. I'm fucking awesome. But I never bring people along with me.'

'You did before.'

'But I don't anymore.'

'Not even for five? Five whole thousand pounds. Into your bank account right now, and I promise to come to Peru but no farther. Whatcha say?' He grinned again.

How could she refuse? There was something about Mateus that was hard to resist.

Also, funds were short. Damo's bar shifts, although welcome, had been a bust. For a penniless waif like her, five thousand quid was a shit-ton of money and, given her usual economical approach to travelling, enough to cover her whole journey to Cambodia three times over and then some. She thought about the flexibility, the contentment of knowing she was covered if things went wrong.

'Okay,' she conceded. 'But only to Peru. After that, I'm going it alone.'

'I know, I know... it's a family thing.'

'Why, though? Why are you so eager to traipse around after me?'

'I did a magazine quiz. And scored thirty-seven out of a possible forty for being a fusty old fart.'

'Can't say I disagree. But, really? You follow me around like a lost kitten because of some stupid magazine quiz?'

'Yes. Well, actually, no. I made that bit up. But I'm soooo bored. And you are out there, chasing down the truth. You're good at it. And weird.'

'I'm not weird. I'm quirky.'

'Okay then... you're *qu-eird*. Anyway, I want to be a part of something. Something important. Producing does my bloody head in. It's just one band after another. I've got all this money and my life is nothing but a tiresome bumhole.'

'I wouldn't call it a bumhole. People would sell their soul for a fraction of what you've got. I'd love to be able to play guitar.'

'You could learn.'

'Yeah, but nuh. Tone deaf, mate.'

'I'm a good teacher.'

'*Yeah*, but I'm a crap student. Ask my lecturers at Uni. Got a 2:1, though. Anyway, I'll take your word for it that your life's a bumhole. You can come... for five grand. But, after Machu Picchu, you bugger off back home again. Move your studio to Dublin or whatever it is you've got planned. Tell you what, you can be my base camp.' Mateus's eyes lit up at the suggestion. 'If you want so bad to be a part of this, you can be the person who – if I need it – does all the library stuff. The analytic hub, if you like. For the big reveal. If I ever find it, that is.'

They flew business class. Mateus insisted on it and, frankly, Ary wasn't in the mood to bicker. When they got to Lima, after a short adjournment for jetlag purposes, they took the cheapest bus to Cusco. As the conspiracy theory guru and expedition leader, she had to maintain at least some authority for the travel arrangements.

They arrived in the morning.

Mateus complained of cramps.

Ary told him to, 'Shut the fuck up.'

They both laughed, got breakfast at a churro bar in Centro Histórico, before booking a day trip out to Machu Picchu.

When they got there, Ary left Mateus with the main tourist group gawking at the *Temple of the Sun* and peeled away to investigate a part of the site she had never been to before but felt she knew every bit as well as the concrete concourses of her childhood. Heading towards a place marked on the official pamphlet as *Templo de las Tres Ventanas*, she turned east along an array of descending grassed terraces where, in her mind's eye, she imagined the hubbub of people in brightly coloured clothes tending their crops. To her left, stood the rest of the ancient city. To her right, a gigantic nub of forest-swathed rock. A clay path taking her to the outer edge of the site and up five steps into the ruins of a small, round, single roomed structure built in stone. She was alone. Far from the other visitors. A bowl-like hollow commanded centre-place of the floor. It looked like a fire-pit.

Appeared ceremonial. Somehow, she knew it *had been* ceremonial. Behind the hollow, hewn into what remained of the circular wall, a shallow recess indicated where something had fallen free or been removed from the stonework. The tablet with the symbol was gone. No remnants remained. By way of speculation, invention, or perhaps some kind of Jungian archetypal recollection, however, Ary knew for certain it had been there...

...the notion of which, even to her open-minded outlook, seemed ludicrous.

On a slow walk back to join Mateus, Ary felt on edge. *Were her visions totally in her head?* Some strange manifestation of her ability to perceive things distinctly. *Or could she really see into the past, recreate it in the present?*

Her first vision, the one where she saw through her mother's eyes, she had put down to a daydream. A vivid one, but nonetheless a daydream. The most recent, however, the details of which she'd kept secret from Mateus, seemed different and her journey to Machu Picchu one of verification, to prove what she'd seen in her mind did in fact exist.

Or not.

Either way, she needed to know.

And, it did exist. Making her discovery of the recess for the tablet even more troubling.

Had someone hacked her phone?

All of her devices?

Were they manipulating her thoughts through them?

A concept that also sounded ludicrous, but she didn't discount the notion either.

The entities behind *the great conspiracy* were cunning, skilful, and had resources far beyond the capabilities of any individual, maybe of governments. GCHQ, the CIA, MSS, GRU, all intelligence services were mere pawns. Willing participants in a global confederacy of vested interests, agitated by a group of interdimensional beings. Through her pseudonym of *Harper T Jackson*, she had thought to reveal this truth while keeping herself hidden. But they had found her. The recurring symbol. The visions. The fact that she was here in Machu Picchu. All proved what she had suspected since the image first popped up on her screen: something she had done, or was still doing, had drawn attention. Plucked nerve. And they were persistent. Powerful. Recent events rubberstamping her premise that nobody really controls their life.

Nor, it seemed, did they control their own thoughts either.

CHINA IN YOUR SAND

Honouring his side of the agreement, when they returned from Cusco to Lima and with Ary withholding the content of her vision, Mateus took a plane home. Actually, she hurried him off. He didn't want to go, but said he respected the reasons why she needed to complete the next stages of the investigation alone. Poor old Mateus didn't have family. As a child of the system, his band, Radon Death had substituted as kin. A partnership that brought wealth and influence, but never the intimate relationships he craved. Ary liked to think she filled the gap. And, by the way he indulged her out-there theories, she reckoned Mateus did so too.

The thought made her smile.

Having pre-acquired a visa before leaving London, she arrived in China just before noon, hoping her usual nondescript attire would deter scrutiny. She wanted to float through. It didn't work. Some people stared anyway and Ary put it down to, when you're born and raised in the UK, it's nigh on impossible to cast off looking Western. Upon leaving Beijing Capital International Airport, she had flagged a taxi to take her to the hotel Mateus had slyly booked in advance and confirmed in his text:

I booked you into the InterOriental - close to the Forbidden City for touristy stuff
Just thought you should start out in luxury (winking face tongue out emoji)

Ary felt the conflicting emotions of irritation and gratitude for his gift.

He hadn't asked.

He was interfering.

But there would be more than enough backpacker hostels in her future. A comfy bed to kick the whole thing off mightn't be a bad idea after all.

A follow-up text said:

You're booked for three nights
Rest up. See something cool. The world will wait (sleeping face with Zs emoji)

The room was massive. In the uber-extravagant price range. The kind of place a Western celebrity frequented when faking a crusade into ethnicity. It had a king-size bed, limitless food brought to the room by deferent waiting staff, and use of the spa, including a masseuse, a sauna, a pool to swim off the sauna, and a hot-tub to soak off the pool, and another masseuse to give a final rubdown if all the marinating failed to achieve consummate relaxation.

Ary gave in, luxuriating in a lifestyle she seldom experienced.

Unlike Mateus, life for her was a rigmarole of scrimping and denial. She worked, she saved, she travelled, she came back home to London, worked, saved, and travelled some more. She liked it that way. The achievement of doing things by her own means. Since the second she met him, standing by the speakers at a Lacuna Coil gig, they had hit it off. Became good friends. Excellent friends. But he wanted to indulge her. Which turned into an ongoing argument. This time, however, she decided to give in. Live it up a little. *Why?* Because Mateus had done this for her. He was a fierce friend. Always there when things got freaky. He was her linchpin. Her co-conspirator in a maelstrom of conspiracies.

The thought of him made her smile again.

And, in the moment, she realised she missed him, and loved him, even if that love was only platonic. It was deep. Deeper maybe than any she had felt for the scarce few relationships she'd had down the years. Mateus was *it*. To quote the movie, he was *the fucking love of* her *life*, and she would tell him... when she saw him next.

After a quick soak – in the bath, a spa visit would *take for-fucking-ever* – she left to buy a Chinese sim for her phone. Although she was VPN-ed to the eyeballs, it was prudent to not draw attention by having a – albeit encrypted – UK sim. Luckily the bloke in the phone-shop spoke English. Limited, but enough to get the job done. As he inserted the sim, he also commented on her wallpaper, said it was *cool*. She asked him had he seen the symbol before. He shook his head. It was worth a try.

Back at the hotel, she ordered a single glass of Shiraz to the room. *And, why not?* It was paid for. Then, sitting on one of the three sofas – yes, the suite came with three bloody sofas – she took a selfie holding a wineglass to her mouth, attached it to and sent Mateus a text of thanks, and told him about the *three bloody sofas*.

He replied with:

> *Glad you're enjoying it*
> ...a thumbs-up emoji and four Xs.

She rang her mother on the hotel phone. No point wasting valuable minutes.

'Well, I got here,' Ary said. 'I'm in Beijing.'

'That's good.'

'Remind me again where I'm going?'

'Your father's sister has moved. She now lives in Xianyang. In the city. It's where the work is.'

'That makes her easier to find. What about the rest of his family?'

'Maybe they still live in their village, north of Xiaohe Reservoir. But I don't know. After Baba died, I don't talk with them. I only had a number for his sister.'

'That's good. Do you have the address?'

'Yes.' Mteay dictated it precisely.

Ary wrote it down on the back of the hotel menu.

'Her name is, Li Xiu,' Mteay added. 'She knows you are coming.'

'Thanks. I love you.'

'Love you too.' Her mother hung up. Ary assumed talking about Baba evoked bittersweet memories.

Draining the contents of her glass, Ary left to get something to eat.

On other research trips, dictated by the most affordable return tickets, she'd had to adhere to strict schedules. Three days in the Chinese capital, however, offered a rare opportunity to look around. She found a food market situated in a courtyard, not far from the Temple of Heaven. On the walk there, she was struck most by the width of the streets, the size and newness of the buildings, the sheer quantity of people but, when she ducked down an alleyway and came out into the market courtyard, the true China came to life for her. On all sides of the small square, smoke and steam imbued sunlight danced across the awnings of a myriad stalls, the heady mix of fragrant and savoury aromas causing her mouth to salivate. Colourful garlands and paper decorations adorned the internal spaces, while shoppers milled, haggled, and sniffed at the rows of produce, from sugared fruits to the large pots filled with soups, stews, and curries. The activity was frenetic. Like Portobello Market in London but with the dial ramped up to eleven. Homing in on the food-stall frequented by the largest concentration of patrons – this wasn't Ary's first dalliance in suchlike places – she bought five *cong you bing* pancakes and a bottle of beer, along with three *bing tanghulu* fruit sticks, because scallion pancakes always gave her a sweet tooth.

As she stood eating at one of the food-stall's four pedestal tables, some people stared.

Others didn't.

It was the way of it.

Finishing her pancakes and beer, she dumped the paper wrapper and bottle into requisite recycling bins, left the square and walked along

Qianmen East Street to the Mausoleum of Mao Zedong. Most visitors to Beijing made a beeline straight for the Forbidden City. But the founder of the nation in which she now stood had been such a big part of her father's, if not her mother's life, Ary thought it honourable to make the pilgrimage for him. Baba had been a soldier in the People's Liberation Army. He had fought in the Sino-Vietnamese War. He often said he was proud to fight for the party, and how he had wept upon receiving the news of the chairman's death. He also said, since arriving in London, that the phone clicked when he made or received a call. Which prompted Ary to question why her parents had chosen to move to the UK in the first place. Mteay said it was for the health service. Baba said it was because of work, offered by a friend who had moved from Hong Kong to open a restaurant in Ladbroke Grove. Whatever the reason, Ary suspected a grain of truth in her father's claims about being monitored. Maybe the British had let him enter the country hoping to snatch a precious Chinese state secret, disclosed by way of idle chitchat. They had picked the wrong target. Baba did little else except work long hours, read the paper, and relive his military exploits during the invasion of Loc Binh. To which end, she would respect him by visiting the tomb of his leader.

She spent the next two days doing the same touristy consumer stuff: the Temple of Heaven, the Art Zone, took a trip out to the Great Wall where the view was as stunning as expected, bought a small bottle of essence and yes, she did visit the Forbidden City. Beijing was an amazing place. Huge. Impressive. She regretted leaving but, when her three days were up, took a cross-country train to Xi'an and thereon out to Xianyang where Baba's sister lived somewhere within a sprawling mass of concrete resembling the Stonebridge estate of Ary's childhood, only much larger and dappled with snatches of leafy inner-city parkland.

After forty minutes searching for and then locating the exact tower block, she took the lift to the tenth floor and went along a narrow corridor running the full breadth of the building. Twenty or more doors flanked either side. Each painted in the same nondescript off-white colour, the frames draped with garlands of green mugwort. Baba had talked of this, decorations for the Dragon Boat Festival, put up ahead of the national holiday coming in late June. Reaching the last door on the left, she cross-referenced the address with the one she written in her notebook, checked a few times more and stood there, staring at the paintwork. On the other side of this unassuming door lived a connection to her beloved father from a time before even her mother had known him. In London, they had been a compact group. Baba, Mteay, Ary, and no one else. The Longs, as the

British might call them. A unit, bereft of a wider family and self-contained by its smallness. And yet, she did have family. One that even her father had lost touch with before his lungs finally packed in and death whisked him away to whatever darkness a person finds themselves when they breathe their last. Less than a few metres away, that family was probably sitting in a chair, or making tea in the kitchen, preparing food, watching TV, reading a book. They could be doing anything. Just leading a normal life. Nothing strange and nothing to get worked up about. And still, her hand refused to obey, defying any instruction to ball into a fist, lift from her side, and knock the door.

The decision, however, was made for both her and her hand.

The door opened and a short, slim, black-haired woman – for some reason, Ary had expected her hair to be grey – dressed in a white blouse and purple skirt, said, 'Hello,' in flawless English, 'I'm Li Xiu. You are Ary. Your mother rang. She said you were coming.'

At first, Ary stayed silent, reaching around into a side-pocket of her backpack for the small bottle she had purchased in Beijing. She held it out. The bottle was made from cream and brown coloured ceramic, embossed with a dragon. The shop assistant had said it was of a style once used for opium, but now contained peony scented essence; the flower that symbolises wealth, honour, and completeness. Ary thought it a good house gift for someone she shared DNA with but had never met.

And she said so: 'It's diffuser essence. Peony.'

Her aunt refused three times before taking it with both hands and saying, yet again in perfect English, 'Thank you. It is very nice.'

She ushered Ary inside, gesturing to four pairs of slippers on the floor by the door. Ary selected the pair she reckoned to be closest to her size and changed out of her boots. The slippers felt tight, but she squeezed them on anyway and, following her aunt through to a compact but well laid out living room said, 'I like your flat. It's very modern, and shows a great eye for detail and home planning,'

The little woman beamed and gestured for Ary to sit on one of the room's two grey sofas. Without saying a word, she then disappeared into another room, returning with a pot of tea and accompanying porcelain, which she served with the traditional etiquette.

Throughout the process, neither spoke.

The tea was offered, accepted, sipped, and finally Li Xiu said, 'For many years we thought Ai had died. He went to Vietnam. We didn't hear much. A *Shang Shi* – what you would call a staff sergeant – came by and said he'd been discharged due to injury, but had decided not to come home. She said he went to Cambodia. No one in the family knew why. And, when he did finally connect, many years later, Ai told us he had met your mother and now lived in England. We thought he'd gone mad. Why would anyone go to England?'

Ary thought about it. 'I don't know. Your country is beautiful. He always said so. And talked about coming back someday. But there were complications with his wounds. Then, he died.' Tears filled her eyes. She noticed Li Xiu's had also. 'Anyway, the tea is lovely. You make it well. And your English is impeccable.'

Li Xiu sniffed, blinked and wiped her eyes. 'I studied at school. And then at university. My undergraduate degree was in general archaeology with English. My doctorate at Stanford focused on the Yangtse Civilisation. I met my husband there. When we returned to China, we both got jobs at the East China Normal University. He will be home soon. He is working late. A few years back, we uncovered a new pyramid. He's documenting the finds.'

Later, and at Li Xiu's and her husband, Qing Yuan's insistence, Ary joined them at a local restaurant for dinner, where they ate noodles, dumplings, and a slew of other dishes. It was obvious they were trying to impress. For two hours, talk revolved around Baba, Mteay, life in the UK and – to Ary's approval – the ancient world. Particularly China, and the significance of the new pyramid's discovery for Chinese heritage. Concealing her, what could be termed less than mainstream, enthusiasm for the subject, Ary mentioned her recent outings to Newgrange and Machu Picchu. She didn't explain the reasons behind the trips. Professionals like these didn't condone cooky conspiracists. She thought it apt, however, to indicate their common interests.

Qing Yuan wondered if she had considered studying archaeology.

Ary told them about her 2:1 in History from London Met and they seemed impressed.

Insisting she spend the night, they invited Ary back home. Rice wine was offered and accepted. Around one in the morning, they all went down for the night. Ary got the guest room. Dropped right off. An undefinable time later, a slight tapping and the words, 'Are you awake?' jostled her from a dense, dreamless sleep.

She sat up. 'Yes.'

'We are going out to the site soon,' Li Xiu said from the other side of the bedroom door. 'You can come if you like. The National Cultural Heritage Administration has recently allowed us to show visitors the main areas. Of course, all the important artifacts have been removed for study. But you can still see the pyramid.'

Before the words *you can come* had left his lips, Ary was up, still clothed in her jeans and tee-shirt, but she would keep this lapse of manners to herself. To use the vernacular, she had totally tied one on last night, and she didn't even recall getting into bed. Rice wine was strong. At least she removed the slippers before crawling under the sheets. The room wavered. Bouncing up had been the worst idea. Her mouth tasted like farts. She needed water.

'Yes please,' she said with a paper dry tongue. 'Just give me a few minutes to freshen up.'

'Of course. It's still only six-thirty. We will eat breakfast first. I have made *báizhōu* with pickled tofu. It's rice porridge. Some people call it *congee*.'

'That sounds lovely. Thank you.' It did – and, then again, didn't, when a person's stomach was rolling a somersault. And, as for it being *six-thirty... what the fucking hell?*

She waited until Li Xiu had gone before she left to scrub up in the washroom. She drank water from the tap, splashed some on her face, brushed and fixed her hair into her favoured K-pop style buns, yellow ribbon in one and red in the other, rolled some deodorant under her arms and joined the others for a breakfast of *dòuhuā* and tea.

The salty tofu pudding was very welcome. Helped settle the tummy.

Thirty minutes later, with Ary feeling somewhat human again, they left together in a white, electric-powered car, bearing the circular red and white logo of the East China Normal University, driven by a man who Li Xiu introduced as their standard driver. They headed south along the G5 past the Golden Monkey Nature Reserve. There was intermittent conversation between the driver and Li Xiu that seemed mundane and workaday, but nothing in English that Ary could get a handle on. Two hours later, just short of Cun'erba, they turned into a side road. The bumpy dirt track took them through forested hills and then out onto open plain, still populated with trees but sparsely, in the centre of which, surrounded by high fences and showing signs of excavation, a stepped pyramid rose from a hilltop.

Ary's jaw dropped. She knew about the usual places: Giza, Teotihuacan, Tikal, but what stood before her took her breath away. Her skin tingled. Hairs stood on the back of her neck and arms. She waited for the vision to begin but nothing happened. She checked her phone, expecting to find something weird there, but nothing occurred to make the moment seem or feel unusual.

'Are you expecting a call?' Qing Yuan asked as the car rolled to a stop before a high gate.

'Just checking the time.'

He looked at his smartwatch. 'Nine thirty-five.'

The guard attending the gate let them through. Li Xiu and Qing Yuan exited the car, indicating for Ary to follow. Before he drove off, the driver glanced once at Ary, as though evaluating or judging her involvement here, before driving away to park inside a wooden structure at the perimeter of the site. As he got out of the car, his stare returned. The attention felt physical, heavy, as if a presence was trying to force its way into her mind.

'Isn't it impressive?' Li Xiu asked, shattering whatever the driver and Ary had just shared.

'It's something else,' Ary replied.

'It's probably, if not definitely the most important site in China. We've dated it to somewhere in the Mesolithic period. Which is a long time before any major civilisation existed in this area. And confusing. We'll be studying the finds for decades. Come look at this.'

With her husband in tow, Li Xiu led Ary across to a long narrow trench, maybe five metres in breadth, running the full length of one side of the pyramid. Dropping two or more metres into the sandy soil, a dozen people dug, brushed, and sifted through the dirt amid what looked like seven rooms. The trench was covered with a tent-like structure. There were two similar trenches, one to each side of the pyramid, and no doubt another beyond as well.

Li Xiu's phone rang. She walked a few steps away, answered, spoke softly, turned to Ary and said, 'My apologies. They want me over at the Situation Room,' before heading off towards a collection of construction trailers close to where the driver had parked the car.

'Li Xiu is Chief Archaeologist for the whole site,' Qing Yuan said. 'We won't see her for the rest of the day. Let me show you around. Our discovery of a human skull has been circulated with the wider scientific community, so we can do that now. You probably heard of a similar one? A couple of years back? Dragon Man?'

'Yes. fascinating stuff. I wrote a blog on it.'

Qing Yuan didn't enquire further. Ary got the impression his focus was confined to one thing: this dig. A site so impressive, she found it hard to keep her mouth closed for longer than a few seconds. Having investigated many comparable sites, albeit from a point of view not shared by the scientific community, she knew certain distinctive features when she saw them. Yet, the monument wasn't what she'd expect to find in China. Li Xiu had said it was Mesolithic, and Ary couldn't help but notice the similarity with Northern European burial sites from the same period. The mixed rough and cut stone construction carried the same traits as Skara Brae in the Orkneys, the Newgrange passage tomb, but also the houses of the Ancient Puebloans in North America, or – dare she think it – the stone towers and dwellings of Anatolia, in Africa, South America, the kurgans of the Steppes; her mind was racing, the connections were obvious, pointing to a mashup of features, seen in all parts of the world, amalgamated within this one single structure.

Her skin tingled. Hairs stood on the back of her neck and arms. Her thoughts blurring, lost within an expanse of clouds and sparkles. Nimbi. Nebulae. Countless dewdrops drifting through an unending mist. Her sight cleared. She was standing before this same pyramid, watching hundreds of workers, dressed in hemp tunics and trousers, stack stones to lay out the walls of the seven roomed structures to the forefront, as well as those on either side and beyond the pyramid. As for the pyramid itself, it seemed work had only started. The footprint was there but with only the first tier constructed. This too was awash with activity: workers clad in similar hemp attire, and others with European features, ginger hair and beards, wearing in plaid linen tunics and trousers. For some reason, in her dreamlike state, nothing seemed unusual about them being so far from their historical home. Nor was the worker sitting cross-legged on the ground carving *the symbol* into a book-sized slab of granite. These slips in and out of reality had become familiar now. As was the whoosh of consciousness that returned her to Qing Yuan and normality. The whole vision had lasted only seconds, as if the message – if that's what these *slips* were – needed only reinforcing. A punctuation point.

Looking across to the right, where the stonemason from her vision had sat, she asked Qing Yuan, 'Have you excavated that area over there yet?'

'Yes. We've completed that section. The trench was backfilled to preserve the site. Why do you ask?'

'Oh, nothing. Just curious.'

'There wasn't much there,' he continued, 'granite shards, a few limestone tools. We think the shards came from the tablet we found close to the pyramid. It was broken into eighteen pieces. Like an unintentional jigsaw puzzle. And carved with a symbol...'

'What kind of symbol?' Ary interrupted, more eagerly than intended.

'We don't know. Circular shapes. A cross or a square. Spirals. It's back at the university for study.'

Ary said no more. The coincidences were piling up. It was as if something had led her here, to this exact place, at this exact point in time. The idea of which both intrigued and disturbed her.

A BRONX TAIL

More than a month had passed since Jordan Burke received five thousand bucks into his bank account. An inquiry with the people at Westchester Trust, a chat with family, coupled with a dutiful citizen report to the cops, and everyone seemed to agree, whether from an anonymous source or not, the money was his to do with as he pleased.

Even the Community Service Officer behind the front desk at the 46th Precinct said, 'Maybe you've got a fairy god-something. Or whatever the *woke* term for it is nowadays.' She added that, if it was causing too much irritation, she would be happy to take it off Jordan's hands, sniggered, and advised it was most likely a big mistake and to take it up with his bank, which brought him back to square one.

Because Jordan wasn't convinced.

No one just gives a person five K expecting nothing in return.

And in what universe does a mixed-race resident of Fordham Heights get a huge, untraceable sum of cash deposited into his account and all the cops say is, *maybe you've got a fairy god-something*?

He didn't need to be a private detective to think the whole thing stank. But he also wasn't about to go poking around and discover it was the work of drug-dealers, gangbangers, or – who knows – maybe the Black Mafia, if they were still a thing, hiding their ill-gotten gains in some unsuspecting person's bank account. So, he opened another, transferred the full five thousand across and left it untouched, hoping the bank might call him some day and admit to having made, as the cop at the 46th Precinct suggested, *a big mistake*.

They didn't.

The money stayed there.

A confusing problem that he kind of forgot about until now when, sitting at his PC, revising an article on *Sonoluminescence*, otherwise known as *Star in a Jar*, for *The Kitchen Sink Magazine*, his cellphone buzzed.

A text popped up on the screen:

> *Go to Crotona Park NOW – Indian Pond*
> *You'll be contacted again when you get there*
> *It's the article of a lifetime*

An instant later, Jordan rang his sister, Jada, and began speaking. 'I got a text. I think it's from the people who deposited the money.'

'I'm in a lecture,' she replied with an angry whisper.

'Sorry,' he said. 'Call me when you're out.'

Eleven minutes later – Jordan was counting – Jade rang back. 'What the flying fuck, Jordan. You can't just go ringing me anytime you like.'

'I thought you'd be free.'

'I'm never free. When I'm not here...' She paused to say *hi* to someone nearby, '...I'm at work. You know this.' She *grr-ed*. 'Sometimes, you just totally screw with my last nerve.'

'Why don't you mute your phone then?'

'Why don't you go fuck yourself.'

'It's just a suggestion.'

'Really? *You* – the guy who can't even download an app without two hours of class-based instruction, is giving me advice on how to use my devices?'

'No. But it would save a lot of hassle if you...'

'Look, Jordan, what do you want?'

'I got a text.'

'Brilliant. I'll bring champagne. We'll celebrate.'

'No. I got a text. I think it's from the people who put the cash in my account.'

Jada went silent, for quite a few seconds. 'Are you sure?'

'I think so.'

'You think so?'

'Yes.'

'So, it might not be.'

'But I think it is.'

'And why is that, genius?'

'Because they want me to go somewhere.'

Jada said *hi* to someone else and then, 'Maybe it's somebody from your magazine. You're always setting up meetings. Me too, on the times I take over for you.'

'But in coffee shops. For lunch. Never in Crotona Park, at Indian Pond.'

'That's where they said to meet?'

'Yep. And *NOW*. Written in upper case. They said they'll contact me when I get there. I'm totally freaking out here, Jada. I'm scared. What if they're going to rob me?'

'What, rob you *and* give you five grand?'

'Good point.'

'I know. I always make good points.'

'What do you think they want?'

'Who knows. If I were you, I wouldn't go. Spend the cash. Get yourself some decent clothes.'

'Hey.'

'Something snaz. You look like one of my lecturers. The really ancient ones. A year or two off retirement. Or, you could go on holiday. But I'll tell you this...'

'What?'

'If it was me, you wouldn't catch me anywhere near Crotona Park.'

'Me neither.'

'Good. You win the *I'm not a fucking idiot* badge.'

'But I'm going anyway.'

'*What?* Why? Why would anyone...? Do you want to be kidnapped? Yeah, *good luck widdat.*'

'Kidnapped? You think they'll kidnap me?'

'Shit ain't fair, bro. So, yes, maybe. It's as good a theory as any. Or maybe they want to give you another five K.' She laughed.

'Not funny.'

'It is a bit. No, you're right. It's not. I'll come with.'

'I knew you'd say that. I was depending on it.'

'Yeah, well, can't have my big bro getting all banged out. Any lame-ass tries anything, I'll skull-fuck'em tong style.'

'Forgot you know Kung Fu.'

'Tae Kwon Do. And I'm a black belt. The real deal. Anyway, I'll protect your sorry ass.'

'How long until you get here? They said *now*. And that they have *the article of a lifetime.*'

'Hashtag eyeroll, bro. Fuck you're dumb. They can say whatever they like, but you stay put until I get there. Give me half an hour. I'll meet you out front of Cute-icles.' She hung up.

Jordan closed down his phone, and his computer, fearful of additional messages coming through. He stood, put on the puffer jacket he wore well into summer, climbed the stairs to the small lobby at the front of the nail bar and waited for his sister to arrive. The street outside hummed. People, squinting under a bright afternoon sunshine, shopped along the precinct. Two women stood chatting by the gate to the community garden. A group of rowdy teenagers smoked cigarettes outside Pop Donnelly's Minimart, and Jordan wanted so much to suck on those acrid fumes more than at any time since quitting. He thought about bumming one. These guys, however, didn't strike him as the types who shared smokes.

Lori Cassano came out to join him. 'You craving again?'

'How'd you know?'

'I saw you eyeing those kids down there. You're like a cat stalking a blue jay.'

'I'm that transparent?'

'Always.' She looked around. 'Are you expecting someone?'

'Just my sister. We're going down to Indian Pond.'

'Nice. An afternoon off.' She peered up to the sky. 'You got the weather for it.'

'It's... kinda like a work thing.'

'Didn't know we had a nuclear plant in Crotona Park. Or people building rockets.'

'No, it's not like that. Got to meet someone.'

'You don't look in the least bit happy about it.'

'I'm not.'

Lori went back inside. Closing the door behind her, she said, 'I'm sure it'll work out fine.'

When Jada arrived, she patted Jordan on the shoulder, said, 'Let's go, bro,' and led him out to and down Grand Concourse.

They took East Tremont to Crotona Avenue. Followed the road into the park. At the Greenway, a group of players had gathered at the entrance to the Tennis Center. Jada advised going no farther, suggested it might be good having people around. Jordan agreed. Not that he was in any shape to formulate logical decisions. His thoughts raced. Had done so since Lori went back into her salon and he spent twenty-three minutes and forty-two seconds waiting for Jada to turn up.

Thoughts like:

Who was the mysterious texter? What did they want? Why him? Why anything?

Were they dangerous?

His imagination played through numerous possibilities, and in none of them did he come out well. Only the worst contacted other people this way. Only those with agendas gave a total stranger a stack-load of money. His best deduction was still drug-dealers, or local gangbangers. His fear said murderers. His reasoning said murderers too.

He nearly jumped out of his skin when his phone buzzed.

Glad to see you came

...the text said...

Don't worry
We mean no harm

Jordan wasn't convinced.

THE TRUTH FAIRY GOD-SOMETHING

The next text said:

> Go back to Grand Concourse & take the Subway to 110 Street
> Follow Tito Puente to the railway bridge
> We will contact again when you get there

It was followed, a few seconds later, by another text:

> And lose your sister

Jordan did as instructed.

Everything except the *lose your sister* part.

Despite what Jada thought, he wasn't naive or stupid enough to go meeting strangers without her. In fact, it disturbed him even more that they knew she was his sister.

When he reached the railway bridge, his phone buzzed again:

> Good. Now go to Central Park
> Nutter's Battery
> Wait on one of the benches.
> I see your sister is still here
> Not what we agreed

This time, Jordan replied:

> I didn't agree to anything
> My sister stays
> Who are you?

'The fuck you doing,' Jada snapped, snatching the phone from his hands. 'Are you stupid. Nobody ever answers the weirdo.'

No reply came.

They waited for over an hour and no one came either.

They went back to the *TKSM* office. On the subway ride there, Jordan suspected he was being watched. Which was understandable, considering he *was* being watched. But no more texts popped up on his phone. They journeyed in silence. Jada, it seemed, had also been unsettled by the day's events. Back at the office, she pulled up her usual wastebasket, sat and, adjusting her glasses from slipping down her nose, said:

'So, it's official. This shit got real. I thought it was just some scumbags picking on the geeky kid.'

Without removing his jacket, Jordan sat in his computer chair. 'Me too. Don't get me wrong, I was scared... but I was also kind of okay with it being teenagers yanking my chain.'

'Maybe it still is. No one turned up. That's probably because they didn't expect two of us. Or maybe the whole thing was to send you on a pointless bug hunt. Or, as I said before, *shit's got real.*'

'It's probably the bug hunt thing. The corner kids are always shouting lame crap at me.'

She smiled. 'Like what?'

'*Braindork. Nerdhead. Parka-sparka*, whatever that means.'

'Yeah. That just making shit up.'

'I think it's because of my puffer jacket. Even though it's exactly the same as the ones they wear.'

'But they don't keep theirs on when it's *heart-of-the-fucking-Sun* hot.'

'They do. But, I s'pose I'm not cool enough.'

Jada didn't reply, just grinned.

'Anyway, I think you're right. It's just some smartass who got my digits and thought it would be a total megablast to mess with the *parka-sparka.*'

'Or, it got real.' She laughed.

So did Jordan.

She stood, flipped the wastebasket upright again, gave him a peck on the forehead, said, 'Stay chill, bro,' and left.

Jordan turned on his computer. A few hours of intensive feature writing might put an end to his unease. Or so he hoped. There was still the matter of the five thousand bucks. And the fact that someone had accessed his supposedly private, protected, off-grid, and totally unhackable cellphone. He contemplated changing phones, relocating the *TKSM* office, or maybe even skipping country for a while. He wanted to travel. The engineering of the ancient Greeks intrigued him. Recent archaeological finds in Africa and South America tweaked his curiosity beyond mere interest. And South East Asia, particularly Cambodia had been on his hit list since his High School history teacher told him about ancient Khmer methods to manage water supply.

Prior to now, the snag had been cash.

There was, however, the five grand. And everyone agreed the money was his to do with as he wanted.

Why not use it to travel?

Why not see Angkor Wat on someone's else's dime?

As the idea turned from thought to resolution, the door behind him opened and, spinning around in his chair, Jordan expected to see his sister standing in the light of the doorway.

It wasn't Jada.

A figure stood there instead; tall, dressed in black, who stared at him and said:

'...And you should leave right now.'

Jumping to his feet, Jordan scurried to the back wall of the office, clipping his hip on the corner of the desk in the process.

He yelped. High pitched and puppy-like.

'Be careful,' the figure said, moving forward. 'We can't have you hurting yourself.' The voice was soft. Female. Foreign. *Asian? Perhaps South Asian?* 'You have a nice place here,' she added, peering around the basement room. 'Dark. Mouldy. With a certain *Stasi* torture-chamber charm.'

He noted the sarcasm and, huddling beside one of the three wipe-boards, nursing his hip with one hand, stared at the intruder but didn't say a word.

The stranger walked to the desk, sat in his computer chair, stretched out her legs, leaned back, looked to the ceiling, and uttered a loud sigh.

'Ah, it's good to sit down,' she said. 'I've been on my feet all day. Mostly chasing you around New York. But it was worth it. We're here now. Together at last.'

Jordan stayed silent. The light of his computer screen confirming the figure to be a woman of about forty years old, with short black hair, greying in places, wearing what looked like black pyjamas, underneath a long raincoat that seemed somewhat unnecessary in the good weather. Then again, who was he to talk. His puffer jacket was hardly summer wear.

Swivelling in the chair, she said, 'It's cold in here,' did up the buttons on her coat and added, 'you should get yourself a heater.'

'It's on the wall,' Jordan replied with a cracked voice. 'Who are you.'

She glanced across to the heater and back to Jordan. 'Oh, yes indeed. You do have one. And I'm a friend... of sorts. We are very interested in you.'

'*We?* Who are *we?*'

'Look, why don't you stop cowering in the corner and come over here. I'll even give you back your seat.' She stood. Gestured with an open hand for him to sit in the computer chair.

Jordan stayed put.

'I won't bite. Well, I won't bite you.' She sniggered. 'Only kidding. We like you. You have an inquiring mind.'

'Who likes me? What are you talking about?' He edged out a few steps.

The woman took a few back to match. 'I suppose we're your future clients. Of *The Kitchen Sink Magazine*. Yes, that'll do, we are clients of your magazine. Although we aren't interested in anything you publish. It's *you* we like.'

'You keep saying that.'

'And we mean it. We're big fans. You are our very own Trey Songz, only without the snazzy fashion sense. I mean, what is it with the puffer jacket?'

'A big deal, apparently. Everyone seems to have a beef with it.'

'I can understand why. Anyway, you won't need it where you're going.'

Jordan darted back to the wall, clenching his fists in readiness for whatever came next.

'Oh, stop that. Don't be silly. You know you couldn't fight your way out of a wet paper bag.'

'Don't come any closer.'

The woman raised her hands, palms out, and smiled. 'Fine. Whatever you want. I'll stay right here. But we really need to wrap this little chitchat up soon. Your flight is booked for tomorrow morning and I'm sure you'll want to pack a bag.'

'What the hell are you talking about?' He felt resolve, maybe a dash of inner courage, but stayed by the wall, scanning the room for a feasible escape route.

'There's no need to flee. I'm not here to hurt you. Would someone who recently gave you a five-thousand dollars want to hurt you?'

'Yes.'

'You're right. I didn't think that one through. I suppose some might. Well, I'm not. I'm here to get you to where you need to be. I'm taking you to Angkor Wat. *On someone else's dime.*' She grinned. 'On *our* dime to be exact. Like you wanted.'

How did she...?

'It's very simple really. But that is a discussion for another day. Let's just say your thoughts are sometimes – well, in your case, quite often – an open book to those with the skills to read them. It's one of the ancient arts. There are many more. I'm not the most adept, but I get by. Which is why, and for my sins...' she chuckled, '...no, that's not true. I don't have sins. No one does. Just psychological shortcomings. Anyway, long story short, they gave me to you. And we decided it would be less frightening if I reached out through a text. We also put a little money in your account as an incentive to be more outgoing. But that didn't work. Not with someone who's afraid of his own shadow. We thought you would at least spend a few dollars on something for yourself. Maybe a new jacket. One with style.' She chuckled again. 'Sorry. That was bad of me. Anyway, today's little jaunt around town was just to see if you would chase the rabbit, so to speak. And, you did. Bravo. You get a gold star. You also get to spend the cash. Think of it as your slush fund. And you'll like Cambodia. It is an ancient and mysterious land.'

Jordan made a dash for the door but, a few steps in, he gave up. He didn't know why, only that it didn't seem urgent anymore.

'Sorry about that. You tried to flee, so I planted a suggestion. We can't have you getting twitchy. We need you. Everyone needs you.'

Jordan relaxed and felt a compulsion to sit in the computer chair.

'Sorry about that too,' she said. 'I needed you to calm down and enjoy the situation. And how rude of me, I didn't introduce myself. I'm Sandhya. Your guide until you get to where you're going.'

'What does that mean?'

'It means, I'm your guide. And I promise I won't influence your thoughts again, unless you give me good reason to.'

'Guide to what?'

'Not what – where. As I said, you are going to Cambodia. You have things to do, people to meet, and it's my task to make sure you get there. It's all very exciting, isn't it?'

'No.'

'Ah, come on. It is a little bit.'

'Whatever. And what happens if I don't go. I could call the cops right now, and say you broke in and threatened me.'

'And you think they'll believe you? Over the word of someone who has the power to influence thoughts? Remember the police person at the 46th Precinct, how accommodating they were? And your bank? We call it a *nudge*. The old ones, of course, had a more sophisticated word for it.'

Jordan let it go. The woman seemed strange but not menacing.

Or was that also an assumption she'd placed in his mind?

And how was she doing it in the first place?

'Come on,' she said. 'You're a scientist. Think. Be science-y. How could a person – and, believe me, I am just as flesh and blood human as you or anyone else – see into or influence the thoughts of another?'

He said nothing. Pondered, but found no answer.

'Fine. I'll do it for you. The universe, including all matter and energy within it, is a vast ocean of potential. The old ones found methods of tapping into this reservoir and exploiting it for the benefit of all. We call it simply *Logos*. The source and resource for everything they built. But it was lost. Well, not exactly lost... hidden. By us. And, with limitations, I can manipulate Logos. Not as efficiently as my colleague who, at this very moment, is guiding your future compatriot, but I can do it. And, I think, because of my quirky but charming character, I add a little pizazz to the process while I'm at it. A wee bit of panache. Bewitchery. In fact, they used to call us witches. Burned us for it too. But that's also a discussion for another day. You need to get cracking, get yourself home and packed. Oh, and, if I was you, I would ask your sister to maintain your magazine while you're gone. It's important. People need to know about the weird and wonderful universe we live in. It will help make what's coming palatable. Not so much of a surprise. Because, there is one thing you can count on with the average human, they don't take well to change. And, for that too, we need you. So, up you get. You have a long few days ahead of you.'

While she talked, Jordan sat there, open mouthed and stunned by the wave upon wave of information he surmised as marginally plausible, but far too ludicrous to fully contemplate. He mused on whether this person was on the level. An actual telepathic. It was feasible. Previous *TKSM* articles had touched upon the concept but most, if not all, had lacked definitive proof.

Or was she just a loon?

A fan of the magazine who had gone so far down the rabbit hole, she'd tumbled head over heels into the murky pit of delusion. *Freakshow territory*, he called it. The place where all conspiracy theorists plied their distorted trade.

'Yes, they are also true,' she said. 'Well, not exactly true. But, to some extent, conspiracy theories are based on reality. Even the lizard people thing. And ancient aliens. It's all a manipulation. The greatest manipulation. But we'll tell you more when we get to Cambodia. Think of it as you'll be uncovering *the article of a lifetime*.'

'That was in the text.'

'Yes. From me to you. Because it's true. So, what do say? Are you coming? For *the article of a lifetime*?'

Jordan thought. *What did he have to lose?* She seemed okay. If she wanted to kidnap or kill him, she would've done it already. In fact, she seemed cool. He had warmed to her. With an uncontrollable urge to do anything she suggested.

'That's the ticket,' she said with a smile.

'Are you really putting thoughts in my head?'

'A bit. But I will stop. Soon. When we are on the plane and I can guarantee you're not a flight risk. Get it? *Flight* risk.' She laughed. Jordan didn't. 'Ah, forget it. My best routines are wasted. You know, I could make you laugh if I want to. Only kidding. I wouldn't do that. Or, would I? Kidding again. Or... no, Sandhya. Stop it. Forgive me, I get carried away sometimes. Anyway, are we all done with the *is she, isn't she, could she, will she* nonsense yet? Can we actually get going?'

Jordan nodded.

'Oh, and leave that god-awful-ugly puffer jacket behind. You won't need it.'

Jordan nodded again, and rang Jada, told her he was using some of his recently acquired bank balance to travel and asked if she would take over management of the magazine while he was gone.

'You do you,' she replied. Which he took to mean *yes*, and her approval.

He said, 'Thanks. You're the best.'

She said, 'I know. I really am. And don't worry. Your stuff is safe in my hands. Go. Enjoy something.'

He grunted.

Jada sniggered.

He said, 'Thanks again,' hung up, closed down his desktop, locked the office, waved to Lori from the lobby and, with Sandhya walking alongside, left for home. He spoke only once on the way there, to ask, 'Was it you who sent me the symbol?'

Brushing her hair back over her ears, Sandhya smiled. 'Yes. That was me. And it's the meaning of everything.'

LENA HANSEN

The Irish bartender smiled as he took her order. Admiring his tight behind, Lena's gaze stayed with him all the way back to the bar, where he began pouring her lager. Out on Amagertorv, throngs of shoppers spiralled from shop to shop like turds circling a toilet-bowl. A whirlpool of baseball caps, sleeveless tops, sweaty skin, and sunglasses. The weather was hot, thirty Celsius and, although dressed in an ostentatiously bright yellow sequined tutu, complete with multicoloured sequins and a lime green, diamante encrusted fanny pack acting as a sash belt – amply airy to deal with the heat – Lena had opted to sit at one of the fourteen tables outside The Dublin Bay bar, sheltered beneath the awning. She checked her bra straps. Fluffed out the tulle in her skirt. Pushed up *the girls*. Did a wiggle. Undid the turquoise blue scrunchy holding back her blonde hair, placed it in her fanny pack, and let her wavy locks tumble down her cheeks.

The bartender returned, set a glass of beer on the table and took payment with a contactless device. Through it all, Lena smiled. Her best one. And, for a second or two he smiled back, before moving on to the two women sitting four tables across.

Jealousy gripped Lena like a punch to the gut.

One of them, a fake blonde in a bob, was smiling up at the bartender through a mouthful of bleached teeth. While the other; squat, with curly brunette hair and, in Lena's opinion, *a face like a shitting cat*, leaned back in her chair and checked out his tight butt.

She might have to kill them.

Or at least punch them out so badly, no one would want to fuck them ever again.

Either option pleased her. She uttered a snicker. The street, however, was the busiest in Copenhagen. Far too many witnesses to embark on such a rewarding but conspicuous strategy. So, instead, waiting until the bartender came with their beers and moved on to another table, she got up and edged past some other tables to stand beside the two women.

Down at Højbro Plads, a street-artist was juggling flaming sticks.

He was good at it. Had drawn a large crowd.

Looking his direction, Lena laughed. Loudly. A guffaw as ostentatious as her garish yellow dress. The women glanced her direction, looked her up and down, shared a silent smirk at Lena's expense, and then, as expected, almost broke their necks to gawp down to the street-artist at the square. While they searched for the non-existent source of the comedy, with a slight of hand worthy of a Las Vegas card sharp, Lena dipped into her fanny pack, removed a small bottle she always kept with her for screwing with the locals, and dropped one drop each into their beer glasses. She sniggered. The two women turned and gazed up with baffled expressions.

Lena said, 'Det var så sjovt,' and went back to her seat. Taking a large mouthful of beer, she held her glass up to them: a greeting, perhaps a salute... to the fun times to come.

The two women reciprocated, albeit with confused expressions.

And it didn't take long.

Blonde Bob squirmed on her chair. Appeared distressed. A second later, she jumped to her feet and dashed into the bar, her right hand clamped to the backside of her pink shorts. An eyeblink later, Curly Brunette followed her, rushing towards the *Toilets This Way* sign. Because she wore black jeans, however, Lena reckoned the outcome of her hurried visit, should she fail to make it in time, would prove much less embarrassing than for Blonde Bob wearing the pink shorts.

All eyes in the bar followed their frantic flight.

Lena laughed.

Curly Brunette peered back as if knowing.

Lena said, 'Det var så lidt,' and laughed louder.

As the two women disappeared downstairs to the cellar lavatories, their joint departures had been so rapid, their handbags still hung, looped over the back of their chairs. Lena downed her beer in two mouthfuls, sidled over their abandoned table and, snatching both bags, skipped off down Amagertorv in the direction of Rådhuspladsen, swinging the bags and whistling as she went.

She didn't want or need anything from the two women.

The theft was purely to add insult to injury.

Their addresses, however, might come in handy.

A job had come through.

In Siem Reap, Cambodia.

A bit of practice wouldn't go amiss. Like trying out the latest poison she had concocted.

Or, if she wanted to get a little more up-close and vicious with it, stabbing one of them through the ear with her shiny new stiletto switchblade.

ONE NIGHT IN BANGKOK

At their home in Xianyang and by their request, Ary Long stopped for an additional day with her aunt and her husband. She learned more about her wider family (the Chinese connection at least) and, when not at work, Li Xiu told her stories about Baba when he was younger, in the years before he joined the army and disappeared from their lives. The effort seemed to sadden Li Xiu. At the mention of some childhood memory, she would look away, and Ary heard the tears catch in her throat. As did Ary's. The only one immune being Qing Yuan, who took on the duty of making sure they all got to the restaurant on time for Ary's final night meal.

The next morning, departing with a good luck gift of rice wine, she took the bus from Xi'an to Kunming, changed onto another going through Laos to Vientaine, before taking one more the rest of the way to Bangkok. The trip, including the requisite visa checks, took five days. Two of them for hostel stops to grab some decent shuteye. Arriving in Bangkok, she decided to use some of Mateus's travel allowance and booked into the Riverside Grand. The hotel had a spa, with all the facilities. After days cramped into buses with what seemed like hundreds of people, she needed a shoulder rub, and a back rub, and a neck rub, a leg rub, with oils, a seaweed soak, that thing they do where they put hot stones on your back, and a... she needed the full bloody treatment.

It might be a long time before another bout of extravagance.

After a steam, a soak, something called a Black Soap Cleanse, and the longest massage in history, she went back to her very grand, very big room and sent Mateus a text. Upon crossing the border into Laos, she had replaced the Chinese sim for her encrypted UK one. She felt safer for it. Hidden. In so much anyone could in this over-interconnected world.

The text said:

You up for a video chat?

As usual, he didn't reply. And, equally as usual, she didn't expect him to. His phone was probably down the back of the couch, beside the microwave, or still resting on the bathroom sink from when he conducted his morning routine of toilet-based tweet-scrolling. While she waited for an answer, she changed into the hotel robe, sprawled out on one of the room's not one, nor two but, yet again, three couches – must be a poshy hotel thing – and browsed the internet for any instances of where or when the symbol might have been documented. She found none. It seemed it had appeared... well, *reappeared*, if her mother and her childhood soldier were taken into account... only for her. An ancient emblem lost to time and unveiled to one single person. Perhaps her questioning, nonconformist attitude had attracted its presence. Because only she possessed the detachment to recognise its uniqueness. The thought struck her as enlightened. Another one congratulated her for being so intuitive.

She smiled.

Strangely, it felt like someone else was smiling through her.

Putting the weird sensation down to tiredness, she closed her laptop, set it aside and switched on the television. The massive device lit up the room like a cinema screen. Ary felt a tad indulged. This was how the rich lived. This was how Mateus lived. Life at the top really was the dog's bollocks. Or, on second thoughts, perhaps not. Sure, it was nice to be pampered but, being a housing estate girl, she reckoned the excess would wear thin after a while. Maybe quickly. It wasn't her. A nice thing to do now and again, but it felt fake, unreal. Scrolling through the television channels, she stopped at a soap opera, in Thai and, although she had no idea what they were saying, she caught the gist: a princess, in some country a lot like Thailand, stripped of her title when her father, the King, was deposed in a coup. The elaborate sets oozed colour and opulence. The costumes were magnificent. The storyline easy to follow, played out in vivid detail through the expressions of the actors. If she could speak the lingo, she felt certain she'd be hooked.

Her phone buzzed. Mateus, saying he was available to chat.

It was mid-morning in London – or Dublin, if he had already relocated Stinky Hole Records – and, with the television switched on but muted, she stretched out on the sofa and opened her laptop.

When the video loaded and Mateus appeared, she said, 'Hey.' He looked a mess. Red face. Eyes struggling to stay open. Hair like Boris Johnson. 'You look functional.'

'I had one of those nights. Only just got out of bed. Your text woke me.'

'Soz, mate. Another band?'

'Yups. Antisocial Bitch Cat.'

'Cool name.'

'Cool band. And talented as fuck. But they're even younger than the last lot. They've got the vibe. The energy. And also, sadly for my liver, the constitution to match. If their stuff wasn't so earwormy, I might finally realise I'm too old for this shit and throw in the towel. The mornings after are like being hit by a truck. I should swap the bourbon for ginger ale.'

'Good for you. Your body will thank you.'

'And my brain, Apparently, according to an article I read, there's no safe level of alcohol that doesn't rot neurons to mush.'

'Explains a lot. You must've been sucking it back since the age of five then.'

'As in the average age of the members of my new band...' he laughed.

Ary joined him. '...As in the average age of the members of all your bands.'

The laughs continued for many seconds. After the heaviness of the reappearing symbol, discovering the connection with her mother, visiting Baba's sister, the freaky visions, and everything in between, a good old giggle session was exactly what she needed.

As the laughs simmered to a few snorted chortles, she asked, 'Have you moved your studio to Dublin yet?'

'Soon. Just waiting to sign this band then it's time to split. Talking about splitting, where are you now?'

'Bangkok. It's the way the bus went.'

'Why didn't you fly? You've got the cash.'

'I like to be frugal.'

'Yeah, right. I can see that. That couch you're sitting on looks totally frugal.'

'I thought I'd spoil myself. On your quids.'

'Spoil away. That's why you've got them. But it's not like you to go throwing money around.'

'It is, sometimes. Even I like a bit of pampering now and again. But I could also get fed up with it too.' She changed the subject. 'Sooo, I went to China. Found my family. Or at least one of them. And her husband. My father's sister. She told me stories about Baba when he was young, before he left, and before he died... obviously.' Tears stung the corners of her eyes. She bit them back. 'Anyway, I also found something else. Which is where you come in. Turns out, my aunt is this bigwig archaeologist. Her husband too. They took me to a dig. A pyramid. Where I saw...' she realised she hadn't told Mateus much about her visions, '...where they found something like the symbol.'

'Wow, cool. And were they able to ascertain where it comes from, what it is?'

'No. And I didn't push. They don't know about the things I'm into, and I want to keep it that way. I get the impression they wouldn't agree with some of my... *most* of my theories. They're establishment types. They put convention and consensus first. Which is where you come in. What with being the research-centre-stroke-analytic-hub part of the endeavour. I need you to do some of that library stuff you so kindly agreed to cover.'

'Your wish-list is my command, Illustrious Leader.'

'Stop that.'

'What?'

'The Illustrious Leader bullshit. It's worse than Team Ary.'

'But we are Team Ary.'

'We're really not. Anyway, I need you to go to the British Library and see if you can find any reference to the symbol there, but with focus on China, particularly the area south of Xianyang. While you're at it, look into Machu Picchu. I'm certain there's a connection.'

'Yeah, there is. I found it remember? But you never did say much about that leg of the trip.'

'Not much to tell,' she lied. 'If there was anything to find, it wasn't obvious. Which is why I need you to delve deeper. It's what you do best.'

'Yes Sir! Right Away Sir!' He mock saluted.

'You can stop that too.'

'Aww! You strip the fun out of everything.'

'What happened to you? You used to be so serious.'

'I suppose I grew up.' He smirked.

'Doubt that. Anyway, do the searches. We can chat in a few days. I should be in Siem Reap by then.'

'Cool. I'll get right to it. Just as soon as my head finds its way back to the real world. Oh, and don't languish too much in the luxury. You're right, it gets tedious after a while. The stuff you get up to is way more fulfilling as it is.'

'I won't. Promise. There are only so many times a person can stare at two unused sofas.'

They shared a laugh and goodbyes.

Closing her laptop, Ary turned up the sound on the television and returned to her soap opera. The princess had changed out of her lavish clothes, preparing for a quest to confront the issues troubling her. Ary felt of the same mind. There was no logical reason why she had taken the bus to Bangkok. Direct buses operated between Xianyang and Siem Reap. And yet, here she was, living it up at an expensive hotel with spa. A distraction. A deferment. An excuse not to confront how freakishly serendipitous and disconcerting her situation had become.

Apart from a lengthy border stop for visa-stamp purposes, the bus trip from Bangkok to Siem Reap turned out surprisingly comfortable, probably because of the air-conditioning and the distance being much shorter than other runs Ary had taken in the past. And yet, although well rested from her stay at the Riverside Grand in Bangkok, she'd slept most of the way and arrived refreshed, apart from the relentless cramp stabbing in her left calf. Hobbling down the aisle, she disembarked, took her backpack from the hold, and walked off the pain by strutting back and forth along the shopfronts of Shivutha Boulevard.

She bought Mateus a thank you present: an incense stick holder shaped like a monkey, crafted by a gifted artisan who fashioned all sorts of beasts and creatures from dark wood. Although Mateus's London flat was fancy-schmancy up-market posh, he appreciated simpler things too; like cultural art, using them as conversation pieces to impress the youngsters he entertained at his *get to know my latest band* bashes.

'They make me look all worldly n' shit,' he'd say. 'They add extra cool to my already uber-cool persona as *Mr Music Producer* guy.'

Ary, however, didn't agree. Mateus needed nothing to add to his persona. He oozed cool the second he tied his shoes in the morning. He was anything but boring. An enigma. Many enigmas. A jumble of emotions, drive, excitement, a childlike flair for silliness, sometimes too serious and, depending on his actions on a previous evening, both a worry and a delight to be around. Thinking about it, insisting he return home after Machu Picchu mightn't have been her best idea after all. If nothing else, his enthusiasm was intoxicating.

A tuk-tuk driver blared his horn, swerved, and skirted around her.

She jumped back, peering around for additional traffic.

Lost in thought, her attention had drifted and, deep within a downer for having forced Mateus to leave, she had unwittingly meandered out onto the road. It was a rooky mistake. She ought to know better. Patting herself down, as though the action might in some way re-establish composure, she moved back from the edge, walked to and crossed at a faded pedestrian crossing, went over the Art Market Bridge and searched for a place to spend the night. Tomorrow, she would seek out the places from her mother's childhood and, in turn, those she had seen in her first vision. Through Mteay's descriptions and by studying a map she'd picked up at a tourist information centre, she reckoned the location to be somewhere north-maybe-northwest of the city, close to Ta Prohm Temple, somewhere out among the rice fields. The whole region was in its rainy season now and, although the intermittent sunshine felt hot as hellfire, grey clouds had gathered, hung low, threatening to burst at any second. Watching the sky, she headed along Achar Sva Street to a hostel recommended on a backpacker website. The Siem Reap River lapped at the thoroughfare's grassy edges, its brown waters evoking memories of holidays with her parents in the Peak District, when a week-long canal break became six days of rain, cold, anoraks, soggy sandwiches, and watching the soil-saturated canal grow ever higher outside the narrowboat's porthole-like windows. She assumed, however, when the rains did break, the experience in Cambodia would prove much more pleasurable. Because of the colour. The patterned tuk-tuks. The bright awnings and myriad wares festooned across shopfronts and market-stalls. Or perhaps due to the splendid, ornate and somewhat regal architecture. This city of contrasts impressed every nodule in her brain. From the dusty side-streets to the paved avenues. From the shiny jewellery stores – no doubt designed with tourists in mind – to the bloke selling green coconuts from the back of a bicycle by the side of the road. Along with the smells; a mix of sweetness, spice, and savoury hanging on the air as thickly as the rainclouds slowly stifling the sunshine overhead, the city had her hooked. She felt a home here. Secure. At this present moment in time, it was where she should be. And, from somewhere in the back of her mind, a voice agreed.

Arriving at the hostel, she booked a room using the best Khmer she could muster from the phrasebook she'd purchased along with the map, while also lambasting herself for not having gleaned at least something more than *suostei* and *saum arkoun* from thirty years of being the daughter of a Cambodian national. As she wasn't in the mood for roommates – backpackers tended to gab too much and wax lyrical about their travels – she asked for a single with its own bed. It was spotless, and surprisingly spacious given how small the two-storey hut-like building appeared from the outside. She dumped her backpack on the bed, sought out the upper floor café, situated on a bamboo-covered terrace overlooking the river, sat at a table and ordered tea.

It was good. She ordered another, ate some caramelised fruits, stayed for more hours than she had intended and ate a dinner of deep-fried banana blossom dipped in curry paste. Throughout, and apart from a cursory hello to the odd punter ranging in and out of the café, she talked to no one. This time was for her. Alone. She mused on how she would get to Mteay's village. If it was still there and, if not, was there any point going. She opened the screen on her phone and contemplated the symbol, its significance, why it had cropped up in her life, around the globe, and contained so many references to supposedly unrelated cultures.

It seemed to be a pictorial representation of oneness in the world.

Again, her thoughts struck her as enlightened. Another showing up on its heels to congratulate her for being so intuitive. She smiled. But felt like someone else was smiling through her. A voice spoke. It came from inside her mind yet sounded as if somebody was speaking directly into her ear.

'*Very good,*' it said. Female, with an African accent; Botswanan, Zambian, definitely from the southern end of the continent, confirmed when the voice added, '*Very good again. You have a knack for this.*'

Ary jumped to her feet, knocking her tea to the floor. Apart from two café staff chatting behind the counter, she was alone on the terrace.

'*That is not totally true,*' the voice said again, '*I will be with you in a moment.*'

Her flight reflex said run. Logic, however, dictated it was all in her mind; tiredness, the long bus ride, the heat, or something in the food. A strange herb in curry dip. Some sort of loopy juice in the tea.

'It is not the curry,' the voice said, this time sounding nearby. 'Or the tea.'

Ary turned to find a woman, wearing a colourful, loose-fitting dress, sitting at the table behind. 'Where the hell did you come from? Can I help you?'

'No, no, no. Not at all,' the woman replied. 'I am here to help you.'

'Help with what? Who are you?'

'I am... well, why don't we discuss that over tea. I see you've spilled yours. Let me replace that for you. Then we can sit here together and wait for the others to arrive.'

'Wait for who to arrive? What are you talking about?'

'I ordered green. It's probably a little late in the day for black.'

'Keep your bloody tea. I'm leaving.'

'Fine. But you will miss out on the answers you are looking for. Especially about that symbol on your smartphone.'

'What? How did you know...?'

The woman smiled. 'Oh, my dear one, I know everything. You might even say I've been in your head for two months.'

VOICES IN MY HEAD

The woman moved up to a chair at Ary's table, gesturing for her to sit back down.

A waiter arrived carrying a tray with a teapot and two cups, which the woman accepted using the words *orkurn chran*, before filling both cups. 'I hope I am doing this right. It is my first time in Cambodia. It's very important to respect another's customs. But I suppose we can't get everything correct.'

'That's bullshit,' Ary said, retaking her seat.

'What's bullshit, dear one?'

'That crap about this being your first time in Cambodia. I just heard you say *thank you very much* in flawless Khmer.'

'Oh. Yes. I can see how that might sound a little confusing. But, it's not really. I simply learned the language as I was coming through the door. It is beautiful. Like music to the ear.'

'I know. I'm half Cambodian.'

'So, you speak then?' the woman asked, with an edge, as if she already knew the answer.

'No. But my mother is Cambodian. I recognise the lingo.'

'This I know too. How is your mteay? Well, I hope? Baba's death distressed her greatly.' She sipped some tea. Seemed able to do so through a smile. Then nodded at Ary's cup. 'Please. Drink. It's at the perfect temperature.'

'My mother's okay. None of your business. And how did you know my baba was...?' Ary left the question there, said, 'Never mind,' but didn't take up the offer to drink tea.

'It's not poisoned. You saw the waiter bring it himself.'

Yeah. Right. He could be in on it too, Ary thought.

'Yeah, right indeed. He could be *in on it*, whatever the *it* is. But I can assure you the tea is just tea. And good tea at that. You really should try some. It's lovely.' She continued sipping, smiling over the top of her cup.

Ary pondered the possibilities: GCHQ, CIA, MSS, GRU, some other group, perhaps inter-dimensional beings themselves. Strangely, she wasn't bothered.

'And you shouldn't be,' the woman said. 'I'm not in the slightest bit dangerous. The answer is also not as sinister as you think. Put simply, I can read minds.' She flicked her head back and sideways. 'I can make people do things too.'

As if by command, the two café staff disappeared into the back kitchen.

The woman nodded down to the street where, along the road, all the traffic took abrupt turns into side-streets and was gone. The pedestrians went too. As did the stall owners and kerbside traders. Only a solitary brown paper bag remained, dancing on a breeze as if joyful for its newfound range of uninterrupted movement.

The fuck's happening? Ary thought. *It's like* 28 Days Later.

'Yes, it does seem that way,' the woman said.

'What way?'

'Like the world has ended. Zombie apocalypse style. But I assure you, it's just in our present vicinity. The world is still out there. Doing what the world does.'

Ary stared down from the terrace, her thoughts a mix of confusion and awe.

'I mean, where do you think your visions come from?' the woman continued.

'*My visions?*'

'Yes. Your visions. As in your little divergences from reality. Machu Picchu. Your mother's childhood.' She grinned, as if with accomplishment. 'What would you say if I told you that scenes – like those of past events – can be planted directly into a person's mind?'

'Is that even possible?'

'You tell me. You are the one who considers herself open to most things. Could it be that, if a mind is malleable enough, a suggestion can be placed to influence a person's actions? Or their thoughts taken to somewhere they have never been? Actually, I'll save you the trouble. They are both true. One is called *nudging*. The other, causing a person to relive someone else's experiences, is called *prescribing*. All part of the ancient arts we call *Logos*.'

'So, let me get this straight, you're saying that you made those people down there to all go home? And a vision of Machu Picchu from hundreds of years ago to jump into my brain?'

'Yes. And it's not hundreds, but thousands. Thirteen thousand to be exact. All builders emulate their ancestors. Nothing is new, my dear. All art is theft, as they say.'

'Bullshit.'

'You like that word.'

'I like common sense.'

'As in inter-dimensional beings taking over the planet?'

Ary paused. 'You've read my blog?'

'I've read your mind, dear one.' She chuckled. 'And your theory is a good one, if not a tad off the mark.'

The reply piqued Ary's curiosity. She gave in, drank some tea, folded her arms and settled in to hear the answer to her next question: 'So, if it's not inter-dimensional entities, then who is behind it all? And don't give me crap about nobody, or governments, or even the fucking corporations. We are so far past that bullshit. And, *yes*, I do like that word. I also like to say *fuck* as well. They add flavour to a conversation.'

'I've noticed. And we will get to explanations soon enough. I promise.' She glanced down to the street, at two people walking along the footpath by the river. 'In fact, very soon. Here they are now.'

'Here who are now?'

'My colleague. And your fellow traveller.'

Introductions were made. Names shared. Wary glances cast. They sat. Drank tea. The two women talking about much but the massive elephant in the room.

'I do love a nice cup of tea,' Ary's recent acquaintance, Nkechi said.

'Me too,' the other one, who went by the name, Sandhya agreed. 'It sharpens the mind.'

The bloke, Jordan Burke, from New York, said nothing.

Ary remained silent too.

'You don't agree, Ary?' Sandhya continued.

'Truth? I couldn't give a shit. I just want to know what this is all about, and why I don't tell you to go fuck yourselves and head back to my room.'

'Because you need answers,' Nkechi said. 'Jordan needs answers too.'

He didn't seem like someone needing answers. No more than a deer needs to know how the headlights on the oncoming truck work.

'So, what's your skin in this game then, *Jordan Burke from New York?*' Ary asked. 'What has you so intrigued you journeyed halfway round the world?'

He glanced at Sandhya then back to Ary. 'My grandfather came here. Died here too. Sandhya says he was important. That I'm important. She can also influence people's thoughts. Like actually influence them.'

'Fair enough. You should get a load of this one I've got.' Ary poked her temple. 'She can plant visions in your head. Great big bloody scenes, like out of a movie, slap bang right there in the middle of your brain. She calls it...'

'...*Prescribing*,' Nkechi interjected with a smile.

'Yeah. *Prescribing*. And it's annoying as fuck.'

'But it leads to answers,' Nkechi continued. 'And Ary and Jordan getting the answers they deserve is why we're here. Isn't that right Sandhya?'

'Yes, Nkechi. It is.'

'Indeed. And important.'

'Yes, very important.'

'The fuck you two doing?' Ary interrupted. 'You're like some sort of fucked-up *Sesame Street* routine?'

The women laughed.

Ary didn't.

Jordan didn't either.

Ary started on him again. 'So, what about you, Jordan Burke? Apart from you and your grandad being important, what's your take on all this? I mean, what do you even do?'

'I publish a science journal. You might've heard of it, *The Kitchen Sink Magazine*?'

'Nope.'

'No, probably not. It's not an everyday periodical. It deals with the stranger side of science: quantum anomalies, hypnosis, sleep and dreams, engineering in the ancient world, that kind of thing.'

'Well, the last one is easy. The ancient builders did it. Very sophisticated. And they're still here. They come from an alternate dimension.'

Nkechi and Sandhya exchanged glances, uttering a slight, joint snigger.

Jordan smirked.

'What? It's true. I've done the research. It's all on my blog...' She stopped, fearing her next words would betray her pseudonym. Then again, the two women likely knew already, so she continued, '...*Hard Truth*. I go by the name, *Harper T Jackson*. But it's me. My place to inform the world.'

'I know that blog,' Jordan said, with a tone of derisive delight. 'It's total horseshit.'

'Fuck you,' Ary snapped. She had met criticism before: a disbelieving look, the odd, *well, that's one opinion*. This prick, however, was downright rude. 'Hope your magazine sucks the big one,' she added. 'Knob-end.'

He grinned, like someone who had found their level and reckoned it above hers.

'I suppose we had better put a stop to this,' Nkechi said to Sandhya.

'I agree. Introductions are fine, but only if they remain mannerly. Do you want to do it, or shall I?'

'I'll do it.'

'Do whatever you want,' Ary said, rising to her feet. 'I'm outta-here. This has gotten stupid.'

'How stupid?' Jordan mocked. 'Flat Earth? Creationism? An ancient civilization I can go with – if the proof is there. I've even seen some. And it's somewhat credible. But, dimension-hopping aliens. It's like something from the comic-books I used to read, before I gave them up for science. Man, you got a bad case of conspiracy-theory-itis.'

'They're not aliens. And don't be a...'

'Enough!' Nkechi shouted. 'And, Ary, sit down.'

She did, but suspected not through conscious intention.

'This has gone far enough,' Nkechi continued. 'No wonder we had problems back in the day, with humans like you two running around. The truth is, you are both right. Yes, Jordan, there was an ancient civilisation, and it was more advanced and sophisticated than anything the world has seen since. And, Ary, you are also right. But the builders came from right here on Earth. There was no need to bring in outside help. The civilisation fell. At its demise, twelve-thousand nine-hundred years ago, steps had to be taken... to preserve Logos. The protectors went underground. Where we remained, drip-feeding the druids and shamans. Keeping eternal knowledge alive. We are Gnostics. We are few. Only the two of us you see here. Selected as small children by our predecessors, like the Dalai Lama. And there is one other. The third Gnostic. But they have their own path to follow. You will meet them someday. As for the people who control everything, even down to manufacturing conspiracy theories, they are called *Ar-yans*.'

'Like *Aryans*?' Jordan asked.

'In a way, yes. But not the ethnocultural group. They consider themselves above such trivialities. And it's pronounced as I said, *Ar-yans*. The name is very old. Before accepted linguistics. And every political, economic, religious, sociological, and medical upheaval since the fall of the old world has been by their design.'

Jordan mulled over what Nkechi had said. The old him, the one that existed before a few days ago, would dismiss her as a loony-tune with notions as implausible as anything *Ary the drably dressed, K-pop haired, conspiracy blogger from London* might conjure. And yet, because of the out-and-out crazy things that had happened since Sandhya barged into his life, he had come to accept more, believe more, his past theories about the structure of the universe being both reinforced and blown to tiny pieces at the same time. Atomic pieces. Subatomic pieces. Quarks. Muons. Gluons.

The pun made him smile.

'You're funny,' Sandhya said, smiling.

'And that's the problem,' Jordan replied. 'Can you please stop reading my mind?'

'Sorry. Maybe we shouldn't Nkechi? Give them a chance to awaken on their own?'

'I agree. We should stop interfering.'

'Thank you,' Jordan said.

'Whatever,' Ary added. She was leaning back in her chair, arms crossed, wearing a sulky expression, probably because of Nkechi's abruptness in making her sit down.

Jordan ignored her. 'Tell me more about this ancient civilisation,' he asked Sandhya. He liked her. She was warm and approachable. As was Nkechi. Ary, the conspiracy blogger... nah, not so much.

'Well, of course, we weren't there. We might both look the pinnacle of good health, but living for thirteen-thousand years is probably beyond even us.' The two Gnostics laughed. Jordan got the impression they'd shared that joke before. 'Much of what we know has been handed down. Through visions and studying Logos. We can safely say it was a paradise. In fact, the original *Eden* of religious scripture. Global, collective, interactive and, most of all, peaceful. No nation states. No wars. No famines. No poverty. Every person, every creature had status. There was meaning. And purpose. Humanity and compassion.' Her face beamed, as if reliving a cherished memory. Jordan felt certain her skin glowed. 'The whole planet was interlinked; in mind, in body, and in spirit. The energy system – some of it electromagnetic – came by way of a network of pyramids and ancient sites, connected through what conspiracy theorists,' she glanced at Ary, 'call ley lines. Adherents to New Age theory, those we view as fellow gnostic thinkers, know about them too but, like so much, the truth has been supressed.'

Ary straightened up at that.

Jordan reckoned because the conversation had strayed into her ideological ballpark.

'The planet thrived,' Sandhya continued. 'Guided by a global community of hominoids: homo sapiens, giants, hobbits, to mention just a few. Each species at differing levels of technological development. Each with a role to play in maintaining *Balance* – the harmony of the cosmos; the *Natural Order*; the basis for all science, spirituality, and even collective consciousness itself. Food was grown in numerous, nature-conscious collectives. Governance came through consensus and advice documented in the *Book of Lights*. Which, along with Logos, preserved the wisdom of the old world. Everything was bright. And optimistic. But, to quote *Max Ehrmann's Desiderata*, we all know *the universe is unfolding as it should*. Periodic dark ages are a given. How long they last depends on how we, as a planet respond.' She paused, appeared sad. 'A catastrophe hit. Threatening to wipe out all that came before. Factions formed. The Aryans split from their hominid cousins and built a rogue society in Asia. They took advantage of the upheaval, wanting to exploit Logos for personal gain, promoting the ugliest intoxications of greed to attain power. They became corrupt. Seeding the post-impact societies, from the flint age through Sumerian and onward to today – always remaining dominant, always fomenting division. They run the world. They are the Caucus.'

'The Caucus?' Jordan asked.

'Yes,' Sandhya clarified. 'Direct descendants of the first Aryans. Heads of the thirteen patriarchal dynasties who – according to conspiracy theorists like our lovely Ary here – govern a secret, behind the scenes organisation controlling world politics, economics, and religion.'

'Knew it,' Ary said with her chin raised. 'Who's spouting *horseshit* now?'

Jordan didn't reply, but did ask, 'I have a question.'

'Anything,' Nkechi said. 'That's why we are here.'

'Okay. You said *post-impact*. What were you referring to?'

'A comet. The one that hit the planet around twelve-thousand nine-hundred years ago, give or take a few.'

'But there wasn't an impact then.'

'Or, is that what you've been told?'

Jordan scoffed.

'Sneer all you want,' Nkechi continued. 'But I can assure you, there was. It smashed into the north American continent. The aftermath of which provided Aryans with the perfect opportunity to make the world in their own image. They are smart and calculating. Working in the shadows behind the shadows. They permit themselves only one child. A male to act as heir. Any females meet "accidental" postnatal deaths.' She did the air quotes. 'Additional male children, when a line is deemed secure, are also killed. Like us, Aryans can utilise Logos – albeit with limited effect. We are much more adept. They can, however, block our influence over them. And, like us, they can control weather, and even seismic activity.'

'No one controls weather. The idea is as ludicrous as your comet impact theory.'

'Not theory. Fact. Whether you choose to believe it or not.'

As if to prove the point, it started to rain. Not full-on monsoon standard, but enough for Sandhya to say, 'We'll stay dry, if we remain beneath the terrace awning.'

Ary smiled.

Jordan gave it no more thought. It was just rain, and a coincidence.

'Aryans are also very good at making devices,' Nkechi continued, as if 'They don't have our adeptness, so they manufacture mechanisms for seeding clouds, influencing dispersal, agitating deep sea rifts and volcanic activity. Believe me, they can do it.'

'But people would know,' Jordan said.

'People know shit,' Ary interjected. 'They see shit too.'

'Exactly,' Nkechi said. 'As Ary so nicely puts it, most people are too busy living their lives to notice such things. Or, in the case of the West, too busy trying to work out which reality-show celeb will hook up with that other reality-show celeb.'

'Smooth brains shagging,' Ary added.

'Yes. Gossip-based misdirection. Very powerful. And Aryans are behind all of it. They even have a doomsday option to slow the planet's rotation by manipulating the Coriolis Effect. Let's hope they never find the cause to use it. Mostly, though, they make instruments of death. Small devices that are indistinguishable from everyday objects. Household utensils. Clothing items. A simple pebble. I mean, who notices a pebble? It's how they ignited the great fires of London, Gomorrah, Mutapa, Edo, and Nero's Rome.'

'Nero was Aryan? What am I asking for... of course he was. The guy was a fucking megalomaniac.'

'All of them were, and are, in so much as they took the bait. And by *them* I mean the usual suspects. Corrupt humans, who desire only power and wealth. But they too were fooled. Their greed made them susceptible to manipulation.'

'My mother mentioned a pebble,' Ary said.

'Ah yes, the lovely Daeny. My heart goes out to her.'

'She claims she saw one start a fire. When she was a child, here in Cambodia. I thought she was just confused or misremembering.'

'She wasn't. She saw it happen.' Nkechi fixed her gaze on Jordan. 'Your grandfather was killed by such a device. What, to him, looked like a simple pebble was the means of his death. It was very sad.'

'After the comet impact,' Nkechi continued, 'Aryans dominated completely. They think it's their universal right to do so. At the same time, however, another faction formed. Us – Gnostics. We prepared for the aftermath, preserved Logos and – apart for the few enlightened teachers we sent out during times of turmoil – hid away for millennia. The time has come, however, for us to begin again. To reinvigorate the secrets of the last Golden Age and sow the seeds for the next.'

'Golden Age?' Ary asked.

'Yes. It was and, if all goes to plan, will be exactly as it sounds.'

'Fair enough.'

'Sure,' Jordan said, with derision. 'And, let's say I believe you... why now? Why us?'

'Yeah,' Ary said. 'Why us?'

'In answer to Jordan's first question, we have been waiting for the correct cosmic conditions to manifest. Aryans believe the old-world misused Logos. They rate power above all else. Don't want to share. And want to stop Gnostics from sharing too. But the Cycle of Universes depends on it. The planet, Solar System, and Galaxy depend on it.'

'And when will these correct cosmic conditions manifest?' Ary asked.

Jordan still wasn't buying it.

'They already have,' Sandhya said. Nkechi nodded. 'March 2023, with the first entry of Pluto into Aquarius. We're getting a three-month hint of what will come. A prophesy of sorts. Nothing much has changed on the face of things. But pawns, like you two, were put into place. The groundwork was laid.'

'So, I'm a pawn now?'

'Yes, Ary, you are. We all are. Cogs in the cosmic wheel.'

'And what happens next?'

'When Pluto makes its second entry into Aquarius on January 20th 2024, the subsequent twenty years will lay the bedrock for the forthcoming age of light.'

'The Golden Age?'

'Yes. The next and final Golden Age.' She was beaming again, before her expression turned serious. 'But everything must be in place before Pluto temporarily returns to Capricorn.'

'Which happens when?'

'June 11th – where he will spend the six months up to the January event. During that time, the initiation process will slow down. A system needs time to propagate. After thirteen thousand years of dormancy, it's not like switching on a bedside light.'

'I see,' Ary said. 'And, today is May 28th. Which gives us fourteen days.' She seemed to genuinely understand what they were talking about.

'Yes,' Nkechi replied. 'That's it. You've got two weeks. Time is upon us.'

'Why did you wait? Not start sooner? Like back in March when Pluto made its move.'

'Astrology again. Tomorrow, Mercury reaches its greatest western elongation for this year. Which has influence, but can be troublesome. It's the Aryan's preferred cycle for disruption. It also stirs up geomagnetic activity. Which is what we are interested in.'

'Electromagnetic activity? What will that do? And how do we fit into all of this?'

'You'll find out soon enough. We prefer for you both to learn in stages.'

Jordan had had enough. 'It's all woo, isn't it?' he butted in. 'Pluto this way. Aquarius that way. Moving into. Returning out of. Doing cartwheels on a bike. It's all bull.'

'For the non-believer, yes. For someone, however, who was shown first-hand the power of Logos by Sandhya, I would reckon it's proof. We thought you'd have come around by now.'

'I have. I think. For some of it. But, astrology? Come on. That kind of crap is for tabloids and crystal ball gazers.'

'It's also a means of prediction. Like dogs sniffing cancer. Or tracking climate change through bird migrations. Every entity in the universe, from super-massive nebulae to ultramicroscopic neutrinos, impart influence upon each other. Gravity. Black Holes. Dark Matter. They all have synergy... and are a tool. The interactions of planets, suns, and galaxies are one such tool. How we use, or don't use them, is up to us.'

'I'm okay with it,' Ary said.

'You would be,' Jordan jabbed.

'And you're a knob-end.' She turned back to Nkechi. 'Actually, I'm okay with everything you've said. But, can I just get one thing straight: all the UFO and UAP sightings, all the aliens, the reptilians, the shapeshifters, fake news and beyond, it was all just one bigass fucking con-job?'

'Absolutely,' Sandhya confirmed. 'All of it.'

'*Illuminati?*'

'All of it.'

'*Hollow Earth?*'

'All of it.'

'*Chemtrails?*'

'All of it.'

'What about Covid-19?'

'For crying out loud... yes. All of it. The entire. The total. It all. *All – of – it*. Even Covid-19. In fact, all the SARS. And the influenzas. And the plagues. They didn't invent or devise diseases. Or viruses. Human rape of nature and animal abuse did that. Under their guidance, of course. But they did take advantage. Helped spread misinformation. Using them as a means of manipulation.'

'So, it did leak from a lab?'

'No. As I said, they didn't invent any diseases. They just exploited their existence for their own ends. As they've always done. Everything you deem as truth was down to them. All of it. For the last thirteen-thousand years. They fed you crumbs. Fake history. Myths and legends.'

'Theseus?' Ary asked 'The Minotaur? That's my favourite,' she said to Jordan as an aside in, what he deemed to be, a rare moment of non-foulmouthed conviviality.

'All of it.'

'Well, maybe not all,' Nkechi said. 'Some of it was us too, throwing around our version of misdirection.'

'True,' Sandhya continued. 'Gnostics did make up a few stories. But only to deter Aryans from poking around where they shouldn't. The main bulk of fake history, conspiracies, and legends were down to them. It was part of their process. A long time ago, they learned that in order to manipulate people, you must give them something to be scared and suspicious about. So, apart from utilising the odd pandemic now and again, they gave you gods and monsters, demons, ancient aliens, Roswell, and time-travelling moon Nazis. Just enough to keep a person doubtful... and distrustful. The stories were pure invention, like shoes, or cat videos, or the likelihood of a certain New York real estate mogul having the common person's best interests at heart. They are intended to keep you distracted. Anything but the truth. As long as the general populace believes the myth, the real con stays on track.'

'But how could they?' Jordan asked. 'People would find out.'

'Some, yes. But most prefer to remain oblivious. Give them enough distractions or prejudices and they'll gleefully let you exploit them till the cows come home.'

'Except me,' Ary said.

'Yes, except you, dear one. And, to some extent, Jordan too. As for other humans, the task was easy to accomplish. Aryans did that old magician's trick of diverting attention to anywhere but the truth. In spite of a person's proclivity to free will, they selected enemies and *others*; scapegoats to blame for all the ills they themselves were causing. Simple, populist answers to complicated questions. It is the *Great Lie*.'

'I call it that too,' Ary proclaimed.

'Yes. We know. You're a star. Anyway, it is the largest, most enduring, most complex secret ever devised. And, if you ever wanted proof of how easy it is to keep a big secret, look no further than the Manhattan Project.

Over one-hundred and twenty-five-thousand people worked on the atom bomb, and not a peep was uttered. Take it from us, for thirteen-thousand years, Aryans devised and maintained everything you know as history. Nothing came about without their input.'

'So, Deep State then?' Ary said.

Both women sniggered.

Ary appeared put out, but didn't respond.

'Yes,' Nkechi replied. Jordan was shocked. Ary grinned. 'And no.' Jordan was less shocked, felt relieved. Ary returned to looking put out again. 'No, Deep State doesn't exist. That would imply that governments are part of the Aryan scheme. But they aren't. Far from it. Ninety-nine-point-nine percent of them aren't even aware the Caucus exists. The other few, the big ones – China, the United States of America, some members of the European Union – are only mildly conscious of something operating at the fringes. Occasionally they'll produce some report or other with regards to Unidentified Aerial Phenomena, fluctuations in the market, the reasons behind the recent pandemic and such. But, as with the average person in the street, they are being manipulated. Greed is also a powerful tool. Pluck that string and whole nations come clamouring for more. Well, by nations, I mean corporations. And they too are oblivious. For the Caucus, it's about the end result. Domination. Simple as that. It has been their only goal for thirteen-thousand years. And has now become more an immutable tradition than it ever was a sense of purpose.' She smiled. 'So, yes. In some ways you are correct, Ary. Only not as you originally envisaged.'

'I knew it,' Ary said, with an air of validation. 'I was right–ish all along.'

'You were. You are.' Nkechi said. 'You both are. And that brings me nicely to your second question, Jordan. *Why you?*'

'It's because of who you are,' the women said in unison.

'Actually,' Nkechi continued, 'it's because of who you come from. Your legacy.'

'In 1975, a US soldier was made aware of our ancient order,' Sandhya added. 'We don't know how. Or who told him. We suspect Aryans, planting seeds, wanting to expand their network of agents searching for us and Logos. Because, if there is one thing that's apparent, it's that, after thirteen-thousand years of trying, their methods have failed. Maybe they wanted to open it up to lesser minds. We don't know. What we do know, though, it wasn't Gnostics who set him on his path. And, deserting the war in Vietnam, he came here to Siem Reap where, somehow, he stumbled upon the symbol.'

'A symbol?' Jordan asked.

'Yes. *The* symbol. You know about this. Don't play the intellectual sceptic. It doesn't suit you, and only delays what I have to say. That soldier was your grandfather.' She turned to Ary. 'And the last person to see him alive was your mother. She witnessed his death. Another horrific experience for one so young.'

Jordan cast Ary a searching look.

She replied with a shrug of her shoulders.

'Through proximity, a bond formed,' Sandhya continued. 'At the moment Jordan's grandfather died, something passed between them. That bond now lives inside both of you. And, as luck or the will of the universe would have it, if you survive, you two will ensure that everything comes to pass.'

ALPHA DOG – OMEGA DOG

When the conversation with the women concluded and they had gone downstairs – out to the still empty street, disappearing into the thickening rain – Ary returned to her room to mull over the points they had thrown out there. She needed to think, dissect their claims. It wasn't that she was averse to their suggestions. Quite the opposite. It all sounded very credible, and bang on for the same viewpoints she'd been pushing since she first dipped her toes in the vast, complex ocean of conspiracy theories. In fact, putting aside the *if you survive* part of the conversation, there was a lot to like, and they agreed on just about everything – in that:

A secret society ran the world.
That society dominated everyone and everything.
It started in antiquity.
They had powers beyond the realms of the ordinary person.
There was once a global civilisation with immense technical ability.

Tick, tick, tick, tick, and – who's fucking kooky now, bitches – *tick*.
Her life's work ratified and substantiated.
The was only one difference: *who was the secret society?*
Ary had always believed it to be inter-dimensional beings and, to her at least, all evidence pointed that direction. But the women had an alternative theory and, if true – that everything spanning the last thirteen-thousand years – meaning *everything* – and, yes, another *tick* for the intrepid Ary Long – had been by design... then, surely, this secret group would also be behind any hypotheses she had previously taken to be true. It would certainly fill a hole in her research. No matter how deep she dug, she never did manage to find the smoking gun, that proof-perfect golden nugget to support her claim of inter-dimensional travellers.
Why? Because the two women, called Gnostics, had proved it false.
The group was human, and ancient, called the Caucus.
As confusion drifted from her mind, Ary laughed. And kept laughing. Big, fat, gurgley guffaws, that bubbled up from her lungs and burst into the air with impressive ferociousness. Her jaw ached. Her belly panged. A stitch stabbed at her side, but she carried on, unable to stem the flow and fervour of her delight.
Her assertions about an ancient civilisation had been vindicated.
She was queen of the bloody world. God of all she surveyed.

As the laughs died, her breath faltering to recoup expended oxygen, she sat on the bed and texted Mateus:

You will totally cack your knickers when I tell you the shit I just heard
More tomorrow
Tired now – and fucking ecstatic (zany face emoji) X

With the joyous part out of the way, she turned her thoughts to Jordan Burke.

He was an odd one. At times, quiet. At others, way too opinionated. He seemed intelligent. Bookish. A bit of a pencil dick, but maybe street smart. He said he used to read comic-books, but gave them up for science. Idiot. Comic-books were the sickest. And, apart from his rude dismissal of her theories, he seemed open minded and didn't balk at the claims the two Gnostics had made. Which must have been difficult for a know-it-all like him. She sensed his dilemma, pictured neurons sparking and fizzling in his brain and laughed aloud again. He was kind of cute. Like a snappy puppy. A person could indulge him for a while but, at some stage, he would need a sharp tap on the nose to realise who the alpha-dog was.

Before they left, the Gnostic women had given them a joint task. They were to go to Ta Prohm Temple and find the place where Jordan's grandfather uncovered the symbol which, in turn, got him killed by agents of the Aryan faction.

Ary's mother had witnessed it all. Thereby creating the bond.

'DNA is a powerful catalyst,' the one called, Nkechi had said. 'It stores energy, purpose and intent. And that's where you two come in. When you rise in the morning, go to the temple. Rediscover the symbol and...' She let it hang.

'And what?' Ary had asked.

'Do whatever comes to mind.'

'Well, that's fucking vague.'

'Yes, it is,' the two women had said, together, before they headed off.

Morning came quickly. It seemed Jordan had only touched his head to the pillow, before sunlight streaked through the bamboo blinds, and birds twittered as if with deliberate intent to rouse him from his slumber.

Taking Ary Long's advice, he had rented a single room. It was her one moment of niceness and, although small, the space was enough. He slept comfortably, dreaming of ancient ruins whereby, upon waking, assumed the images had been put there by one or both of the Gnostics. A difficult notion to accept. In the past few days, everything he'd thought to be fact had been both simultaneously proven and, with the same breath, thrown into disarray:

Time was mutable.

The fabric of the universe was fluid and non-defined.

Matter was collapsed probability.

These he already knew. What he didn't realise, however, was that certain individuals, and even whole groups of people, could manipulate phenomena to their own ends. Descendants of an ancient civilization. Heirs to a mystical *Logos*, handed down over thousands of years.

The concept had thrown him a curveball.

Jada would most likely say something like, *that shit's whack*, bro.

And, while still in the company of the two women, to clarify a niggling problem, he even found himself asking the simple yet, previously for him, unconscionable question, 'Can Aryans influence minds too?'

'Yes,' Sandhya had replied. 'But not as well as us. Our predecessors managed to keep much of Logos from them. They got fragments: certain technologies, the secrets of science, but not enough to converse over large distances or manipulate the inclinations of others. In that respect, they can only place mild suggestions. Hypnotism in a way.'

'So, they *could* be in my thoughts?'

'Yes. But no. We placed a blocker there. Think of it as a big steel barrier, with an uncrackable lock and a combination known only to Nkechi and I. They can try to break through but will fail. On occasion, you might even sense their futile attempts. Like a heavy weight, banging a door inside your mind.'

'I know that,' Ary had said with enthusiasm. 'When I was in China, some bloke was staring at me. It felt like he was trying to get inside my head. Thumping.'

'Exactly,' Sandhya had continued. 'When you were at the pyramid site. But his efforts were pointless. He could never get in. They, especially agents, don't have the skills. This is why Aryans embraced a more direct, long-term approach to achieving their aims. They depend on tangible things, like political influencing, shadow economies, fossil fuels, corporate industry, and war. They can't shape matter through will. And, except by way of devices, they can't muster or reform energy. If they got access to Logos in its entirety, however, it would be game over. It's why they have been hunting us. At the moment, they dominate the physical world. With Logos, they could have it all.'

'Uncool,' Ary had said.

'Yeah. I know. Totally,' Sandhya had replied, and smiled.

Jordan remembered remaining quiet, and feeling uneasy. Apparently, while humankind busied themselves with trivialities, two ancient factions had been going at each other for thirteen millennia. Some or both of whom had the power to screw around with his thoughts. To quote his sister again, that was *some mad heavy shit right there*. So, setting the notion aside for later consideration, he put on a light-fitting shirt and shorts, left his room and went out to the terrace to order something for breakfast. Ary Long was already there, alone at a table, eating something from a bowl.

'What's that?' he asked, sitting down beside her.

'Bobor.'

'*Bobor?*'

'Rice porridge with shallots.'

'Nice?'

'It's lovely. I don't think it's for you, though. It's not a pancake, or a burger, or a pizza, or a pizza-burger, or a pancake-pizza-burger. This is actual food. Like, real food. That takes time to prepare. My mteay... *my mother* makes it.'

He let the wisecrack slide. It was too early in the morning. 'She was born here?'

'Yup, like that Gnostic woman said. My baba was from China. So, I'm only half Cambodian.'

'Was?'

'He died few years ago.'

'My condolences.' He left it there. 'Should I order some?'

'Absolutely. It's the dog's bollocks.'

'*The dog's bollocks?*'

'The cat's pyjamas. Amazeballs. The bomb.'

'Ah. It's good?'

'Yuh-huh. It's *the dog's bollocks*.'

'Okay, then. I'd better get some.'

'You do that.'

He stood, went halfway to the counter, before returning again. 'Look, is there something I've done to you?'

'Un-fucking-believable,' Ary said, with a roll of her eyes.

'Well?'

She set down her spoon, wiped her mouth with a napkin. 'Being a weapons grade prick might have something to do with it. Oh, and being a total fucking arsehole might be something to do with it too.'

'You're still sore about the blog thing, aren't you?'

'No shit Sherlock. But I'm over it now.'

'You don't sound over it.'

'Well, I am. The nice ladies said we should do stuff together, so that's what I'm going to do. Even if you are a total bell-end.'

'*Bell-end?*'

'Knob. Helmet. Glans penis.'

'Sheesh, your mouth is foul.'

'Your face is foul.'

He smirked. 'You remind me of my sister.'

'She sounds terrif. Not a prick like you. And better get used to it, mate. My language isn't changing anytime soon.'

He drew closer. 'Look, I'm sorry. I didn't mean to insult you. It's just that, before the last few days, I had everything tight. Had it all worked out. Even the weird science parts. Now? Well, that's been blown out of the water. *Truth be told*, as my father would say, I haven't got a clue what's going on.'

Her expression softened. 'Yeah, tell me about it. I've uncovered some freaky shit in my searches, but nothing like this.'

'So, you actually believe *the truth is out there?*'

Ary glanced down at her tee-shirt. 'Yes. Definitely.'

'Me too. But maybe not in the same way. I suppose that makes us travel buddies.'

Ary returned to her bowl, 'You really should get some of this,' gazed around at the empty tables and added, 'before there's a run on it.'

For the next hour, they stayed on the terrace, eating breakfast and sharing details about their upbringings; hers in London; his in the Bronx. Their backgrounds seemed similar: mixed-heritage parents, close family, not downright poor but no big-ass holiday home in the Hamptons either.

He told her about his fascination with the stranger traits of the universe, heavily plugging *The Kitchen Sink Magazine*, which she checked-out on her phone and seemed impressed.

She talked about her blog. Jordan had to bite hard not to snigger. Without prompting, however, she accepted she might have been wrong about a few things, but not totally. Called herself a *Schrödinger's Conspiracy Theorist... simultaneously correct and incorrect at the same time.*

The physicist in Jordan appreciated the reference.

As for him, the problem stemmed from everything the Gnostic women had proposed.

Ary said, 'Don't sweat it, mate. The universe is a messed-up place.

Chaos Theory and all that.'

'I know. I've spent years researching it. All physicists have. And it throws up more questions than can be answered. But what next?'

'Next, we do as we're told. We go to Ta Prohm Temple.'

Without discussion or argument, Jordan nodded. Resignation was a funny thing. His new reality. An acknowledgement that, to paraphrase Socrates, *he knew that he knew nothing.*

With breakfast and their chitchat concluded, they stopped by their respective rooms to grab sunglasses, met by the front desk and tracked down the correct tourist bus – transferring to the next because, a hundred yards into the journey, the first one abruptly broke-down. Twenty-five minutes later, they arrived at Ta Prohm Temple and Jordan beheld something magnificently old and beautiful. Before now, a high-school daytrip to Niagara Falls had been the extent of his expeditions beyond *the City*. And New York didn't have ancient sites. It should. Because of its Native American past. But urban sprawl had crushed any trace of the original inhabitants. Which was a shame. And shameful.

'It's the fucking bollocks, isn't it?' Ary said.

'It definitely is. Look at the detailing. The stone columns. The intricate spires. When was it constructed?'

'Sometime in the late 12th and early 13th centuries. But I've always reckoned it was built over a much earlier site. If our two new best friends are right, maybe even as far back as their ancient civilization.'

'So, we're believing that now?'

'I do.'

'You would.'

'Don't go there.'

'I wasn't. Just stating facts. You find it easier to believe this kind of thing.'

'Because of my open mind.'

'I have an open mind.'

'Yeah. That's right. You're soooo easy to convince.'

'Well, maybe I am convinced. Maybe I believe all of it. I mean, what's crazy about that?'

'Exactly. You are in my world now, chum.' She smiled, walked off towards the temple's central door and shouted back, 'C'mon. Let's go a hunting.'

UNPLUCKY THIRTEEN

Exiting the lift, the three ushers peeled away, whereupon the Caucus Consigliere – Yuze Shun's personal assistant – escorted Vilmos Gildermere into the meeting chamber, bowed and left. Gildermere took his designated armchair. The other twelve members were already seated.

'Why am I here?' he asked.

'For my update,' Rothbauer replied.

'What, we can't use phones?'

'Not for internal business. And you know I disapprove of us using *plebian* tools. That's for them. We meet. As we always have. Here. In private, where our business can't be overheard.'

The rest of the room mumbled agreement.

Gildermere shrugged and smirked. 'Fine. Only asking. So, what's the big update.'

'The usual. I am merely reporting back to the group.'

'And...?'

'...And, everything is under control. I am monitoring the situation and, even if the plebian populace start adopting Gnostic notions of togetherness and cooperation, we will tire them out with war, disease, and economic turmoil. Same as always. They'll be so distracted; they won't have the mental space for lofty ideals like unity and collaboration. The Bubonic Plague worked...'

Gildermere scoffed.

Rothbauer snapped him a look, '...The medieval mini-ice-age surpassed all expectations. World wars one and two were pure genius.' He nodded across to Bertram Saxe-Gothe, the mastermind family behind both catastrophes.

Saxe-Gothe returned the gesture.

'This time, however,' Rothbauer continued, 'our plans will be final. The Gnostics will lose.' He paused, smiling as if expecting applause.

'Is that it?' Gildermere said. 'Is that your big update. You brought us all the way here to tell us that our plan is *same as always*?'

'In a nutshell, yes.'

'Good. Now we've dispensed with that wonderous declaration, there is a food packaging company in Brexit UK desperately needing receivership.' He made to rise.

'Sit down,' Rothbauer yelled. 'I'm not finished.'

Gildermere sat. 'Go on. Enlighten us.'

'The Gnostics are working with plebians,' Rothbauer said, addressing the room.

'And so?'

'They intend to use them to *reactivate*.'

'And they'll fail. They're just plebians.'

'But they're not just any plebians.'

The mood of the room changed. The mumbling recommenced.

'They can't be. It's impossible. We dealt with that strain millennia ago.'

'Yes, we did. But it seems the Gnostics kept the genus going. Secretly. Not even the plebians themselves know what they are.'

'And you think they are capable of *reactivation*?'

'Not think... *know*.'

'So, get rid of them.'

'I'm working on that.'

'Good. I can go then. And, when it's done, there's no need to trail me all the way back to South Korea to inform me. A simple text will do. You know, saying something along the lines of: *job done*.'

'You will come when I tell you.'

Gildermere was about to snap back, but let it go. No point upsetting the harmony of the Caucus. Not when he had plans brewing.

And, while Gildermere annoyed his Patriarch and brewed plans, across the Pacific Ocean, at the New York Headquarters of the UN, the Secretary General was having a good day. In fact, he was having a great day... week... month... year. Excluding a handful of stonewalling nations, a bout of previously inconceivable cooperation had prompted a post-pandemic bounce. Six of the seven members of the G7 had pledged increased funds for medical research, and even to combat climate change. And, despite the differences and ongoing conflicts, an unprecedented mood of collaboration seemed to have taken hold of the world.

It felt eerie. Unnatural. But very welcome.

For the first time in a long time, the future looked bright.

WE'RE GOING ON A KHMER HUNT

Trapped amid knots of tentacle-like banyan roots, shadows crept across the temple's moss-mottled walls like centipedes slinking before the morning sun. The weathered sandstone blocks seeming sad and abandoned, and yet elegant in their dilapidated charm, made stately by the history radiating from every twist of timeworn masonry. Through combined effort, time and the enveloping forest had embellished this place of beauty. Nature enhanced grandeur. Stone and branch melding as one, creating a vista both raw and graceful.

Having followed a group of sightseers up to the main complex, Ary and Jordan listened to a tour-guide deliver, in English, an obviously well-rehearsed screed on Ta Prohm's lineage. When he began listing Jayavarman the Seventh's other feats of great architecture, however, they peeled away and headed towards the main courtyard.

The guide noticed them leave. 'We will be going that way soon,' he shouted after them.

Ary turned and faked a smile. 'I know. We were eager to look, is all.'

'You'll miss my talk.'

'It's okay. We've taken the tour before,' Jordan said. 'This is not our first visit. And we had to return because the temple is so magnificent.'

'Look at you going all Pinocchio on it,' Ary whispered from the side of her mouth.

'Shut up,' Jordan replied. 'I don't make a habit of it.'

'It is magnificent,' the guide said, gazing around. 'And should be visited many times.'

The tourist group muttered among themselves. They seemed to approve.

As did Ary. 'Yup, it's magnificent all right,' she said to Jordan. 'But I didn't have you down as the dishonest type.'

'Only when I have to. Anyway, drop it. Why do you think we're here?'

'That's easy. We must *rediscover the symbol...* and *do whatever comes to mind*, whatever the fuck that means. I take it – what with you being all in with the weirdo Gnostic women n' all – you are familiar with the symbol?'

'I am.' He didn't elaborate.

'Shweet,' Ary said. 'Then, I suppose, all we have to do is locate it. I've found one before, in Ireland. And another in Machu Picchu. And I'm pretty sure my aunt, she's an archaeologist, found one at a pyramid near Xianyang in China. Oh, and I had better get this out of the way now... I get visions.'

'*Visions?*'

'*Visions.* You know, like Lady Macbeth, only without the blood and death... for now, at least. I'm not wobbly in the brain, though. I reckon those two Gnostics just like fucking with my head.'

'Tell me about it,' Jordan said, again without elaboration. It seemed, when he wasn't being a condescending prick, the bloke preferred the cat-got-your-tongue approach to conversation.

'Anyway,' Ary continued. 'It makes sense that, if the symbol is anywhere, it'll be in an ancient site like this. Probably here in the main, central, column-y part of the complex. That said, the one at Machu Picchu, which I only saw through a vision, was at the outskirts of the city. The one at Xianyang, if it even is the symbol, might have been situated inside the pyramid itself. Or maybe on the outside wall. Perhaps it's over there,' she pointed to the tallest in a row of domed structures, 'carved into one of the reliefs.'

'So, you think it's over there?'

'What? Yes. Don't you listen. That's what I bloody said.'

'Why there'

'How the fuck should I know. I'm pissing in the wind as much as you are here. But it's a good place to start.'

'*Start?*'

'Well, I don't see any *Weird Symbol This Way* signs around the place. It's a process. You never know, it might be the first thing we come across.'

It wasn't. And, for the next two hours – smiling with feigned politeness as they dodged the other sightseers drifting in and out – they scoured the walls of the domed structure, checking the columns, scrutinising reliefs, but with no success. Ary tried the phone flashlight trick she'd used at Newgrange. The glow picked out many details of the decorative stonework but no symbol. Working their way around the outside facias, they came upon a stone head, peering out from a tangle of banyan roots. On the ground, blocks lay strewn where they had fallen. The symbol wasn't there either. Whatever Jordan's grandfather had found here; it wasn't within the main area. They moved on to other enclosures. Searched the entire complex. Four hours later and none the wiser, they gave up.

Ary tried a new approach. Assuming she had only to think a request and one of the Gnostic women would answer, she inner-voiced a question: *Are we looking in the right place?*

No reply came. She asked Jordan to try.

He did, reluctantly, before announcing, 'Didn't we tell them not to do that?'

'Oh, yeah. I forgot. Well, that's buggered it. What do we do now?'

'Me? I want to go home. Did you hear me there... talking about mindreading as if it was an actual thing?'

'It is.'

'It can't be. And I'm having a real hard time with this.'

'Me too. But it's where I live. Honestly, I think we are going to find something soon. I sense it in my gut. So, why don't you try being open to the prospect? Maybe it's you. You're the problem, and being up your own arse is fucking with the vibe.'

'What vibe?' he snapped.

'There you go again. Being a massive prick. After all you've been told – never mind the whole mindreading thing – you still don't get it. You should lighten up. Ya know, chillax a bit. What more proof do you need?'

'None. And that's what's scary. I can accept it, but I don't have to like it.'

'I feel you. I really do. Even someone like me can have doubts. But, you gotta get over it. For good or ill, we're slap bang in the middle of something here. Together, apparently. You have to let it go. Think of it as giving into science.'

'There's nothing science about any of this.'

'Or, maybe there is. What would you do if this was an experiment?'

'First of all, I'd weigh the options.'

'Do that then. Imagine you are going through the steps.'

'Why? What's the point?'

'You heard the women. Everything is the point. We are it. Me and you; the dream team. Didn't you hear, we're the centre of the goddamned fucking universe. And, if they're right, for the big thing, whatever that *big thing* is, to happen, we both need to be up and at it. Like finding the symbol. Here. In this place.' She walked off, away from the main site and into the surrounding brush. 'Actually, I think it's over here.'

'How?' Jordan asked, trailing after her. 'How could you know that?'

'I don't. Not for definite. But it might.'

'What? Like everywhere else we've just spent the last whatever hours wandering around.' He gazed into the maze of trees, roots, and tumbled walls with a look of futility. 'So, what comes next? A four-day hike through Alaskan forest? An expedition through the Skull Island jungle?'

'Pr'aps. I always wanted to see the world... real or fictitious. And, you know what, I reckon my spidey-senses aren't far off the mark either.' She climbed over a section of collapsed wall and dropped down into a grassy hollow at the edge of the trees. A pile of metre-cubed, root-encased stone blocks lay alongside the ruined wall. They were smaller than those from the actual temple complex, but exhibited similar signs of having been worked. These were not random boulders. Scurrying back and clambering up to the edge of the ridge, she shouted, 'You need to get over here,' back to Jordan. When he answered, 'Why?' she added, 'I think I've found something.'

Jordan craned around, expecting to see or hear a security guard, berating them for entering an unsanctioned part of the site. There were none. No tourists either. Just two macaques, watching from atop a solitary column, occasionally gesturing to the rest of the troop nestled among the niches of the entablature bridging the other five columns. Any prior sounds of birds and insects had ceased. The only noises were his footsteps crunching through the dry earth and Ary shouting, 'Come on, dingbat. Get your arse down here. I think I'm onto something.'

'Really?' he asked, scaling the wall and jumping down.

'Yeps. I do. See this here...?' she was pointing to a pile of stone blocks, '... do they seem off to you?'

'In what way?'

'Off. Out of place. As in, shouldn't be here.'

'No. They're stone blocks. There's a berzillion of them. The whole temple is made of stone blocks.'

'Yes. They *are* stone blocks. And you are back to being a prick again. But these are smaller, a different kind of rock, grey granite instead of red sandstone which, in my opinion, makes them older.'

'And you drew this conclusion how?' He walked up to join her.

'Dunno, really. It just came to me. Like through a hunch or something. I think, when the builders were constructing the temple, they uprooted them and discarded them over here. And, if I'm right, one of these might even be where your grandad found the symbol back in the day. You see, I've had a bit of a brainstorm. I feel drawn to this place. Right here. Right now. Weird, huh? And I also think, the reason we're here together, is because we each possess half of a *symbol-dar.*'

'A what?'

'A *symbol-dar*. Radar for finding the symbol. It's an upgrade to my normal *freaky-shit-dar*.' She laughed.

'Yeah, I see what you did there. But I don't have one.'

'Give it time. As for mine, I'm getting some kinda weird attraction to these stones. Usually...' she said aloud, as if shouting to someone within earshot, '...a certain someone would help me by inducing a vision.' Jordan had an inkling who, but didn't press it. 'No?' she asked the air. 'Not going to help then? Suit yourself.' She turned back to Jordan. 'Bloody Gnostics.

They're like fucking buses. First, you didn't know you needed one, then two of 'em come together, then you're back to none again. But something is definitely giving me a tingly feeling. I can't quite put my finger on it. And I think this is where you come in.'

'Me? Why?'

'Duh! Coz you're the other half of the dream team, mate.'

'But I don't feel anything. Nothing. And this, of course, is bullshit.'

'Give it a go. What have you to lose? I promise I won't blab about it to all those sciency types who read your magazine.' She smiled, a wide one, brimming with expectation and coercion.

'Okay then.' He stepped closer to the stones. 'So, which one do you think is out of place?'

'That one there,' she said, pointing to a moss-coated block set apart from the others. 'To me, it doesn't look right. The granite is darker, greyer. It's not as sunken into the ground. As if someone rolled it away from the rest. Not recently. But not centuries ago either.'

Jordan studied the block. 'You know, I think you're right.'

Ary stepped up to join him, laid the palm of her hand on the stone. 'Nope, nothing. By now, I'm usually deep into a time-trip or some messed-up journey through my mother's memories. And believe me, that is not a place you want to go. She was brought up during the Khmer Rouge period. Not a nice time.'

'I'm sorry to hear that,' Jordan said with genuine sympathy. 'Is she okay now?'

'Yeah, yeah. Mightn't have a metaphorical pot to piss in, but she's peachy. A bit bossy is all. If I wanted to choose a place and time to go tripping down, though, my mother's childhood in Cambodia wouldn't be it.'

'No. I reckon you wouldn't. So, why don't I get visions?'

'Dunno. Ask the Gnostics. They seem to be controlling this shit.' She removed her hand. 'Well, now we've confirmed that's a bust, why don't you have a crack at it?'

Jordan's logical side bubbled up again. This was nonsense. *Malark-hooey*, as his Thermodynamics lecturer used to say. Incongruous solutions to unproven concepts. Like New Age Physics. Astrology. Auras. Mindreading. With time, science – *real* science – would get there, disproving all of these groundless, and to Jordan's mind, dangerous suppositions. And yet, that's exactly what the two Gnostic women had thrown up: incongruous solutions to, not one, but all unproven concepts.

He glanced across to Ary.

She was smiling and, as if noting his reservations, said, 'Go on then. Touch the bloody thing.'

He did. And, for a while, nothing happened. A split-second later, he was alone. Ary was gone. It was dark. The moon's rays rippling across the banyan canopy, its pale glow interspersed with pinpoints of light, undulating like waves of glittery smoke or dewy night-time mist. Stark yet blurry. Difficult to discern but becoming clearer. Amid a sparkling haze, the moss-coated granite block appeared by his side. He was wearing green fatigues. A patch above the left breast pocket said: *US ARMY*. He was confused. Scared. Attempted to move, but couldn't. A passenger in someone else's body. His consciousness trapped behind another. Holding a spade, and through eyes that weren't his, Jordan watched the alternate him dig dirt from around the stone block before, using the shaft as a lever, he – *they* – lifted the bottom edge high enough to wedge a rock the in gap. Sweat dripped from his brow. He felt its chill. Standing like a stalker in someone else's mind, he observed the body he occupied repeat the task three more times, wedging increasingly larger rocks alongside the first until, with one last effort, the block flipped onto its side and the vision disappeared.

He was back with Ary.

'Better get used to those,' she said. 'They sneak up on you like a bitch.'

Jordan knew what she meant, and her confirmation made the experience all the more unsettling. But, what the hell. Mind-manipulation, acceptance of spurious theories, and now visions, it seemed, were to be his new reality.

'We need to turn it over.'

'Thought as much. But have you seen the size of the bloody thing? It's massive.'

'My grandfather did it.'

'Your grandfather? So, you took a trip down the family memory lane, then?'

'It would seem that way. Anyway, he managed on his own, and it's the only way to see what's underneath.'

'Spoken like a true believer.'

Jordan rolled his eyes.

Ary laughed. 'Okey-dokey then. I'm in.'

Checking the surrounding area for a branch, Jordan found one thick and straight enough to use as a lever, rammed the tip under the bottom edge of the block and said, 'When I lift, you wedge a small stone in the gap. I'll lift some more. You wedge a bigger...'

'Okay. Got it,' Ary snapped. 'I know how to lift heavy things. What is it with blokes? Always overexplaining everything. I have one just like you back at home. He's as annoying as fuck too.'

Jordan didn't respond to her rebuke. In any case, she was probably right.

He just said, 'Let's do it,' and, following the planned procedure, they went about raising and wedging, raising and wedging, and so forth until the stone block teetered and fell back with a thud.

'There it is,' Ary said with a grin.

And it was. For the first time since appearing on his desktop computer, Jordan had proof the symbol was real and not someone *fucking with* him, as Jada had eloquently proclaimed. The carving looked old. Maybe thousands of years old. The notion disturbed him.

'It's the first one I've seen complete,' Ary continued.

'What do you mean?'

'When I found the one at Newgrange, the whole pattern was only revealed because I shone a light on the wall. The carving at Machu Picchu came through a vision... as I said, you better get used to those. And the one at the Xianyang pyramid was on a tablet that had been removed for study at my aunt's university. I didn't get to inspect it up close. Her husband said it was broken or something. Anyway, long story short, this is the only one that's been fully formed.'

'I see. So, I suppose that makes it special.'

'Or maybe they all are.'

'Maybe. But what if it's a scam? I mean, what do we really know about those two women anyway?'

'What, you think they might be baddies?'

'Yeah. *Baddies.*'

'They seem nice enough.'

'All charlatans seem nice. At first.'

'They sound legit about all the ancient ancestor stuff.'

'To you. I'm still processing.'

'They can do things with our minds.'

'Exactly.'

'So, you reckon they've gone to all this trouble, got us here, to do what... clear our bank accounts? Steal our identities? Build a big-ass fucking space-death-laser?'

'No, not that. But... well, you know... something sinister.'

'I suppose they could. They have the ability. I don't see it, though. I like them. Even if that's only because they're farting around in my brain.'

'Okay. I'll bite. So, let's say that's the case, what do we do next?'

'Shit happened when you touched the stone. Maybe you should do the same with the carving. What with you being your grandad's heir n' all.'

'You think?'

'Sure. Touch it.'

'But what if something happens?'

'Isn't that the whole point?'

'Maybe we should...'

'Just touch the fucking stone, Jordan.'

He did, laying his palm on the triskele at the centre. Nothing happened. 'Maybe you should touch it too. They said we're in it together.'

'True,' Ary replied, setting her hand alongside Jordan's.

The effect was instant. A blaze of blue light erupted from the stone, tracking the lines of the symbol, bursting through the gaps between their fingers. Needle-like tingles surged through Jordan's body. He shivered, tried to pull his hand away but it wouldn't move, stuck there as if another hand was pressing it into the stone. He attempted to step back but this too was denied to him. A power had taken possession of his muscles. Glancing across at Ary, he saw her also shiver, and grin, appearing to relish the situation. The light flared again, and again, pulses of blinding brilliance that struck out in beams of incandescent blue energy, streaking across the forest; energising the soil, traversing others, racing onwards and outwards, until they became glows in the distance. The trees glittered. The ground gleamed, throbbing as the blue light settled into the dry dirt like water sinking into sand and became a faint flush, contained to a network of lines that snaked through the forest and temple.

When the pressure released and they removed their hands, the glow disappeared.

'What the living fuck,' Ary said.

'Exactly what I was thinking.'

'It was cool, though? Right?'

'It was definitely cool. But I have zero idea what just happened.' He heard voices. Tourists milling about at the outer regions of the temple complex. 'Better flip this back over. Don't want anyone else to find it.'

Ary glanced across to the tourists, nodded and, by repeating the raise and wedge technique, they flipped the block into its original position with the symbol facing downwards. Throughout the task, Ary maintained her smile. Jordan felt much the same, even though deciphering the events of the last few minutes would take some serious scientific assessment. Using the branch, he scraped earth around the base of the stone to disguise any disturbance. He stepped back to assess the finish, overextending in the process, tripped on a root and fell backwards onto his butt.

Ary sniggered.

'Don't laugh,' Jordan said, reaching up for help.

'Laugh? I think I shat myself.' She grabbed his hand, pulled him upright.

Midway, a wisp of dust puffed up from the granite block. A muffled crack followed.

'Did you see that?' Jordan asked, steadying on his feet.

'Yeah,' Ary replied. 'Freaky.'

Another puff. Another muffled crack. Someone cursing from atop the entablature where the macaques had sat. The monkey troop were gone. As were the two from atop the solitary column. Their collective howls fading through the trees as shuddering branches marked the route of their flight. A figure, human, wearing black clothes and a biker's balaclava, had taken their place. Crouched on one knee. Hurling obscenities at the rifle in their hands.

'That's a fucking gun,' Ary shouted and dashed into the forest.

For Jordan, it took a few seconds longer.

Then it hit. Adrenaline rushed and he was streaking after her.

A bullet whizzed past his ear, punched a hole in a tree trunk. Another splintered branches to his righthand side. Ary was yards ahead, leaping over brush and banyan roots. A third bullet whizzed close to Jordan's other ear, followed by another. He paid them no heed, just ran, head-down, sidestepping, leaping, dodging roots and bushes, following Ary for what seemed like a good quarter mile before the shooting seemed to stop and he found the courage to glance behind. They were deep into the forest. Ta Prohm Temple lost to the density of trees. As if with the same mind, they slowed, together, and then ducked. Well, Ary ducked. Jordan slumped completely to the ground and shimmied belly-down behind a knotted clump of banyan roots.

When Ary moved in alongside him, she peeked over the top. 'I think it's over,' she said.

Jordan didn't reply. Panic gagged his throat.

Ary turned to sit with her back against the knot of roots. 'So, that's just fucking brilliant,' she continued. 'Now we got someone taking pot-shots at us.'

Jordan remained as he was, and still said nothing.

Words refused to come.

LIFE OF PAIN

Lena Hansen cursed loudly, disassembled her Paratus-16 sniper rifle and placed the constituent parts into her Luis Vuitton backpack. Making sure the coast was clear, she then clambered down the endmost column, took a roundabout route via the forest edges to the public toilets, nipped into one of the cubicles and changed into a yellow Valentino summer frock. She put on a blonde wig. Swapped her army boots for Gucci loafers. Secured her black *work* clothes and balaclava with the rifle in the backpack and, exiting the temple complex, took a taxi to the Golden Angkor Hotel and the plush room she had made her HQ – and cover – for the duration of the assignment.

On the journey, she spoke to the driver as might any tourist, lauding the magnificence of Angkor Wat in a feigned but flawless, English public-school accent. Pure fabrication, of course. Everything she had learned about the place had come from information pamphlets and a handful of YouTube videos made by previous visitors. It was part of the ruse. And, as she blabbered on about *this amazing place*, promising to tell all her *friends at the country club about the wonderful Khmer culture*, she faked awe and fabricated interest, when all she could think about was the badly calibrated sight on her rifle, and how Nimo – her South Asian weapons guy – who usually was so meticulous, had totally fucked up this time.

He would regret it.

He should have prepared better.

She should have prepared better.

It was careless. Sloppy.

Siem Reap Objectives 1 and 2 were still alive. Her employers would require an explanation. She would have none. Only a vow to make good on the assignment or face the consequences.

Back in her hotel room, she dumped the backpack on the floor and kicked the coffee table, which toppled with a thud but remained undamaged. These fancy hotels really did have quality gear. She laughed. It came from deep in her lungs and erupted in a spray of spit. She felt a failure, but laughed all the harder for it. Over the next half-hour, amid bouts of disappointment-tinged laughter, she worked on the holographic sight until it was calibrated and, raising the weapon to her shoulder, focused through the window on a waiter serving cold drinks to a table of people at the bar across the street. Aiming at his head, and allowing for distance and the deflection of the window glass, she pondered how, with the slightest pressure of her finger, the happy tourists could so easily spend the evening washing blood and waiter brains out of their hair. The thought made her snicker. She almost pulled the trigger just to experience the outcome. Poor guy. Going about his life and never knowing how close he came.

Breaking down the rifle, she set the parts back into the backpack, ready for her next attempt on the two marks, walked to the bathroom, removed her expensive clothes and threw them on the floor. Standing before the backlit mirror, she took off her blonde wig. A chin-length bob. Coiffured to a high standard. Selected out of dozens to fake the persona of a rich, British socialite. She rubbed her bald scalp. Followed by her shoulders. Her skin was shaved from head to toe. She needed to be untraceable. A ghost. No stray hairs. No trackable history. No accounts. No online presence. No birth certificate. Even Lena Hansen was an alias. And, it had been so long, Lena – for want of a better name – wasn't sure who she was either.

She was merely *assassin*.

Which was good.

Her actions today, however, were not.

Removing a razor from the pack of four disposables that came with the room, she detached the upper cartridge, snapped it open, removed one of the five blades and sliced a single word, three times into the skin below her breasts. From her upper thighs to her chest, the signs of previous admonishments furrowed her midriff like the ridged landscape of an alien world.

All of them said the same word:

BEDRE

And she would do that; be *better*.

It was the enduring lesson of her life.

An hour later, with her wounds cleaned and covered, Lena Hansen awaited a response from the handler (or handlers) she had never met. Any communication came via a secure phone, through a specific app she assumed had been designed for the purpose, wherein details and images for any given assignment could be studied free of external scrutiny. It was slick tech. Totally under the control of the mysterious people who ordered the hits. Untraceable. Or so they told her. Unhackable. And, so far, she found no reason to disagree. In her occupation, anonymity was paramount. She didn't know them and liked it that way. Trusting them to keep their end and she, in turn, delivered the goods with the shrewdness and stealth they required. Her marks despatched without fanfare. She left no trace,

This time, however, she failed.

The message on the app simply read:

Make good on the contract

It was enough. She knew the consequences.

Putting the blonde wig back on, along with a cream Gabriela Hearst maxi, she placed her work clothes and some listening gear in the backpack, went down to the lobby, drank mocktails for appearances sake, smiled at a chihuahua, sneered at a bellhop to keep with the persona, waited for night to fall and headed out to the hostel where the assignment app showed the two marks were staying. In a disused building off Achar Sva Street, she changed into her professional attire, ducked down a side alley, climbed onto a rooftop and approached the terrace café where Ary Long and Jordan Burke were sitting at a table with two women. The women weren't Lena's problem. Only *Objectives 1 and 2*. Tonight, however, she intended only to observe. Lack of planning had caused the fiasco at Ta Prohm Temple and, although the fuckup had been technical, she would take a while to get to know Long and Burke's habits before making another attempt.

Reaching into the backpack, she took out a parabolic listening device, switched it on, inserted the accompanying earpiece into her ear, and shimmied across to the edge of the roof overlooking the terrace where Long and Burke chatted with their two friends.

Long sounded agitated. 'Someone was shooting at us. They were actually bloody shooting at us. With bullets. Real fucking bullets.'

Burke nodded. He appeared less agitated than Long, but his hands shook and, every few seconds, he glanced from side to side, as if searching for the someone in the darkness.

Lena almost laughed out loud. *I'm up here, you idiot,* her internal voice said. *Right above you. If I wanted to, I could put one clean through your eyeball and you'd be deader than disco before the others even realised the gook on their faces was the back of your skull.*

She sniggered, also internally. Mocking them from inside her head.

One of the two women, who Long had earlier called Sandhya, merely smiled.

The other, called Nkechi, seemed equally nonplussed, as if someone having an assassin on their tail was as natural as taking a piss. And that annoyed Lena. Her business was serious business. Well, at least for the mark. She didn't take too well with it being trivialised. People should fear her. All of them. She was a shadow. The Grim Reaper. If these two women ever came up on her hitlist, she would take the greatest pleasure in offing the bitches. Up close and personal like. So close, they would die with Lena Hansen's spit dripping down their faces.

The group talked for another half-hour. Which meant Long ranting like a lunatic for most of it, Burke contributing next to fuck all, and the other two offering little more than a smile, or a nod. They seemed to be holding something back. It occurred to Lena they might be aware of her presence.

As if speaking to the ether, the one named Nkechi said aloud, 'Nothing to see here. You're finished.'

Lena felt the instruction was meant for her, but shrugged it off. There was no way any of them could know she was nearby.

'I'd say I'm finished,' Long snapped. 'I'm out of here. Nothing's worth getting my head blown off for.'

'I thought you were the great conspiracy investigator,' the one called Sandhya said.

'What? You're bringing that up now?'

'Yes. I thought this was what you wanted. Your life's work. To find the truth.'

'I did. I do. But, at this present moment, I can think of nothing better than getting arse-faced with my mate, Mateus.'

'Ah, *the music person*. He's very talented.'

'Yes, the music person. I want to go to the pub, drink a stack of shots, throw up, maybe shag something, and never think about this place again.'

'Like a true investigator.'

'Oh, get fucked.'

'She's right,' Burke chirped up.

'So, now you speak?'

'Yes. Because you keep going on about how you're this mega-level conspiracy theorist, but want to pack it in at the slightest hint of trouble.'

'Trouble I can do. I'm used to trouble. What I'm not used to is bullets... flying past my fucking head... blowing chunks out of the surrounding foliage.'

'Neither am I. But something major has happened.'

The two women smiled but remained quiet.

Lena had no idea what he was taking about and didn't care either.

'We should see it through,' he continued.

Long huffed. Rolled her eyes. 'So, now you're the brave one. Two seconds ago, we could've used you as smoothie-shaker, now you're all: *we should see it through – the loony women are right – stuff is important.*'

'It is important. And I think you'd regret it if you gave up now.'

'I'd stay alive longer.'

Better believe it, Lena thought with a smile.

'But you would never find out the truth.'

'I was of the impression we already have,' Long said, glancing across to Nkechi.

'It's just the start,' the woman replied. 'You need to find the last piece.'

'What last piece? There's a bloody last piece, now?'

'You already know about it. At the pyramid site. Your aunt's husband was right. It's a puzzle. All the parts are there. You only have to put them together.'

'Why?' Burke asked.

'In the days before *the Fall*, various sites around the world acted as junction points for the global network. Three were disabled by the Aryans. One in Ireland. Another at Machu Picchu. And the one you found and activated today.'

'The bursts of blue light?'

'Exactly.'

'But we did that. It worked.'

'Think of it as an electrical circuit. And, yes, you repaired a junction. Energy went out. Coursing through other junctions in the grid. Places you'd know as ancient sites like Nasca, Mereo in Nubia, Stonehenge, etcetera. There is even one at the Yonaguni monument, but that one is a *Core Hub*. As is Bimini. And Santorini, also a *Core Hub*, an *Activator*, completely destroyed by the Aryans. Only Yonaguni remained intact, albeit underwater. But we'll come to those later. Anyway, there are many junctions: El Giza, Gobekli Tepe, Lake Baikal in Russia, Évora in Portugal, Chichin Itza, Kashan, many many more... and also the pyramid Ary's aunt uncovered south of Xianyang. And, therein, lies the problem.'

'What problem?' Long asked. She seemed less anxious and more engaged.

'To energise the full network, each junction must be activated by way of a complete and unbroken symbol. Like diodes in a circuit board. It's a power thing. Jordan would understand.'

'You calling me thick?' Long snapped.

'No. Not at all. I only mentioned it because Jordan is the physicist among us.'

'I am,' Burke said with a smile. 'I am that.'

Long smirked, then smothered it. 'I know how electricity works.'

'This isn't just electricity, though. I only used that as an example. It's more like what, in previous centuries, they called *the ether*. We call it *Logos*. It is potential. The energy beneath all matter, and light, and thought. It's what charges galaxies. The whole universe. And the old ones used it for... well, everything.'

'But it needs a circuit?'

'On Earth it does. Logos evolves. It is never granted or given by others of higher intellect or ability. They only observe. Never interfere. The world would be quite a different place if they did. Never mind if the impact hadn't happened. But that's of no matter now. We are where we are. The universe has spoken and we can only follow.'

'I think they want the point,' the one called Sandhya interrupted.

'Yes. Sorry. I get carried away when I think about the brilliance of it all.' She sat up straighter. 'So, anyway, the next bit is actually quite easy. You must go to Xianyang. Both of you. It only works when there's both of you. Find the pieces of the symbol, put them back together... at the pyramid, and make everything good again.'

'Xianyang?' Long said.

'Xianyang.'

'At the highly classified dig my aunt oversees?'

'Yes. That one. The pyramid.'

'You want us to get the bits of the symbol without being caught, and do all that other stuff you mentioned?'

'Exactly.'

'Your head's cracked, missus.'

'We can do it,' Burke said.

Ary Long shot him a wry look, before addressing the women, 'There's no way he's saying that on his own. You guys are defo messing with his head.'

'No,' Sandhya said. 'Not at all. Well, maybe a little. Just to calm his nerves.'

'You said you wouldn't do that. And what about me?'

'You're a tougher nut. It's a gender thing. We got you with persuasion, through visions. But it won't work now you know. We need you to agree of your own accord. No influencing.'

'I agree,' Burke said. 'Let's do it.' His eyes looked glazed, as if daydreaming.

'Does he know?' Long asked, poking a thumb his direction.

'Not a jot,' Nkechi said. 'But we need both of you. It's the way things have turned out.'

The conversation paused. Ary Long appeared to be thinking. 'Okay,' she said, after a while. 'And I need you to teach me some of those tricks.'

The women glanced at each other. 'All right. But just a few. We can't have humans playing with Logos too soon.'

Long smiled, and thumped Burke on the shoulder.

He flinched, said, 'Ow.'

'Did you hear that?' Long said.

'Hear what?'

'We're going to China. You'll like it there. I have family.'

'Burke said, 'Okay.'

Long turned to face the two women. 'Still doing your thing?'

'Oh, that? Yes,' the one called Sandhya said. 'A small tweak. We'll probably let him out when you get him to Xianyang.'

'Me too?'

'A little. Just to calm your grouchiness.'

Throughout the whole exchange, Lena had wondered what the hell they'd been discussing but, at the same time, didn't care. It wasn't her problem, or business or, apart from discovering their next location, of any importance.

Only the job mattered.

Placing the parabolic device into the backpack, she shimmied back across the rooftop, dropped down into the alleyway, changed into her rich Brit attire at the disused building, and went back to the hotel. For the duration of the surveillance, she had muted the assignment phone. Turning it back on, a message popped up in the app asking:

Were there two women with the targets?

She answered:

Yes

Seconds later, an instruction followed:

Don't make another attempt until targets are alone

She didn't reply. The message was clear.

NO BLUE LIGHTS FOR MATEUS

That night, back in her room, Ary made a video-call with Mateus. He was in Dublin. The studio and offices of Stinky Hole Records already dismantled and shipped across the Irish Sea to a loft-style building on the south side of Samuel Beckett Bridge. It was afternoon there. The clatter of builders banging and grinding in the background making it difficult to hear his words. With an apology, Mateus walked downstairs and out to the street, where the day emerged sunny behind him. Not Siem Reap sunny, but that hazy, cloudy, rain might drop at any moment sunshine she loved so much about Ireland. To her, it always seemed fantasy-like. Tolkienesque. Even if all the concrete, brick, cars and buses shattered the illusion.

He mentioned he had put his fancy London flat up for sale.

'You're actually doing it?'

'Absolutely. I've found my new place. Just as pricey as Loftus Road, but I love it in Dublin. I feel at home here.'

'Good for you. You deserve a break. What with having to suffer being a stupid-ass rich-bitch n'all.'

'Yeah, and fuck you too,' he said with a smile. 'So, what's the big deal that will have me *cacking my knickers* then?'

Ary took her time, relating everything the two Gnostics had told her. Sensing a hint of jealousy, she also informed him about her new partner, Jordan Burke and how she – *they* – were going back to Xianyang to attempt, *however the fuck that might happen*, to access the tablet her aunt and uncle found at the pyramid site. Throughout, Mateus's face went through an assortment of expressions; from surprise, through intrigue to wonderment, especially when she mentioned the part about activating the ley lines.

'Did you see anything over there in Ireland?' she asked.

'Nothing.'

'No blue lights?'

'Nope.'

'No streaks of energy?'

'Nope again.'

'Just as I thought. It was only myself and Jordan who saw them. Must be something to do with the power being hidden, and us being special or something.'

'You're definitely special.'

'Yeah, and you're still a prick.' They laughed.

'You sound happier. Less snarky.'

'Just had my life's work confirmed, innit.'

'*Nearly* confirmed.'

'*Totally* confirmed. Except for the bit about who's behind it all.'

'Yeah, you missed the mark there. But, congratulations anyway. I look forward to reading the blogpost.' The conversation went flat. After many awkward seconds, Mateus said, 'Look, I'd better get back inside. These guys are good but I need to keep an eye on things. Don't want to find my mixer desk nailed to the ceiling or something.'

Ary didn't push it. She wanted to chat all the way until morning but realised her revelations might be causing envy-issues for her oldest friend. It wasn't the first time she'd left him out. He was probably used to it by now. But, this time, she had a replacement and she could sense his hurt. She felt it too. Deeply. And she missed him.

Mateus said, 'Gotta go. We'll do this again soon,' and finished the call.

His abruptness punched her heart. Her eyes welled, a few tears rolling down her cheek, before she sniffled them back, put her phone in her pocket and went down the corridor to Jordan's room.

When he opened the door, she said, 'I have something else to do before we leave for China.'

'What's that?'

'I want to go to where my mother used to live. The place where your grandfather died.'

Jordan nodded, and closed the door.

He hadn't said it, but she knew he would come.

MONDAY – MAY 29th

Two Weeks Earlier

Huxley Slick refilled his coffee cup, set the breakfast tray aside, said, 'Open TV,' to his virtual assistant, and waited as the fake wall beyond the end of his bed slid down, revealing the large television hidden within. Outside the windows of his bedroom, beyond the infinity pool, the gentle waves of the Pacific Ocean played tag with sand and seaweed on Huxley's own personal slice of Malibu Beach. Early morning sunshine blazed. The smart glass in the windows adjusting tints to match the ebb and flow of the wispy clouds moving overhead.

He said, 'Find *Money Bags*.'

The television switched from the home screen to where his good friend – well, as good a friend as anyone could be in his line of business – Alan was on the *Money Bags* show, talking about an unexpected solidity in global markets. Although a handful of soundbites and ad hoc predictions could never replace his team of financial gurus, Huxley liked the show, it provided a comforting overview of the markets and, on occasion, one of the guests let something slip. Small. Seemingly unimportant. Nothing recognisable to the average Joe, but a hint of what direction they were taking some, or even a fair amount, of their holdings.

Today, Alan seemed his usual self.

Huxley, however, knew different.

Of late, unknown to the hoi polloi, things had been going far from planned.

Sure, only an idiot failed to make a killing during the lockdowns. Chaos really was the best earner. Such gambles, however, depended on a subsequent upturn which various governments said had happened but, down in the dark sewers of financial risk, the real players knew had failed miserably.

Trends had been unpredictable. Hard to pin down. Seemed almost manipulated. And, at present indicators, Huxley Slick looked set to lose just short of thirteen billion dollars.

When his coffee cup hit the television screen, it bounced with a splash of brown liquid, staining the room's cream-coloured carpet.

Huxley hated flat-screen TVs.

Almost as much as he hated losing.

Two Weeks Earlier – minus three days

Through the full-width windows of his office, the windows of the Guangzhou CTF Finance Centre twinkled in the night sky but, vexed to the point of depression, Cheung Li hardly acknowledged them. They were wallpaper. A backdrop to ruin. *Why?* Because Cheung Li followed trends. Something he used to be good at. Of late, however, Li-Lin Jīnróng – known to the markets as LLJ – had seen dismal performance in both their own and client investments. Combined, seventeen and a half billion had been wiped from their most lucrative speculations. And that was just the post-pandemic losses.

Sure, only idiots failed to make a killing during the lockdowns. Chaos really was the best earner. Such gambles, however, depended on a subsequent upturn which various governments said had happened but, down in the dark sewers of financial risk, the real players knew had failed miserably.

Trends had been unpredictable. Hard to pin down. Seemed almost manipulated.

He popped a pill. A mood enhancer that never worked.

He tapped his virtual keyboard. His business partner, Jian Lin's face appeared on the screen and, for the next hour, they discussed the diabolical forecasts.

Jian was furious.

Cheung was close to smashing his smart-desk.

Their reputation was in tatters.

Two Weeks Earlier – minus five days

Giles Hufferston Windthorp III finished his dry sherry. For him, the sweet variety was something one drank with dinner. Dry was for calming the nerves. Or dealing with bad news. He shuffled in his armchair, set the empty glass on the side table wherein, as if by magic, Henry, his personal waiter, arrived and replaced it with another, two-thirds full of the same Barbadillo.

Giles said nothing.

Henry smiled and left.

There were only two other members at the Midas Club this day:

Samuel Pickering, the historical fiction author of much acclaim... fifty years ago.

And Jeremy Chandler Forsythe; ex-general, conflict expert, and war story bore.

They were sitting together, quaffing malt whisky and, although many yards away, Giles heard their ludicrous solutions to the ills of the world as clearly as if they had taken up position on his lap. The harsh vagaries of life never ravaged the leafy lanes of Hampstead Heath or the palatial walls of the Forsythe House Estate, Wiltshire. A lifetime of privilege had afforded them the wherewithal to postulate nonsense. And Giles had been no different. Until his brother enticed him with the promise of even greater prosperity, he had been happy, lounging away the day, awash with wealth, watching the oiks pass by.

They had even done well in the pandemic.

Only idiots failed to make a killing during the lockdowns. Chaos really was the best earner. Such gambles, however, depended on a subsequent upturn which various governments said had happened but, down in the dark sewers of financial risk, the real players knew had failed miserably.

Trends had been unpredictable. Hard to pin down. Seemed almost manipulated.

Lifting the sherry-glass to his lips, Giles committed the greatest indignity one can when drinking an exquisite beverage. He downed it in one. Such was his anger. Such was his rage. If trends persisted, he was set to lose over twenty billion. Most of his inheritance. He would be left with only the estate, the stables, the holiday villas in San Marino and Monte Carlo, and the twenty-two million he considered pocket money. The whole enterprise had been a debacle. A tragedy. His brother was a moron. As was he for listening.

He smashed the empty glass on the floor at his feet.

Henry arrived, with a dustpan and brush, and another glass of Barbadillo.

Giles Hufferston Windthorp III paid him no heed.

Two Weeks Earlier – minus a week and one day

Azima Hussain enjoyed her first hours as Visiting Chair in Systems Theory. She received the expected reception, a meet and greet with the faculty, a tour of the campus, and a one-to-one with Gerd Bauer, the Head of School, who peppered her with gratitude for deciding to bring her research and reputation to the University of Munich School of Economics, Finance & Accounting.

Azima said she was likewise grateful for the opportunity. Mentioning – on several occasions – that equal, if not most of the credit should go to her collaborator, Keerthi Chopra, at the Mumbai School of Business and Finance. Gerd Bauer beamed, uttered another round of thanks, and showed her to her office.

Her phone buzzed.

It was Keerthi.

She sounded agitated.

Two Weeks Earlier – minus a week and three days

Wiltbridge Caulder Global had numerous offices on every continent bar Antarctica and, in Estevo Pinheiro's opinion, if the researchers at each of the seventy or so research bases there ever wanted to speculate on the markets while digging their half-tracks out of the snow, then WCG would set up offices there too, situated between the residential quarters and the area where they did all the financially insignificant science stuff. In fact, they would probably rip the stations down and repurpose the sites for futures, investments, and the wanton rape of a totally exploitable and lucrative landscape. Oil was good. Minerals were better. Land sales the best.

There wasn't a single environment WCG wouldn't exploit or dominate.

Everything was up for grabs. People and places were dust to be swept aside.

In the world of finance, they were a – no, *the* – lesson in how to become number one, and stay there. It was why he worked for them. Achieving the position of VP of Corporate at the chief South American office in São Paulo. Four years of eighty-hour weeks had paid off. He was exactly where he wanted to be.

Until today.

Today, the South American division of WCG crumpled.

Other divisions stayed firm but, sparked by a surprise lack of confidence in WCG São Paulo's inability to safeguard their major client's investments, stock haemorrhaged at an alarming rate. The father company in New York cut them adrift. Everyone and anyone who had a stake either pulled their cash, sold their shares, or found a lifetime of investments suddenly lose ninety-eight-percent of their value. Estevo Pinheiro also lost – *big time* – the Brazilian Real equivalent of twenty-three million US dollars. His only twenty-three million US dollars; leaving him with just the apartment in São Paulo and his holiday place in the Maldives, both of which he'd double-mortgaged to buy extra WCG SP shares. Another bad decision that would catch up with him within a couple of days.

He did have a ten or so thousand Reais in *chump change*, lodged in a current account he'd had since leaving university. At one time, it had been his emergency fund. Now, it wouldn't even pay an hour's interest on the loans he had accrued.

In the space of seven hours, he had lost everything and owed millions.

Never put all your money in one place, his father, also a banking professional, had told him. *Always diversify. Always have multiple streams of income.*

Until recently, Estevo had listened but, buoyed by his successes as newly appointed VP of Corporate, he had hoped to make a short-term killing: a two-week deal where he transferred all of his holdings into WCG SP stock, massaged the numbers a little and then, as stock skyrocketed, he would sell high and jump ship, hopefully to an even better position with a rival company.

He would have it all. King of the hill.

In a blink, that aspiration, however, had gone.

His husband-to-be would never forgive him. He liked nice things. Deserved nice things.

The pills tasted sour on his tongue. He felt woozy. Nauseated. His desk-chair felt cushiony. The sunlight pouring through his office window strangely beautiful, a brilliant kaleidoscope, fading into grey, darkness and death.

Two Weeks Earlier – minus a week and six days
Azima Hussain and Keerthi Chopra were conducting their seventeenth video call in five days. This latest one in conference. With the Presidents, Chancellor, King, and Prime Ministers of the G20.

They didn't look happy.

For the umpteenth time, Azima and Keerthi related their findings.

The blank stares peering back at them said everything.

Minus no days – May 29th – Crash Monday
Market collapse.

All of them.

COUNTRY ROADS...

It rained overnight. Wave after wave of heavy showers, pummelling the roof of Ary's bedroom as if a giant with major bladder issues had specifically picked the vicinity around the hostel to relieve itself. Finally, hours into the effort, she achieved sleep, descending into blissful darkness until, what seemed like only moments later, she woke to knifelike shafts of sunlight splitting the bamboo blinds on the window, with one impertinent bastard lingering bang-smack on her eyelids.

She got up. Checked the time on her phone.

Six forty-fucking-two.

The rain had stopped. Like the sunlight, having committed the utmost annoyance.

She dressed, tied her hair in ponytail buns, went to the terrace café, and found both Nkechi and Sandhya sat at a table, drinking tea.

'Ah. Here at last,' Nkechi said.

'At last? It's the middle of the bloody night.'

'You slept well?'

'No. I didn't.'

'Yes, the summer rains can be a little intense in Southeast Asia,' Sandhya said, sipping from her cup.

'A little? It was a fucking torrent. I didn't catch a wink. Next time, I'll use some of Mateus's money and book a room with a roof that's more than just beams and wanky wafer-thin tiles. I've had it with slumming it. Everyone knows I need proper sleep to function. And remain rational.'

'So, it would seem.'

'How is your friend?' Nkechi asked. 'I take it his move is going well.'

'How do you know...?' Ary began and left it. Of course, they knew about Mateus. This pair knew everything. It was freaky – and disconcerting. 'Good. I think,' she replied. 'Busy doing his thing. I'll get some tea.' She went to the kiosk, ordered a smoked green with coconut milk, and returned to sit alongside the two women at their table. She had warmed to them. Or, at least she thought. Maybe they were just messing with her head. When neither of them replied to the notion, she relaxed and asked, 'So, guys... what's happening then?'

Jordan, rushing out onto the terrace, holding his phone aloft, answered her question, 'They've crashed?'

'Who crashed?'

'All of them: banks, stock markets, currencies. Even the big coporations. They all went belly-up over-night. They're calling it *Crash Monday*. History's biggest financial breakdown.'

'Must've been the rain,' Ary said with a snigger. 'Lack of sleep can really damage a person's cognitive abilities.' Then, she saw the sober look on Jordan's face. 'Fuck... you're serious?'

'Yes, I'm fucking serious. The world economy has collapsed.'

'Who cares. It's always doing that. Like in 2008.'

'This is different. This time it's everything.' He held out his phone. 'Look. *The Washington Post* says practically every economy was decimated in a single sweep. Major sell-offs. Developing nations in recession. Reserves activated. They're talking about special measures. The EU has already begun brokering gold as a bulwark. The United States have moved to bonds. China. India. South Korea. Japan. Russia. All of them. Their all bankrupt. Not that Russia had far to fall due to sanctions. But they're saying the WTO has lost control. The IMF too. It's a complete disaster.'

'Pah! It's always a disaster. Until it's not. Maybe it'll force one of those shite-hawk centibillionaires to finally cough up some moolah and do their bit for a change.'

'They're gone too. Their fortunes demolished in a matter of hours.'

'And all this while I was aslee... while I was *trying* to sleep. Hey, maybe it was my entities. You know, the ones you don't believe in. A dimension-travelling *Ocean's Eleven*. Hopped in – stole the lot – and hopped out again.' Ary laughed. Jordan didn't. Fuck, he was a real doom-gloomer. 'Never mind. Everything will be okay,' she continued while sipping her tea. 'I'm getting breakfast. You want me to order you some bobor?'

'You're not listening.' He thrust his phone closer to her face. 'It's gone. The whole world of finance has disintegrated. Does that not concern you?'

Ary looked at the screen and the front-page quote:

Trillions Wiped from Global Markets

'Meh!' she replied.

'You are unbelievable.' Jordan turned to the Gnostics. 'And do you two not have anything to say about this.'

The women sipped their tea. Then, with a slow glance upwards, Sandhya said, 'It's the Aryans. They like to do this kind of thing from time to time.'

'*This kind of thing*?' Jordan shouted. '*This kind of thing*? It's a complete catastrophe. Did you know it was going to happen?'

'We had a hunch. They tend to go a bit doomsday-ish when they suspect we're making headway.'

'*Doomsday-ish? Headway?* Headway with what?'

The women smiled at each other. 'The symbol? What you did yesterday? It started a chain of events. A global shift. Positive vibes, so to speak. They were aware we were up to something, and needed to hinder it. Seeding negativity. Like destabilising the world economy. Sometimes it's a plague. Or a revolution. World Wars – both One and Two. All they need to do is suggest shooting some Archduke and, next thing you know, whole populations are blowing each other to smithereens. Twice. Julius Caesar's decision to cross the Rubicon. Genghis Khan feeling a bit cramped in Mongolia. It's not hard. They generally go for the simple approach. People are easy. Greedy people more so. Like I said, they do this kind of thing from time to time. They don't have our sense of decorum, or level-headedness.'

'But how can you take it so... well, so...'

'...Couldn't give a fuck,' Ary interjected. 'You looked like you were struggling there, mate. Thought I'd help.'

'Well, yes,' Jordan said, appearing to ignore Ary and directing his attention to the two Gnostics.

'But we do – give a fuck, as Ary eloquently put it,' Nkechi said. 'And this is not the first time. Aryans didn't get to control everyone and everything by being soft-handed. It's what they do. This is just the next instalment in a long line of global fiascos, brought on by their need to keep a tight rein.'

'And, you are okay with this?' he asked Ary, setting his phone on the table.

'Like the woman said, it's what they do.'

'So, now you're all knowing about Aryans.'

'Not all knowing. But more than you. And I trust these guys.' She smiled. The women smiled back. 'They know their shit. And, if they say it's no sweat, then fair enough. That's cool with me. Tea?'

'No! I don't want tea. Or breakfast. Or anything else, for that matter. I need to get back to New York. While there's still such a thing as airlines. Don't you understand, the world has no financial base. We are at the whims of chance.'

'Nothing new there, then.'

'Not exactly true,' Nkechi interjected. 'Remember, everything is controlled.'

'Sorry. Forgot that. So, what now? Seeing the world has gone totally handbasket.'

'We carry on as planned. The Aryans will move to exploit the downfall they have put in place. Those cryptocurrency fluctuations you saw last year...'

'...All down to them?'

'Exactly. In fact, cryptocurrency as a concept is down to them. And, if previous behaviour is anything to go by, they're next move will involve stirring up religious fundamentalism. Moreso than they've done already. It's a playbook as old as the ages. That and fear of the other. Racism. Xenophobia. Homophobia. Misogyny. The usual trappings of political oppression. Tools of domination. They will rank it up a notch now. If they weren't so conspicuous, they might even be smart. But, as the great Gnostic infiltrator, Sun Tzu said, *In the midst of chaos, there is also opportunity.*' Then, Nkechi's expression turned sombre. 'Still, though, never take them for granted. They've tried to kill you once and they will again.'

'Nice,' Ary said.

'More reason to go home,' Jordan added.

'Conspiracy theories will also be dialled-up a notch,' Nkechi continued. 'You will hear rumours about fifth columnists, devil worship – always a firm favourite – underground terrorist cells and, when the time is right, an extra-terrestrial visitation of some sort. Maybe even an invasion.'

'Oooo! Cool,' Ary said.

'Not really. It's lies. To foment unrest. Create obstacles so we Gnostics can't finish our mission.'

'So, I'm Gnostic now?' Ary asked.

'You always were. You just didn't know it. Jordan too. In the scheme of all that is, has gone before and will be, you two are probably the most important people in the history of this planet.'

'Oooo! Cool,' Ary said again. 'No, supermax cool.'

Jordan remained quiet, stood staring into space.

'Are you doing that?' Ary asked Sandhya. 'Have you, like, switched him off or something?'

'No. That's all him. My thinking is the penny has finally dropped. I don't reckon he's happy about it. But it has dropped.'

For the next couple of hours, they sat at their table, drank tea and cold drinks, watched as a thunderstorm shattered the bustle down in the streets and talked about what the future might hold when the rain abated. The Gnostics reaffirmed that something major was coming. They called it *The Fall* – and the *Rise of Aquarius*. Ary knew the terminology well. Pluto entering Aquarius had been high on her list of things to happen before interdimensional beings took over the world. She'd just misinterpreted the data. As in the interdimensional beings part of the equation. Bog-standard humans were behind it all. People with the power to play with other people as if extras in the cheap, shitty reality show of existence. *So much for fucking freewill, eh?* The two women also used the *The Fall* to describe a comet impact that wiped out the great civilisation thirteen-thousand years ago. They spoke of three regions: Atlantis, Lemuria, and Arcadia. The first two, lost Pacific and European lands. The last as a coverall title for the civilisation that encompassed the whole world.

They also told Ary and Jordan to delay their trip to China for a few days:

Take a break.

See the sights.

Throughout, apart from an occasional grunt of acknowledgement, Jordan Burke remained quiet. And did so through the following day, when they took a joint trip, with the two women, to the main Angkor Wat complex, and also the day after that, when they took another trip, again with the Gnostics in tow, to see the waterfalls at Phnom Kulen National Park. He did stay, though, following along like an abandoned kitten. He seemed anxious and, at the same time, keen to hold their company. As for the Gnostics, they were Dalai Lama calm. Pointing at things. Marvelling at the splendour of ancient Khmer architecture. For people on a deadline, they seemed distinctly unhurried.

The next day came with a four-hour thunderstorm, so they stayed in the hostel, watching CNN News on a small, thick-framed television in the common-area. They were alone. This backpacker hostel apparently had no backpackers. Ary assumed it was because of the two women; their skills and need to have her and Jordan Burke to themselves.

On the TV, a carousel of doom rolled from one story to another.

The world really was turning handbasket.

Uprisings had erupted in Gaza, spilling into Tel Aviv and Jerusalem. The war in Ukraine took an even more violent twist. Riots broke out in Ankara, Chechnya, Budapest, Belarus, Rio de Janeiro, London, Manchester, Dallas, Portland, Kansas City, Los Angeles, and Mumbai, with severe unrest in most of the major capitals and prominent cities, including the Cambodian capital, Phnom Penh. True to prediction, fundamentalists of all the main religions, and a fair few of what could be classed as moderates, claimed the end of days was nigh. God's retribution. Blaming everything from gay marriage to veganism and multiculturalism for the *damnation of man*. And right wing nutjobs came out from under their stones too. Not that they had ever really been under it. But here they were, spouting their bile and rhyming off lists of ethnic groups who held the downfall of humankind in their hands. Also, to prediction, cryptocurrencies soared. Then collapsed. Then soared again. And, on the Friday following *Crash Monday*, the online editions of a raft of tabloids around the world carried frontpage articles on *strange lights seen over five continents* and *close encounters* and reports of an alien spaceship crashing in the Australian outback.

It was super weird to witness the very things the two women had predicted coming to pass. Ary asked them if they were clairvoyant. They said they weren't. That their prognoses came, in the most, by way of statistics.

Over millennia, they and their Gnostic predecessors had studied Aryan actions to the point they became proficient at predicting their next moves.

Sandhya said, 'Greed crazes the mind. Power destroys it. Simple, emotional reactions which, in turn, make forecasting human behaviour a process of merely mapping trends.'

Nkechi confirmed this with examples of the most narcissistic, socio-psychopathic and manipulated humans of all time: Nero, Caligula, Adolf Hitler, Torquemada, Qin Shi Huang, Tamerlane the Great, King John of England, Attila the Hun, Pol Pot, and all the other arseholes of the world, current and historical. They took the bait, swallowed the pill, and went about their escapades of death and destruction completely oblivious to the Caucus who were puppeteering their strings.

They wanted power.

And they were given it. As long as they did so to the Aryan grand scheme.

Otherwise, they were off-ed, and another was found to replace them.

It was playing out again. Only ramped up by X-to-the-Nth.

Midpoint in a CNN News pundit's views on the implications of the crash for global unity, Nkechi turned to Ary and said, 'You should make your trip to your mother's village tomorrow. Take Jordan with you. Go in the morning. Early. You will know the way.'

Ary didn't reply to that, returned to the programme and watched Jordan's expressions swirl in a mishmash of alarm, dismay, and resignation. He was getting there. Slowly. The dominoes were falling and he appeared lost, set adrift on a sea of doubt and fear. She felt somewhat responsible for his swings. Vowed to be less judgemental, and more caring. *Yeah, as if that would ever happen.* She did, however, make an internal promise to be more tolerant. He was a nice bloke. Stiff as a board but likeable. He deserved answers too and, if what Nkechi and Sandhya had said about their family links were true, he would get them, tomorrow morning, at the village her mother left many years before.

Rain returned that evening. A cascade. And Ary spent another sleepless night listening to the clatter on the roof and the thoughts tumbling through her brain.

If the village was still there, how would she feel when confronted with her mother's painful past. Would it look the same as it did in her mother's memory? Would she know if it didn't?

She expected a vision.

None came.

She also thought of Mateus, sent him a message:

Going out to Mteay's birthplace tomorrow
Wish me luck

He didn't reply and, checking first thing in the morning, still no answer.

She felt its loss.

She ate breakfast alone on the terrace. No Gnostics this time. Jordan arrived. They discussed how to get out to the village, Jordan saying little and Ary advising that they *just wing-it*. He seemed happy to go along. They hired a tuk-tuk, with a smiling driver called Sok Phon, who drove them out to Srah Srang and gave Ary his mobile number for booking their return journey. The rain had stopped and, as if in deliberate antithesis to the night of torrents, the early sun blazed so brightly her sunglasses strained to filter its intensity. The air smelled of rain-swept grass and drying earth, interspersed with the aroma of spices coming from the numerous small cafés and produce vendors flanking the northern embankment of the Srah Srang Reservoir. Sok Phon dropped them off alongside one of the stalls, where they bought and drank coconut water before heading out to the countryside, purchasing an additional carton each for the journey. The girl behind the counter smiled. Everyone smiled around here. Everyone smiled in Siem Reap. Ary got the opinion that, if her mother's childhood hadn't been so traumatic, she might smile more often too.

With the coconut water secured in their respective backpacks and following the course of the northern end of the reservoir, they headed out along a tarmacked road until they reached a side road, veering to the left and what, to western eyes, might seem little more than a soggy dirt track but Ary knew to be the main road north to a place marked on her map app as Rohal Village. The green scent of foliage filled her senses with longing.

The puddle strewn boggy track evoking memories of both happier and horrific times. Not her memories. Mteay's. No doubt planted in her mind by Nkechi, or maybe the other one. Which Ary leaned into. Took in and relived as if her own.

Three-hundred metres farther, they turned right onto a similar looking dirt track. All roads looked the same around here. Overhead, a duck egg blue sky capped a vista of earthen trails cut through trees and brush, on occasion opening onto rice patties, beside which they encountered the odd house, some built on stilts, with palm-leaf roofs, thatched walls, and fresh-faced kids playing on the threshold steps or paddling in puddles by the side of the road. The kids stared. Jordan seemed in awe. His own less-than-affluent past challenged by the comparative poverty and idyllic calmness of the lives unfolding around him. She sensed conflict. His predetermined notions of what it meant to be poor and happy being called into question.

People. Living. Doing their thing.

Being here.

Ary also sensed these last few phrases had come from the Gnostics. She viewed it as a lesson. Part of her training. She wondered if Jordan was getting training too.

'A person could live here forever,' Jordan said as they rounded a bend. It was the first words of any significance he'd spoken in days. Sudden. As if he'd just been switched back on. 'It's so quiet. The Bronx is loud. Very loud. And messy. Confrontational. Not in a *punch you in the face* kinda way, but how people speak. Their body language. The way they associate with each other.'

'Yeah. London's a messy place too. Some areas can be quite dangerous.'

'Can't be that bad. I've seen *Four Weddings and a Funeral*.'

'Oh, fuck off. Love the film, but it's so wide of the mark from the *real* London it might as well be a different place. London is inner-city. It's concrete estates, teeny tiny flats, and walls so thin you can hear next door taking a piss while you're eating your dinner at the kitchen table. It's dirty. Smelly. Rough. And I love it. Apparently, nearly a hundred languages are spoken in London. It's a melting pot. Like New York, I assume?'

'Yes. And I love that too. You have to see it sometime.'

'Likewise. You'll have to do London. I'll show you where I grew up. Introduce you to my mother.'

'I would like that.'

'So, are you good, now? Back with us n'all?'

'What do you mean?'

'Nothing. You've just been out of it a bit.'

'I was processing.'

'Processing?'

'Yes. There's a lot to work with. Big changes.'

'And that took you days to process?'

'Yes. Why?'

'No reason, but there was a time there – maybe yesterday – when I thought the mothership would come to beam you up.'

'I don't know what you mean.' He looked confused.

'Never mind.'

'So, how far now?'

'I don't really know. I guess we just keep going until I feel like we're there.'

They walked for another forty minutes. Ary led them through a wooded area thick with rubber, papaya, and milk fruit trees, arriving at a palm grove and a village of stilt-houses she recognised, from visions, as her mother's former home. A breeze blew. The trees swaying like dancers. Grass and coarse dirt covered the ground between the tall trunks, and the grove itself was so densely packed it was difficult to see through. There were rocks. Big, grey ones. Beyond the grove, far in the distance, Ta Prohm temple popped-up like a page from a child's storybook. A patch of grass-covered land looked out of place amid the trees.

Without a word, Jordan walked to the patch and stood there, staring at the ground as if reliving a memory. The village hived with activity. As much as anywhere in Cambodia *hived* with anything. Life seemed more serene here than in the West. Ary watched the villagers go about their tasks. Some were laying leaves and small fruits over wide metal platters. Others stewed a soupy concoction in a large metal pan atop a clay-built fire pit. Wafts of steam and smoke rose in clouds. A sugary aroma filled the air and her nostrils. As the villagers worked, they also watched. The children at play, eyeing Ary and Jordan as if an invading army of two, here to take away their calm and contentment.

She expected a vision.

Again, none came.

What came instead was Jordan saying, 'This is where he died.'

'Who? Your grandfather?'

'Yes. He died right here. By this tree. Where the trunk is scorched.'

'How do you know for sure? It's totally overgrown.'

'I know. I feel it. This was where it happened.' He reached his phone from his pocket and took photos of the area. 'For my mother. She never knew him. It will make her happy to know what happened and see where he passed.'

With his actions, Ary took out her own phone and called her mother. It was after midnight in London, but Mteay always answered when Ary phoned. Since Baba died, she slept little. When her mother answered, Ary told her to expect a video call in a minute or so and hung up, before making another video call, whereby a bleary eyed Mteay appeared on the screen.

'It's nice to see you,' she said. 'Are you okay?'

'Good. Better than good. I have something to show you.' Flipping the camera perspective to face away, Ary took a slow scan of the area. When she flipped the camera back, she saw her mother was crying. 'I'm at your village,' Ary said. 'I got here.'

Her mother spoke. 'You're at the grove. Where the American soldier died.'

'Yes. I'm here with his grandson.' She snatched shot of Jordan, who appeared lost in thought.

'How?'

'It's a long story. Let's just say it's been an interesting journey. I met Baba's sister. I will tell you everything when I get more time.'

'Sopheak?'

'No. I haven't found him yet. But I am looking. It's why I came out here today. If they can understand English, I will ask the villagers. You were right, I should've learned to speak better Khmer. Any Khmer, actually. Anyway, I'll do my best. See what I can find out. You never know...'

They were interrupted. A man with grey, almost white hair, standing halfway down the steps of the nearest stilt-house, was shouting at her. He seemed agitated, yelling something in Khmer and then English, 'Private property. No tourism.'

Ary approached him, went to the bottom step. 'I'm sorry. My mother comes from this village. She was born here. Maybe you know her?' She held up her phone with the screen facing the irate gentleman. He looked familiar.

'Go away,' he yelled again, before his expression changed. Staring at the phone, his face showed alarm and confusion. For many seconds, he stared without saying a word. Then, as if falling from his lips, one word emerged... in the form of a question... a name:

'Daeny?'

Ary spent the next couple of hours with the man – Sopheak – Mteay's bother – at his house, chatting about – among other things – 1975, when the Khmer Rouge took him away. For as long as her battery held out, she kept the video link open, so Mteay and Sopheak could spend a while, face to face, sobbing, weeping, making up for their separation. It seemed as if everything had happened at exactly the right time, and Ary knew full well it wasn't by coincidence. Nothing was, these days. In this case, however, she didn't resent the Gnostics placing the impulse.

Sopheak revealed the events following his disappearance.

The Khmer Rouge had press-ganged him into service. A teenage soldier. He fought in the war with Vietnam. Got injured. Like Baba. A shot to the chest, and Ary couldn't help but think of the similarity. Maybe the same war. Bullets whirling. Turmoil. Terror. Fear. A thudding impact. Knocked back. Bleeding into the dirt. Both bound in an unknown commonality.

A voice in her head agreed.

The words: *synchronicity* and *Balance* came to mind.

Sopheak spoke of how he spent many years in Kampot. More *synchronicity*. How, after a lucky break and a job in marketing, he saved up enough to reclaim their house and plot, returned home and carried on under the impression he was the only one in his family still alive. His smiled as he spoke, even through the tears, until the phone battery finally gave its warning and Ary promised to bring Sopheak to London. They talked for another while before her uncle headed out to work in the rice patties, Ary feigning that she had come to Southeast Asia to track down family, suspecting that her real motive would sound too out-there at this early stage of their relationship. He hugged her as he left. Ary joined Jordan who, for the time she'd been away, had stayed by the tree in the grove. She found him scrapping in the dirt with his boot.

'Did it go well?' he asked.

'Very weepy. Including me.'

'So, there is a heart in there after all.'

'Bite me. How are you getting on out here? Has anything plucked a memory? A feeling or something?'

'I don't have those. Seems you're the only one who gets visions.'

'Shame. It helps.'

'I'm okay as I am. I've gotten used to Sandhya poking around in my brain but I'm glad she's not sending me off on journeys into Loopaloopaland.'

'And that's how you think of it?'

'Yes. Totally. This whole thing is Loopaloopaland. I accept it. But it's weird.'

'Ah well, at least you're getting there.'

'Maybe.'

'No, I think you are. Soon you'll be getting visions like me...' A sudden swirl of confusion hit Ary like a punch in the head. It steadied. Solidified. Amid a hazy glittering mist, she saw the soldier, Jordan's grandfather, sitting by the palm tree, his hut aflame, gusts blowing cinders, ash, and pieces of burning bamboo into the air to merge with the glitter-mist. The blaze flared white. Heat seared her face. She was behind a rock. Ammunition exploding inside the burning hut. Bullets whirling, squealing, punching holes and stripping bark. The soldier was singing. As he burst into flame. The palm tree at his back went with him, followed by the grove. As suddenly as it came, the vision disappeared.

When she came too, Jordan was staring.

'I've just had another one,' she said. 'I saw your grandfather.'

After a long pause, all Jordan asked was, 'Did he suffer?'

'I don't think so. It was very quick.' She placed a hand on his shoulder. 'And, one thing I now know for certain is we are definitely linked.'

'It would seem so,' Jordan replied, as Ary witnessed his last doubts wither.

They walked back to Srah Srang and, apart from Ary's occasional utterance of: *this way* and *almost there*, they didn't talk much. Ary called Sok Phon the tuk-tuk bloke. When they reached the reservoir, he was already there, waiting at the same spot he had dropped them off. He drove back to the hostel, where they went to their respective rooms, arranging to and meeting later in the terrace café for dinner.

The two Gnostic women were there. The streets below the terrace devoid of people and traffic that Ary assumed might have something to do with the trouble in Phnom Penh. Or maybe the Gnostics.

Ary asked them about *synchronicity* and *Balance*.

Nkechi, with Sandhya nodding alongside, told her – told them both – of the *connectedness of existence*. How everything, down to the smallest parcel of energy, smaller even than a photon, was a dot of potential in an ocean of probability.

'Indeed,' Jordan said. 'Waves, particles, matter... it's basic quantum mechanics. I'm just not sure how it pertains to synchronicity, though.'

'The universe is playing out exactly as it intends to,' Nkechi continued. 'There is purpose to everything.'

Jordan rolled his eyes.

'Really, after all you've been shown, you still act with derision?'

He looked like a schoolboy chastised.

'There is purpose to everything,' Nkechi repeated. 'Nothing is by chance. Even this latest global crisis and the machinations of the Aryans.

The universe adapts and realigns, ensuring it keeps on track to its final end. And restart. End… and restart. *Synchronicity* is nothing more than evidence that an event or events are in line with that purpose. The rest readjusts.'

'I kinda get it,' Ary said, 'but, apart from the blah-blah-yackity-smackity particles and matter stuff, what does it mean?'

'It means that you, Jordan, his grandfather, his mother, your mother, her family, your father's family, all of it, from London and the Bronx in New York to a tiny little unobtrusive village north of Srah Srang, Cambodia, are all doing what you should, when you should, and how you should. It's as simple as that.'

'And, what's this big end you speak of?' Jordan asked.

'*The Cosmic Cycle.*'

'The what?'

'You are a physicist. You should know the concept: a universe is born, the Big Bang, it expands, grows, galaxies, stars, solar systems, planets, life, intelligence, it all follows, and then – with the aid of *dark matter* – it reaches *critical density* and the *Big Crunch*. The universe folds in on itself. All the way down to a super dense pinpoint of potential and… *Blamo!* – I love that word – another Big Bang, followed by expansion, another Big Crunch, and so on, so forth, on it goes into infinity.'

He scoffed again. 'That's conjecture. What about *dark energy*?'

'You know as well as I do, it only appeared six billion years ago and began driving the universe apart. Before which, gravity put the brakes on expansion. But, like all energy, it is wholly dependent on that which generates it.'

'And what's that?'

'The universe, of course.'

'So, you are postulating that the universe is conscious?'

'In a way, yes. And also, no.'

'Yes? And no?'

Nkechi nodded.

'Why is everything always so damned cryptic with you guys. You never give a straight answer.'

'Some things don't have straight answers. It's the beauty of the universe. Like Heisenberg's observations of *uncertainty*. Or *Quantum Entanglement.*'

'Well, everything you say has no founding in proof. Or at least not unambiguous proof.'

'Doesn't it?' Sandhya chipped in. looking uncharacteristically peeved by his rudeness. 'Would you stake your education and reputation on that? You, the person who hosts *The Kitchen Sink Magazine*? A journal dedicated to uncovering theories the science-world is slow to accept?'

He said nothing.

'Thought not. And, do you know why? Because, deep down you suspect – no, I'll go one further... you *fully accept* that we are right. We can't be anything else. It is the way of things and everything we – *you* – are undertaking right now has one single purpose: to ensure the universe unfolds exactly as it intends too. Without tampering. Or having to make adjustments because a power-hungry group of Earth humans see fit to spend thousands of years perverting the natural course of existence.' She paused and, with a softer tone, said, 'Look, I know it's hard for someone like you to accept this version of reality. But, I'm afraid my good friend, you have no choice. You can either roll with it, or get rolled over. The future depends on it. We are already decades behind. Pluto into Aquarius was supposed to cement the new age into place, not instigate it. But it is where we are. Our job – *your job* – is to make sure it happens.'

'By lighting up the symbols,' Ary said.

'Yes,' Nkechi replied. 'Thanks to you, the network is alive and almost linked. Tomorrow is a full moon. Coupled with the geomagnetic upsurge of Mercury Max, the conditions will be perfect to reconnect the grid.'

'That explains these last few days hanging around then.'

'Yes. We couldn't have you moving too quickly and encountering obstacles. And, anyway, you were safer here with us. But the time is now. In China, you will fix the final junction. It'll be easy.'

'Why don't you two do it? You're the ones with all the mind tricks.'

'We can't. We don't have the necessary... what could you call it?' Nkechi addressed her Gnostic colleague.

'*Psychic acumen.*'

'Exactly. We don't have the necessary psychic acumen. We might have skills, but we're not attuned. You *are* attuned. To the planet. To existence. You are *Star Children*.'

'I've heard of those,' Ary said. 'I did a blog on it last year. Fascinating stuff.' She sat up straighter.

'We know. We read it.'

Ary looked across at Jordan, 'Well, fuck me sideways, whatcha know, I'm a bloody Star Child.'

'Yes, you are,' Sandhya said. 'And we have a confession to make. Your visions weren't all down to us. Most of it you did yourself. We just guided. *Nudged* you the right way.'

'So, why did you say otherwise?'

'Ease of acceptance,' Nkechi said. 'We thought you would handle it better if we drip-fed the truth instead of pushing too fast.'

'Makes sense,' Ary agreed. 'I can be a bolshy bastard at times. I know that.'

'What the hell are Star Children?' Jordan butted in.

'Jeez, mate. Don't you know anything? They're the next evolution of humans...'

'Or, more correctly,' Sandhya interrupted, 'the *stalled* next evolution of humans.'

'Stalled?' Ary asked.

'By the Aryans.'

'But it didn't work, right?'

'It did. For quite a few millennia. But recent astronomical trends have switched those parts of the human genome back on. And you are both participants in that reawakening.'

'Cool. Always knew I was special,' Ary said with a laugh, before turning again to Jordan, 'which makes us – me and you – the next evolution of humankind. Empathy. Generosity. Intuition. Star Children, mate. We are goddamned fucking Star Children.'

'Never heard of them. I've more important things to think about. Like the world economy melting down.'

Ary cast him a withering look.

Jordan shrugged and mouthed, 'What?'

'Yes, Ary,' Nkechi interrupted. 'You are absolutely right. Empathy. Generosity and intuition. And, it's your intuitiveness – now joint – that gives you both an edge. You instinctively know where to find hidden things. You also have the ability to redirect energy. Like with the symbols. In your case, Ary, just by being in their vicinity. As in Newgrange and Machu Picchu. At Ta Prohm, however, it needed you both. And, while we suspect Ary might be able to locate and activate the Xianyang symbol alone, we are not sure how closely meshed you have become. By sheer damned luck or, as we like to say, *the way of the universe*, you have been thrown together. From here on, we would like you to work as one, do what is necessary at Xianyang, then it's on to Santorini.'

'Santorini? Why the hell would I go to Santorini?' Jordan asked.

'To reactivate one of the three *Core Hubs*, of course. We will take care of the one in Bimini. As for the third...'

'...Because all important things come in threes,' Ary interrupted.

'Yes, exactly. It's in Japan. An underwater monument known as Yonaguni. Still intact. Still active.'

'The blue light you saw,' Sandhya said in clarification.

'Under the guise of archaeologists, we have been working at Bimini for decades. Rebuilding. It is ready to go. Luckily, in spite of comet destruction, it remained connected to the grid. Leaking energy and doing all sorts of crazy things to the surrounding waters.'

'The Bermuda Triangle,' Ary said.

'Yes, the very same. Just like Yonaguni, which the locals call the Dragon's Triangle, at the periphery of the lost land of Lemuria. Because the network is broken there – that is until you make the connection at Xianyang – that energy has nowhere to go. So, temporal vortices occur, parallel universe incursions, rips in time and space. And, because the Bimini Core Hub is still functioning, albeit haphazardly, it doesn't require the assistance of a Star Child to be reactivated. One of us can do it. You, however, have a harder task. The complex at Santorini was destroyed by the Aryans... twice. Once before the comet impact. And again three-thousand six-hundred or so years ago, when they caused a volcanic eruption. The site was completely ruined.'

'Because it's Atlantis.' Ary said.

Jordan scoffed.

Nkechi ignored him. 'You know your stuff, Ary Long.'

'I wrote a blog on it.'

'We know. And yes, the Romans called it Atlantis. But it wasn't the total civilisation they assumed. Just a small but important part of the homogenous whole that provided Arcadia with energy. The power beneath – actually beneath – a magnificent civilisation.'

'And what exactly is it the great Gnostics want us to do when we get there?' Jordan asked.

'Lose the churlish attitude for a start,' Sandhya snapped.

'Don't be hard on him,' Nkechi said. 'He's homo sapiens. The most distrusting and difficult to teach species on the planet.'

Sandhya nodded, while shooting Jordan a disapproving stare.

He looked away.

Ary smirked.

'You need to find the entrance to a cave,' Nkechi continued. 'It won't be easy. No one has found it in millennia. Your special instincts will come in useful there. And, if the way is not too ruined, or completely demolished, it will lead you to the Core Hub complex, where you must insert this into the correct recess.' She set a ten centimetres square granite tablet, carved with the ancient symbol, on the table. It was pristine. As if recently made.

'What is it?' Ary asked.

'The ON button.'

'It looks new.'

'If by *new* you mean over twenty-thousand years old.'

'Bloody hell.' Ary reached out to touch the tablet but snapped back. It seemed alive. Electrified.

'Our ancient predecessors managed to snatch it away before the comet hit. We have kept it safe. Hidden. The world's greatest secret.'

'And the Aryans know about it?'

'Yes.'

'And they know you have it?'

'Yes.'

'And that we will have it?'

'Yes.'

'Brilliant! And, how will we know where to place it?'

'You are Star Children. Your intuition will guide you. It's as easy as that. *No problemo*, as they say.'

'Okay.'

'Okay?' Jordan snapped. 'That's all you have to say? Okay? The world is going to shit and it's just okay?'

'No need worry about the world,' Sandhya said, seemingly over her bout of pique. 'Like the universe, it will be here until it isn't.'

'That's what I'm worried about.'

'Well, don't be,' Nkechi chipped in. 'Even if humanity was wiped out tomorrow, the planet will survive. It always does. Until, as Sandhya has already explained, it doesn't.'

'And, will humanity be wiped out tomorrow?'

The two women laughed. 'No. Not tomorrow. The universe needs them. But, one day they will disappear. Everything does. Thus continues...'

'I know, I know, *The Cosmic Cycle*.'

'You got it, bro,' Sandhya said, and turned to Nkechi, 'Don't you just love all this modern speak. It has great... er...'

'...Descriptiveness?'

'Exactly descriptiveness. And simplicity. Like the universe itself.'

'Anyway, take that with you,' Nkechi said to Ary, who slipped the tablet into her pocket. Its electrical charge now muted. 'That's all for now. Let's have some tea.'

The women ordered. They drank a lot of the stuff.

Ary was partial to the odd cup, but these two knocked it back as if it was the elixir of life. And, maybe it was. These last few days, her eyes had been opened to many weird realities and, it wouldn't seem at all strange if tea turned out to be some kind of chemical key that unlocked the mysteries of existence.

She laughed at the thought. Aloud.

Both Nkechi and Sandhya smiled at her.

Before they left to deck down for the night, Nkechi told them to leave for China first thing in the morning, informing them of another Gnostic who had *nudged* Ary's uncle into taking the pieces of the symbol home from the university lab. Her aunt knew nothing of this. In fact, her uncle was unaware too. He was merely following a hunch. All Ary and Jordan had to do, apart from getting into the country in the first place – a task Ary reckoned well taken care of by the Gnostics – was get the pieces, go to the pyramid site, set the assembled symbol into the exact spot – she would know when she got there – lay hands in the same way they did when out at the temple, and then return it back to her aunt's flat where *nobody will be any the wiser*. Nkechi smiled as she told her this, said, *simples*. Actually said it. As if the task was as easy as going to the corner shop for sweets. Ary asked why they shouldn't leave the symbol in its spot. She was told the network does the rest. The symbol is only a switch of sorts. Then, Nkechi's tone turned serious. She told them to be careful. That the person who shot at them at Ta Prohm temple was still around, following them and, because she and Sandhya had somewhere else to be, they wouldn't be able to supply the same protection as before.

'And how did you do that?' Ary asked.

'Just a tweak,' Sandhya replied. 'A suggestion to ignore or forget to do certain things. But we don't like messing around in people's brains. It's a negative use of Logos.'

'You *knew* there was an assassin?'

'We suspected. And sent out a *wide nudge*. A lot of people in Siem Reap had mechanical issues that day.'

'So, that was you? When buses and cars are having a fucked-up day, it's all down to you two?'

'Us three. And, no. We're not that good. But we can make people half-hearted about performing certain tasks. We suspected the Caucus might send an assassin, so we induced, how can I say...?'

'...A lackadaisical approach to checking equipment,' Nkechi said.

'Exactly. We're not proud of all the broken-down buses and tuk-tuks, but it had to be done. And we only use the *wide nudge* in extreme circumstances. As I said, we don't like messing around in people's brains. It's a negative use of Logos. And not encouraged.'

'Except for us,' Jordan said.

'You are different. You have a job to do.'

'And being hunted by an assassin is part of that?'

'No. That's not what I said at all. What I mean is, for good or ill, people's minds should be their own. With you two, we are pointing you in a direction you were destined to travel anyway. We're just moving events along. The assassin doesn't have a purpose in all this. They are an outlier. And, this time, if something happens, we will be too far away to do anything to help you.'

'Great!' Jordan said.

'Which is why you promised to teach us how to do the mind-brain-thought-manipulation trick,' Ary said, more so as a question.

'Yes. But not yet.'

'Not yet? Some loony is running around trying to blow our bloody heads off, and you say *not yet*?'

'Yes. It's not time. And I didn't say never.'

Ary threw her hands skyward. 'Fair enough then. I s'pose we're on our own then.'

'Not on your own. You'll be watched but, if something does crop up, you will have to keep your wits about you. Be careful. Cautious. Don't take chances.'

The women handed them each a visa for entry into China, wished them both well, pledged to get in touch soon, and left, whereby, for the first time since meeting them, Ary realised they had never spoke of having rooms at the hostel, never paid a bill and, when the rest of the planet had been turned upside down with strife, the area around the hostel appeared calm, empty in most cases.

She wondered if Xianyang might be the same.

PYRAMID STREAM

Ary felt relief when the plane touched down at Xi'an Xianyang International Airport. Even before departure, without the Gnostics nudging his thoughts, Jordan Burke had morphed into *Captain Neurosis*, reacting with uncalled-for twitchiness to any loud noise, speaker announcement, and the two shaved-headed blokes carrying black sports bags who looked more like athletes than cold-blooded murderers. Whispering in her ear, he voiced his theory they were assassins, imploring her to keep an eye on them. Ary assured him she would, suspecting that any killer worth their salt would determine an airport, bristling with armed police, to be the worst of places to take a pot-shot. She told him as much. It didn't help and, although the plane was only a quarter occupied, he spent the journey from Siem Reap to Xi'an squirming in his seat, his eyes darting this way and that, like a cat weighing up the vet's thermometer.

By the time they reached the outer concourse, however, he had calmed.

Ary patted his shoulder.

He smiled.

She said, 'You're doing great. We'll be okay. Nkechi and Sandhya are watching over us. And, if not them, I'm sure they have someone looking out for us while we are here. Remember, they have skills.'

Jordan nodded.

A moment later, Ary's uncle, Qing Yuan pulled up in a white car. It bore the circular red and white logo of the East China Normal University, but had no driver this time. Only Qing Yuan and, apart from a cheery welcome and some bland chitchat about the weather, he didn't speak much as he took them to his apartment, where he immediately handed them the pieces of the tablet carrying the symbol. Ary placed them in her backpack. It was a simple as that. The whole process turned out to be as easy as buying sweets at the corner shop after all.

Throughout, Qing Yuan remained placid, uninvolved, almost robot-like.

Ary knew why and assumed Jordan did too.

She asked her uncle, looking around, 'Where is Li Xiu?'

'Beijing. A last-minute conference of the National People's Congress. They are discussing budget cuts. Closing down excavations. Including ours.' He seemed more engaged now. As if, by handing them the pieces of the tablet, the first part of a task had been completed. Relating this information was the second.

'So, there's only you?'

'Yes.'

'She's not at the excavation?'

'No.'

'Good. Now, about that. Can you take us there?'

'Of course.'

She hadn't expected the answer to come so quickly. 'And, could we go now?'

'Of course. The guards know me.'

Jordan cast Ary a sideways glance.

She returned it. '*Don't like messing around in people's brains*, my arse. Those two women are totally full of shit.'

Jordan nodded, said, 'Let's go. This cloak and dagger stuff is giving me the jeebies.'

'Me too,' Ary agreed. She turned to Qing Yuan. 'Okay then, uncle, let's do this.'

On the way there, Jordan requested an English language radio channel. Qing Yuan tuned to *CRI, China Plus*. The news was bleak. Out in the greater world, events had moved quickly. Governments toppled in Zimbabwe, Nigeria, and Brunei. Contrary to EU policy, Hungary introduced autocratic *special powers*. Other EU member states called a meeting to address the breach. In the USA, in response to federal cutbacks and presidential executive orders, former civil war states in the south were talking secession, with the mid-west up to Montana expressing interest in joining them in their New Confederate Union of America. Some northern states had approached Canada for inclusion in their federal system. A secession bill was already doing the rounds in the Californian state assembly. Needless to say, the US economy tanked. Adding extra pressure on already fractured global markets. Similar tensions had exploded in post-Brexit UK. Russia moved its remaining divisions to the Ukraine border. In the Middle East, a coalition of Sunni states declared *al-harb* on Israel. Skirmishes blew up along the disputed territories between India and Pakistan. Japan reclaimed *Sakoku*, closing off the country to the rest of the world. And the People's Republic of China reintroduced the same national strategy it had implemented during the Covid-19 pandemic, which made the ease of how Ary and Jordan had journeyed to Xianyang even more surprising. Passport control had been a breeze. The border guys hardly even checked their visas. It had been too easy.

Or not.

Again, Ary could feel Gnostic influence in everything they did.

When they reached the dig site, Qing Yuan spoke with a guard, who opened the gates to let them through. Unlike her last visit, there were no workers on site. Not that she'd noticed how many there were before anyway. The sheer magnificence of the place had commanded her whole attention. She'd felt drawn. Did so again. As if the place had cast a spell.

Qing Yuan parked close to the stepped pyramid. Jordan and Ary got out. Qing Yuan remained in the car, sitting in the driver's seat, staring into the distance.

'That's weird,' Jordan said.

'It's all fucking weird,' Ary replied.

'You're telling me.' He gazed around. 'It will take me years to get my head around the events of the last few weeks. Look, the guards aren't even looking at us. It's like we're invisible.'

'Good. Better that way. So, don't sweat it. Let's get this done and the fuck outta here, before Qing Yuan comes around, realises what's happening, and we spend the rest of our lives in a Chinese prison. I have a very delicate disposition. I wouldn't do well in a Chinese prison.'

'Me neither.'

'They might hang us.'

'Way to get me not sweating it.'

'Sorry.'

'So, what now?'

'I s'pose we put the bits in the right place. Feel anything?'

Jordan shook his head.

'Nope. Same goes for me.' She crouched, took the tablet pieces from her backpack, laid them out on the ground and arranged them into what she deemed to be the symbol pattern. 'Anything now?'

'Nope. And that's wrong.'

'What's wrong?'

'You've arranged them wrong. Look...' He was pointing at gaps in the tablet. '...There should be no spaces. Smooth. And the symbol doesn't look right.'

'What about this?' She rearranged the pattern.

'Still not right. The lines going southwest to northeast should be straight. There are gaps. And the edges are wonky.'

'You're wonky. What about now?' Another attempt.

'Still not right.'

Ary stood. 'Fuck it. You do it.'

Jordan crouched, disassembled the puzzle, laid the eighteen constituent parts in a semicircle on the ground in front of him and, with his expression fixed in concentration, began slotting the pieces into place. 'See. The upper corner goes here. The spirals should be even. And this spot right here in the centre... that should form a quasi-representation of yin and yang.'

Ary huffed.

Jordan remained stoic, focussed on the puzzle. For the next five minutes, he moved the pieces around, sized the edges, set them aside, put them back, in, out, in again. Stopped. Looked bemused. Mumbling to himself 'That doesn't look right.' Followed by, 'Ah... now I see it... the south orientated line should be *between* the bottom two triskele spirals... indicating balance. Makes sense now. How did I miss that. Must be losing my touch.'

As he worked, Ary scanned the area. This was taking too long. The guards appeared uninterested but that could change.

'Now would be good,' Ary said. 'These guys might wake up at any minute.'

'Shh!'

'Did you just fucking shush me?'

'Shh!'

Ary shushed. Jordan continued, placing and displacing parts of the symbol, in, out, sizing up, laying down again until, taking the eighteenth and final piece, he slotted it into place, creating the yin yang pattern he had mentioned earlier.

'There,' he said, looking very pleased with himself.

'Done?'

'Yes. Feel anything now?'

'No. Bugger all. Maybe we need to bring it closer to the pyramid.'

'Maybe.' Jordan lifted the tablet. It was a solid block now, as if, through the correct assembly, the parts had fused together.

'Well, that's impressive,' Jordan said, as they approached the pyramid. 'How old do they say it is?'

'Mesolithic.'

'Whoa! That's amazing.'

'It is. And surrounded by armed guards. So, let's get moving.'

'Okay. Yes. You're right. It's just, I could devote a whole issue of my magazine to this place. Which reminds me. I must call Jada.'

'Jada?'

'My sister. She looks after things when I'm away. Not that that happens much.'

'Well, it does now. So, feel anything?'

'Nopes.'

'Nah, me too. Maybe we should touch it, like the last time. Together.'

Before she had finished, Jordan had leaned down, placed the tablet on the ground and laid his right hand atop the symbol, left of centre.

'Now you,' he said, with uncharacteristic confidence.

She liked this less whingy side of him. It made a nice change.

Crouching and laying her hand alongside his, Ary braced for the flashes of blue light they'd witnessed back at Ta Prohm. None came.

'What's wrong?' Jordan asked.

'Fucked if I know.' She glanced across at the nearest guard. Checking to see if they'd been noticed yet. The guard stood there, chipping the ground with his heel. All good, so far.

'Do a vision then.'

'Do a what?'

'One of your visions. Do your thing.'

'You think I can conjure them up just like that? By thinking about it?'

'Worth a try.'

'S'pose.'

'We can do the lay hands thing again, while you meditate where it should go.'

'Meditate? What are you? Some kind of new-age guru?'

'Hardly.'

'Anyway, last time was easier. It just came. Trust the Gnostics to be awkward bastards. It's always half-instructions with them. And *your intuition will guide you* bullshit. Okay. I'll do it. Let's give it a whirl.' With both their hands on the tablet, Ary closed her eyes and tried to visualise where the symbol might fit on the pyramid. Nothing came. 'This is crap... totally loopy.'

'Everything is loopy. This whole escapade is loopy.'

'True. I suppose. Welcome to my world.'

'Just clear your mind. Breathe deeply.'

'What the actual fuck,' she said, with her eyes still closed but smirking. 'Are you my yoga instructor, now. Shut the fuck up. I'm trying to concentrate.'

She felt the now familiar skin tingle. Hairs standing on her neck and arms. A vision was coming. Blurred thoughts. Clouds and sparkles. This time she took it all in. Took control. Willing her mind to go deeper. Her sight cleared. She was standing in front of the pyramid – alone. It looked new. Clad in bright limestone. Magnificent. And utilitarian. She was herself and, at the same time, someone else. Someone with influence. Duty.

Holding a stone tablet in her hands. The symbol tablet.

When she returned to the present, she said, 'Follow me,' stood and, taking the tablet from under Jordan's hand, guided him around to the righthand corner of the pyramid, passing two indifferent guards in the process who didn't even glance their way.

Halfway along the eastern face, one metre above pavement level, a centimetre deep recess, the shape and size of the assembled tablet, had been carved into one of the pyramid blocks. It was weathered. The edges bevelled. Ary glanced around. There were guards everywhere but none of them seemed the slightest bit interested in them or what they were doing.

'Let's get this over with,' Jordan said, with another burst of uncharacteristic confidence.

Without hesitation, Ary set the tablet into the recess. They laid their hands onto the triskele at the centre and the response was instant. Needle-like tingles, followed by a burst of blue light, surging, tracking the curves and lines of the symbol, flaring between their fingers, exploding with blinding radiance, beams of electrically charged energy streaking upwards to pick out the gaps between the stone blocks of the pyramid, all the way to the top, filling the entire space of the excavation site, striking out in all directions and racing onward through the surrounding forest until faint glows danced on the horizon and blue luminescence percolated into the distance. The tablet felt cold. Icy. It pulsed. Then it blazed white. Melting into the recess, granite fusing with limestone, appearing as if tablet and cover-stone had been carved from the same rock. Inwardly, she knew the final connection had been made. She suspected Jordan knew it too. They removed their hands. The blue light disappeared, the tablet pieces separating from the limestone, falling to the ground, and the area around the pyramid appearing as uneventful as before they began.

'Fuck, that never gets old,' Ary said.

'Totally awesome.'

'And not so hard to do after all.'

'As easy as pie.'

They shook hands, and laughed.

Gunfire shattered their complacency. Rapid bursts. A second's pause. Followed by more bursts. Pause. More bursts. Bullets ricocheting off the pyramid stones, squealing as they carried on hopping and spinning across the dry ground. Out by the gate, while others rushed from all sides of the site, a group of guards were exchanging fire with a shooter nestled among the tall grass beyond the perimeter fence. Ary and Jordan jumped into the nearest excavation trench and hunkered down. The shooting continued.

With Jordan at her side, mouthing voiceless disapproval, Ary snatched a peek over the edge and saw a guard drop like a sack of stones, a crimson halo misting the air where his head used to be. Two more guards reeled, their backs bursting open like melons smashed with hammers, dropping with similar stone-sack-like efficacy as their now skull-less comrade. Those who had scurried across the site to take cover behind a wooden outbuilding, carried on the exchange, the timber walls, dirt and bushes in their vicinity bursting with tiny explosions of wood, dust and leaves, as bullets peppered the air around them. One of them, with a bloody hole gaping in the middle of her chest, slid down the outbuilding wall. A long red, somewhat artistic smear, worthy maybe of Jackson Pollack, marking the track of her descent to the ground. Another guard's head exploded, splattering bone, blood, and brains over the polished white bonnet of Qing Yuan's university staff car. The left wingmirror went next. He seemed unbothered, sitting in the driver's seat as though calmly waiting for grandma to return from picking up her pension at the local post-office.

The shooting stopped.

Ary released her breath and heard Jordan do the same.

He was trembling.

As was she, too scared to get up and terrified to stay put.

'That was meant for us,' she said.

'Yeah, you think?'

'Don't get snippy with me, Mr *Easy as Pie*.'

'Sorry. I'm not used to getting shot at.'

'Me neither.'

'I need a cigarette.'

'You really don't. It's the same thing as getting shot, only slower.'

'I know. But that's not how nicotine addiction works. You can't just switch it off.'

'Suck it up. We have bigger problems.'

They remained in the trench for several minutes before they stood up. Guards were checking the dead, attending to the injured, and warily scouting the whole site – except for the area around excavation pit where Ary and Jordan sat cowering.

'How's your uncle?' Jordan asked.

Ary looked across to Qing Yuan's car. 'He seems fine. I'm not even sure he knows anything happened. I also reckon the shooter has gone now. I don't think they expected guards with guns. We should split. The sooner we're out of here, the better I'll feel.'

Jordan nodded. He was still trembling.

Ary climbed out of the trench, helped Jordan up, nipped over to the pyramid, gathered the tablet fragments, dropped them into her backpack and led an edgy looking Jordan Burke by the hand over to the car, where they slid into the back seats.

'All finished?' Qing Yuan asked her.

'Yes.'

'Thankfully,' Jordan added.

Without instruction, Qing Yuan started the car and drove them back to his apartment where he requested the return of the tablet pieces. Ary complied. She assumed their part in the scheme to be over now. The thought prompted her to check if the other – ON switch – tablet that the Gnostics had given them the night before was still in her pocket. It was. Ready for the next task in Santorini. The thought also chilled her. The assassin would no doubt be there too.

Qing Yuan took them to the airport. The whole process from pick-up to drop-off, complete with deadly gun battle, taking no more than a few hours. Neither Ary nor Jordan questioned this, and Ary was pretty sure her uncle would have no recollection of the happenings of the day either. There would also be no repercussions. The Gnostics would see to that and protect him.

Dropping them at Departures, Qing Yuan drove away.

Ary vowed to call later. She suspected he didn't take it in.

Jordan's phone buzzed. A text from *No Caller ID*.

He read it and said, 'There are tickets waiting for us at the Sky China desk. Athens via Bangkok and Dubai. We also have a hotel booked in our names when we get there. The message says to *take tomorrow for yourselves. Relax*. And apparently, in the total understatement of the year, we've *earned it*.'

Ary's phone buzzed too. A message from Mateus:

Studio finished – but label in massive diffs
Bad time to shift countries
Wish you were here – hard to go through alone (sad face emoji)

Her heart broke. Here she was living her conspiracy theory dreams but, although very real, it also seemed illusory, and scary. She longed for easier days, parrying with Mateus over whether aliens had visited the Earth in antiquity, or if interdimensional beings were the core instigators of world history. Back then – just a handful of weeks ago – *proof*, as they saw it, had in truth been little more than conjecture. More aspiration than evidence.

Now, she had that proof. Categorical confirmation that there was a new – *old* world order. A mind-blowing revelation. She just didn't have her confidante and best friend to share it with.

She replied with a simple:

Will be in touch soon (2 heart emojis)

For all she knew, the Aryans were monitoring her messages. The Gnostics said their abilities were limited but, these days, any old geek could hack a mobile phone. For now, it was better to go dark. She would leave giving Mateus a proper answer for a few days. Get the job done. Head back home, and physically be there to help him through his troubles. On a television in the pre-departure area, a news report – in English – stressed caution when taking non-necessary international travel. Only now did Ary notice the near empty airport. At most check-in desks, a single attendant dealt with only a handful of passengers. The rest were shuttered. There were no queues. No jostling or agitated people dashing for flights. No families spread out across the common areas. No kids begging attention, or weary parents corralling them onto seats in the hope of snatching a moment's peace before the inevitable turmoil of seven hours aboard a plane with a squad of unruly progeny.

The place was a graveyard.

Jordan picked up the tickets. They checked-in, waited, boarded, and took off for Athens, their plane empty bar themselves and the air crew, and seeming the only flight without departure issues. Ary settled back. Jordan read newspaper headlines on his phone.

His expression didn't look good.

'FOR FANDEN!'

Lena Hansen limped back to the all-terrain, offroad 4x4 she had stolen in Siem Reap, which had also proved its worth for the long drive up through Vietnam, and for her night-time fording of the Red River into China without being detected. Blood saturated her cargo-pants. The wound in her right thigh, although just a graze, had cut deeper than she'd like. Delving hastily into her backpack, she took out her field service first aid kit, sliced her right trouser-leg with a scalpel, disinfected and stitched the three-centimetre-long laceration, and changed into a fresh pair of cargo-pants. She shrieked, shouted out, 'For fanden!' and shrieked again. Over and over. She punched the dashboard until her knuckles bled. She head-butted the steering wheel. Shrieking. Punching. Shrieking. Headbutting. Flailing around in the driver's seat of the stolen car. Willing the tiny cramped space to do her injury. With the scalpel, she sliced the word *BEDRE* three times into the skin below her breasts. The scabs of her previous three carvings cracking open in the process. She sucked in the pain. Pain was good. Pain was punishment. And ecstasy. Redemption. A lesson to do *better*.

Be *better*.

Once again, she had failed. Totally miscalculating the number and proficiency of the guards at the pyramid site. She didn't even get close to taking out the two objectives. She should have waited until they left, got ahead of them, found a position by the side of the road, and popped three through the windscreen while they were on their way back to Xianyang. That would have been the sensible approach. One she had used often. She had no idea why she had chosen such an open, well-defended place to make the play. The thought just came to her. Proving its worth by insisting; at the pyramid site, they would be vulnerable, slow, unwary, and feeling protected. An easy hit. Simple, clean, and absolute. But it wasn't. It was a major fuck-up. Her employers would disapprove, might take measures, remove her from the equation and set another operative to the task.

A more able one. *Better*.

She shrieked, punched the dashboard, turned the assignment phone back on, and waited for the inevitable correspondence which would decide her future. Instantly, the phone beeped and buzzed. A message came up on the app:

CONTRACT DISCONTINUED

Again, the message was clear.

RIDERS ON THE STORMS

The first earthquake struck at 02.35 on the morning of Monday 5th June 2023. The accompanying destruction and tsunami slamming into the Tōhoku region of East Japan with almost carbon-copy similarity to the one that devastated the same region in March 2011. The second earthquake came three hours later. Not an aftershock, but another magnitude nine, doing further devastation to a region wracked by the destruction of coastal towns and villages. The death toll crossed forty thousand.

Tropical Cyclone Lynsey blossomed from a minor storm in the Caribbean Sea. Hurricane Emma-23, named because of its similarity to one in 2008, grew out of low pressure forming close to Newfoundland. On Monday 5th June 2023, like destructive old friends, they met over the Mid-Atlantic Ridge, combined intensities and headed westwards, making landfall on the North American Coast at the Outer Banks, North Carolina. The neighbouring states of Virginia and South Carolina were also ravaged, as was Georgia when it headed south to finally peter out in the northerly half of Florida.

On December 10th 1856, a powerful earthquake struck Rhodes and Crete and, with the subsequent tsunami, claimed the lives of five hundred and thirty-eight people, injuring six hundred and thirty-eight, and destroying nearly seventeen thousand homes. The earthquake and resulting tsunami on Monday 5th June 2023 were more devastating by a factor of ten.

In Asia, on the same day, a batch of freak tornados took the lives of over a hundred people in Hyderabad, India – seventy-three in Sing Buri – nearly fifty in Muscat, Oman – and seventy-nine and counting in southern Syria.

Apart from a few tremors, Santorini was untouched by the Rhodes earthquake and, although having generated there, apart from a few strong winds, the Bimini region of the Bahamas was unaffected by Hurricane Lynsey-Emma-23. Yonaguni also escaped major damage from the Japanese quake. To Ary's reckoning and based on what the Gnostics had told them about Aryan capabilities, it appeared as if those areas had been targeted for destruction but the attempts failed. The same went for the tornados, which looked suspiciously like they had been planned to hit Bangkok and Dubai, their two short stopovers from Xi'an Xianyang to Athens, and the others to disrupt the onward course of their journey.

The thought terrified her.

Jordan looked visibly shaken by the news, and expressed as much. He also indicated his sadness at the climbing death counts, and his revulsion that anyone would kill so many to attack just two people.

Ary agreed, but without adding, 'That's the way of the world, bruv. Humans can be sick, murdering bastards.' She didn't think it necessary to further agitate his delicate emotional state.

She held his hand during all three flights. As much for herself as for Jordan. She wished Mateus was here. When facing a crazy-arsed killer, he might be as useful as a knitted condom, but she did like him being around. He calmed her. For now, Jordan would have to do. Jittery, nervous, unable to accept reality until it smacked him up the side of the head Jordan, who she also reckoned might have finally come to terms with what was happening to them both, and why they were so important.

Arriving in Athens, they took a taxi to the hotel where, having collected the keys from reception, Ary went straight to her room and slumped into bed. It was still daylight, but the trails and travels of the past day or so had her dead beat and, despite the fat bluebottle relentlessly banging against the window – reminding her of a previous bluebottle, the one in her bedroom in London; back when life was simpler, more about revealing secret, nefarious organisations than being hunted by them – she passed out, waking at dawn the next morning to her phone buzzing and a dream where Nkechi and Sandhya were ordering her to get up.

They seemed determined, albeit in the dream.

A message on her phone said:

Get up
Time to go

So much for having a time to herself.

Jordan arrived at her door moments later. He'd had the same message – and dream.

The situation felt urgent. Core of one's soul urgent. A gut feeling, like when sensing a mother's sorrow... or a father's death.

JUNE 6th

The Caucus Consigliere bowed once and left the meeting chamber, closing the door behind him. Gildermere crossed the room and sat in his designated, blue velvet armchair.

'Do you always have to be so tardy?' Rothbauer snapped.

'Are your frustrations meant for me,' Gildermere replied, 'or for the failings of your designated operative? I've been informed that they missed their targets... twice. How is that possible? I thought you hired only the best. Maybe if your son was older, he could displace you and do a better job. He couldn't do any worse.'

Rothbauer gritted his teeth. 'At least I have a son. Your line has stalled. Maybe not a bad thing either. There would be less bickering with the rest of us.'

'My line is fine. All in good time. What has stalled is your ability to accomplish the simple task of killing a couple of insignificant plebians.'

'It's a trifle,' Rothbauer replied, exhibiting strained reserve. 'Believe me, the next attempt will be successful.'

'Well, that's good then,' Gildermere replied. 'As long as you have a handle on it. At least the other aspects of the scheme are going well. The financial meltdown. Nice. Effective. It's working as sweetly as the one I instigated in 2008. Then again, the best ideas are always worth copying. And how did the seismic attack go? The hurricanes? Your big backup strategies?'

Rothbauer ignored him, instead addressing the whole room with, 'It's all going as planned, fellow members. The Gnostics have only days left to reactivate the *Core Hubs*. I doubt they'll succeed.'

'Is this before or after they successfully linked the global network?' Gildermere asked with as smirk. 'By my reckoning, all they have to do now is turn it on. They are that close.'

'But out of time.'

'It doesn't take long to flick a switch.'

'You are beginning to annoy me,' Rothbauer snapped. 'Why do you have to be so obtuse.'

'It's my nature. A sign of genius. If it wasn't for my ingenuity, half of your schemes over the last four decades would've come to nothing. Every recession was down to me. The Gulf War. Iraq. Afghanistan. Ukraine. Earthquakes and tsunamis – all down to me. While you lot sat around here like Arthur's knights, pontificating and dreaming about the world you might inherit when the Gnostic aspirations fail, I was getting on with business. I'm sorry to say it, but I am the actual link that holds our little group together. While you talk – I *do*. Who was it that saw the potential in the SARS virus, and set about coaxing infected animals out of the wild? Who was it that, among other triumphs, *nudged* a US Democratic president to revoke the Glass-Steagall Act? And nudged a communist party to embrace the neoliberal economy? Me. That's who. Gildermere. The family that has been controlling the markets since the Knights Templar had the bright idea to issue money-drafts to pilgrims. Gildermere invented coins. Gildermere invented banks, turned simple agrarian farmers into soulless, money-grubbing traders. The whole world order is down to us. You should be grateful for it.'

'And I suppose the rest of us have done nothing,' Rothbauer said to the room.

The other members nodded, some casting daggers at Gildermere, he assumed for bringing discord to the group.

'No. I didn't say that,' Gildermere replied. 'You have done much. But only as a result of my new ideas.'

'There are no new ideas. Look around. Bookcases filled to bursting with more than twenty thousand years of collective Logos.'

'But not the right *Logos*.'

'No. But that will be ours too... soon enough.'

Again, the others nodded in agreement with Rothbauer, but they also appeared uncertain. An almost negligible tone of disquiet that they probably didn't even notice themselves but Gildermere picked up on.

Rothbauer had failed to deliver. More than once.

Something Gildermere could and would exploit.

While the Caucus sat in their subterranean meeting chamber plotting their continued world dominance, at the New York headquarters of the United Nations, an emergency conference of member states – their delegates having flown in the night before – were animatedly discussing recent events, with three distinct sessions planned throughout the day:

The Climate Emergency; to discuss new data claiming Arctic ice shrinkage of 35% and Antarctic shrinkage of 27%. Also on the agenda: the Atlantic hurricane, the Asian tornados, the earthquakes in the Mediterranean and off the coast of Japan, and the sharp increase of temperature in the Northern Hemisphere seeing a heatwave in Siberia and readings in excess of 51C in Washington State and British Columbia – higher even than the unprecedented heat dome of 2021.

The Market Crash; to discuss the dire state of world finances, bailout packages, and hopefully gain some level of consensus to halt mass sell-offs and the downward spiral of the global economic sector.

Unrest; to find ways to bring stability to those parts of the world seeing a rise in violence and insurrection. Through internal measures, most nation states were managing to keep such unrest to local areas. But worrying trends were emerging in assumed stable economies. Not least the USA, with the separatist aspirations of the proposed New Confederate Union of America. The EU also had difficulties, Hungary's autocratic *special powers* being of greatest concern. Russia and Ukraine were still at war. Brazil, Ecuador, and Nicaragua were in open rebellion. As were a number of sub-Saharan countries. North Korea was on the verge of collapse, threatening war with the south. And, across the world, disorder and chaos reigned supreme.

To the logical, technical and scientific mind of the UN Secretary General, if recent events were an experiment, all data would point to deliberate actions. A situation he reckoned to be as ridiculous as it sounded. And yet, the notion still niggled.

How could so much go so bad so quickly?

Weather and climate catastrophes, plunging markets, violence and war. His Roman Catholic faith spoke of a Judgement Day. The Book of Revelations, although cryptic, had chronicled suchlike events as the final outcome for a sinful humankind.

Was this truly it? The End of Days?

Addressing the first session and delivering his duties under the directive to inform the body of *any matter which may threaten the maintenance of international peace and security*, he gave a brief, one hour precis of the state of the world at present. Bickering and allegations peppered the speech. Lines were drawn. Wars officially declared. A third of the chamber walked out, including the Russian Federation, North Korea, Belarus, Hungary, Brazil, the Philippines, Turkey, India, Pakistan, Nigeria, Uganda, Iran, the United Arab Emirates, Saudi Arabia, many others, and a member of the US delegation claiming his own colleagues no longer represented his home state of Texas.

Japan didn't attend.

STRANGER THAN PARADISE

The Athens dawn was breath-taking; clear blue skies streaked with wisps of cotton-white cloud, backdropped by an orange sun, and the ancient pillars of the Acropolis flooded with radiant yellow and deep deep amber. The sense of history was palpable. The quiet city streets evoking the age and longevity of their existence. Even the glass and stone modern block of Ary and Jordan's hotel seemed to fit the venerable metropolis.

In a text to Jordan, the Gnostics instructed them to check out.

A taxi arrived, took them to a secluded airport outside the city, where a deluxe private jet flew them the forty-five-minute journey south to Thira Airport on Santorini.

For the whole way there, apart from a few cursory instructions on where to sit, seatbelts and the like, nobody spoke to either of them. Not even the taxi driver in Athens and, disembarking, except for the small tablet with the symbol – which the two cabin-crew seemed to know about – they were told to leave their backpacks at the airport office, after which they were brought to a rainbow-coloured helicopter, with *GROUP TOURS FROM 595€* written on the side and a single occupant, the pilot, who flew them out to Nea Kameni, an island at the centre of the Santorini caldera. Amid a cloud of dust, the pilot dropped them down atop the highest point on the island, Tholos Naftilos, formed when, around three thousand six hundred years before present, the Thera eruption secured the demise of the Minoan civilisation.

Ary had studied it well, had been fascinated by the myth of the Minotaur.

If it was myth. At one time, her theory had been pan-dimensional being.

To her, but now knowing otherwise, Santorini was one of the main portals for crossing dimensions. Her viewpoint had changed. Apparently, it was some kind of mega-functioning electricity generator or something. And, despite all they had done, Jordan – even after everything they had encountered – still professed his suspicion of this theory.

Sometimes he *got it*. Other times he didn't. He was a bit fucked up.

Ary put him right with three words: *big blue lights*.

Jordan said, 'Okay. Okay. Science bad... malark-hooey good.'

Ary didn't dignify that with an answer. He would come to it on his own.

When they exited, in another eruption of dust, the pilot took the helicopter up and headed back towards the main island. Just a couple of hours into morning, it was already hot atop the ash strewn landscape, and open, with no shade, like standing on the Moon... but with heat-lamps.

Ary asked, 'So, what do we do now?'

'Dunno. Same as always, I s'pose.'

'Feel anything.'

'Nada. You?'

'Not a fucking jot. We're supposed to look for a cave.'

Jordan walked to the edge of the flat peak and looked over the edge. 'Maybe it's down there somewhere. At sea level.'

'Could be. But why drop us off up here?'

'Couldn't land the chopper. This is the flattest, highest part of the island.'

'Duh! Fuck sake! I'm thick as a ditch. Of course that's why.' She joined him at the edge. 'There's a path going down.'

'This place gets millions of tourists every year. It's probably for them. But where are they all.'

'Too early in the day?'

'Maybe. Or are the Gnostics doing their thing.'

'Probably that. *Definitely* that. Should we go then?'

'Ladies first.'

'Yeah right. You're a real fucking gentleman. It's not as if it's steep and crumbly as shit or anything.' She laughed.

Jordan sniggered. The more they got into things, the easier it seemed for him to accept weird situations. And this was weird. To say the least. Even for her, who had waited her whole life for proof of her conspiracy theories.

As they took a zigzagging, cross-and-back approach to descending the gravely incline, Ary noticed another helicopter, flying in from the main island. It crossed over, circled around Nea Kameni and hovered, engulfed in plumes of volcanic dust, above the same spot they had been dropped off a few moments earlier. It was shiny black, with no markings, occupied by soldier types, dressed in dark blue body armour, visored helmets, carrying assault weapons. The soldiers jumped down and fanned out. Ary grabbed Jordan by the arm and pulled him behind an outcrop of jagged rocks, watching as the helicopter set down and the soldiers went about placing small pebble-like objects around the perimeter of the hilltop.

'That does not look good,' she whispered. To their right, a narrow path descended between two crags to the coast. A small cabin cruiser was moored alongside a concrete jetty at the bottom. 'Come on,' she said, tugging Jordan to follow her down the path.

As they scurried down, another six helicopters landed alongside the first. Blue-clad soldiers were swarming over the hilltop. On the jetty, a woman in her mid-forties was untying the boat mooring. She seemed hurried, and Ary feared they might not reach her in time.

'Stop. Wait.' she shouted, as she and Jordan covered the last few metres.

'Please. Wait,' Jordan added. 'Can we come with you?'

The woman hesitated, then she nodded and, minutes later they were aboard, heading out to sea, before turning landwards in the direction of Santorini Old Harbour and Thera. Whether through language difficulties or wariness of strangers, the woman didn't speak. Ary and Jordan thanked her in English as they disembarked. She nodded, turned, walked up steps to a street of whitewashed houses and dipped into an alleyway between two cafés. Ary and Jordan followed. It seemed the right thing to do.

Ary checked her phone. Jordan did likewise.

As expected, they both had messages from *No Caller ID*:

ABORT
Rooms booked in the hotel at the end of the alley
Wait for instructions

In her room at the new hotel and for the first time in a while, Ary thought about Charlie, the curious but nice bloke with the overzealous addiction to a certain movie. She wondered how he was getting on. *Did he work in finance? Or have finance? Did he lose money in the crash? Or was he just holing up in his East London flat watching the world crumble around him?*

If only he knew the truth.

Which was the self-same thought she'd had back then, but without the added bonus of having her theories proved to her. She pondered on how he might react to the prospect of secret caucuses, ancient rivalries, and people with powers to influence other people's minds. Or, indeed, people like her: *Star Children*. And she felt for him too. A prime example of sleeping nobodies. Not even pawns. Just grains of sand, buffeted by the uncaring waves of a malign dominating faction on one side, and a dispassionate group of two maybe three manipulators on the other.

Did Charlie even know he was a nobody?

Did Mateus?

She missed Mateus. Messaged him, saying:

I'm in Thera, now
Santorini
Doing my thing (smiley face emoji)

Silence.

She phoned him.

He didn't pick up.

She messaged again: saying (lying) that she was *enjoying* a stopover in the Hotel Villa Spiros. She didn't mention the soldier-types invading the island, or the person trying to kill her and Jordan.

Not that it mattered anyway.

He didn't reply.

Seeing the soldiers overrun the island had and still terrified Jordan. Armed NYPD were one thing. Professional military were something else. Although brought up street, even he admitted he wasn't good with dangerous situations, and the lunacy he was now living had jumped to a whole new level. He called his sister. To check on *The Kitchen Sink Magazine* and also to hear a friendly voice; one that wasn't caught up in his absurd reality.

She didn't answer.

He messaged.

She didn't reply.

He called again.

This time, she answered, telling him to *calm the fuck down, everything is good.*

He didn't tell her about the Gnostics, what they had said, the soldiers, or the person trying to kill him. He would panic over those alone. Or with Ary. For good or ill, the only person he could depend on.

In the outside world, events had surpassed the UN Secretary General's worst predictions. The Middle East was more volatile than ever. A special Security Council meeting had failed to de-escalate the impending conflict. The Russian Federation fell in with Iran. The EU – with Hungary abstaining – now the world's biggest economy, refused to take sides, but leaned towards supporting Israel. China, the second biggest economy, also refused to take sides, meanwhile increasing activities in the South China Sea by moving naval forces close to Indonesia, the Philippines, and Papua New Guinea. In the UK, the ongoing Brexit-related decline had caused so many problems for the recently elected Labour-Liberal-Green coalition government, their only concern was getting enough food into the country.

And, dealing with growing secessionist movements, the US President, calling a special session of Congress, had little time for issues outside of United States borders. There was a heat spike in the Sahara. Another in South America. Icebergs the size of Trinidad were breaking away from both the Arctic and Antarctic. A massive storm – Hurricane Jeet – ravaged the Indian subcontinent. Melting permafrost in North America and Siberia released tonnes of CO_2 into the atmosphere. And the Secretary General's optimistic outlook from early June had well and truly disappeared.

You can't put the shite back in the horse, Colm Magee, his Irish born advisor had said.

The Secretary General agreed. At seventy-three, and with an exhausting lifetime of politics behind him, he realised he didn't have the stamina or psychological wherewithal to deal with so many crises. It was time for someone new. Someone who knew how to work with the *shite*. Someone with financial experience. Someone with a fiery personality. Someone determined and, although it pained him to even consider such a notion, someone who was not from the world of politics. A pragmatist. A controller. Someone who could influence the Security Council, and right the boat. Someone with energy.

And he knew the very person.

With more wealth than anyone should have in an equitable society.

But practical. Always putting the world to rights.

Now he'd have his chance.

HARSHING THE MELLOW

Sandhya and Nkechi turned up at the hotel in the afternoon. They appeared concerned. Not a usual look for the two Gnostics. Jordan ushered them into his room. Ary showed up seconds later from her room next door, stating she had been summoned by way of a thought in her head and seeming not too pleased about it either.

'Stop doing that,' she barked at the Gnostics. 'It's fucking creepy.'

They didn't reply.

Jordan reckoned he would never get used to the Gnostics' abilities. Especially the mind-talk-influence-thing they did. It defied his logic and learning, but was undeniable. His previous notions on reality – now so far removed, it wasn't even a dot in the distance – had turned into an implausible but unambiguous *new reality* and, the truth was, in Sandhya's own words, he could *either roll with it, or get rolled over.*

The jury, however, was still out as to which way he would go.

Or he could run home.

Sandhya, however, had already told him once before, on the flight to Cambodia: *There is **pureness** in being right – but true **purity** comes from knowing you are wrong.*

Running home would be right ... for him at least, for Jordan Burke.

But was he knowingly being wrong by doing it?

Of course he was. Staying, seeing whatever this was through, was the only *pure* option.

The thought lingered.

Sandhya and Nkechi sat side by side on the sofa. Ary took a chair by the window, sat peering out to the street below. Jordan sat on the edge of the bed. It seemed apt. On the edge was where he lived these days.

Sandhya spoke first, appearing to struggle to sound upbeat. 'Your bags will be with you soon. They're on the way from Santorini Airport.'

Ary said, 'Thanks.'

Jordan added, 'Yeah, thanks.'

'We included a guidebook for the Santorini islands. One each. Study it. Get to know the lay of the land.'

'And then what?' Ary asked.

Sandhya glanced at Nkechi. In unison, they nodded, as if in unsaid agreement.

'Then... you try again,' Nkechi said.

'Suck my dick,' Ary burst out.

'Beautiful turn of phrase,' Jordan said. 'You have a sweet mouth.'

'Yeah. As I said before, live with it.' Ary turned back to the two Gnostics, 'How the bloody hell do we *try again*?' She used a slowly spoken, mocking tone, like a child ribbing her buddies. 'The place is totally gagging with soldiers. With big-ass fucking guns.'

'Guns are the least of your problems,' Sandhya said. 'They have booby-trapped the whole island.'

'The pebbles?' Jordan asked.

'Yes. Like the one that killed your grandfather. It's their go-to weapon. It's kind of like a landmine, but can focus on a person's – *your* specific DNA.'

'Well, that's not fucked up or anything,' Ary said. 'So now we're up against anti-personnel mines that are totally personal.'

'I see what you did there,' Sandhya said, chuckling. 'Very good.'

'That's what you got from that. The joke. Not the *I'm scared shitless* bit. And how did they get our DNA in the first place?'

'From the air... maybe. The tiny particles of skin you leave behind as you walk around. Perhaps they had an agent working in the Siem Reap hostel. They could've collected samples from your bedsheets. There are any number of ways. But that's not important. The objective is to get you back to the island to do the necessary. Flick the switch. Reactive the Core Hub.'

'Yeah. Nah-ha! Not happening. The world go to fuck itself. It's full of wankers anyway.'

'You don't mean that,' Nkechi said.

'Yes, I do. No. I don't. But I want to.'

'We all want to,' Jordan interjected, feeling a sense of clarity and bravado. 'But we don't have that luxury anymore.'

Ary cast Nkechi a questioning look. Nkechi shook her head.

Ary said, 'Really? That's all him?'

Nkechi nodded.

The exchange seemed weird, but Jordan let it go. They had a job to do. He knew that now. And, if the Aryans were willing to throw so many resources to stop them, it must be an important one. Ary and his involvement seemed to have rattled them. The pebble booby-traps proved as much.

'Well,' Ary said. 'I've had my rant. Sometimes that's all I need.'

'We've noticed,' Sandhya said with a smile. 'Actually, every remaining Gnostic – all three of us – have noticed.'

'Good. I like a reputation of being the *out-there one*.'

Jordan sniggered.

'What?'

'Nothing. Just that you're definitely the out-there one.'

She reached across, play-punched his shoulder. They all chuckled. And then they stopped. A sombre silence falling upon the room with all the heaviness of an approaching storm.

'When?' Jordan asked.

'Soon,' Nkechi replied. 'Later. We will get you to the island. Our data is over three thousand years old, but we think the cave entrance is somewhere on the north side near Ákra Stáchti.'

'You don't know for certain?'

'No. That's what we needed you for. No Gnostic has set foot there for thousands of years. In fact, except for the really ancient texts, we eradicated all references to an entrance. If the Aryans suspected we were investigating the area, they might also deduce that the Core Hub still held potential. It's why we focussed on Bimini. They know, just like us, that all three are necessary to reactivate the grid. By using their own tricks of misdirection, we kept them distracted. While we waited for you.'

'What do you mean, *waited for* us?'

'A prophesy of sorts. The unfolding of the universe. Everything has led to you two, here, now, in this place, doing what you need to do to get the next age back on track.'

'A prophesy?' Ary asked.

'Yes... of sorts. Handed down by our predecessors.'

'A prophesy? Like we're the chosen ones or something?'

'Yes.'

Ary smiled. 'Fucking boom!' she muttered to herself. 'A Star Child and a chosen one. Brilliant.'

Jordan ignored her. With each passing moment, the prospect of going back to the island felt evermore terrifying. It was a task for brave people. Capable people. He was just a physicist, an academic who ran a science magazine. This type of activity was more suited to a soldier.

'Yes, it would,' Sandhya said. 'A soldier would be much more suited to the task. But there aren't any who are also Star Children. They don't have empathy. They are killers and neither we, nor Star Children ever kill. Anyone or anything. Or hurt. We only nudge. True strength is knowing how to effect a change through compassion. Take Ary here. She might come across gruff and angry, but she is a real softy at heart. You both are. That will keep you safe. The universe flows through you.'

'Coz we're the goddamned frickin' chosen ones, bruv,' Ary said with a wink. 'We're the fucking *Skywalkers*... apart from the shitty ones, that is.'

Jordan smiled, still unconvinced but getting there. 'So, this cave – will the soldiers be there?'

'Most likely. I'd go as far as say, *definitely*.'

'Great. And can we get around them?'

'That will be up to you. You don't have any special abilities, but you do have excellent intuition.'

'We could learn the *nudge* thing,' Ary said. 'You know, like you promised.'

'You don't have time,' Nkechi said. 'It would take too long to teach you.'

'Aww!'

'Yes, aww... but needs must.'

'And what if you are wrong?' Jordan asked. 'What if the cave can't be found?'

'Then,' Sandhya began, 'the world is fucked, to use Ary's terminology.'

Ary sniggered. 'Oh dear, the Gnostic said a bad word.'

Jordan didn't snigger. Levity might help ease tension, but the graveness of their situation had a nasty habit of *harshing the mellow*, another phrase his undergrad Thermodynamics lecturer liked to say when faced with a difficult day.

They were heading into dangerous territory. Both physical and psychological.

They were ill-equipped – both physically and psychologically.

Star Children or not, they were just two ordinary people, more inclined to write about a threatening situation than actually run headfirst into one, but he believed the Gnostics. Had fallen for their pronouncements and the direness of the situation.

'When exactly do we go?' he asked again for clarity.

'Later,' Nkechi said. 'We will fetch you when we think it's best.'

'Tonight?'

'We don't know. Maybe tomorrow. Or another day. Whenever is safest.'

'We have less than five days,' Ary said.

'We know.'

'It's not much time.'

'We know.'

'What if we fail?'

'You wouldn't like the outcome. A world of unrestricted Aryan rule would be worse than the last thirteen thousand years.'

'Bad then?' Jordan said.

'Yes, very bad... for everyone and everything.'

'And what if the soldiers see us firs...' Ary began.

'Look, we'll fetch you when it's time,' Sandhya snapped.

Jordan hadn't seen this side of her.

Ary, however, seemed unphased. 'Jeez looeez, no need to go all Galadrial on it,' she continued. 'I was only asking a question. So, I'll try again, what if the soldiers see us first?'

'We won't lie,' Nkechi replied in a calmer tone, 'it's possible. But we will do our best to cloud their awareness. We estimate there are around fifty agents on the island. If not interrupted, we should be able to nudge a handful at the same time. But it will consume all our attention. You'll be on your own.'

'Okay. So, we'll have at least some level of protection.'

'Of sorts. But don't get cocky. You're not dealing with normal humans here. Aryans are adept, resourceful, and have certain skills.' She cast Sandhya a worried look, adding, 'Most of all... they know you are coming.'

It's a strange noise – the sound of bullets piercing the pillow beside your head.

Pumfs.

Or *piffs.*

Perhaps a combination of both.

At first, they don't register. Confusion. *What's that? Was it? Is it? Can't be.* Followed by blind panic. Rolling off the bed onto the floor. Crouching. Peeking over the edge of the mattress. Noticing the three tiny holes, surrounded by cracks, in the glass at the upper end of floor-to-ceiling window on the opposite side of the room.

The next bullet punctured the mattress edge.

The fifth did the same, missing Jordan's shoulder by inches and splintering a large notch from the exposed floorboards by his knees. He scurried against the wall, his legs clutched to his chest, chin buried into his kneecaps, heart beating fiercely, pulse gagging in his throat. He dropped on one side, just in time for the sixth bullet to burst a hole the wall behind him. His body was a quivering mass of trembles and ticks. His thoughts confused, running wild, without focus. In contradiction to itself, fear had rooted him to the spot while simultaneously urging him to flee. The door to the washroom was open, kept that way in case he needed to pee in the night. He steeled his will. Without looking back, he scampered across to and through the doorway, hoping he wouldn't cop one in the fanny and amazed by the thoughts that crossed his mind when his life was in danger. He smirked. The need for self-preservation returned, seemingly unbothered to be away for the period when he needed it most. The washroom had no windows, was at an acute angle to the rest of the room. Out of eyeline.

Safe.

Leaning against the toilet, reclaiming his knees to chest pose, he stayed that way for a good few minutes... until he heard commotion in the corridor outside.

Moments earlier, Ary had been lying on her bed, reading one of her old blogs titled: *THEY WALK AMONG US – Shape-changers in our midst*, amused as much by the ridiculousness of her previous assumptions as she was by her prior naivety.

It really was heady stuff.

Nonsense. She knew that now. And yet, not too far off the mark either.

There was a knock on the door.

Expecting to hear Nkechi, Sandhya, Jordan, or all three of them reply, she shouted, 'Who is it?'

'Surprise,' came the answer.

She jumped up, ran across the room and threw open the door.

Holding a duffle-bag in one hand, wearing the world's biggest grin, Mateus said, 'Guess who?'

Without a word, Ary threw her arms around him. Hugged him close. So tight she sensed the impropriety of the gesture but didn't care if he got the wrong – or *right* – idea. It was Mateus. And she loved him. More than she'd admit, or wanted to declare, especially to herself. For so long, she had denied her feelings for this wonderful man. Too wrapped up with ancient cults and interdimensional travellers to think of personal happiness. Now the truth of the universe had been revealed to her, it seemed foolish to dedicate so much of her life to obsessions. And, through it all, he had been standing right beside her. Indulging. Encouraging. Being her crutch and her greatest promoter.

He was handsome as fuck too.

Easing her grip, with all the nervousness of a teenager contemplating her first kiss, she stared up into his beautiful face. 'Why are you here?'

'I came to see you,' he said.

'But why?'

'I needed to be with you. Things aren't going great with the label and I had to see you. You're the only one who understands.' He paused. 'I also came to tell you...' He paused again.

'Came to tell me what?' She tensed, so much wanting his answer to be the right one.

He drew in a breath. Sighed. 'I came here to...'

'To what?'

'Please don't interrupt. Let me get it out – say what I came to say.'

'And what's that?'

He breathed in again. 'What I came to say... why I came here is...'

'Yes?' She leaned back, awaiting his presentation.

'Oh, fuck it. I came here to tell you that I lo...'

Her initial awareness was of something whizzing past her head, followed by a popping sound – of warmth – and wetness – and ringing in her ear. Splatter. A spray of red. Holding Mateus upright. His deadweight, slipping through her arms. Into the puddle of blood, spreading across the floor like crimson oil from a burst canister. More wetness, dripping down her face.

Her next, and first conscious thought, was to howl.

At the delayed shock.

At the prospect of a future without her best friend. *The love of her life.*

How hard could it be? Five years of military training. Sniper school. Elite forces. Successful secret missions. Numerous hits without detection. The best rifle for this kind of job: a foldable, semi-automatic Paratus-16 with holographic sight. A prime spot in a church belltower overlooking the targets' hotel, with direct eyeline to their respective rooms. And the marks just there, as if waiting to be shot.

So, why was it so hard to simply pop a bullet through someone's head?

She had come close. Missing the first one by centimetres, the other by much the same, taking out that stupid guy who happened to turn up at the wrong door at the wrong time. If he had only stopped to tie a shoelace or take a shit, he would be alive now. Not that it mattered. It was his own fault for distracting her target. And infuriating. Now, she would have to hurt herself again. The fucker deserved to have his brains splattered for the inconvenience and pain she would have to endure.

As for objective one, that was just sloppy.

For that, she deserved the pain.

It would take many cuts to make amends.

On top of which, even though the contract had been discontinued, with the inevitable consequences of her failures most likely already on the way, before they caught up with her, (*alias*) Lena Hansen would see the contract through. She would put an end to *Siem Reap Objectives 1 and 2.*

SPLITTING THE RELATUM

Vilmos Gildermere was making moves. He had plans. Overnight lobbying of fellow Caucus members had switched five families: Jomon, Romanovich, Hanno, Abram, and Mansa to his side, with Pachacuti, Patidar, Soma, Roquefeuil-Borgius, and Saxe-Gothe professing loyalty to Rothbauer, citing the current leadership as the most conservative, and therein always better option for solving the Gnostic problem.

It was five to five, with Shun – as the traditional host family – holding the casting ballot. The present Patriarch, Rothbauer and the prospective contender, Gildermere didn't get a vote. Which meant, he only needed to flip one more, and his attention was drawn to the de facto Caucus Chair himself, Yuze Shun who, a few meetings back, had seemed more questioning than Rothbauer's usual bunch of sycophants. He had queried the current state of the world. He seemed open to persuasion. There were only days left for the Gnostics to achieve their objectives. They were adept, resourceful, had better skills than the Aryans and Rothbauer's answer was to flood the island with agents and traps. Hardly the most inventive approach for a society at the pinnacle of thirteen thousand years of world dominance. It was weak. Kneejerk. And puerile. Gildermere could exploit that.

Using a private contact he retained for off-grid calls, he invited Shun into a one-to-one video-chat. Moments later, the host family had flipped, expressing support for Gildermere's claim.

A meeting was called.

Planes flew, helicopters landed, and an angry-faced Rothbauer welcomed the family delegates into an unprecedented, emergency voting session of the Caucus. As with all elections, the meeting was short, and tense, but the expected decorum held. Each delegate placed a small stone disc – bearing their family crest – into one of two ornamental jade bowls at the centre of the Caucus-chamber table which, prior to the ballot, had been designated as either Rothbauer or Gildermere. The whole process took less than thirteen minutes to complete.

The vote did not go well for Rothbauer.

His gammon-hued expression illustrated his disappointment and anger... but he conceded.

The meeting folded.

Before the delegates left, however, as his first action as Patriarch, and the overture he had put forward to win over the other six families, Vilmos

Gildermere stated his plan for more Caucus involvement in plebian matters.

Direct action, he said. *Hands on steering. Down in the trenches, so to speak.*

Events were unfolding nicely.

HERE IT COMES... HERE IT COMES

The next couple of days came and went without major incident, and Jordan was thankful. The shooting attempt had left him jittery, to say the least. Actually, he was a bag of nerves, staying out of eyeshot to any window, making sure the bathroom door always stood between him and the hotel personnel calling to his newly acquired room on a lower floor. The manager said it was the least they could do. Seemingly as pleased as a dog with two tails that he and Ary hadn't opted to move out and find alternative lodgings.

Where the Gnostics stayed, he had no idea. On occasion, they just appeared, informing him of increased activity on Nea Kameni. More Aryan agents had arrived:

Swarming like a disease, Nkechi had said.

Whereby the island was, to all intents and purposes, under military occupation.

Not that Ary showed any interest. Since the death of her friend, she had become aloof, never venturing from her own newly acquired room, which the manager had moved, with much sympathy, to side-by-side accommodation with Jordan's. The Gnostics ordered her food, that remained outside her door uneaten. Jordan phoned, knocked her door, but Ary didn't answer. He had known her for only a few weeks. Thought her an arrogant shrill. In her present circumstances, however, he felt for her, suspecting Mateus might have been more than a friend, or at least she had aspirations for as much. Sharing a wall, he heard her crying for a large portion of the day. The nights seemed worse. He wanted to go to her but thought it impolite to intervene on another person's grief.

The police investigation was a bust.

They came. They made some cursory attempts at gathering evidence. They went. The hotel staff washed the walls, door, and floor. Ary was moved to her new room. The manager sent a gift basket with a condolences card. It also stayed outside her door. The Gnostics did something *nudge*-ish to help her with the heartache, citing that their attempts might have only a modest effect... something to do with emotions being hard to break through. It didn't work. They were, however, able to leverage the detectives and their investigation into Mateus's murder. Turned them onto other things. And Jordan agreed, the last thing they needed was the local police department snooping around, asking awkward questions. The Gnostics still hadn't come up with a time to go back to the island, though, and Jordan was in no hurry to embark on the journey either. It was important. He was resigned to that. It was, however, also dangerous. They might fail. Or die. Not a prospect to inspire enthusiasm in anyone with a logical mind. Jordan was one of those play it safe guys. Academic and prudent. He might have come to terms with his new reality but, no matter how hard he worked on convincing his scientific instincts, reason always broke through. And caution. Gut wrenching, fear induced, *just want to go back home to play with his magazine and not go poking around in matters that might get him killed* caution.

He was no hero, but he was smart.

There was job to do and he wanted to get it over with, he just didn't like the idea of starting.

As if reading his thoughts – and they could – the two Gnostics came to his room.

'How is she?' Sandhya asked, empathy written across her face.

'Not good. About every half-hour, I can hear her crying.'

'Us too.'

'And there's nothing you can do for her?'

'Nothing that's safe.' Nkechi said. 'Tinkering with someone's grief can have terrible adverse effects. It is an important part of healing. We need her, but must let her go through this for as long as circumstances will allow.'

'And, how long is that?'

'Today is Thursday. The Core Hubs must be reactivated by midnight on Saturday, before Pluto goes temporarily back into Capricorn.'

Jordan still had problems accepting the astrology part of the plan, but remained quiet.

'I sense you still have issues.'

'Of course I do. Until a week or two ago, stargazing was for loons and harem-pant wearing hemp-weavers. Now you've got me believing it.'

'Because it's science.'

He screwed his face. 'Yeah, but no. Not really.' He sat on the bed. The Gnostics took the sofa. 'Look, I know you have all these powers. And I fully accept the *nudging* and influencing people. But you have to give me some slack here. Someone like me doesn't drop a lifetime of scientific outlook just like that. I need time.'

'You've got time.'

'I don't think so. As you've already stated, we have a little over two days... tops.'

'And, being a physicist, you already know time is relative, depending on the observer. And also constant. And unreal. All at the same time, forgive the pun.' She chuckled. 'It would be safe to say that time is a secondary sense, without any direct sensory percept or reason for its existence. It is, therefore, a creation of perception. Its measurement open to interpretation.'

'I get that. Did so as an undergraduate. But what relation does it have to our task? To me, all your astrology stuff just sounds like more *malark-hooey.*'

'See, you are doing it again. Closing your mind. Let's put it this way; if time is constant and relative to how the observer – *you* – create it through perception, it would be safe to assume that, if you change your definition of time and any event within it, you could also change its effect on your reality. Think of it as a mass of potential. Never linear. Never broken into segments like, seconds, minutes, weeks, months, years, eons, etc. If that's the case then, with the right mindset, you should be able to slow time down, or speed it up with respect to your desired outcome.'

'Yeah, right. But no one can do that.'

'No human can do that... yet.'

'And I'm human.'

'You're a type of human.' She sighed. 'All I'm saying is, over thousands of years and with the right *Logos*, we have become unbothered by deadlines and linear time. Yes, the task must be complete by midnight on Saturday. The fate of everything depends on it. But, in the same way we understand the universe is playing out just as it intends, we also take it for granted that, by sending us messages – as in the recent Mercury Max and Pluto into Aquarius – certain factors have been, are, and will be set in place. It's not for us to determine how those messages come to us. And, when it comes to time, or lack thereof as you believe, we merely sit back and wait for a signal. Because, within the constant, the event has already taken place. The information just hasn't reached us yet. Synchronicity. Like what happened to Ary's friend.'

'His murder? Blowing his head to bits? That was part of the big plan?'

'Probably,' Sandhya said. 'Maybe.'

'You don't sound sure.'

'We can't be. We just wait. And observe. To us, apart from being heart-breaking for Ary, her friend's death wasn't random.'

'Tell her that. I'm sure she'll appreciate your sympathy.'

'We will. When she's ready to hear it.'

'And we will get her back on track too,' Nkechi added. 'Soon. But when the time is right and not...'

'…Random,' Jordan interrupted.

'Exactly. When it fits with the scheme of things.'

'Now you definitely sound like a pair of harem-pant wearing hemp-weavers.'

The two Gnostics laughed, stood and walked to the door.

'So, why didn't they just kill us ages ago?' Jordan asked, as Sandhya reached for the handle. 'And why an assassin? Why not just send a bunch of troops and burn us up with a couple of those pebbles of theirs? Same as they did with my grandfather.'

'It would be too obvious,' Sandhya said. 'That kind of thing draws attention. Especially when you've been hopping from city to city. Cities have people. Lots of people. Aryans work behind the scenes. And they don't have our talents for covering up behind them. Their methods are coarse. Lack finesse. Another reason why they are so keen to get the hands on the *Book of Lights* and *Logos*. With it, they'd be unstoppable. Additionally, until their agents saw us with you, they had no idea you were part of the plan. We can allude them – for a while – but they are many, we are only two.'

'Plus the third Gnostic, who is otherwise engaged,' Nkechi added.

'Yes. The power of three,' Sandhya continued. 'Even so, by the time the Aryans caught up with us, you were already recruited. And you're Star Children. They know that now. It has them rattled. It's why they've updated their approach. Sent so many agents to the island. They are desperate. Panicking.'

'They looked pretty together to me,' Jordan said.

'But they're not. And that makes them dangerous. More dangerous than usual. They will do anything to stop you.'

'And, of course, they will fail,' Nkechi said. 'Anyway, try not to think about them. Relax. Enjoy your day. Clear your mind.'

'Easier said than done. I'm terrified to stay here. You know, because of the assassin. And I have no desire to return to that damned island either.'

'We know, dear. But you'll be magnificent.'

'I wish I had your confidence.'

'You do. You just need to find it.'

Jordan wasn't so sure. In fact, he was the opposite of sure. 'Yeah, not feeling it. And I must say, I don't enjoy our chats. They seem very one-sided.'

'We know that too.' Sandhya opened the door. 'Anyway, we will come for you and Ary soon.'

'And then…' Nkechi began.

'...And then all hell lets loose?' Jordan said.

'Or not.'

'Depending on my perception of time and events.'

'Exactly,' the two Gnostics said in unison, smiling. 'Now you're getting it.'

As a child, while other kids struggled with young reader storybooks, Ary was brain-deep into Greek legends. Gods. Demigods. Monsters and mythical beasts, she gobbled them up. Always the oddball at school and bullied for her social anxiety, the *Classics*, as her grammar school teachers called them, gave her an out, somewhere to hide, something to investigate, a child with an imagination... who then discovered comic-books and Sci-Fi novels, spaceships, galactic empires, invasions fleets, and alien manipulation of the human species. For a mind loitering somewhere between the improbable and the possible, taking the leap to conspiracy theories required only the slightest tweak of how she viewed the world around her. Not that the Classics, comic-books, and Sci-Fi novels were the cause of her misconceptions – as she saw them now – they had, however, activated her enquiring mind. She had always seen herself as a scientist. A historian. A seeker of facts and purveyor of wisdom. Tales about the Minotaur fuelled a curiosity for the Minoan civilisation, Crete and the surrounding islands. Theseus, Perseus, Jason, Hercules, and Aeneas all provoked an unstoppable urge to broaden her scope, taking in South America, Asia, Africa, where she found increasing overlap in how ancient cultures explained their genesis. Tales of floods. Adversity. Of quests and unnavigable labyrinths. So, when her preferred choice of reading proved to be the perfect marriage of the improbable and the possible, she felt certain she had found the answer. A way to finally explain why she felt so different to others.

Mateus had taken a similar route. A geek, searching for answers, seeding his musical creativity and sparking his inquisitiveness. For most of her journey, he had been by her side, indulging her hypotheses and supporting her batshit claims. Now he was gone. The tang of his blood still lingering on her tongue. Four showers doing little to wash the stink from her hair, or shift the anguish from her heart, which brought on the tears, throwing up bittersweet memories, reliving that moment, and the cycle beginning all over again.

She tried gin, without tonic. Two bottles. No glass.

She attempted to sleep, but woke in sweat and shock.

So, she stayed awake, and drunk. Repeatedly reading his last message, staying with the final sentence:

...with its accompanying sad face emoji.

She blamed herself for not being by his side as his record label suffered, inwardly berating her decision to travel the world chasing mysteries instead of telling the person she loved how she felt. She never would get the chance to feel his arms around her, the softness of his breath on her neck, or the pleasure of lying together on ruffled sheets. It was all gone. The desires. The fantasy. The dream of what might have been. Blown to pieces by a bullet. Lost somewhere in the fug of alcohol, sleeplessness, and a heart cleaved in two.

On more than one occasion, she shouted out loud, 'Fuck'em. Fuck all of them.' As far as she was concerned, the Aryans, the Gnostics, the whole planet could go and fuck themselves right up their own fucking arses.

With Mateus's death, the shit had got real.

It was her fault he got killed. She was the one who got him into the conspiracy game in the first place. If she had left well alone, not gone enticing him with her way-out-there theories, he might still be pushing hits and discovering the next big thing, instead of lying, head blown open on whatever passed for a mortuary on these shit-arsed little islands. And she felt guilt for thinking that too. The Santorini population weren't to blame for what was happening to the world. But they were complicit. By not seeing. Or questioning. Just blind sheep lapping up whatever the Aryans fed them.

So, fuck them too.

The door knocked.

Ary took a swig of gin, rubbed her eyes, wiped the snot dribble from her nose on the sleeve of her hotel gown and answered it.

It was the Gnostics.

She told them to, 'Piss off!'

They didn't. Not right away.

'How are you?' Sandhya asked.

'How the fuck do you think I am? I'm whooping it up. Having a ball. It's a total party in here.' She looked at the near empty bottle in her hand. 'Well, it is. In a way. Just not a good one. So, fuck off. Leave me alone.' She slammed the door in their faces.

'We'll come back later,' Nkechi said from out in the corridor.

'Don't.' Ary went back into the room and dropped onto the bed, spilling gin on the sheets. She didn't care, another bottle – courtesy of the hotel manager – was at the other end of the phone. 'Oh, and I won't be doing any of your symbol shit either,' she shouted out, knowing the two women would be lingering. 'You can find someone else. Or not. Let this arsehole world burn, for all I care. They're all wankers anyway.'

There was no reply.

'Good,' she said inwardly, downing the dregs of the gin, lifted the hotel phone and ordered another.

...AND, THE CHAOS NEVER ENDS

Two Weeks-ish Earlier – one day after Mercury Max.

In recent years, given the uptick in their occurrence, the fine, upstanding, broadly Tory-voting residents of the English county of Leicestershire became no strangers to the concept of periodic flooding. With almost clockwork accuracy, the River Soar burst its banks on several occasions in any particular year. Whether summer or winter, it didn't matter. Houses filled to knee level. Snazzy hardwood floors and showy combi-steam ovens were ruined beyond repair. Insurance pay-outs were made. Premiums rose. Which was what the fine residents mostly griped about. Fire safety personnel spent their days ferrying the flood-stranded elderly and infirm to safer ground. *The same as always* returned every year. Expensive. Problematic. Yet handleable, as long as a fine, upstanding, broadly Tory-voting resident of the English county of Leicestershire disregarded the debilitative climate factors causing the calamities in the first place. Bumbling along in the face of adversity was deemed a virtue. No need for action. It might cost something. Don't let anyone convince you otherwise. Natural gas is good. Oil is better. Factory-farmed meat. Petrol for the multiple cars. Don't let the bastards grind you down. Keep a stiff upper lip. Except for the griping, that was. So much griping.

June 2023, however, proved a different matter altogether. Starting with reports of possible thunderstorms over the East Midlands. The morning began sunny. Parks frequented. Cafés filled. Tea. Sandwiches. Swiss Roll. And the threat of a downpour given as much credence as any other during the now common occurrence of a rainy June. The purple-black clouds moved down from the north over Nottinghamshire. A growing, churning, writhing mass of hellish potential. They spread out. Got fat and angry until, with earth-shattering intensity, they boomed and burst, brilliant white lightning illuminating the sky as though a fleet of alien attack-ships were doing battle somewhere up there in the vastness of space.

Seventeen centimetres of rain gushed down in the space of twenty minutes, continuing without letting up for the next four hours. Riverbanks broke. Sheets of water pouring over the hills, surging onto roads from sodden farmland, immersing traffic and dwellings in an almost instant and rising lake, which stretched across two counties.

Two-hundred and six people drowned. Over three hundred were missing. Multiple thousands of animals lost their lives. Nearly twenty-five thousand houses were destroyed by overruns and landslides. Three times that number were deemed as only borderline repairable. Whole villages became stranded. Disruption to mobile phone networks exasperated the problem. Emergency services coped, but saw their resources strained to breaking point. The bill to taxpayers reached into the tens of billions, as insurance premiums went through the roof, leaving many bankrupt and destitute.

The floodwater remained for the best part of a week.

Deniers and slow learners said it was *the same as always*. Arguing human-generated climate change to be mere conjecture, bunkum, and the stuff of snowflaky, woke-ist, virtue-signalling doom-mongers. And yet, as the waters washed away their valuable properties and possessions, even those naysayers had to face up to the notion of things being definitely *not* the same as always. Getting used to an annual occurrence was one thing. Seeing it grow to the level of chaos... well, that had the touch of perilous predictability to it. Overnight, one-time resolute opinions became open to persuasion. Discussions were had. Government ministries met. Research groups consulted. Action plans put in place.

They didn't work.

Action plans require dedication and commitment. And, as usual with these kind of knee jerk actions, it was too late.

The next thunderstorms inundated most of the South East and London.

More on the way.

One and a Half-ish Weeks Earlier – a few days after Mercury Max.
Ask any five-year-old snot-picker the simple question, *how hot is the Sahara Desert?* and they'd reply with a single word, *very...* or something else of similar inference. It was a known fact. Water was wet. Ice was cold. The Sahara Desert – and indeed all deserts – were *very* hot, the highest recorded temperature in the region peaking at 57.78° Celsius. Definitely hot, but nowhere near the 69.56° C and rising recorded on the last day of May 2023.

A mass exodus of surrounding areas ensued.

Tens of thousands of refugees fled North Africa, taking to flimsy boats, drowning en masse in the Mediterranean Sea and, those who made it to European shores, were met by crowds of angry locals, wielding everything from broken chair legs to shotguns and dusty Beretta semi-automatic pistols Bisnonno had tucked away in the attic during the closing days of the last world war. Italy called in their army. As did Greece and Spain. Something akin to warfare broke out along coastal territories.

The EU declared a state of emergency.

One Week-ish Earlier – seven days after Mercury Max.
In June 2021, Germany and Belgium had one of the most devastating floods in recorded history. The flood of June 2023, a carbon copy of the one still destroying large parts of England, caused even greater damage and loss of life.

The EU declared another state of emergency.

Zhengzhou, China – July 2021; record-breaking rainfall flooded underground railway tunnels, trapping commuters in rising water. Properties and premises were ruined. Power outages caused problems for hospitals. Critically ill patients had to be transferred. The waters threatened dams.

Many people and animals died.

Worse followed in 2022.

The summer floods of 2023 made them both look like warm-up acts.

Pakistan – from June 2022, heavier than usual monsoon rains caused destructive flooding in more than one third of the country, with massive loss of life, injury, and devastation

The following June brought more of the same.

The June 2023 eruption of the Hengill volcano didn't just cause devastation all the way to the Icelandic capital of Reykjavik, it caused a chain reaction, setting off Hekla, Laki, Grímsvötn, Öræfajökull, Bárðarbunga, and Hofsjökull, cutting the island in two.

Many died. The economy was trashed. The EU, China, and USA airdropped food parcels. Plans were put in motion to evacuate the remaining population.

In the US state of Hawaii, the Mauna Kea volcano also erupted. As did Erta Ale in Ethiopia, Bagana in Papua New Guinea, Ebko and Karymsky in Russia, Baratang in India, and many more around the world, not least one of the most famous, Mount Vesuvius in Italy.

The EU declared their next state of emergency.

Most states, however, didn't.

THE UNREFUSABLE OFFER

'So, this was your big *secret* plan?' Gildermere shouted at Rothbauer. 'Drowning and incinerating the whole world?'

Rothbauer remained silent. As did the others sitting around the Caucus table.

'What's the point?' Gildermere continued. 'How can we control things if there nothing left to govern? It's good we deposed you before you did any more damage. What happened to *discrete*? And *consummate efficiency*?'

'I did what was necessary,' Rothbauer said. 'And there's still the doomsday option of slowing the planet's rotation by manipulating the Coriolis Effect.'

'Which would leave a scorched earth, you idiot.'

Rothbauer didn't reply.

'Genius. Wipe it all out. Come on... admit it, you messed up. It's a family trait. You Rothbauers were also the bright-sparks who thought wiping out a third of the European population through Bubonic Plague would be a good solution to peasant uprisings. It only made them more resolute. The result was the Renaissance. The death of feudalism and the downturn of the religious dominance the Gildermeres had spent millennia putting in place.'

'We do what is necessary,' Rothbauer said, again with an air of defiance.

'What you did was idiotic.' Gildermere looked around the rest of the group. 'Anyway, global destruction aside, I may have a way to deal with all of this... as well as Gnostic plans to reactivate the Core Hubs.'

The whole group, including Rothbauer, sat up straighter.

'For the first time since the comet,' Gildermere continued, 'the Caucus will move into plebian politics. The UN Secretary General has stepped down and, given the urgency of the current world situation, the Security Council has called a special conference to elect a new one.'

'When will this happen?' Yuze Shun asked.

'It already has. This morning. Via tele-conferencing.'

'And the election?' Kritik Soma asked. 'They have selected someone?'

'Yes, they have.'

'And who is it?' Rothbauer asked. 'Some stiff-shirt, pencil-pusher no doubt. Just like all the others. Easy to influence.'

'Better.'

'*Better*? Better how?'

'In all ways.' Gildermere replied, letting the statement linger for a moment, then added, 'Because it's me. I am the new UN General Secretary.'

A bout of mumbling rippled around the table. Side conferences were had. Romanovich and Abram laughed aloud. Rothbauer look visibly shocked.

'You can't do that,' he said. 'No Caucus member has ever taken up a political position. When you proposed more involvement in plebian matters, I – and I'm certain everyone here – expected you'd set up some type of body. Another fake think tank. A phony research group. The usual. But this... this is...'

'What – sacrilege?'

'Yes, for want of a better word. Sacrilege.'

'Now you sound like a plebian. There is no sacrilege. Just as there are no religions unless we design them. We are everything. Everything is us. And now, so too is the world of plebian politics. With direct involvement, I can tweak at the edges. Make things in our image. Undo the total clusterfuck you caused.'

'How?' Rothbauer scoffed.

'Easily. Apart from all the floods and volcanoes popping off left, right, and centre, Siberia is enduring its fifth wildfire in as many years. Landslides in India and Turkey. Famines in North Africa and South East Asia. European food production severely crippled by changing weather. The UK, once a great empire, can hardly feed itself. You have created a mess, but also the conditions, if handled directly and in the right way, to distract and control the plebian population. The world is in chaos. And leaderless. All I did was step in... take control, whereby I will twist the knife... give them false hope.'

'And what about the Gnostics? What about their Star Children and the Core Hubs?'

'We have our agents on Santorini. You put them there. It's probably the only smart thing you did. So, they are more than well placed to take care of the Star Children.' He leaned across the table, closer to Rothbauer's face. 'Look, everything is in hand. And not in the bumbling, inefficient way you go about things. Really in hand. Even though it's fake, I will mollify and modify their politics. Propose unity and a common approach. Then, when everything is nice and calm, we will focus all of our attention on Santorini. They have only days left to accomplish their task. Our agents will thwart them... take them out.'

Rothbauer scoffed.

'Don't worry, my good friend,' Gildermere said with a smile. 'Events will unfold nicely.'

MAN WITH A PLAN

On top of the other dilemmas Vilmos Gildermere had to deal with on his first day as UN Secretary General were even more floods in South East Asia and northern Europe, volcanic eruptions in Tanzania and Kenya, a strange sudden freeze event in Antarctica that baffled scientists, and wildfires raging in Southern Europe, Australia, Turkey, Brazil, and California. In fact, the USA got it worse than most; hurricanes in Florida and Georgia, tornadoes laying waste to just about every Midwest state, wildfires up the western seaboard, and the Yellowstone Caldera threatening to finally blow. A spiritual person might conclude they were punishment for bad deeds. Or perhaps a way to realign priorities. Vilmos, however, followed no such fantasies. Nor did he fret. Through centuries of promoting environmental mismanagement, the Caucus had set these events in motion. Feeding the greed. *Pumping the gas*, to use an apt and topical idiom.

He did, when faced with the global magnitude of the situation, though, understand why the former chap had jumped ship. The situation (for plebians) was dire. Too dire for a mere plebian to handle. Part of the plan. The Caucus convincing people that rearranging the deckchairs would be enough. Wipe out most of humankind to more tolerable levels. Death to the world as known.

A scorched Earth.

His first incentive was to appear as if the problems were not intractable. As head of the United Nations Secretariat, he sent out a directive, instructing the tens of thousands of UN staff members working at duty stations all over the world to up their game, address issues of natural catastrophe by advising the appropriate groups, supplying aid, bringing warring factions to the table, and emphasising the serious implications of pursuing the same old politics. He projected a good image. Appearing sensitive, caring, and as a person with a workable plan. For the first time in a long time, by way of a short virtual meeting, the Security Council had agreed without argument. They rubber-stamped his suggestions. UN member states backed them unanimously. Task forces, specific to each problem, were put together. Global cooperation, on a scale never seen before, set about relief efforts. Ceasefires were called. Weapons put down. Markets made policies for greater regulation. The world was in a serious place, needed serious solutions, and Vilmos Gildermere was the person to deliver.

As his scheme played out, the other Caucus members had questions, worried by the coordinated and symbiotic relationships growing among the governments of the world. They feared it might become lasting, something they couldn't reverse. Gildermere told them to relax. That plebians were plebians. Sure, they might cooperate for a while, but good old greed and lust for power would always seep back in. It was human nature. Scorpions to frogs. And, better still, time was running out for the Gnostics to instigate their plans for global concord. The Core Hubs were still *inactive*. Agents on the ground reported the murder of someone close to one of the Star Children, emotionally crippling said Star Child.

It was already the evening of Friday, 10th June.

The Gnostics had only one day to complete their task.

All would be fine.

A FAST BOAT FROM THERA

Saturday Morning – eighteen hours before Pluto returns to Capricorn

Ary woke with a banging headache, a clawing taste in her mouth, and the two Gnostics staring down at her, silhouetted against a searing bright light. They had pulled open the curtains. Something Ary hadn't done for days. The sunlight hurt her eyes and pissed her off no end.

'Get fucked,' she said, rolling onto her side and pulling a pillow over her head.

'It's time to go,' Nkechi said.

'Didn't you hear me? I said, *get fucked.*'

'We'll give you time to change,' Sandhya said. 'Your hair's a mess. You haven't tied your pretty ponytails. And that dressing gown looks like it's been through the trenches.'

'So what?' Ary replied. 'None of your business what I wear. Or how grubby it is.'

'True. It's not. But, quite frankly, you smell bad. The whole room stinks.'

'Take a shower,' Sandhya added. 'Freshen up. We'll wait.'

'Wait all you like. I'm not doing shit... ever again. Not for anybody.'

'And what about the world? What about the plan?'

'Fuck the plan. And the world. You can't polish a turd. There's no point to any of it. So, piss off and leave me alone.'

The pillow was snatched from her face. Nkechi glared down. She looked angry. 'We don't have time for this.'

'Augh! You're so annoying.'

'You need to get up. Get to it.'

'Get to what? Saving the planet? Yeah, well, fuck that. Here you are with all these powers, and you couldn't even save one person. I'm talking about Mateus here; in case you didn't know. You know, my friend. The one who got his head blown off.' She sat upright. Felt tears welling, but swallowed them.

'There was nothing we could do,' Sandhya said. 'We can't monitor everyone. Our whole focus is on protecting you. And Jordan. And getting the job done. Which is why you have to get up. Everything depends on you reactivating the Core Hub.'

'So what. Don't care.'

'If you don't, the Aryans will win.'

'Let them.'

'And everyone and everything will pay the price.'

'As I said, *don't care.*'

Sandhya sat on the edge of the bed, laid a hand on Ary's shoulder. She didn't flinch. It felt good there. In her mind's eye, she saw Mateus. He seemed at peace, but the pain of his loss still stung.

'You will feel this way for a long time,' Sandhya said.

'Get out of my head.'

'I'm not in your head. It's painted as plain as day on your face. Acceptance of death is tough... but also inevitable. We exist in a world of suffering, some of which can be too painful to bear. Or so it seems while we are experiencing it. But, when time has passed, we come to terms with our agony. It settles. Becomes more memory than emotion.'

'Oh, fuck off with your schlocky self-help wisdom.'

'Where the wisdom comes from isn't the issue – only that it is... *wisdom.* All sentient beings feel pain. It is by acceptance that consciousness is truly freed.'

'See. I was right: *schlocky.*'

'Well then,' Nkechi said, 'think of it this way; what about your mteay? Her brother, Sopheak? If you don't do what you must, they never will get their reunion.'

'You bitch.' Ary flashed her an angry glare. 'That was a cheap shot.'

'But no less correct. If we – *you* – fail, the people you love will suffer. It will be feudalism on steroids. There will be only two ranks: Aryans... and everyone else who serves them.'

Ary pulled her knees to her chest. Sat there, staring at the two women. Their inference that, by doing nothing, she was hurting her mother had cut to the bone. It was uncalled for. Callous. Spiteful. But true. She wanted to snuggle up inside another gin bottle, let the world greed and war itself into oblivion. The Gnostics, however, had a point. The future balanced on a knife edge. Time was short. The implications for her mother and family, severe. There were two actions she could take this day. She could get to it. Or wallow in alcohol and self-pity.

If asked, she preferred the latter.

It was safe and predictable.

The first one, however, was the right thing to do.

How did that old saying go again? Cometh the hour, cometh the man... or woman... or person... or whatever the fuck came when *hours cometh.* It didn't matter. The nub of the phrase meant, when faced with an unsavoury task, do the deed...

'...Just get on with it,' she said aloud, and then asked the Gnostics, 'Are you doing this? Is this you putting ideas in my head?'

'No,' Sandhya said. 'We wouldn't. Not when you are grieving.'

'And the task is too big,' Nkechi added. 'Too important. You must come to it on your own.'

'So, you decided to shovel me a fuck-ton of emotional blackmail instead.'

'Yes,' Sandhya said, with a frankness Ary didn't expect.

'Because it's that important?'

'Yes again. It's all about you. And Jordan. And, eventually, Pluto moving into Aquarius. Pluto is the planet of transformation. Aquarius the sign of progress. We don't have time to give you the full breakdown, but let's just say it's all about society and trimming the dead branches. Ushering in healthy growth. When they come together the old world – the old ways – fall, become something else. Something better.'

'Sure thing, Sand-elf.'

'This isn't some fantasy tale, Ary. This is fact. And transpiring... now.'

'So, astrology is fact?'

'It's a guide. As are all things in the universe.'

Ary shrugged, but found her thoughts drifting to her aunt in China; Baba's sister, who she'd only just met. To her uncle, Sopheak, sitting in his stilt-house. And to her mother, waiting for the day she would be reunited with the brother she'd thought was dead.

Her eyes watered. She sniffed back the tears. 'Okay. I'll do it. But, afterwards, we're done. You can take your save the world, Golden Age, Pluto going into fucking Aquarius bullshit and piss off into the night.'

'Good,' Nkechi said.

'That's both of them,' Sandhya added, speaking to her Gnostic colleague as if Ary wasn't there.

They helped Ary get up from the bed, and waited while she showered and changed into jeans and her favourite black *Truth is Out There* tee-shirt.

Their smiles said they approved.

They probably knew it made her feel safe – or as safe as anything could when faced with murderous assassins, mercenary armies, and a rapidly diminishing timescale into dystopia.

An hour later, on a sea as calm as a millpond, they – all four of them: Jordan, the two Gnostics, and a cleaner, fresher, as drably dressed as always but back to sporting her coloured ribbons, Ary – were sitting in the galley of the same cabin cruiser that had rescued them days earlier, heading out from Santorini Old Harbour towards the southern edge of Nea Kameni. As they approached, the boat's pilot took a sudden swing to port, picked up with a passenger ferry, followed alongside for a while, before hooking for a slip of land at the southwestern end of the island. Jordan hardly noticed. Ary worried him. She was still in bad shape. That much was obvious by the bags under her eyes and the hangdog look that had set up home in her normal cynical but upbeat expression. He felt for her. Apart from his grandparents, two on his father's side who passed at home on their seaweed farm (of all things) in Donegal, Ireland and his mother's mother who breathed her last in her own bed in Jamaica and, of course, barring his GI grandfather who had set this whole nutjob chain of events in process in the first place, the only other person he knew who died was Mr Poznanski, the old wheezy guy who used to live in the first-floor apartment of his block. Smoking had caused it. Cancer. The reason Jordan decided to pack in the coffin nails. The poor old guy collapsed on the stairs. Lungs riddled with black lumps. No one knew. Only Mr Poznanski and his doctor. Jordan found him slumped over the bannisters. It was shocking, but he doubted as shocking as seeing someone's head blown open. He had no idea what witnessing something like that could do to a person. Especially when, to his eyes at least, the witness also had an emotional attachment to the victim. It was obvious Ary had feelings for the guy. More than platonic. It was painted larger than life across her face. In the way her shoulders drooped and the vacant stare searching the horizon for a cure to her heartbreak.

'Are you okay?' he asked her.

Still staring out to sea, she said, 'No,' at a whisper, and nothing else.

He wished he could take her pain away. For all their bluster about possessing powers, the Gnostics were as useful as a glass hammer.

'Is there nothing you can do?' he asked Sandhya.

'It's never wise to interrupt a person's grieving process. We told you this.' She seemed distracted, her gaze searching the approaching shore. 'I think we were right,' she said, turning to Nkechi. 'The Aryans have forgotten about this place.'

'Good. Our ruse worked.'

'What worked?' Jordan asked. 'What ruse?'

'For a scientist you're not very observant,' Sandhya said. 'And you don't listen.'

'We are at a different island,' Ary spoke up. 'The one back there,' she pointed with her thumb over her shoulder, 'is where they took us a few days ago. Nea Kameni. This one is its sister island, Palea Kameni. Didn't you read the guidebook?'

'Yes,' he lied. 'Actually, no, I didn't. I was too busy being shot at.'

'Well,' Ary said, 'this one isn't crawling with agents. Look, it's empty. Not a soul.'

'Ary is correct,' Sandhya said.

'And I suspect,' Ary continued, 'all that bull they told us, about their data being over three thousand years old and the cave entrance being somewhere on the northern side of Nea Kameni, was only to throw the Aryans off the scent.'

'Very good,' Nkechi said.

'Yeah right. And I don't like being manipulated.'

'It was necessary. For your safety.'

'It didn't help Mateus.'

Neither Gnostic replied to that.

'So, is this where we are supposed to go?' Jordan asked, in the hope of breaking the tension.

'Yes,' Sandhya said.

'And where's the cave?'

'We don't know. The part about our data being over three thousand years old is correct. We only know it's here, somewhere, but not the exact spot.'

'Fucking great,' Ary said. 'The indomitable Gnostics strike again.'

'We never said we were *indomitable*,' Nkechi said. 'Only that we have certain skills.'

'Skills that are needed elsewhere,' Sandhya added.

'You're leaving us?' Jordan said.

'That would figure,' Ary snipped. 'It's what they do.'

Sandhya glared at her, then smiled. 'Yes. Our task lies in Bimini. And, as for the third Gnostic, they have their own assignment to complete.'

'Which is what?'

'Something else.'

'Something what?'

'Else. Important. We all have our part to play.'

'You see, good things do come in threes,' Nkechi interrupted. 'Even when it comes to us.' She chuckled, before her expression grew serious. 'But time is running out. And we still need to get there.'

'I thought time was immaterial,' Jordan asked.

'That's nonsense,' Sandhya replied.

'But you said...'

'We said, *time is a constant...* and *relative*. We didn't say it could defy the laws of physics.'

'Okay. We agree on something. So, what about your premise that Pluto going into Aquarius impacts our daily lives? Surely it follows the laws of physics too?'

'Of course it does. Everything follows the laws of physics. Planets. Constellations.'

'But you said it would cement the next age. You used that exact word, *cement*. As if the movement of planets have direct ramifications for events here on Earth.'

'You mean, events everywhere in the universe. And you are taking us too literally. At the end of the day, planets are planets, constellations are constellations, and some things are mere consequence. That's it. No conjecture. No place for speculation. Just plain science. At its core, the universe is a simple mechanism. Bound by the laws of physics. Except when it's not.'

Jordan let it go. Their twisting logic had become exhausting. 'And what about us?'

'You will do what you must,' Nkechi said. 'You are Star Children. *The* Star Children. And, as soon as our amiable, but completely unaware, skipper here lands you ashore, you will find the entrance, enter the cave, seek out the Core Hub and place the tablet in the required place...'

'*The tablet!*' Jordan snapped. 'I forgot about the damned tablet. Do you still have it?' he shouted at Ary.

She shrugged.

'It's fine,' Sandhya said. 'Don't worry, we have it covered. Because of the turmoil over the last few days, we suspected certain details might lapse. The tablet was in Ary's possession but, because of her...' she hesitated, seemed to measure her words, '... sensitive situation, we took it back for safe keeping.'

Ary said nothing. Jordan shot her sympathetic smile. She didn't seem to notice.

A second later, like a stage magician pulling a card from thin air, the small square tablet appeared in Sandhya's hands.

She gave it to Jordan. 'You can hold onto this, for now. But, because she has a greater affinity for the symbol and its inherent potential, it will be Ary's job to find the right placing.'

'Fucking brilliant.' Ary mumbled. 'Knew it would be me.'

'It has always been you, dear one. You're special. Unique. And, although you are hurting right now, even in the darkest night, light finds a way to get through. It's what makes heroes out of ordinary people. The person saving a child from a burning building. The volunteer digging a well so others can drink clean water. The nurse. The doctor. The carers, animal rescuers, and charity workers. They do it not for the glory, but because it's right. Through the courage of compassion, they seek out the light and find the strength to go towards it. That is the true measure of the will. That is the measure of you, and Jordan. Your heartbreak reveals your empathy. And therein your courage. The Aryans don't have that. They don't even understand it. All they have is envy and violence, greed and hate.'

After a pause, Ary replied, 'Yeah, whatever,' but it sounded less contentious, her tone perkier, not as acerbic – more like the old, pre-death-of-her-friend Ary.

Jordan slipped the tablet into his pocket and shot her another smile before, in an attempt to ease the awkwardness, he asked the Gnostics, 'So what does the symbol actually mean?'

Sandhya looked at Nkechi.

They shared a nod and Sandhya replied, 'It means all things. It is a representation of the guiding influences in the universe. In the centre sits the triskele depicting the Fibonacci Sequence, otherwise known as the Golden Ratio, and the Power of Three, which Ary has documented in her blog.' If Sandhya had mentioned this as way to make amends – sitting, stone-faced, Ary seemed unwilling to accept the gesture. 'The four outer pillars,' Sandhya continued, 'which is often seen in South and Southeast Asian architecture, represent the four points of the compass, both physically and philosophically speaking; the pillars themselves depicting the four metaphysical concepts of Wonder, Faith, Doubt, and Scepticism... the basis of thought. There is Yin Yang in the centre, depicting balance – the Balance – with the main body of the symbol contained in a circle, which is the easy part to explain... the Circle of Life and Death. Then we come to what is presently referred to as an Incan Cross, but can be found across all cultures; the cross itself being a symbol of death and renewal, or also the permanence of existence and the inevitability of the Cosmic Cycle, which we told you about before.' She paused, then said, 'So, that's it. That's the Organon.'

'Organon?'

'The symbol's name.'

'As in Aristotle's works on logic?'

'Yes. And no.'

'Dammit, why are you always so cryptic?'

'Yeah, do you guys ever give a straight fucking answer?' Ary added.

'Yes.' Nkechi smiled. 'And no. Because we mimic existence... which is cryptic. It's both simple and complex. In the words of the late great Bill Hicks, *just a ride*. As a physicist, you should know this, Jordan. And, like

Siddhartha, Yeshua, Confucius, and all the other Gnostic teachers, Aristotle was just one piece in a multi-millennia cycle of drip-feeding *Logos*. Seeding metaphysical enthusiasm, so to speak. For when the time was right. For now. Whilst, at the same time, not revealing too much. Keeping the Aryans in the dark. The Organon is the other part of that plan. It's the key that unlocks. Actually, Organon is its modern name.'

'Doesn't sound very modern? And, who the fuck says, *whilst?*'

'Organon is its Greek name. In the old times, the symbol went by what can be loosely translated as the *Tenet*. But Organon is a much better fit, we think.'

Sandhya nodded.

'So, why haven't we seen it before? I've studied everything there is to know about ancient secrets and never once came across the symbol until you guys showed up.'

'You have. In its constituent parts. As a conspiracy theorist, you should know that some things are kept hidden... until they are revealed.'

'I get your point about them being cryptic,' Ary said in sideways comment to Jordan. 'File it under *a bloody fucking nuisance* or *you couldn't make this shit up.*'

'There is also another, more complex rendition of the Organon,' Sandhya continued, apparently ignoring Ary's slight. 'With greater detail and meaning. The one you've encountered so far is the most common interpretation. You might discover the other as your journey continues.'

'*Continues?*' Ary snapped. 'No, no, ladies. This is it. I do the thing and you fuck off. That was our arrangement. For my mother. Sopheak. Baba's sister. But nothing more. If we're lucky enough to survive what comes next, that's it. I'm retiring. From all of it. The blogs. The theories. Your mad shite. I'm giving up.'

'Yes, dear one,' Nkechi said. 'Whatever you say.'

A thump on the hull indicated that the boat had reached land. Jordan turned, gazed out a porthole and saw that they were in a narrow inlet, by a craggy shore, not totally shielded from the view of the larger island but hidden enough to remain unseen by a passing boat.

The Gnostics ushered them out on deck.

'This is it?' Jordan said, scanning the rugged, vegetation-sparse terrain. 'This is the centre of the world?'

Sandhya giggled. 'No, silly. Just an island, that houses a Core Hub.'

Nkechi giggled too.

'It's not very impressive.'

'Why should it be impressive?' Sandhya looked genuinely confused.

'I was expecting more... well, more bells and whistles.'

'What would be the point of that? Why hide something and then put a big sign up saying, *Here It Is?*'

Ary snorted a snigger.

Jordan let it go, she was hurting.

'Anyway, off you trot,' Nkechi said. 'We believe the cave entrance is somewhere north of here. Up there maybe.' She was pointing along the coast to a cliffy outcrop, bristling with jagged rocks. 'We don't know for sure. But Ary will find it. We have faith.'

Ary glared at them both. Then at Jordan. An instant later, she was out of the boat and saying, 'C'mon then. Let's get on with it.'

Jordan followed. The Gnostics waved. The pilot turned her small vessel seaward, powered away from the shore and became a dot, cresting the water towards Thera.

Jordan and Ary walked up the coast in silence. Apart from the slightest sea breeze, the air was eerily still. Soldiers talked about the inhaled breath before battle. Athletes spoke of the quietness of the mind. The pause that comes when about to undertake an onerous task. The island was as barren as its sister five hundred yards across the bay. A rugged mass of dacite, pumice and pebbles. Hopefully not the exploding kind. There was little greenery. It was sweltering hot. Even for Jordan. They had no water. The Gnostics had insisted they travel light, leaving them with just their clothes, no belts – they didn't explain why, but buckles were a problem apparently – a white tubular-shaped object each, made of stone and supplied by the Gnostics, which they called a flashlight, and the symbol tablet in his pocket. Definitely no phones. The women were adamant, said it was to avoid distractions. Jordan could see their logic, but doubted their reasoning. Something else was at play. Dangerous. The phones would be back at the hotel when they returned from their task... *if* they returned from the task.

That damned *if* was always there.

Niggling.

Causing doubt.

Striking fear.

'Stop lagging.' Ary barked, from a few yards ahead.

Jordan didn't reply, just followed her along the shore to the spot where Nkechi had indicated might harbour an entrance to a cave. They stopped. There was no cave. Just rocks and, for now at least, no sign of the armed agents he expected to fall upon them at any second.

COME TOGETHER RIGHT NOW

Of course, only the deluded or insanely optimistic could believe that hundreds, in some cases, thousands of years of intercommunal enmity might be wiped away through the simple matter of collective necessity but, with practically every region on the planet experiencing some level of catastrophe, unbeknownst even to their own populaces, it was amazing what previously adversarial nations could achieve in very little time. By freak of circumstance, the planet was simultaneously burning, flooding, and being blown away. To which end, and after some intranational soul-searching, a newly cooperative *United* States of America joined Canada, the South American nations, Asia – apart from the Democratic People's Republic of Korea (DPRK) – along with the Oceanic islands to create a supermax version of the Trans-Pacific Partnership. The Russian Federation rolled back its malign ambitions in Ukraine. The UK became an associate member, or *re*-member, of the EU. Unaffiliated Eastern European countries followed suit, along with all the nations of Africa. Any country, not aligned with one of the two groups, merely joined the closest alliance. Both of which were administrated by the overarching supervision of the UN.

By the morning of Saturday, 10th June 2023, and following long hours of discussion and compromise, the whole world – bar the DPRK, who joined soon after, along with Japan who were coaxed out of their kneejerk isolation – had acquiesced to at least some level of UN oversight, with the proviso that the General Assembly had sign-off on any resolutions. It truly was democratic and as fair as circumstances might allow. Sure, there were disagreements. Old rivalries came to the fore. And there were many excuses for how, what scientists had predicted for decades and, to some extent, the Caucus had instigated, *circumstances took us by surprise* and *no one saw it coming.* Like one of those movies where a massive alien fleet swoops in from a far-off galaxy and begins blowing up all the major cities, though, for the first time in its history, the world appeared to act as one. Made decisions as one. Cooperated as one. Focusing on the problems they held in common

A sceptical person or, in particular, a member of the Caucus, might say it was too good to be true, that it worked. People really could pull together and pool resources when need demanded. Which was troubling. It threatened to upturn thirteen thousand years of sustained and deliberate manipulation.

The calls came thick and fast.

First, Saxe-Gothe. Followed by Mansa, Patidar, Soma. And finally, Rothbauer.

He didn't sound happy. Or convinced of Gildermere's methods. They seemed to fly in the face of everything the Caucus wanted to achieve.

Gildermere ignored their protestations, claiming his scheme was to keep the plebians distracted. While he, as an Aryan, focused on thwarting the Gnostics at Santorini. He sent three additional helicopters, crammed with agents, to support those already imbedded on Nea Kameni. They had better gear. More sophisticated and deadlier devices. If the two Star Children were stupid enough to embark on their quest, he doubted they would make it farther than the shore.

Everything hung on stopping the reactivation of the Core Hubs.

All focus, both Aryan and Gnostic, was on that barren little island.

Rothbauer signed off. To Gildermere, he appeared unconvinced.

It didn't matter. The Caucus had always been a tad twitchy when it came to playing in a new age. They were too obsessed with the past. With tradition and the old ways of doing things. The future called for a different outlook and Gildermere, in spite of their resolute conservatism, would deliver.

They could either roll with it, or get rolled over.

Sitting at his desk in the office assigned to him at the UN Headquarters in New York, Vilmos Gildermere picked up the phone, called an encrypted number, spoke to the Chief Field Agent for the Aryan taskforce at Santorini and enquired as to the situation on Nea Kameni.

'No change.' The Chief Field Agent informed him. 'No one has landed on the island since our occupation. There are no signs of the agitators. Or their Gnostic handlers. Our sources state that, since the rogue shooting, they haven't left their hotel in Thera.'

'Has anyone actually checked the rooms?'

'No. But we've...'

'Then you don't know.'

'We are pretty certain...'

'But you don't know for sure.'

'No. Not for sure.'

'So, what are you doing about it?'

'I'll despatch an investigator right away. We already have boots on the ground. Members of the hotel staff. I'll get one of them to check the rooms.'

'Get all of them... to check all the rooms. Then call me back right away. The Gnostics are running out of time but, like cornered rats, that makes them dangerous.'

'*Dangerous*? Gnostics? They're not even allowed to kill.'

'That's true. But – and I want you to listen to this very carefully – if they do manage to reach the Core Hub... and they could... and if they manage to reactivate it... and they could... then it's game over for everything we've spent the last thirteen millennia setting up. Over. Out. Done and gone. Do you get that, Agent *They're-not-even-allowed-to-kill*? Do you understand the implications? With that kind of power, and also having possession of the *Book of Lights* and *Logos*, we could do nothing to stop them. So, I suggest you check the rooms. Swarm Nea Kameni with personnel. This is supposed to be the dawn of the *New Aryan Age*. Your job is to make sure that happens. So do it. Do your job.'

He slammed down the phone, rubbed his face with his hands, sighed, picked up the phone again and rang the pilot of his private jet, telling him to get ready for departure.

He was going to Santorini.

Time was waning.

The two Star Children were hours away from achieving, or failing, in their goal.

CLASSICAL EDUCATION

As they stood on the gravelly shore, Jordan found himself scouring the ground for round pebbles. There weren't any. Palea Kameni was just jagged rock upon jagged rock. To hide their explosive devises, the Aryans would have had to disguise them as clumps of pumice or dacite, and anyway, the Gnostics had said they were still on the other island, across the bay; nearby, but not on this one.

Yet.

'We need to move,' he said. Since arriving at the spot, Ary's mood had changed. She seemed downcast again, reticent.

'Wow,' she replied. 'Look who's all up and at it. I thought this was all woo. Not real science.'

'I changed my mind.'

'So, the super prick changes his mind and I have to follow.'

'Yes. You do. It's just the way of it.'

'Now you sound like one of those fucking Gnostics.'

'Well, apparently, we are now.'

'Fucking yay. Hope they give us a medal.'

'Look, if they can convince a sceptic like me, then they must be onto something. You saw the blue lights. You know what is at stake.'

'Yes, I saw the blue lights. But I'm not the one who needed convincing. And, yes, I know what's at stake. I just don't care.'

'So, why are you here then? Why are you not still back at the hotel working-up your sclerosis?' Before Ary could snap a reply, he continued, 'because of your family. That's why. They matter. And, you know what, my family matters too.'

'That was a low punch.'

'What? Making you responsible for my family's future? Yes. Too right. The way I see it, you either get your head outta your ass and into the game, or we both go home and watch the world fall down around us. Your family. My family. All families. Whatever effects one, effects all. Save one, save all. And, you know what, it's all up to you.'

'And, you know what... you're as big a grade-A shitbag as the Gnostics. They played the guilt card too. It's cruel. Not fair. Or nice.'

'But does it mean you'll do it? Are with me?'

After a few seconds, she said, 'Yes.'

'Does it mean you'll see it out?'

'Yep. Yeah. Yes. I'll fucking do it, okay.'

'Good. Now help me find the entrance to this goddamned cave they're talking about.'

'Don't need to.'

'Why?'

'Because it's up there.' She was pointing to a clump of ragged black rock rising slightly higher than the others. 'See that shadowy bit?' Jordan nodded. 'It's an optical illusion. There's a gap there.' She scrambled up the gravel rise. At the top, she stood and stretched out her left arm, which disappeared into the rock as if amputated at the shoulder. 'See. An illusion.' She peered into the shadow and back to Jordan again. 'The gap looks big enough to slip through sideways.'

'That can't be the entrance,' he said. 'Anyone could stumble across it.'

'I get the impression people don't come here. The Gnostics probably put a curse on the place. Come within fifty metres and your stomach explodes in a fit of vomits. Or it gives you boils or something.'

'They can't kill.'

'No, but they could induce a temporary affliction.'

'Yep. They could do that. How did you know it was there? Never mind. I shouldn't ask. Anyway, nice one.'

'Yes. I found it. And, to quote Bilbo, *I do believe the worst is behind us.*'

Jordan wasn't so convinced. 'So, do it then. Go inside.'

'You go inside. Why does it have to be me?'

'Because you found it.'

'As if that's a reason. You come up here and do it.' She gazed into the shadow and back to Jordan. 'Never mind. I'm on it.' She smiled, stepped sideways and vanished into the cliffside. Locating the entrance seemed to have lifted her spirits. After the chase was over, though, if they survived, Jordan expected a collapse.

When she didn't reappear, Jordan scrambled up the incline, found the shadow, but not the gap. A hand, on the end of an arm, manifesting from the rock, grabbed his tee-shirt and yanked him into darkness.

'Keep moving sideways,' Ary said from the other end of the arm. 'It's narrow. The stone is sharp. And breathe in, if you don't want to strip the skin off your belly.'

Jordan snatched a breath, went farther in and, testing the uneven ground with his feet, followed Ary along a winding crevice through the rock. They travelled for many minutes, following the weaves and turns of the cramped passage, wider in places, narrow in others, but always heading down. Ary kept hold of his tee-shirt the whole way. Only letting go when they emerged into a circular open section, dimly illuminated by the faint backlight coming through the crevice and similar in size to his basement office in New York. It smelled the same too. Musty, but with a hint of sulphur. Ary took out her weird-looking stone flashlight. It was already lit. Jordan did likewise. His was shining too. The devices seemed to know when to switch on:

'Impressive.'

'And freaky,' Ary added.

In the better light, a set of steps, hewn from the rock and descending a sheer passage, came into view. Unlike the rocky area around them, the walls were smooth, squared to the same height and width, the steps themselves exhibiting properties of having been chiselled from the bedrock and rarely, if at all, used.

Ary took off down them, her lack of caution making Jordan twitch.

Ten or so steps down, she turned, shined her flashlight in his face, said, 'Come on then,' swung around again and disappeared into the void, her torchlight bouncing in the darkness like marker buoys bobbing upon midnight harbour waves.

He hurried after her. She turned a corner, the bobbing torchlight vanishing. He followed, down a spiralling stairwell, watching her torchlight, no torchlight, torchlight again, no torchlight, and so on, as he trailed after her.

Occasionally, she shouted back, 'Still with me, Marco Slow-mo?'

He replied with a simple, 'Yeah,' and carried on.

All in all, Jordan reckoned they descended three-hundred steps which, by estimating the height of each riser, put them somewhere around nineteen to twenty standard floors below ground level with no sign of running out. The air grew colder but not frigid. Ary continued her checks, using the alternating nicknames of, *Marco Slow-mo, Sir Francis Flake, Zheng He-can't-keep-up.* Jordan understood the inference but it got tiring. He also guessed it was part of her coping mechanism. They carried on, winding downwards for the same, if not more steps than they had already taken until they reached a wall that wasn't a wall but another shimmering optical illusion similar to the shadowy entrance to the cave above. Ary piled through. Jordan hesitated. A hand gripped his tee-shirt and, an instant later, he was on the other side, standing in a passage, as neatly hewn from the bedrock as the spiral stairwell but long and narrow, like one of the halls at Ta Prohm temple, with the ceiling high above and a large bronze door at the far end.

They continued down the passage together and with caution. Even Ary, the capricious and carefree one of them both, appeared wary and yet in awe of everything she saw. Her eyes were like dinner plates. Wide and disbelieving. Jordan felt it too. The formidable pressure of knowing you were somewhere very old, very important, and untouched since before the fledgling annals of history. As they neared the door, the first thing Jordan noticed was a three-feet diameter representation of the Organon, embossed centre-place of the bronze, and containing the same basic design as the symbol he had seen before but with more detailing. The bulk of the pattern, including the Incan Cross, was now enclosed within a square and the outer perimeter within two additional circles. The mandala aspects were more defined, reminding him of the reliefs at Ta Prohm, and the symbol for yin and yang appeared closer to something an archaeologist, anthropologist, or even a mystic might recognise. Each corner held what looked like a Dharma Wheel, and additional lines, radiating from within the configuration, marked the cardinal points of northeast, southeast, northwest, and southwest. It was the same but more. *The other* Organon Sandhya had mentioned. More complete. Perhaps more powerful. Hidden here for millennia, away from prying Aryan eyes.

Ary said, 'Wow!'

Jordan added, 'It's still shiny. In fact, the whole door is gleaming. How can that be? This long down here, it should have oxidised by now. Green not glossy, and...' He caught himself. 'Never mind. I know already...'

'The Gnostics,' they said together, sharing a giggle.

It was good to hear Ary laugh. He missed it. And her.

She was standing back, her torchlight fixed on the symbol. Jordan did likewise, but also jabbed the door with the tip of his finger, half-expecting to get an electric shock and, when it didn't happen, touched the door again, this time finding the courage to lay his left palm flat on the surface. The bronze was as cold as expected for a big metal door situated forty-odd floors underground... and smooth, as if regularly polished. Passing his hand over the outlines and creases, he noticed they were sharp, delineated. If he didn't know better, he might assume they had been made by machinery or a 3D printer. It was amazing. And unsettling. Everything he had accepted as history was thrown to the winds. Sliding his hand around the outer perimeter, he reached up and, standing on tiptoes, tracked the upper border and then beyond, where his fingers picked out smooth metal again, followed by another, smaller relief, a few inches in size, not as prominent as the Organon but defined enough to show there was a second motif there.

'What's this?' he asked himself as much as Ary.

She stepped closer, shone her flashlight directly onto the relief. 'Well, fuck me sideways. Can't be. Who'd've thought it'd be here? Then again, I suppose it makes sense. Thera was part of their civilisation after all. But here? Can this be the actual place?'

'What? What is it?'

'A bull's head.'

'A what?' He stepped back, joined Ary in shining light directly onto the motif.

'A bull's head.'

'Which means what?'

'Well,' she began, 'what I think this is... this bull head... here... on this big bronze door... down the bottom of a deep staircase...'

'Stop rambling. Tell me!'

She drew a breath, smiling broadly like the Cheshire Cat, and blurted out, 'I think this might be the entrance to Daedalus' labyrinth.'

'What? The Greek legend? Theseus? The Minotaur?'

'The very ones.'

He looked up at the motif again. 'Well, that's definitely a bull's head.'

'I know... eek! This is fucking awesome. The Gnostics said myth and history overlap. What better way to avoid unwanted attention than to create a yarn about a big ugly monster that can rip a person's arms out of their sockets.'

'Good point.'

'But it's in the wrong place. King Minos commissioned the labyrinth to be built on Crete.'

'Maybe it's another misdirection.'

'Sounds about right. Those Gnostics do love themselves a good old misdirection. So, if the legend is in some way true, and the actual place where the fictitious – at least I'm hoping it's fictitious – Minotaur was kept prisoner is here and not Crete, that would mean, on the other side of this door lies Daedalus' labyrinth.'

'And maybe a huge giant with a bull's head.'

'Fuck off. There's no way.'

'You're the conspiracy nut. You tell me.'

'Bite me.' She gazed at the door, awe beaming in her eyes.

Jordan smiled. It was good to see her inquisitive again. 'So, you want to go through?'

'Do I ever.'

Apart from the reliefs, the door was set flush into the surrounding stone. There were no gaps, or obvious hinges, or handles, knobs, levers, or any mechanism to indicate a way the door might be opened. 'So, push it then,' Jordan said.

'You push it.'

'Nope. You're the myth worshipper, it's all yours.'

'Can't. I'm too small and slender.'

'Yeah right.'

'Anyway, you've already done it once. I'll stand back, keep an eye on things. In case it shoots out bolts of electricity or something.'

'Exactly what I was thinking.'

'Good. Then we're on the same page. Push it.'

'Okay. I'll do it. But it's all on you if I die in a ball of blue flame.'

'I'll write your obituary.'

Jordan scowled, took a second to muster his courage, laid both palms on the door and, when no lightning bolts came, he pushed. 'It won't budge.'

'Do it again.'

He tried. A few times, without success. It was like pushing against a mountain.

'Maybe you have to say, *Speak Friend and Enter.*'

'What? Why? I haven't seen anything that...'

'Never mind. Okay then, perhaps there's a button. The bull's head.'

'I don't reckon that would be the case. It wouldn't be much of an impenetrable door if any old Aryan could come along, press the motif and get through. I presume it's another Gnostic barrier.'

'Meant only for us.'

'Good one. Yes. Meant only for us. Maybe, we should be feeling something. Like we did before. Do you feel anything? Surely, we must feel something. Anything. Same as all the other times. Or maybe not. What do you think?'

'Do you know, it's an absolute pleasure to watch your mind in action. But you're right. And, no. Apart from knowing how to get into the crevice up there, I don't feel a damned thing.'

'Which would mean we're doing something wrong. Perhaps we should push together. Like with the other symbols. And, you never know, maybe this is it. It's not really a door but the actual Core Hub. Maybe we made it... in time.'

His theory didn't pan out. When they laid their hands on the symbol, it glimmered with a faint blue light but nothing major happened. The door did open, though. It split in the middle, slickly, as if oiled at its invisible hinges, and slid to either side, revealing a large, triangular shaped hall, hewn from the rock, with smooth walls and floor, at the farther, narrow end of which, a person-wide passageway led off into yet more darkness. As if sharing the same thought, they shone their flashlights around the walls. Jordan estimated the hall to be ten yards wide on either side of the door, twice that again to the entrance to the passageway, with the ceiling too high to measure.

'I think it's the entrance to the labyrinth,' Ary said.

'After you then.'

'Why me?'

'I pushed the door.'

'We both pushed the door.'

'But not until after I played guinea pig. So, off you go. You're the one who loves a mystery.'

Ary grinned. She was *in her element*, as his father liked to say. Childlike. Eager. And, for once, a pleasure to be with. Tripping off down the hall like a kid heading for the candy-store, for now at least, she seemed devoid of the sorrow that had plagued her for the last few days.

She glanced back once before stepping into the passageway.

Jordan recognised it as his cue to follow.

Which he did, only with much less enthusiasm and great deal more wariness.

MAKE IT HAPPEN

When he touched down on Santorini, Vilmos Gildermere immediately contacted the Chief Field Agent with two requests: an update on the Star Children's whereabouts and a helicopter to fly him out to Nea Kameni.

The answer to his first question was, 'We don't know. They're not in their rooms.'

The second, 'Right away.'

Twenty-five minutes later, he was atop the highest ridge on Nea Kameni, sitting on a canvas chair in the mess tent of a makeshift barracks, drinking coffee. The Chief Field Agent, clad in dark blue fatigues and body armour, had accompanied him on the flight. Vilmos, however, waited until he arrived before barraging his Aryan subordinate with additional questions.

Sipping from a brown paper cup, and wincing at the world's worst tasting coffee, he asked, 'Is this the best you can get.'

'Yes,' the Chief Field Agent replied without emotion. 'We don't require luxuries.'

'Spoken like the faithful. You truly are a loyal Aryan grunt.'

The subordinate didn't reply. Remained standing and rigid.

'And what about the populace? The tourists? I take it they've been taken care of?'

'Before we set out, I instigated an eruption scare. As far as the locals are concerned, we are a scientific team assessing the caldera for volcanic activity. The recent quake at Rhodes helped solidify the claim. The Greek government were quick to accommodate. We have complete autonomy.'

'And what about all the weapons? Did they raise suspicion?'

'No. We told the authorities they're for security. They seemed to buy it.'

'Good. We don't want anyone poking around. And, what are your thoughts as to our missing Star Children.'

'We don't know. One minute they were at the hotel, the next they were gone. We suspect the Gnostics are using one of their mental cloaks to hide their whereabouts.'

'That's not an excuse,' Vilmos snapped. 'We trained you how to deal with mental cloaks.'

'I know. But they're very adept.'

'Two of them? Just two Gnostics... can influence a fully trained, fully functional squad of highly skilled field agents... who, it just so happens, are also family members of the most elite dynasties in history? Is that what you are telling me?'

The Chief Field Agent paused, said, 'I suppose.'

'You suppose! Get it together. I want them found. Take half your squad back to Thera. I don't care what it takes: money, bribes, do what is necessary.'

'But that would mean weakening our forces here.'

'It might also mean you find them. Before they actually succeed. You can redistribute your resources. We already know the entrance to the Core Hub is somewhere north of here, near Ákra Stáchti. Our sources say the Gnostics think so too. Focus there. Time is running out. I suspect they'll get desperate. Sloppy. Which will bring them into the open.'

'Anything else?'

'No. That's it. Make it happen.'

The Chief Field Agent didn't salute before he left. Being from the same families as the Caucus members, Aryans, no matter how lowly, didn't do that kind of thing. He did, however, bow. A mark of respect for the Patriarch and a tradition carried over from ancient times. When he was gone, Vilmos tipped his god-awful coffee out onto the sand, handed the paper cup to the agent standing guard by the tent-flap and instructed him to make ready an inflatable dinghy, with an outboard motor, and no security detail.

Vilmos would pilot the boat himself.

AMAZING SPACE

On closer inspection, the passageway was of black basalt. Shiny like glass and reflecting Ary and Jordan's silhouettes in bobbing stripes of shadow and torchlight as they strode towards a point, about ten metres in, where the passage took a sharp turn to the left. Although little more than shoulder width between them, the walls stood around three metres high, with no ceiling apart from that which covered the whole complex many tens, perhaps hundreds, of metres above. They seemed to be on a platform. A massive one, set within a bigger chamber, with no light, no breeze, no way to determine where it began or finished, and no echoes – not even their footsteps. Just eerie silence. A sense of dormancy. As if the whole place had held its breath, waiting for an opportunity to exhale.

Glancing back to Jordan, Ary took the left turn.

He was right there behind her, his head swivelling like a radar dish, scanning the claustrophobic space around them and seemingly wide-eyed amazed by the vaulted space above. He looked scared. Or, if not scared, at least wary. Ten metres farther in, they met a turn to the right, followed by another, ten metres farther again, to the left. Followed by another, to the right, and another, to the left. And on it went for dozens of turns until they faced a choice.

Three directions opened for them: left, right, and forward.

Ary looked back at Jordan. 'Whatcha think?'

He shrugged.

'I mean, do you feel anything.'

He shrugged again, said, 'No. Nothing.'

'Fucking brilliant. Me neither.' She peered into each of their options. 'But, I suppose, when in doubt, take the middle one.'

'What if it leads us over a cliff?'

'We'll be careful. Baby steps.'

'What if it leads us into a big ugly monster with horns on its head?'

'I'll throw you at it.'

Jordan smiled. In the torchlight it looked creepy, but his whole falling off a cliff notion had plucked a nerve and she appreciated the gesture. Stepping into the passage, the floor didn't fall away so, with shuffling baby steps, Ary carried on, discovering, ten metres later, that Jordan was right. They reached an edge, dropping straight down into a pit so dark the light of their torches failed to penetrate more than a few metres.

'Fuck.' Ary said. 'I can't tell where the floor ends.' She pushed back against Jordan. 'Soz, mate. Heights give me the heebies.'

'Good job we were careful then.'

'Too right. We'll have to go back.'

'Want me to take the lead?'

'Hell yeah. I was all up and at it for a while there, but plummeting to my death wasn't on my list of things to do by forty.'

Jordan said, 'Okay,' turned and, with Ary practically clipping his heels, walked the ten metres back to the crossroads. 'So, where to now?'

'I'm not sure. That's the thing with labyrinths, there's no logic. And, as for feeling something, it would appear we're both lacking that little nugget.'

'Do another vision then.' He took the tablet out of his pocket, shone torchlight on it. 'Touching the symbol worked back at your aunt and uncle's pyramid. Maybe if we lay our hands on this together... then shazam, it's vision time.'

He had a point. 'Seems about right.'

'Can't hurt.'

'Let's do it, then. But *shazam*... really?'

Jordan smiled. He smiled a lot, usually instead of talking. Ary guessed it was his coping mechanism. She had her fucking and blinding all over the place. He had his grinning like a gormless idiot. Fair enough. Each to their own. Whatever got him through the day... or the next upshot of touching the tablet. Laying their palms onto the symbol, Ary closed her eyes and tried to visualise arrows pointing the way through the labyrinth. Her skin tingled. Hairs stood on the back of her neck and arms. The vision was coming. Her thoughts blurred. An ocean of clouds and sparkles. Nebulae. Constellations. Billions of suns flaring in darkness and planets rolling through the void. She took it all in. Took control. Peering deep into her mind. When her sight cleared, she was standing in a vast chamber. Overhead, a huge, twinkling representation of the heavens hovered mid-air, which she intuitively recognised as the constellations of Capricorn and Aquarius. A small planet, third last at the outer end of a stylised depiction of a solar system, moved slowly from one to the other. *Pluto returning for six months into Capricorn.* The thought came as soundly as any she accepted as fact, confirming that the planet was on the cusp, which appeared as a white laser-like line marked upon the black sky, delineating the threshold between the constellations. All but the last sliver of the planet had traversed the boundary, and she understood the whole vision for what it was: a clock of sorts, representing the astronomical event taking place in the cosmos and the urgency of its message. She then saw the labyrinth from above, laid out as if carved in stone, ninety percent in darkness, the remaining ten percent depicted as an illuminated route, meandering from the triangular shaped hall at the entrance all the way to the chamber containing the hovering map of Pluto crossing the constellations.

A sudden jolt returned her to the present.

'Got it,' she said, with more certainty than she felt. 'We follow the lines of the symbol, east to west, as if multiple Incan Crosses have been set one atop the other... but also slightly askew.'

'I'll take your word for it.'

'Yeah. Me too. Those bloody Gnostics never make it easy.'

They headed left and Ary guided Jordan along passageway after passageway, deeper into the labyrinth. They walked for what felt like hours. Sometimes they met a dead end. She had a rethink, changed direction and, with Jordan tripping along behind, strutted off with feigned confidence in another direction. At other times, they met a precipice, freaking her out. She continued with measured steps, Jordan holding tight to the back of her tee-shirt. At one point, he stated his theory that, given the askant cross upon cross motif she had seen in her vision, the maze was all but limitless and suspended within a boundless, hollow orb. Ary agreed. The thought terrified her. Searching for the truth was one thing, but getting lost in Daedalus' labyrinth was something she hadn't reckoned on when she began her journey into conspiracy theories.

'How long do you think we've been down here?' she asked.

'Four, five, maybe six or seven hours. I can't really tell. This place has my thoughts in a spin. I don't know if we're up, down, around, or sideways.'

'Me too. And fuck.'

'What?'

'We can't go wandering around down here forever.'

'True. But what can we do about it? We're stuck here. Traipsing through this damned maze.'

They carried on. Meeting more dead ends and way too many cliff edges for Ary's liking. Her inner guidance was working, but not as keenly as before. After her visions at the Xianyang pyramid, Ta Prohm and Machu Picchu, and even when she revealed the triskele at Newgrange, the air had seemed electrified; potential on the brink of being released. Here, she sensed a great force, but subdued, as if imprisoned behind a wall. There – yet unable to reach out. The lack of clarity was throwing off her *symbol-dar*. She laughed at the memory of creating the name. And at Jordan's confusion.

'You okay?' he asked.

'Yes... and no. I think we're lost.'

Vilmos Gildermere estimated he had been following the labyrinth for seven hours since he first landed his dinghy on the shore of Palea Kameni. Tracking the Star Children had been easy. Their aurae lingered like a bad smell, colouring the ether in trails of blue mist, invisible to plebians but plain as day to those with the skills to see. He had followed them through a cleft in the rocks, down the stone stairwell, through an open bronze door and onward through a maze of narrow passageways.

The might, influence, and military power of the Caucus had failed to stop them.

Vilmos, however, knew exactly where they were going.

The Chief Field Agent at Santorini paused before stepping through the mess tent flap, dreading the report he would have to give of how, yet again, his forces had found no trace of the Star Children in Thera.

The new Patriarch wasn't there.

'Where did the Patriarch go?' he asked the duty guard.

The young lad stood to attention, bowed, and stood to attention again. 'He asked me to get him a boat, Chief. He requested one without a security detail.'

'That's strange. Why did he do that?'

'I don't know, Chief. He seemed in a hurry.'

The Chief said, 'As you were,' walked the path down to the inlet housing the taskforce's temporary pontoon harbour and asked the dockmaster if he had seen the Patriarch.

'He took a dinghy, Chief,' the dockmaster replied with a bow. 'Went off in the direction of Palea Kameni.'

'Did he say why?'

'No, Chief. He just got in the boat and headed off.'

The Chief said, 'Carry on,' and peered out across the bay to the nearby island.

Something didn't fit. The Patriarch had told him to search the hotels in Thera and to focus attention in the north of Nea Kameni. He hadn't said a word about anything to the south. And nothing at all about the sister island. It seemed off. Unusual. Questioning the Patriarch about his activities, however, was the biggest Aryan no no. The Chief wanted to let it go. A decision that would serve better for his career, and maybe his health, but it still niggled.

He called for a boat, and a five-man detail.

Perhaps the Patriarch had some information previously unknown.

Maybe he had taken it upon himself to deal with the matter in person.

Whatever the reason, the Chief thought it prudent to lend support. To his knowledge, there were only two Star Children, and three Gnostics, all of whom were forbidden to injure or kill anyone but, in his experience, it was always better not to take chances. If the Patriarch's life was in danger, he would be there, ready, able and, if he took out the enemy in the process, then better still.

It might even advance his standing within the Pachacuti family.

LOST IN SPACE

'This is arse,' Ary said, staring into yet another passageway with its shiny black walls. 'I haven't the foggiest which way's which. We've been going around for hours. I think my *symbol-dar* is broken.'

'Maybe you just need to focus harder,' Jordan replied.

'So, you really are a true believer?'

'I am now. But I want out. I want it over with. And, like it or not, you're the only game in town.'

'You might've backed a loser there, mate. What time do you think it is?'

'Evening... maybe.' He looked drained and crestfallen. Not once, however, did he blame Ary. Throughout the hours of wandering, he remained pragmatic, citing, 'This place might seem like some kind of arcane mystery, but logic dictates that there must be an end. All we have to do is find it.'

Ary was thankful for his gem of wisdom. Without it, she feared her confidence might falter more than it had already. She needed a break. She needed Mateus. Not for his help, but just to be here. The memory made her cry and Jordan consoled her as best someone like Jordan could. He obviously didn't deal well with matters of the heart but, in his own cack-handed way, he did try. With clichés. Actually saying the – relatively unhelpful – phrase, *things get better with time*. And she appreciated his efforts, sniffing away her tears and patting his arm in her own offhand way of showing gratitude.

They walked on. Legs aching. Eyes tired from squinting through the gloom; the reflective stone walls strobing the waning glow of their flashlights. The light flickered. Ary's went out. Followed, a few seconds later, by Jordan's. Gnostic devices or not, they evidently had a lifespan. They were in darkness. The absolute kind. She raised her hand in front of her face but saw nothing.

'Not good,' Jordan said. He sounded calmer than expected.

Ary reached around, touched his arm. It felt good. Familiar. And then the thought came: *what if we are trapped here forever?* She said it aloud.

Jordan answered with, 'Let's deal with the present. There must be a way to trace our way back out.'

She felt neither convinced nor eased. A second thought came: *back out to what... we failed?* This too Ary said aloud.

'You haven't failed,' a voice said from behind them in the darkness.

Torchlight came into view, radiating from the hand of a middle-aged man wearing a smart suit. 'I know,' he continued, in a nondescript accent, maybe Germanic, 'I'm a bit overdressed for stumbling about in caverns. But I've always been of the mind that, no matter the circumstances, one must keep up appearances.' He laughed.

Ary took a step back. Jordan did the same.

'So, you're the Star Children,' the man continued. 'When Sandhya and Nkechi told me it was you two, I wasn't so sure. You've always seemed mismatched to me. *Bucket-mouth and the Nerd.* Which would also make a great name for one of those buddy cop shows you North Americans love so much.' He was looking at Jordan. '*Hey, Bucket-mouth,*' he carried on, affecting a New York dialect, '*where's my science stuff... and doughnuts?*' He switched to mimic a London accent, '*Get them your-effing-self, Nerd. I'm not your blinking flipping effing baker.* Ah, priceless. I'd make a terrific script writer.' He laughed, and then stopped. 'Forgive me. Where's my manners. Let me introduce myself – my name is Vilmos... Vilmos Gildermere.'

'As in the new UN General Secretary.' Jordan said.

'Yes. But I'm not one to brag.'

'Great,' Ary said. 'That's cool. But who are you?'

'I told you, Vilmos Gildermere, UN General Secretary... to the United Nations.' He smirked at Jordan, then back at Ary. 'Oh. I get it. You want to know *who* I am. As in why I am here. That's easy. I'm the third Gnostic. I'm sure Nkechi and Sandhya mentioned me. It would really hurt my feelings if they haven't.'

Ary glanced to Jordan, who shrugged. 'They did. Not much, though. Only that you exist. But how do we know for sure? You could be anyone. An Aryan.'

'I am Aryan,' Vilmos said, smiling.

Ary and Jordan took another step back.

'But, don't worry,' Vilmos continued. 'Only a pretend one. It's a generational thing. I sit on the Caucus of the thirteen Aryan families. All the Gildermeres have, for millennia, and we've been right under their noses all the time. Other than that, I'm one hundred percent, grade-A, industrial strength Gnostic. Also, if I wasn't, how do you think I found you all the way down here?'

'The mind reading thing?' Jordan said.

'Exactly. Well, actually, more of a mind and aura trailing thing. Very useful when tracking a pair of Star Children through an unfathomable maze. As well as wading through the unbalanced thought patterns of the average Aryan. A few of them can develop strong wills, but most are not very bright, you see. They think they are, but it's just their delusions playing with their brains. Anyway,' he shone his flashlight around the walls, 'I take it, it's safe to assume you are lost?'

Ary nodded, still not sure about the new guy.

Jordan appeared more satisfied, said, 'Yes, can you help?'

'Are you doing that to him?' Ary asked Vilmos, which, bizarrely, Jordan didn't seem to notice.

'A bit. But only to take the edge off. Otherwise, he'd be all suspicions and queries. And the last thing we need right now is Jordan Burke going all twenty questions, *Inspector Nerd* on us. We don't have time. What about you? Do my explanations tally with your conspiracy theorist mind?'

'I'm open. But, you're right, we don't have time. And we are lost.'

'The old *symbol-dar* not working then?'

'A bit. Got us this far. But, at the moment, no. Can you help?'

'I'll try. It's why I'm here. Nkechi and Sandhya, however, are the big hitters when it comes to Logos. The Gildermeres – not my real surname – were always the poor cousins in that respect. Probably why we got the Aryan Caucus gig in the first place. Harder to detect. I do have powers, though, just not as honed as theirs.'

'So, what is your real surname?' Jordan asked.

'I don't have one. Gnostics invent them as needs arise: *Salvus* in ancient Rome, the Egyptian Nubian family of *Echnaton*, *Huangdi* in China, *Cahuachi* in the Americas. In Sumer we were known as *Utu*, when we wrote Gilgamesh. *Sun Tzu* was one of ours too, a brilliant infiltrator. *Siddartha* was another, and maybe our best example of sowing hope amid Aryan discord. In fact, most of the great human teachers were Gnostics.'

'But what about you?'

'Thousands of years ago, an adept of my particular line wheedled their way onto the Caucus as the thirteenth family and we've been there ever since, waiting for the right circumstances to act. But, don't get me wrong, it wasn't all roses. A fatal dalliance within the Templar Knights meant the other lines had to go deeper underground. Whereby, until Pluto moves fully into Aquarius next January, even they don't know they're Gnostics. The people with intuition. The psychics. Mystics. Shamans. They sense they have abilities but aren't certain. In the aftermath of the Templar tragedy, it was decided to only empower a single Gnostic from one of just three lines, chosen by the predecessor, in secret and unknown even to their own family members. The reasoning was, by keeping everyone in the dark and with fewer adepts working in the shadows, the Caucus would be none the wiser. And it worked. Here we are, gabbing away in dark passageways, wasting time and holding back the dawn of a fantastic new world that won't happen if we don't reactivate the Core Hub.'

'The Core Hub,' Ary said. 'With all this getting lost and your mad story, I had forgotten about the bloody Core Hub.'

'Do you know how to get there?' Jordan asked the Gnostic.

'No. Only Ary does.'

'So, we're fucked then,' Ary said.

'Not necessarily. I can help. Use my mindpower to give you a jolt, so to speak.'

'Okay, what are we waiting for?' Jordan said.

'Nothing at all,' Vilmos replied with a smile. He nodded towards their flashlights. With a sudden flare, they became bright again. 'I can only keep that up for a short while,' he added. 'Which is fine, because we only have a short while.'

'Better get our arse in gear then,' Ary replied.

Vilmos nodded. Jordan shrugged. And Ary reckoned they might even make it.

The Chief Field Agent and his assault detail moved quickly. Elite training and previous deployment experience had them across the strait, on the Palea Kameni beach and searching for the Patriarch's whereabouts in less than fifteen minutes. Following footprints through the volcanic sand and up a jagged cliff, they discovered a crevice. On first inspection it seemed shallow but, poking his weapon into a shadowy fissure in the rock, the Chief saw the tip disappear, followed by the barrel.

He ordered two of the squad to stand guard and the remaining three to squeeze sideways through the gap, on the other side of which, the agents switched on their flashlights, shone them back into his face and one of them said, 'It's clear.'

The Chief followed through. With weapons raised and splitting into a two-by-two travelling formation, they wound their way down a rocky passage, crossed a circular open section, and descended a spiral stone stairwell for what felt like hundreds of steps, where the air grew colder and a long narrow hall led to a large bronze door hanging ajar.

'Stay here,' he ordered one of the agents. 'Monitor the staircase. You two, go ahead. I'll cover your six.'

The two agents complied without question, took point positions at four and eight o'clock and, a few metres ahead of their Chief, crossed a triangular room.

They stopped at the entrance to a passageway.

The Chief drew up alongside them. 'It looks narrow. I'll stay back. You two file in. Five metre gaps. If there are side spaces, I don't want to get caught in crossfire.'

'You think there's someone down here?' the taller of the two – a Mansa family member – asked.

'Perhaps. We know the Patriarch came of his own accord, but I don't want to take any chances. Maybe he was coerced. Gnostics are slippery bastards. Always using their mind-fuckery to get people to do stuff. We need to be careful. Remember your training; the blocking techniques you were taught. Use them. Don't let them in.'

With the Chief taking the rear, the team headed into the passage. They came to a corner. Followed by another. Another. A dead-end. A corner. A choice of directions. A sudden cliff edge. The drop was steep. The ceiling overhead so elevated their high-intensity torchlight disappeared into the darkness. Another corner. Followed by umpteen more, with numerous dead-ends, choices, and precipices to match. They continued for hours, taking their rations on foot, lost in a maze of polished black stone.

'Chief?' the Mansa agent, at one point, asked. 'Do you know where we are?'

'Yes,' the Chief lied. 'We continue going forward.'

The agent nodded, but appeared doubtful.

'We'll get to it soon,' the Chief added.

'It?'

'The Core Hub. I reckon it's down here, and why the Patriarch came. It never was on Nea Kameni. That was obviously just a rumour put out by those Gnostic fucks.' He reached into his belt-pack, took out a pair of goggles with one clear and one opaque, mica-like lens, and put them on. 'This tracks the Patriarch's aura. Aryan energy is very distinct. If I'm right, and he is on the way to the Core Hub, we'll get a double hit. Provide support to the Patriarch for whatever. And, if the Star Children are down here, a couple of bullets will put an end to them too. No reactivation. Problem solved. We just need to keep going.'

The two agents gave their customary nod, and they carried on... deeper into the maze.

For Ary, Jordan – and now, Vilmos, their new travelling companion – progress continued much the same as before: passageway leading to passageway, the odd dead-end, an occasional choice to change direction or, now and again, a cliff-edge, promising a precipice fall and almost certain death. They'd been down here most of the day. Hunger groaned in Ary's belly. Thirst raked in her throat. She felt weary, of the walking, and the endless black walls that brought on feelings of delusion and hopelessness.

'Hey, Vilmos Gilder-whatever-ya-call-ya,' she shouted back. 'Did you bring any grub with you?'

'No. I don't have any *grub*. But I promise to buy you a falafel when we get back to Thera. I know a great place. Fried to perfection. Homemade sauces.'

'That's not helping. Later doesn't cut it. What about you, old mate?' she asked Jordan. 'When the Gnostics were stripping us of our stuff, you didn't happen to slip an energy bar into your pocket, did you?'

'Nope. I have a few, but they're back in my pack at the hotel.'

'Brilliant. I'll starve then.'

They came to another crossroads. Ary studied the options. Instinct told her to steer left.

'I agree,' Vilmos said. 'I think we should turn left.'

'Stop that,' Ary snapped. 'No poking around in my thoughts.'

'I'm not. It's more that I sense your impulses.'

'Yeah, well don't. Do it the normal way, with your eyes and ears.'

'Sorry. Force of habit.'

'Now, shut up,' Ary continued, pausing to summon a mental image of the pathway through the maze.

'You could do another vision,' Jordan said.

'Fuck sake. What is it with you and visions? I am a person you know. Not a bloody compass.'

'Sorry. I only wanted to help.'

'Well, shut your trap then. Let me think.' But he had a point. So, she did as he suggested but no vision came. A strong sense of direction, however, did, flaring like kerosene thrown on a fire. She pointed left, said, 'It's definitely this way,' and led them down the passageway. When they reached the next corner, she said, 'Turn right,' followed by, 'straight ahead,' and they carried on, 'straight ahead again. Don't turn left. If you do, you'll plummet over the edge and burst like a melon on the floor down there. If there even is a floor. Who knows, could be bottomless.' The thought made her cringe. They moved on, Ary giving directions, the others following close behind, trusting every word she uttered, 'Turn right. Turn left. Left. Right. Left. Straight on. Left.' There were no dead-ends, because, from within, Ary instinctively knew she was leading them towards the chamber she'd seen in her vision. They took a few more turns. The passageway stretched out, maybe three or four times the length of the previous passages, before it opened into a triangular hall, equal in size and the mirror image of the one that had led them into the maze in the first place. 'I think we're here,' she said.

'Where?' Jordan asked. 'This looks like the first hall. Only in reverse.'

'The chamber is at the end,' Vilmos said. 'I can feel it's latency.'

'Yes. I feel it too,' Ary said and stared at her hands. 'It's like tingling... in my fingers, up my arms. In my head.'

'Me too,' Jordan said, clenching and unclenching a fist. 'Pins and needles. And buzzing in my ears.'

'That's the natural valence of the planet you are sensing there,' Vilmos said. 'Raw. Unchanneled. And operating at only yocto-fractions of its total capability. Even at full capacity, the Earth only utilises a micro-amount of its own potential.'

'That's so cool,' Ary said, followed by, 'yeah, we're here all right.' And then, with the reckless confidence of knowing the goal was in sight, she took off across the hall and came to at a wall, made from the same polished black basalt as the passageways and rising up, like a huge monolith, to the vaulted ceiling overhead. There was an archway in the centre. An entrance. Open. No door. Dark. On the other side of which, faint lights sparkled.

ELECTRIC BEAMS

The chamber was huge, constituting what appeared to be the last tenth of the massive hollow orb. Vast. Awesome. The wall ahead curving upwards and outwards. The collective gloom dousing their torchlight, as if absorbing the energy to fuel the myriad pinpoints of glittering light peppering the polished black basalt all around. They were standing on glass. Thick. Sturdy. Beneath which, the bottom half of the inner orb descended down and out, creating another huge void and giving Jordan the willies like he'd never felt before. This place was too big to fathom. And, other than the Gnostic's wackadoodle pronouncements, his mind faltered to find a logical reason for its existence. Which, in turn, made him uneasy. He longed for his safe, predictable desk-chair, in his safe, predictable office, in the safe, predictable basement room beneath Lori Cassano's Cute-icles Nail Bar in Fordham Heights, the Bronx, where he made safe, predictable hypotheses, based on safe, predictable science.

Life had been easier then. Less baffling, and way, way less weird.

Overhead, casting enough light to illuminate the immediate area, a glowing map of the celestial sky hung mid-air, stretching the full width of the chamber and depicting a planet, crossing a highlighted borderline between two constellations. Jordan determined them to be Aquarius and Capricorn, and the planet as Pluto. Mostly because – allowing for Eris and Planet-X – it was third last in a textbook-like representation of the Solar system. Never mind that he had totally fallen for Sandhya and Nkechi's fantastic doctrines.

'Good,' Vilmos said, coming up to join him. 'We need to be on the same page. Time is tight. Pluto has almost returned to Capricorn. If that happens, we won't be able to prepare before it settles into Aquarius again in January. We need the months. We need all three Core Hubs activated. During that time, the initiation process will slow down. The network needs to propagate. After so many thousands of years, it's not like switching on a light.'

'That's almost exactly how Nkechi puts it,' Ary said.

'Well, we are of the same mind... kind of.'

'I noticed.' Then, she was off again, dashing around like a kid on her first trip to Disneyland. 'This place is the fucking bollocks,' she shouted back.

'Apparently, that's a good thing,' Jordan said to Vilmos.

'So I'm told.'

'But she's right. I mean, just look at this place. It's awesome. Who could have built something like this?'

'The old ones,' Vilmos said. 'Tens of thousands of years ago, the three Core Hubs were at the heart of everything. Energy. Communication. All of it possible because they powered the global network. It was the perfect system, for the perfect society... until the comet hit.'

'And what powers the Core Hubs?'

'The planet. Earth is a seething ball of potential energy. All that's required is focusing it through the hubs and via the network that people call ley lines. If channelled right, there is more capacity in a tiny crystal than twenty nuclear power stations. It's all about manipulating the subatomic. We're talking quark and boson level here. Smaller still, with manipulation of wave potential. Creating realities.'

Jordan felt his jaw drop. His mouth was dry. He swallowed spit.

'So, where is it then?' Ary asked, walking back to join them.

'Where's what?' Vilmos replied.

'The big massive thingamajig that runs it all.'

'You're in it.' Vilmos said, gazing around in wonder. 'The whole orb is the Core Hub. And the maze we just came through, that's its central circuit... to use modern, technical parlance.'

'Okay. Fair enough. But where's the switch?'

'Oh. I see. You want to know how to turn it on.'

Ary rolled her eyes.

Jordan said, 'Isn't that why we're here?' and took the tablet out of his pocket.

'Yes. That's easy. Like all switches, it's over there on the back wall.' He peered up at the constellation map. 'And I suppose you had better get to it. The crossover is nearly complete.'

Ary was off again, torchlight bouncing. Jordan followed, but slower, unsure about the structural integrity of the see-through floor under his feet. Vilmos came with him. He was smiling, as if the sheer strangeness of this place and their situation were just another day at the office.

'Are you really here to help?' Jordan asked. 'My impression was we could've done this alone.'

'Yes and no. My main job is to let Nkechi and Sandhya know when you have flicked the switch, so they, in turn, can do their part. But they are very far away, so the network needs to be up and running before I can use my mental doohickies to get the info through.' He glanced at the floor, gesturing a thumbs-down. 'Oh, and I'm also here to hinder any Aryan attempts to erupt that massive volcano bubbling away down there.'

'Volcano!'

'Yes. Beneath the bottom shell of the Core Hub, there's a massive volcano just aching to blow its top. The Aryans have been popping them off left, right and centre but, as well as sending their agents off chasing shadows, I've been keeping this one in check.'

'Well, that's just great,' Jordan said, and left it there.

Ary had disappeared, merging with the darkness. Only her bobbing torchlight remained. When they caught up with her, she was scurrying around at the back wall.

'There's nothing here,' she said. 'Just shiny black stone.'

'What did you expect?' Vilmos asked.

'I don't know. Hieroglyphs. Runes. Symbols. A big fucking control panel, like something from one of the Alien films. An altar, maybe.'

'An altar. What do you think my ancestors did down here? Human sacrifices?'

'Hmm! It's possible.'

His mood changed. He looked genuinely angered by the suggestion. 'That was the Aryans. Or, at least, their followers. Gnostics don't kill. Ever. *Balance* depends on it.'

'Sorry. I didn't mean to piss you off. I'm just curious is all.'

He calmed. 'It's fine. I understand. It's probably tough for you, having to catch up on the true nature of things so quickly.'

'So, where is it? What do we do?'

'You do what you always do. Locate it. Somewhere here is the exact place where you must insert the tablet and start reactivation. I don't know the mechanisms of how it works – just that the old ones secured it so only a certain kind of Star Child could find the right spot. It was yet another of their ingenious ways to thwart the Aryans.'

'So, there are different Star Children now. Which one am I?'

'A seeker. And, of course there are. Everyone and everything is unique.'

'Did you hear that?' Ary said to Jordan. 'He said *unique*.'

Jordan let it go. He had learned to not indulge her.

'So, how do I find it?' Ary asked Vilmos. 'It's all wall. There's bugger all here.'

'Use your talent.'

'Fuck it, I actually thought you were going to say *use the force*.'

'I could. It's much the same. Art imitating reality.' He looked up at the glowing constellation map, his expression changing to one of alarm. 'And you had better get to it quickly. We're down to minutes. Ten, fifteen at the most. Pluto has all but crossed the cusp.' He stepped back. 'I'll stay away, so as not to interrupt your process. Him too.' He tugged Jordan's arm. 'We'll let you work in peace.'

Placing the tablet back in his pocket, Jordan followed the older man's directions, and watched as Ary closed her eyes and took on the same tranquil appearance he'd noticed on other occasions she invoked one of her visions; a pious quality that seemed alien to her usual brashness.

A few seconds later, she came out.

'Did you find it,' Jordan asked.

'I think so. It's quite simple really. There's a notch bang slap in the centre of the wall.' She began rubbing her hands over the polished stone, a yard or so above the floor and centre of the massive concave wall. 'Help me,' she then barked at Jordan. 'It's somewhere around here.'

He joined her, feeling with his fingertips. The stone was warm to touch, imbued with static, as if an enormous energy crackled below the surface, emanating as the countless glittering pinpoints dancing within the black rock. The sensation unnerved him. His fingers tingled. His hands trembled, eardrums buzzing, heart thumping at the prospect of releasing such awesome potential.

'It shouldn't be high up,' Vilmos said. 'The old ones would've planned it so a Star Child born to any homo-species could perform the reactivation.'

Together, Jordan and Ary felt their way around the wall. Ary looked troubled, but said nothing. Jordan continued caressing the warm stone, hoping to find the correct place, as well as being simultaneously eager and anxious about what might happen when they did.

Ary smiled. 'Got it. Where's the Organon?' It was the first time she had called it by its proper name.

Jordan took the tablet from his pocket and gave it to Ary, who set it into a recess with the exact matching dimensions.

She stood back, said, 'So, I guess we lay our hands on it now,' and glanced back at Vilmos, as if requesting his confirmation and permission to carry on.

Vilmos nodded.

Ary turned back to Jordan. 'I suppose we do it then.'

'I suppose so.' He took a breath, noticed that Ary did likewise. Together, they gazed up to the overhead map and back at the wall again. Ary smiled. Jordan reciprocated. They reached out to touch the symbol... as the crack of a gunshot echoed through the vastness.

Three spots of light came into view, shining from the arched entrance into the chamber. Jordan was crouching against the wall. Ary got down beside him. Vilmos seemed unbothered.

'Don't worry,' he said. 'It's just some Aryan agents.'

'*Just?*' Ary whispered. 'They're fucking shooting at us.'

'I doubt that. It's probably a warning.'

'It's still a fucking bullet.'

A male voice, with a Spanish twang, shouted in English. 'Are you okay, Patriarch?'

'I'm fine,' Vilmos replied, adding a side whisper, 'That's what the Aryans call me now.'

Ary didn't care. There was someone with a gun over there. Maybe three, given the spots of torchlight, and who knew how many more back in the triangular-shaped hall.

'Is it the assassin?' Jordan asked with a hushed tone.

'No,' Vilmos said. 'These are my people. Well, they think they're my people. Leave them to me.'

The Spanish twang said, 'You two stay here. Guard the entrance.' Ary assumed he was speaking to his compatriots. He then said, 'I'll come get you, Patriarch. Are the Star Children here too?'

Vilmos replied, 'Yes. We're all here.' And Ary had a gut-wrenching feeling that maybe this Vilmos guy wasn't a real Gnostic after all. Instead of infiltrating the Aryans, he had deceived the Gnostics, played the long con, his intention to stop the Core Hub reactivation. He turned to her. 'You're not being played. These Aryan agents are. They think I'm their leader.'

A single beam of torchlight moved out from the darkness, held by a helmeted soldier clad in dark blue fatigues and body armour, carrying an assault rifle and wearing a pair of goggles, which he removed and unceremoniously threw aside.

With a sharp bow, he addressed Vilmos. 'We tracked you down.'

'I didn't ask you to. You have compromised the whole operation. Your job was to secure the other island, and find these two before they got here.' He said it with a sneer, as if Ary and Jordan were of no matter and the agent had failed in his task.

'You went without protection.'

'I don't need second guessing.'

The agent gave another sharp bow.

'Now, go away,' Vilmos continued. 'Take your team back to Nea Kameni and wait for my instructions. I'll deal with matters here.'

'I could bring them with me.' The agent said, twitching the barrel of his rifle in Ary and Jordan's direction.

'Just do as I say. Take your men and go. Everything is in hand.'

The agent turned, began walking back to the chamber entrance then stopped. He looked overhead at the constellation map. 'It is nearly over,' he said, turning around.

'It is,' Vilmos said. 'That's why I'm here.'

The agent appeared quizzical. 'Why didn't you take a team with you, though? Why come on your own?'

'That's my concern. Now, go away. Leave me to my business.'

The agent winced, as if shaking off an unwanted thought, and pointed his weapon at Vilmos. 'Raise your hands. You two, move away from the wall and do the same.'

'Well, wouldn't you know,' Vilmos whispered. 'There are only a handful of strong-willed Aryans and this guy had to be one of them.'

'What?' Ary said.

'Never mind.' He glared at the agent. 'Are you out of your mind?' he snapped. 'Put down that weapon. I'm your Patriarch. I'll have your family disgraced for this.'

'But are you my Patriarch?' the agent asked. 'Or are you helping the Gnostics reactivate the Core Hubs? Why are you so cagey? And, if I've broken the rules of obedience, why haven't you called the guards over there to come arrest me?'

'I keep saying, that's my concern. And only my concern. As for you, your conspiracy theories will cost you your life.'

Amid her fear of the angry guy pointing a gun at them, Ary felt somewhat vindicated for her years of having misunderstood the truth of things. Apparently, Aryans were susceptible to conspiracy theories too. And *they* were the shifty bunch creating them.

'Don't move,' the agent said. 'I'll radio my commander to see what the Rothbauers know about this.' He looked up again, and then back at Vilmos. 'In the meantime, we can watch Pluto traverse into Capricorn. After which, it all over for you two,' he said directly to Ary and Jordan. 'For the short time you have left to live, you'll bear witness to the dawn of the *absolute* Aryan age.'

'This is ridiculous,' Vilmos said, also peering up at the map.

Ary did the same. Time was ticking down. Until now, the representation of Pluto had obscured the glowing borderline, but a chink of light had appeared, like the corona of a solar eclipse. She feared it meant they didn't have long. Maybe only minutes. Vilmos's voice, speaking inside her mind, confirmed as much.

The agent continued, 'It may well be ridiculous, Patriarch... if that's who you really are. But, if that is the case, and you are who you say you are, then I'll take the consequences. For the moment, however, we wait.'

For the first time since encountering him in the maze, Vilmos Gildermere looked edgy. Not a good omen. He glanced at Jordan, who gazed across at Ary and then back at the tablet in the wall. Ary, guessed his intention, responded with a nod.

'Don't even think about it,' the agent said, straightening his weapon. He peered up.

They all did. What came next happened quickly. In a sudden, coordinated dash, Ary and Jordan ran towards the tablet. The agent rushed after them. Vilmos blocked his way. The agent shoved the older man aside and raised his weapon. A shot rang out. Jordan slammed against the wall; one hand clasped to the side of his chest. He careened back. Slumped.

Ary screamed, but stayed where she was, her palm pressed firmly on the symbol.

Getting to his feet, Jordan said. 'I'm okay,' stumbled and sank to the floor.

Ary shouted, 'Jordan!' – the memory of Mateus's dead body flashing through her mind, bringing with it the agony of his loss. She glared at the agent.

The agent smiled, said, 'Now, come away from there, little girl. Can't have you messing around with things your imperfect female brain could never understand.'

She stayed put, said, 'Fuck you,' and pressed her hand tighter against the symbol.

The agent peered overhead. 'Suit yourself, bucket-mouth. It'll be over soon.'

Vilmos grabbed his arm. Another shot rang out. Vilmos dropped. Ary looked across to Jordan. With weak eyelids, he gazed up, smiled, got to his knees and crawled across the floor towards her.

The agent said, 'Nah hah! You can stay right there.'

Vilmos grabbed his trouser-leg. The agent booted him away with a kick upside the head and pointed his weapon at Jordan. But it was too late, Jordan slapped his hand onto the symbol and the chamber trembled.

At first, the tablet glowed, flickering with faint blue light as if no more than an ordinary household bulb straining to brighten, and then it flared, struck out, tracing circuit-board-like patterns across the polished black stone as it expanded and streaked across all the surfaces of the vast chamber. The glass floor shook. Rumbling from deep below. The constellation map had vanished, replaced by a holographic-like blue cube that pulsed and grew. It became solid. Ary dropped her hand and moved away from the wall. Jordan collapsed and lay there. The agent turned his weapon on Ary. She raised her face upwards to the cube, waiting for the bullet that would end her life, and was okay with it. Something about this place put a person at ease. The cube rippled. It shuddered, split into sections, reformed, split again, became a dodecahedron, an icositetrahedron, then morphed in and out of consecutive and copious multisided shapes known only to mathematicians, and perhaps Jordan. As the shapes transformed, within the vault of the ceiling, lights of many hues flashed through the air, spinning, whirling, some hanging there as if suspended from invisible threads while others romped around the massive space, dancing to the melodic humming emitted by the ever-changing geometric mass. Every surface of the immense hollow orb pulsed in a kaleidoscope of coloured fractals, winding over and through each other, their structures shattering under the impact of twirling, curling motes of brilliant blue light, as if the result of numerous particle collisions whereby, as quickly as the fractals splintered, they reformed and continued their frolics, spreading into the distance where, in the area above the labyrinth, the particles coalesced, strafing the maze with bolts of electricity, the consequence of a colossal energy released from multi-millennial long confinement. Ary lowered her gaze. The bullet hadn't come. As the floor shook, the agent was staggering around, trying and failing to find his feet. The guards at the entrance to the chamber dashed across to join their colleague. They made it only a few metres. The electricity surging through the labyrinth lashed like whip and, in the blink of an eye, they were dust floating upon the charged air. The agent spun around, his expression one of disbelief before, returning to face Ary, he snarled, raised his weapon, another razor thin lightning bolt struck the barrel of his gun and, in an instant, he too became cloud of drifting dust.

The humming grew louder, throbbing with a melody Ary instinctively recognised but couldn't name. She settled for "Song of Nature." It seemed apt. Her skin tingled. Hairs stood on the back of her neck and arms, and her thoughts became sparkles, merging with the motes and fractals swirling around her. She was within and part of the display. And, then again, she wasn't, she was somewhere else, somewhere past. Her mind cleared. She was standing before a newly built pyramid and then, with a woosh of her senses, she was standing before another, and then another, and another, followed by buildings, all newly constructed, yet old, teeming with throngs of people. Some in warm climates and wearing tribal attire. Some dressed for the thick snow coating the ground around them. Some not homo sapiens, but short, or tall, brawny, or svelte. Some at work, playing sports, teaching, learning. She knew them all, as if siblings, and when it was: thousands of years in the past. In the blink of an eye, she had traversed the world as it once had been. Seconds later, she was among the constellations, making a similar journey through star systems, as far as Earendel, traversing planets. Solid ground, soil, rock, forests, and oceans of blue, and green, red, and yellow. There was architecture, similar to that of ancient Earth. With tall, short, and numerous species of hominid peoples swarming through and around them. She knew them all too, as if they were family. The thought brought warmth, and returned her to Earth, to a forested valley where a battered metal sign said *Loon Creek*. It seemed important. Then it was gone and Ary was back in the massive hollow orb. Jordan was there, and Vilmos, both lying on the glass floor. The lightning had settled. The fractals recoiling to reintegrate with the glowing, multi-faceted body hovering overhead and the symbol on the Organon tablet fading, becoming one with the shiny black stone. The chamber had returned to its former semi-darkened state and, apart from the glowing shape and the faint tune humming around her, all was tranquil.

She gazed across at Jordan. He wasn't moving. Panic punched her heart but then he groaned, 'I'm okay,' and she ran to his side, throwing her arms around him.

He said, 'Ouch,' followed by, 'the bullet only grazed my rib. It's not serious.'

Ary looked down. He was right, there was blood but the cut looked superficial.

'It's bad enough,' she said.

'Call it a war wound.' He smiled. 'Just knocked the wind out of me is all.' He staggered to his feet. 'I'm fine. See to Vilmos.'

Ary hesitated.

Jordan said, 'Do it. I'm okay,' and she dashed to kneel by the older man's side.

Vilmos was flat on his back and barely conscious. Under the kaleidoscope gleam of the body pulsating overhead, she noticed a large red patch spreading over his expensive white shirt. 'Shit. He's bleeding. Bad.'

'How bad?'

'I don't know. I'm not a doctor. But it's bad... like could be dead soon *bad*.'

'But I'm not dead yet,' Vilmos said, opening his eyes and wincing as he tried to sit up.

Ary helped him, cradled him against her chest. 'Yeah, right. You're fit as a fucking fiddle.'

'An old fiddle plays the sweetest tun...' he coughed midsentence.

'Stay quiet. Don't move. We'll get you out of here.'

'So, it worked,' he said. 'I passed out, didn't see the Core Hub reactivate?'

'Yes, we got the job done?'

'No,' Jordan said. 'We didn't.'

'How not?' Ary said. 'We activated the symbol. We got it working.' She pointed upwards with her thumb. 'That big fucking thing up there... all the swirling, the throbbing, the lightning, it must've done something.'

'Vilmos was knocked out. There's no way he got the message through to the others.'

Ary felt crestfallen. All the weeks, months, injury and death had been for nothing.

'Is that so,' Vilmos then said with a grin. 'I did it the second you touched the Organon. The third Gnostic doesn't have to be compos mentos to speak with the others. It's all about using the subconscious.'

Ary smiled. 'Well, fuck me pink. Aren't you the hardy old duffer.'

Vilmos smiled back. 'Not just a pretty face.' He coughed again, spluttering flecks of blood-filled spittle down his chin.

Ary checked his torso. Like Baba, he'd been shot through the left side of his chest.

'I'll be fine,' he said.

'Don't think so.'

'We definitely need to get him out of here,' Jordan added. 'Can he walk?'

'Yes, he can,' Vilmos said and, together, Ary and Jordan lifted the older man to his feet, straddled him between their shoulders and, with slow staggered steps, headed back out through the labyrinth.

NORMAL

If ever queried about how he got from the giant hollow orb back to surface, Jordan reckoned his recollect would come up patchy. He remembered helping Vilmos through the maze, the trek seeming much shorter going out than it had on the way in. He recalled the bronze door, the spiral stairwell, the crevasse, the fissure in the rock closing behind them, the cabin cruiser waiting for them in the darkness by the shore, and the ambulance on the empty dockside in Thera. It was, however, hazy – a hotchpotch of images and activity, before it faded, the route to the Core Hub withering from his memory. On the dockside, Ary kissed Vilmos's head before he was ferried off to hospital. She kissed Jordan's cheek too, ordering him to take the same ambulance to get his wound checked.

She seemed enlivened, yet also calm.

Jordan felt it too, as if a bright sun had risen within his mind.

When he returned to the hotel, pain-relieved and suitably bandaged, he and Ary ate salad sandwiches and drank mocktails together in the hotel bar, marvelling at how quickly a fleet of black helicopters could evacuate the island of Nea Kameni. They discussed the ramifications of their actions. Speculated on what came next, had no answers, and circled round to their dwindling recollection of their journeys through the labyrinth.

'I remember big lights,' Ary said.

'But no bull-headed monster,' Jordan replied.

'Nah. It would've been cool, though.'

'Yeah, for the few seconds before it ripped us limb from limb.'

Ary laughed, and yawned.

The bartender told them the bar was open all night but, halfway through their second Virgin Sunset, the events of the day caught up with them and, taking to his bed, Jordan remarked inwardly how the world around them seemed unchanged. The guy in the room across the corridor took a coughing fit around three in the morning. Some rowdy revellers, returning from a night out, giggled and failed to whisper as they passed the door to his room. It was... well, it was all pretty much *meh!*

Where was the fanfare? The big bang burst of fireworks to indicate that things were about to change?

Exhausted but wide awake, he switched on the television, found a news channel and, although he didn't know a single word of Greek, worked out that, in the political world, countries were cooperating somewhat more than usual. An unprecedented occurrence to address serious issues but, again, nothing mind-blowing. He flicked channels. No change there either. Shows looked normal. Adverts looked normal: long haired girls risked whiplash to advertise the ultimate shampoo, insurance companies guilt-tripped old folk into parting with their hard-earned pensions, a new car brought eternal joy. Life was... well, normal. No one, anywhere seemed in anyway whatsoever concerned that massive bolts of electric blue light had circumnavigated the planet and launched the countdown to the next age.

The *long* countdown, Vilmos had said before the paramedics hurried him out of the ambulance.

How long, though?

Within that thought, another came to him.

It said: *twenty years from January 2024 for the foundation. And then, another two millennia.*

Jordan recognised the words as Sandhya's, not in a vocal sense, but at a base level, the voice behind her mind, spoken inside his, yet not intrusive, but direct, as if physically communicated from somewhere in the room. It didn't bother him. Seemed natural. Over the past months and weeks, he had come to accept much, and this was just another addition. They were connected. Him. Ary. The three Gnostics. They were one and, outside of their groupthink, he sensed others – many others – becoming aware that the countdown to the Golden Age had finally begun.

Sitting on her bed, wrapped in the hotel dressing-gown and recalling Mateus's murder, Ary broke down. Along with Jordan, she had done this magnificent deed but felt as abandoned and heartbroken as before she set foot in the labyrinth.

Where was her moment of compassion? The relief from her sorrows?

Where was her glorious future?

So far, she had witnessed nothing but the same. Still grief-stricken. Still yearning warmth, comfort, and the kind words of a friend.

They came, but within her thoughts.

Saying: *you have friends. And soon, many friends. We're here with you.*

Ary recognised the words as Nkechi's, not in a vocal sense, but at a base level, the voice behind her mind, spoken inside hers, yet not intrusive, but direct, as if physically communicated from somewhere in the room. It didn't bother her. Seemed natural. Over the past months and weeks, she had come to accept much, and this was just another addition. They were connected. Her. Jordan. The three Gnostics. They were one and, outside of their groupthink, she sensed others – many others – becoming aware that the countdown to the Golden Age had finally begun.

BALANCE

Having slept well into the next afternoon, Jordan called by Ary's room, encouraged her to come down to the bar, at which point, Sandhya and Nkechi arrived with broad grins on their faces.

They hugged Ary. She smiled.

They hugged Jordan next and, for once, it didn't feel awkward.

As the Gnostics sat and ordered tea for four, Ary asked them, 'So, where is it, then?'

'Where's what, dear one?' Nkechi replied.

'The big fucking thing?'

'Yes,' Jordan added in support. 'Where's the big fucking thing?'

'We don't know what you mean,' Sandhya and Nkechi said in unison.

'We mean,' Ary snapped, 'where's the crescendo. I kinda expected to see global harmony or some such shit by now.'

'It's on its way,' Sandhya said. 'These things take time.'

'How much time?'

'Two millennia,' Jordan said.

'Ah! I see you got my message. Yes, two millennia.'

'You're taking the fucking piss,' Ary said. 'You told us, all we needed to do was switch the thing on and everything would be tickety-boo. World peace. An end to hunger. Vampires and werewolves shagging each other.'

'It will,' Nkechi said. 'Except the last one, of course. It just takes time.'

'And time is relative,' Jordan added.

'Yes.'

'What the fuck does that mean?' Ary said. 'Relative to what?'

'Relative to you. And Jordan. Me, Sandhya, Vilmos. The sentience of the world... of the universe. All over the planet, people are becoming awake. They don't know it yet, but they will. Change is coming. But, to be effective and permanent, it needs time to settle and solidify. Even now, with the Core Hubs activated, the future balances on a knife edge. Any misstep will regress us backwards. We must be diligent. The Aryans still have powers, and influence. Not least a doomsday option of slowing the planet's rotation by manipulating the Coriolis Effect. But, Vilmos, when he's better, will take care of them. He says hello, by the way.'

'How is he?' Ary asked.

'Good. Recovering. He is back in New York. Playing his role as UN General Secretary. Once we knew he was stable, he was flown to a hospital there. The story goes, he was shot by an anti-climate change conspiracist.'

'Nice one,' Ary replied. 'They're total fuckwits. It's supposed to be about uncovering the truth. Not denial of reality.' She shot Jordan a look, as if daring him to say something.

He remained quiet. Some of her theories had merit.

'And it was that kind of thinking,' Nkechi continued, 'your open mind, that brought you to us.'

'For what?' Jordan asked. 'What was the point? To me, and I think Ary too, nothing seems any different.'

Ary nodded.

'As it should,' Sandhya said. 'Permanent change only comes about through small, incremental alterations that, in turn, bring about greater but undetectable transformations in the bodies and minds of all sentient creatures. It is *Balance*. You just need to wait.'

'Was there ever such a thing as *Balance*, as you call it?'

'Once. In as much as humans are able. Aryans are proof of how greed lies just below the surface, and that is the lure of imbalance. To have imbalance there must be the prospect of *Balance*. Cooperation. Globally. And fellowship. Yin yang. We wish to bring that back.'

'Yeah, and we'll all be dead before that happens,' Ary said.

'Yes, you will. In some sense. But the planet and the universe won't. And that is what it's all about. You were and are the progenitors of the future. One day, they'll sing songs about you.' Sandhya smiled. Nkechi too.

A waiter arrived with the tea. Nkechi thanked. Sandhya poured. They sipped and continued smiling. There was much to be gleaned from a smile. Sometimes it meant joy. At other times, sudden elation. And, here, Jordan expected it meant the satisfaction of a job completed. Because of their connectedness, he imagined Vilmos was smiling too, and maybe even all the *awake* but unaware people around the world.

'You are growing wiser by the day,' the Gnostics said together.

Jordan shirked and asked an unrelated question. 'So, what happened to the Aryan agents in the orb? I thought killing wasn't allowed?'

'That wasn't us,' Sandhya said. 'And as tragic as it always is to lose a sentient being, their deaths were all their own doing. Another two, standing guard on the surface, met the same fate. Thus is the consequence of always being prepared to take life.'

'Their weapons?'

'Yes. The metal acted like a lightning conductor. It's why we told you to leave your phones behind. To travel light. If they'd come without their tools of death, they might've lived. They should have lived. All creatures have that right. Even those seduced by violence.'

'A tough lesson.'

'Most lessons are.'

'So, what do we do now?' Ary asked.

Nkechi reached across and brushed a strand of hair from Ary's cheek. 'Now, dear one... you go home. Continue on. You've made a connection and I'm sure Jordan would love your help with his magazine. You should collaborate.'

Jordan thought about it. 'S'pose it can't hurt,' he said. 'As long as you stay away from the wacky stuff.'

'What,' Ary replied, 'wacky stuff like ancient civilisations and mega-gigantic power orbs?'

'Point taken.'

Nkechi continued, 'Good. That's that then. You can collaborate until we need you again.'

'Again?'

'Yes,' Sandhya said, reaching across to hold Jordan's hand. 'But first, when Vilmos is back with us, we must prepare for January and Pluto re-entering Aquarius.'

'Oh yeah. I forgot about that.'

'Well, you shouldn't. It's the true main event. Now the Core Hubs are active, we begin the last six months of the old world. In January, we come of age.'

'And, what happens then?' Ary asked.

'Then...' the two Gnostics said in unison, '...*it begins!*'

DECEMBER 2023

Despite disagreements over which countries footed the bill, on the whole, the two, new global economic zones, supported by a focused UN General Assembly, managed a great deal in the six months since its restructure. The climate was still a major concern. Turning back hundreds of years of spewing detrimental molecules into the atmosphere was as difficult a task as expected. There was, however, consensus. The real kind. Not the half-arsed approaches of earlier efforts. The Paris Agreement was reworked and signed-off. The IPCC were given powers.

As for war, the world didn't exactly break out in peace. In some conflict zones, antagonists resumed their prior condition of beating seven bells of shite out of each other. In most, however, ceasefires were called, round table talks initiated, and common ground found with regard to refugees. There were, of course, skirmishes. No one expected anything less. Rockets fired into and from Gaza. There were scuffles at the Kashmir border. In all parts of the world, anger swelled around food distribution. Disputes occurred. Rivals clashed. And yet, despite the uphill battle, nations – as a collective – seemed to be getting their shit together.

Ary liked that. It helped defuse the cynic in her, reaffirming everything the Gnostics had prophesised about Pluto's final move into Aquarius in January. Of course, Jordan still had issues. No matter how much proof they laid before him, he just couldn't see the connection between the universe, science, thought, and destiny. To him it was an unsolvable enigma. Reminding her of the religious nuts who blamed everything on God. He played it safe. So, winding down her blog, she hopped across to New York and spent a month breaking down the walls he erected when reality clashed with his perceived ideas about existence. It worked. Somewhat. *The Kitchen Sink Magazine* became less safe. Dare she say, contentious. Now, he seemed looser, less stuck up and academic-y. He'd even started a relationship with the woman who ran the nail-bar above his office. Good for him. The one thing Jordan needed more than most was to lighten up.

As for Ary, she was heading home. Christmas was coming and, even though they weren't Christian, Mteay had always made an occasion of the holiday. Ary also had a gift. On the way from New York, she had taken the roundabout route via Cambodia and, when the plane touched down at Heathrow, she exited Arrivals accompanied by Sopheak. It was a secret. A surprise. And, walking through ankle-deep snow to her mother's flat, she thought about the time, months before, when Mteay had shown her the symbol. She recalled the story about the GI – Jordan's grandfather – and the horrors her mother had endured in the years that followed. Sopheak had suffered those too. It was etched in every wrinkle on his face, in the wither of his eyes, and the slight hang of his head. Today, however, he held that head high. There was excitement there, also reticence and, upon reaching her mother's door, the reunion went much as expected. Lots of gasps. Floods of tears. With enough hugs and kisses to wear down the rugged skin of any hardened South-east Asian rice farmer. It was all but impossible to stop smiling. And crying.

Jordan phoned, asking how it went.

Ary blubbered through that conversation too.

She thought about Mateus. His smiling face lingering at the edge of recollect. A future glimpsed but never possessed. She missed his charm. His wit. Mostly, though, she missed him being there when she discovered something cool about the ancients. There were many of those, now. All part of the Gnostic world. The strangeness. Which brought her to Charlie, the nice bloke with the over-obsession for one particular movie, who had also been her last point of normalcy before the Gnostics and their Organon stormed into her life.

In the bizarreness of her new reality, weird guy Charlie represented the everyday ordinary.

Then again, *who was she to judge?*

Leaving her mother and uncle to their tearful memories, she went for walk through the snow and hordes Christmas shoppers. Winter was colder than usual this year. Something to do with climate change. The Gnostics, however, said they were on that too. Ary just feared she'd be dead before she benefited from their efforts.

On the Harrow Road, she stopped at a minimarket, got in line, bought an avocado sandwich and ate it underneath the shop's awning. Later, she would order take-away. Her mother would argue. She preferred to cook and, no doubt, would be gagging to impress Sopheak, but they needed time, and Ary would insist. Dumping the sandwich wrapper in the recycle bin, she tightened her scarf and began walking back to Mteay's flat. The window behind her exploded in a shower of glass. There was a pop. People looked bemused. Then reacted. Some rushing down Harrow Road. Others up side-streets. A few hunkering behind the charity hoppers dotted along the footpath. As the scattering unfolded, Ary was already back in the minimarket, cowering with the shop-keeper behind the counter. Another bullet punctured the cash register. Two more shattered wine bottles on the shelves above her head.

The shooting stopped.

Ary peeked over the edge of the counter.

She was shaking, soaked and stinking of booze.

Seen through the open doorway, on the other side of Harrow Road, a figure wearing black clothes and a balaclava was pointing a rifle at her.

The voice that spoke in Ary's mind was her own.

It said a foreign word, *bedre* – followed by a command: *fuck off*.

With a few swift and seamless movements, the figure dropped the rifle, stepped back into a garden, went through a hedge and was gone.

'Well, what do you know,' Ary said aloud, smiling. 'I can fucking nudge after all.'

EPILOGUE

Pennsylvania – January 2024

Kathy Jackson was desperate. Mom had been totally hounding her about prepping for a college place and Kathy needed at least one good grade to get her off her back. So, in the pursuit of her next 10th Grade assignment, she focused on USA in World War II. Always a safe bet when Fox News watching, *minimal government, God bless the flag*, ultra-Christian, might actually be a member of Dominion, Mrs Carlson was the history teacher.

Through her research, and with her mega-geek best-friend, Josh Miller encouraging every rabbit hole she went down, Kathy stumbled on the curious disappearance of Flight 19 in the Bermuda Triangle and the belief – backed up by an online blog called *Hard Truth* – that, at one time, a massive energy transmitter, perhaps known as Atlantis, was situated somewhere in the Caribbean islands of Bimini, with another in Yonaguni, Japan and one more at Santorini in the Mediterranean Sea. The concept intrigued her. She researched more. Josh got totally obsessed. Men in black cars turned up outside the house. Josh thought they were secret agents, but Kathy disregarded them as unimportant. That kind of thing only happened in movies and, anyway, *who would be interested in a nobody like her*. With inquisitiveness niggling at her brain, however, she uncovered a connection to the Founding Fathers who, seemingly aware of this *truth*, chose bury it beneath a mountain of fabricated superstition and conjecture. There was also a local connection, relating to the Iroquoian speaking people who once inhabited the forests around her own town. An awesome story. Steeped in folklore, mystery, and intrigue. They were the *Seneca*. Called the place: *ë:ní'ta:' o:ne:ka'* – or *Moon Water* – because it was where *the Moon people danced with the Earth people*. Kathy, her mom, dad, Josh, and all the inhabitants of the sleepy little town, simply knew it as home... or *Loon Creek*.

Acknowledgements

Thank you to my wife, Lynsey, who is my first and constant reader, to my family and friends, who are always there for me, and to my daughter, Emma, for her unending encouragement.

A special thanks goes to the guys at Fire Hornet Codex, without whom this book would never have made it to print:
Marg, for having faith in the whole Fall of Ancients concept.
Brett, for his knowhow and calm demeanour in the face of my unending list of questions.
Sandra, for her editor insights.

Also to my daughter's fiancé, Niall, for all the mad conspiracy theory chitchats.
The internet, for being such a wacky, way-out place.
And, finally, my late, dear friend, Sal Nensi, the other brain behind the Fall of Ancients universe. You are missed.

About the Author

Martin Treanor enjoys all things historical, archaeological, metaphysical, and has developed a strong interest in quantum physics which he likes to introduce into his books and stories. He has a fondness for the dark and macabre.

Over the years Martin has worked as a university technician, trade union representative, engineering tutor, lift installer, labourer, bar manager, bookseller, and a writer.

Previous works include his illustrated, political satire series, The Tales of Trumplethinskin, his urban fantasy novel, *Hellmaw: Dark Creed*, released as part of D&D Forgotten Realms creator Ed Greenwood's Hellmaw series, and his Amazon bestselling in metaphysical fiction, debut novel, *The Silver Mist*.

From Ireland, Martin now lives in Lisbon, Portugal with his wife Lynsey and their overdramatic cat.

MartinTreanor.Com

FallOfAncients.Com
TheKitchenSinkMagazine.Com
HardTruthHarper.Wordpress.Com

MartinTreanor.Com

About the Author

Martin Treanor enjoys all things historical, archaeological, metaphysical, and has developed a strong interest in quantum physics which he likes to introduce into his books and stories. He has a fondness for the dark and macabre.

Over the years Martin has worked as a university technician, trade union representative, engineering tutor, lift installer, labourer, bar manager, bookseller, and a writer.

Previous works include his illustrated, political satire series, The Tales of Trumplethinskin, his urban fantasy novel, *Hellmaw: Dark Creed*, released as part of D&D Forgotten Realms creator Ed Greenwood's Hellmaw series, and his Amazon bestselling in metaphysical fiction, debut novel, *The Silver Mist*.

From Ireland, Martin now lives in Lisbon, Portugal with his wife Lynsey and their overdramatic cat.

MartinTreanor.Com

FallOfAncients.Com
TheKitchenSinkMagazine.Com
HardTruthHarper.Wordpress.Com

MartinTreanor.Com